## 'Do you have to leave?'

to, please… I have to think about my career. Can we…'

ant, do you have to leave the room?'

ou didn't mean that.' Usually she rebuffed any flirting
asily; it was just a little harder to do this morning and not
ast because they were on a bed in a very dark room, more
because she felt as if she had glimpsed today the real Santo,
the one behind the very expensive but very shallow façade.

Remember how you told me you would never get involved
with someone you work with…'

I do.'

Her second day at work, they had gone for dinner, had sat
side by side and pored over his diary, Ella trying to be
efficient but terribly aware of his beauty, trying to ignore it,
trying to work when his hand had reached for her face.

'If you try anything like that again, you'll have my notice
with immediate effect.'

How she rued those words now.

We have a problem.' Santo said and she looked at him and,
though it was terribly hard to think of Santo and morals at
the same time, Ella realised he did actually have some; for
apart from a few stunning suggestions, apart from the odd
gentle flirt, not once since that day had he put so much as a
finger wrong.

he just wanted him to put that finger wrong now.

And he did. Just one finger dusted her forearm and Santo
waited for her hand to halt his, gave her every opportunity
to stand, to change her mind. She'd been very clear as to
her boundaries them tumble
down.

D1584100

# SICILY'S CORRETTI DYNASTY

*The more powerful the family...the darker the secrets!*

### Sicily's Most Scandalous Family!
Young, rich, and notoriously handsome, the Correttis' legendary exploits regularly feature in Sicily's tabloid pages!

### The Scandal
How long can their reputations withstand the glaring heat of the spotlight before their family's secrets are exposed?

### The Legacy
Once nearly destroyed by the secrets cloaking their thirst for power, the new generation of Correttis are riding high again —and no disgrace or scandal will stand in their way...

### The Correttis: Sins (May 2013)
A LEGACY OF SECRETS – Carol Marinelli
AN INVITATION TO SIN – Sarah Morgan

### The Correttis: Revenge (June 2013)
A SHADOW OF GUILT – Abby Green
AN INHERITANCE OF SHAME – Kate Hewitt

### The Correttis: Secrets (July 2013)
A WHISPER OF DISGRACE – Sharon Kendrick
A FAÇADE TO SHATTER – Lynn Raye Harris

### The Correttis: Scandals (August 2013)
A SCANDAL IN THE HEADLINES – Caitlin Crews
A HUNGER FOR THE FORBIDDEN – Maisey Yates

# THE
# CORRETTIS
# Sins

## CAROL MARINELLI
## SARAH MORGAN

First published in Great Britain 2013
Mills & Boon, an imprint of Harlequin (UK) Limited,
Eton House, 18-24 Paradise Road, Richmond, Surrey TW9 1SR

THE CORRETTIS: SINS © Harlequin Enterprises II B.V./S.à.r.l. 2013

A *Legacy of Secrets* © Harlequin Books S.A. 2013

Special thanks and acknowledgement are given to Carol Marinelli for her
contribution to the Sicily's Corretti Dynasty series

ISBN: 978 0 263 90615 8

53-0513

Harlequin (UK) policy is to use papers that are natural, renewable
and recyclable products and made from wood grown in sustainable
forests. The logging and manufacturing processes conform to the legal
environmental regulations of the country of origin.

Printed and bound
by CPI Group (UK) Ltd, Croydon, CR0 4YY

# A Legacy of Secrets

## CAROL MARINELLI

**Carol Marinelli** finds writing a bio rather like writing her New Year's Resolutions. Oh, she'd love to say that since she wrote the last one, she now goes to the gym regularly and doesn't stop for coffee and cake and a gossip afterwards; that she's incredibly organised and writes for a few productive hours a day after tidying her immaculate house and a brisk walk with the dog.

The reality is, Carol spends an inordinate amount of time daydreaming about dark, brooding men and exotic places (research), which doesn't leave too much time for the gym, housework or anything that comes in between. Her most productive writing hours happen to be in the middle of the night, which leaves her in a constant state of bewildered exhaustion.

Originally from England, Carol now lives in Melbourne, Australia. She adores going back to the UK for a visit—actually, she adores going anywhere for a visit—and constantly (expensively) strives to overcome her fear of flying. She has three gorgeous children who are growing up so fast (too fast—they've just worked out that she lies about her age!) and keep her busy with a never-ending round of homework, sport and friends coming over.

A nurse and a writer, Carol writes for the Mills & Boon® Modern™ and Medical Romance™ lines and is passionate about both. She loves the fast-paced, busy setting of a modern hospital, but every now and then admits it's bliss to escape to the glamorous, alluring world of her Modern heroes and heroines. A bit like her real life, actually!

# PROLOGUE

'PLEASE.'

Ella wasn't sure how many times that word had been said to her in the past, but she knew that she would forever recall this time.

'Please, Ella, don't go.'

She stood at the departure terminal of the busy Sydney International Airport, passport and boarding pass in hand, and looked into her mother's pleading eyes—the same amber eyes as her own—and she almost relented. How could she possibly leave her to deal with her father alone?

But, given all that had happened, how could she stay?

'You have a beautiful home....'

'No!' Ella would not be swayed. 'I have a flat that

I bought in the hope that you would move in with me. I thought that you'd finally decide to leave him, and yet you won't.'

'I can't.'

'You can.' Ella stood firm. 'I have done everything to help you leave and yet you still refuse.'

'He's my husband.'

'And I'm your daughter.' Ella's eyes flashed with suppressed anger. 'He beat me, Mum!'

'Because you upset him. Because you try to get me to leave…' Her mother had been in Australia for more than thirty years, was married to an Australian, and yet her English was still poor. Ella knew that she could stand here and argue her point some more, but there wasn't time for that. Instead she said the words she had planned to say and gave her mother one final chance to leave. 'Come with me.'

Then Ella handed her mother the ticket she had secretly purchased.

'How?'

'I've brought your passport with me.' Ella pulled it out of her bag and handed it to her mother to show that she was serious and that she really had thought this through. 'You can walk away now, Mum. You can go back to Sicily and be with your sisters. You can have a life....' She saw her mother wrestle with the decision. She missed her country so much, spoke about her sisters all the time, and if she would just have the courage to walk away then Ella would help her in any way that she could.

'I can't.'

There was simply no point, but Ella did her best to persuade her mum. Right up to check-in, right up to the departure gate, Ella tried to convince her mother to leave, but she had decided now that the subject was closed.

'Have a nice trip, Ella.'

'I'm not going for a holiday, Mum,' Ella said. She wanted her mother to realise how serious this was, that she wasn't just going to be away for a few weeks. 'I'm going there to look for work.'

'But you said you will visit Sicily.'

'I might.' Ella honestly didn't know. 'I don't know if I can, Mum. I'd hoped to go there with you. I think I'll stay in Rome.'

'Well, if you do get to Sicily, give my love to your aunts. Tell them...' Gabriella faltered for a moment.

'*Don't* tell them, you mean.' Ella looked at her mum, who would be in trouble for even coming to the airport, and couldn't believe she was expecting

Ella to tell her aunts how fantastic her life was in Australia, to keep up the pretence. 'Are you asking me to lie?'

'Why you do this to me?' Gabriella demanded, as she did whenever Ella didn't conform or questioned things. Possibly Ella was more Sicilian than she gave herself credit for, because as her mother used the very familiar line, Ella was tempted to use it herself. *Why you do this to me? Why did you stand and scream as you watched your daughter being beaten? Why didn't you have the guts to get up and leave?* Of course she didn't say that. Ella hadn't shared her feelings with anyone, not even her mum, since that day.

'I have to go, Mum.' Ella looked up at the board— she really did have to, customs would take forever— but at the last moment her voice cracked. 'Mum, please…'

'Ella, go.'

Gabriella wept as she said goodbye but Ella didn't—she hadn't since that terrible day two months ago. Instead she hugged her mum and headed through customs and then sat dry-eyed on the plane with an empty seat beside her, nursing her guilt for leaving her mother behind, but knowing deep down there was nothing more she could do.

She was twenty-seven years old, and had spent enough of her life trying to get her mother away from her father. Even her job had been chosen with money, rather than passion, in mind.

Ella had worked as a junior assistant for a couple of CEOs, then moved through the ranks, eventually becoming a PA to a politician. She'd spent the past two years in Canberra, dreading what she might come home to in Sydney.

Unable to live like that, she had swapped a very good job for a not-so-good one, and bought a home nearer her parents. Now, after all those years of trying to help her mum, Ella knew she just had to get away.

She had references in her bag and could speak Italian.

It was time to get a life.

Her life.

It never entered her head that she might need some time off to heal from all she had endured—instead Ella's focus was on finding work.

Except it was just rather more intimidating than she'd first thought.

It was January, and she had left the hot Australian summer for a cold Italian winter. Rome was busier than anywhere Ella had ever been. The Gypsies seemed to make a beeline for her every time she ventured from the hotel, but she took in the sites, stood in awe in the Vatican and threw a coin in the Trevi Fountain, as her mother had told her to do. But what was the point, Ella thought, for her mother would never be back.

She took a train to Ostia Antica, visited the ruins and froze as she walked along the beach, wondering when the healing would start, when the revelation that she had done the right thing by leaving would strike.

It didn't.

So instead of sitting around waiting, Ella set about looking for work.

'You have a lot of experience for someone your age, but...' It was the same wherever she went—yes, her résumé was impressive, but even though they were conversing in Italian, Claudia explained at her interview, as the others had yesterday, Ella's Italian simply wasn't good enough for the agency to put her forward to any of the employers on their books.

'You understand it better than you speak it,' Clau-

dia said. She really had been nice, so Ella chose not
to be offended. 'Is there any other type of work you
are interested in?'

Ella was about to say no, to shake her head, but
with nothing to lose she was honest. 'The film industry.'

'We don't handle actors.'

'No, no...' Ella shook her head. 'I'm interested in
directing.' It was all she had ever wanted to do, but
saving up enough money to give her mother the option to move had been her priority. Instead of trying
to break into the industry as a poorly paid junior,
Ella had gone for better-paid jobs. But this morning,
sitting in a boutique Rome employment agency, Ella
realised she could perhaps focus on herself.

'Sorry.' Claudia gave a helpless shrug and as Ella
went to thank her, she halted her. 'One moment. We
have a client, Corretti Media—they are in Sicily—
Palermo. Have you heard of them?'

'A bit.' Ella was obsessed with the industry.
'They've done well with a few blockbusters recently.'

'Alessandro is the CEO, and there is Santo—he's
a film producer.'

'I have heard of him.' Ella said, though chose not
to add that it wasn't his producing skills he was fa-

mous for—more his scandalous ways. Still, Claudia seemed quite happy to discuss them.

'He goes through a lot of PAs!' Claudia rolled her eyes as she pulled up the file. 'Yes, it is Santo who is looking for someone—you would go with him when he is on location. You would need an open mind though—he is always getting into trouble and he has quite a reputation with women.'

Ella didn't care about his reputation, just the thought of being on location. Maybe she could get some experience—at least it would be a start. 'Perhaps he would be more forgiving of your Italian if I tell him that you are familiar with the industry.'

'My Italian is improving,' Ella said.

'And you'd need to seriously smarten up.'

This time Ella was offended. She was sitting in a very expensive grey suit—one that had been suitable for Parliament, she wanted to point out—but then again, it was three years old and politicians weren't exactly known for their stand-out fashion.

'Santo Corretti expects immaculate.'

Ella forced a smile. 'Then he'll get immaculate.'

'One moment.'

Ella sat as Claudia made the call, trying to quell the excitement that was mounting. Because for the first time she actually wanted a job, wanted it in a way she never had before, though her cheeks did burn a bit when Claudia looked her over and said that yes, she was good-looking. Was honey blonde hair really a prerequisite for this job? Ella wondered as she heard her hair being described.

As it turned out it didn't matter.

'Sorry…' Claudia shook her head. 'That was his current PA, and though she is very keen to leave, she says there is no point even putting you forward. He is very particular.'

'Well, thank you for trying.'

Leaving the agency Ella stopped for coffee. Gazing out the window at a busy Rome morning, she told herself it was ridiculous to be so disappointed about a job she hadn't even been interviewed for.

And even if she had… Ella looked out at the women. There was just an effortless elegance to them and if Santo Corretti went for immaculate then the bar was raised very high here in Italy. He would have taken one look at Ella in her rather boring interview suit and the answer would have been the same.

Anyway, Ella asked herself, did she really want to work in Sicily, did she really want to go and revisit her mother's past?

Yes.

Ella's heart started a frantic thump, because she simply wasn't ready. Except she was walking out of the café and instead of tackling the next agency on her list, she found herself peering into the beautifully dressed windows, wondering what a PA for Santo Corretti might wear. And a few moments later she was asking a shop assistant the same.

Well, she didn't say his name, just said that she had a very important job interview. A little while later Ella sat and had her long curly hair trimmed and tamed and then loosely tied at the nape and her make-up and nails done too.

By early afternoon she checked out of her hotel, and took the short flight to Sicily. She looked out at the land she had seen in endless faded photos that had been described to her over and over by her mother. Despite the beauty of the snowcapped mountains, the glistening azure sea and the juts of buildings vying for space on the coastline, Ella wasn't quite sure that she was ready for this. But she was here to work, she reminded herself.

While the bravest thing she had ever done might have been to leave Australia, Ella thought as she checked her luggage into storage and stepped out into the winter sun, this felt pretty brave too.

Or foolish.

She'd find out soon enough.

Ella climbed into a white taxi. 'Corretti Media.'

Ella held her breath, worried he might ask for an address, or say he had no idea where she meant, but the driver just nodded and Ella pulled out her mirror from her handbag, smoothed down her hair and touched up her make-up. Her newly capped gleaming white smile felt unfamiliar. No one would ever guess the price she had paid to get it—and not in money.

Snapping the mirror closed, Ella refused to dwell on it, just pushed all thoughts of her father aside. As the taxi pulled up outside the Corretti Media tower it was a very determined woman who paid the driver and then stepped into the sleek air-conditioned building and told the receptionist that she was here about the PA vacancy.

*'Un attimo, prego.'* The receptionist reached for her phone and a few moments later Ella stepped out of an elevator and was somewhat stunned by the response she received.

*'Buona fortuna!'* An exceptionally pretty and very

tearful woman thrust a black leather-bound diary and a set of car keys at Ella as she wished her good luck dealing with Santo and then shouted over her shoulder an old Italian proverb that Ella had heard a few times from her mother. 'If a man deceives me once, shame on him. If he deceives me twice, shame on me.'

'I take it that's a no, then?'

A deep, rich voice had Ella turn and, as he walked out of his office, she could, for a dizzying second, understand his PA's willingness to have given this man a second chance. She clearly wasn't giving him a third for, with a sob, she ran for the door, leaving Ella alone with him.

Green eyes met hers and there was a hint of an unrepentant smile on a very beautiful mouth and, on his left cheek, a livid red hand print.

'Are you here for an interview?' he asked Ella in Italian and when she nodded and introduced herself, he gestured to his office and she followed him in.

He needed no introduction.

# CHAPTER ONE

SANTO JERKED AWAKE, his heart racing, and reached out for familiar comfort, but rather than in bed with a lover beside him, he was asleep alone on a couch.

What happened last night?

His mind was a cruel trickster.

It did not tell him what had happened—it showed him little clues.

There was an empty whisky bottle on the floor, which Santo stepped over to get to the bathroom, and when he looked down he saw that he was still wearing the wedding suit, but his tie was off and the shirt torn and undone.

He checked the inside pocket of his jacket, re-membered Ella double- and triple-checking that he had them before she left and he went off to be best man at his brother's wedding.

The rings were still there.

He splashed his face with water; his face and chest were a mass of bruises.

Santo looked at his neck and grimaced, but a few love bites were the least of his concerns as yesterday's events started to come back to him.

Alessandro!

Santo picked up the phone to arrange a driver, but he got the night receptionist who, perhaps unaware that she should not ask such questions, enquired where he wanted to go and Santo promptly hung up.

Looking out of the window, from his luxurious vantage point, Santo could see the press waiting. Rarely for Santo, he couldn't stomach facing them, or his brother, alone.

'Can you pick me up?

Despite the hour, Ella answered the phone with her eyes closed. After four months working for Santo Corretti she was more than used to being called out of hours, though he sounded particularly terrible this morning. His deep, low voice, thick with Italian accent, was still beautiful, if a touch hoarse.

Yes, beautiful and terrible just about summed Santo up.

Peeling her eyes open, she looked at the figures on her bedside clock. 'It's 6:00 a.m.,' Ella said. 'On a Sunday.' Which should have been enough reason to end the call and go back to sleep. Yet, all night, Ella had been half expecting him to ring, so much so she had sat with her giant heated rollers in last night and had already laid her clothes out. Like the rest of Sicily, Ella had watched the drama unfold on television yesterday afternoon and had seen updates on the news all night. Even her mother in Australia, watching the Italian news, would know that the much-anticipated wedding of Santo's brother, Alessandro Corretti, to Alessia Battaglia had been called off at the last minute.

Literally, at the last minute.

The bride had fled midway down the aisle and the world was waiting to see how two of Sicily's most notorious families would deal with the fallout.

Yes, Ella had had a feeling that her services might be required before Monday.

'Look, this is my day off.' She did her best to hold firm. 'I worked yesterday...' Of course, as just his PA, Ella hadn't been invited to the wedding. Instead her job had been to ensure that Santo arrived sober, on time and looking divine as he always did.

The divine part had been easy—Santo made a beautiful best man. It was the other two requisites that had taken up rather a lot more of her people skills.

'I need to pick up Alessandro from the police station,' Santo said. 'He was arrested last night.'

Ella lay there silently, refusing to ask for details, while privately wondering just what else had happened yesterday.

She had raised a glass to the screen as she had seen Santo arrive at the church, talking and joking with Alessandro, privately thinking that the gene pool had surely been fizzing with expensive champagne when these two were conceived.

They could, at first glance, almost be twins—both were tall and broad shouldered, both wore their jet-black hair short, both had come-to-bed dark green eyes—but there were differences. Alessandro was the eldest, and the two years that divided the brothers were significant.

As firstborn son to the late Carlo Corretti, Alessandro was rather more ruthless, whereas Santo was a touch lighter in personality, more fun and extremely flirty—but he could still be completely arrogant at times.

'Come and pick me up now,' Santo said, as if to prove her point. Ella let out a long breath, telling herself that in a few weeks, if she got the job she had applied for, then all the scandal and drama of the Correttis would be a thing of the past. Working for Santo was nothing like she'd imagined it would be. 'The press are everywhere,' he warned, which was Santo's shorthand to remind her to look smart—even in a crisis he insisted on appearances. 'Take a taxi and then pick up my car and drive it around to the hotel entrance. Text me when you're there.'

'I hate driving your car,' Ella started, but was met again with silence. Having given his orders, Santo would assume she was jumping to the snap of his manicured fingers, and had already hung up.

'Bastard,' Ella hissed and then she heard his voice.

'You love me, really.'

Ella was too annoyed to be embarrassed. 'I love lying in on a Sunday morning.'

'Tough.'

This time he did hang up.

In a few weeks you'll be out of it, Ella told herself as she rang for a taxi. The woman on the other end of the phone sounded half asleep as well and told Ella it would be a good fifteen minutes to half an hour, which suited her fine. She climbed out of bed and headed straight for the shower and then to the mirror, but Santo could forget it if he thought she was going to arrive in full make-up. She changed her mind, because like it or not, Santo was her boss and Ella took her work very seriously. So, instead of a slick of mascara and lipgloss—which were usual weekend fare, if she wore any make-up at all— Ella set to work with the make-up brushes and then smoothed out her hair a touch and tied it into a low ponytail. She pulled on a dark grey skirt and sheer cream blouse and added low heels.

One good thing about working for Santo was her clothing allowance.

Actually, it was the only good thing.

And Ella wasn't even particularly interested in clothes!

Hearing the taxi toot outside her small rented flat, Ella checked her appearance one more time and then grabbed her 'Santo Bag' as she called it, making sure that she had his spare set of car keys, before heading outside. She squinted at the morning sun and took in the vivid colours of a gorgeous Palermo in May. The ocean was glistening and the city still seemed to be sleeping. No doubt the whole of Sicily had had a late night, waiting for updates in the news.

*'Buongiorno.'* Ella gave the taxi driver the address of the smart hotel where Santo was staying and then sat back and listened to the morning news on the radio.

Of course the jilted Corretti groom was being talked about long after the headlines had been read.

And, of course, the taxi driver was more than delighted with the news. 'Trouble!' he told her. 'As if a wedding would ever unite the Corretti and Battaglia families...' and happily he chatted some more, unaware he was driving her to meet with Santo. Ella chose not to enlighten him. Santo didn't exactly keep her informed about the goings-on in his family. If anything, his Italian picked up pace if he ever had to speak with one of them, just enough to make it almost impossible for her to work out what was being said.

'They have always fought?' Ella checked.

'Always,' the driver told her and then added that even the death of Salvatore Corretti a few weeks ago would not bring peace between the two families. 'The Correttis even war with themselves.'

That much Ella knew. Even though Santo didn't reveal much about his family, Ella was forever having to deal with the feuding Corretti cousins. The family was incredibly divided and they were all constantly trying to outdo the other, under the guise of the family empire. They were all trying to outmanoeuvre one another in the bid to become top dog, not just at work, but with cars, with women, with horses. Ella was sick of it. She was tired of the dark secrets and mind games they all played.

She'd have put up with it for a while longer though, if Santo would just give her a small step onto the ladder she wanted to climb. Over and over she had asked him if she could work on just one of his films as a junior assistant director.

'*Presto,*' Santo would say and then, as he did all too often when he spoke to her in Italian, he would annoyingly translate for her. 'Soon.'

Well, soon, she'd be gone.

Ella asked the driver to stop while she bought some coffee and then climbed back in.

As they approached the hotel Ella told the driver that she wished to be dropped off in the underground car park. As they approached she saw that Santo was right—there were a lot of press around and security was tight. Ella was more than happy to show her ID before paying the taxi driver and telling the concerned valet that she wanted to personally take the car up to collect her boss.

Ella slipped into the front seat and smelt not the leather, but the familiar, expensive scent of Santo. Before she started the engine she texted him, letting him know she was in the basement and on her way to collect him.

The engine growled at the merest touch of her foot and she jerked her way through the car park, doing her best to ignore the flash of cameras as the paparazzi stirred at the new activity taking place.

Come on, Santo, she muttered as she sat with the engine idling, glad of the effort she'd made as cameras clicked away, worried, too, that he might have fallen back to sleep after he had called her. But then, still wearing last night's suit, she saw him, walking just a little unsteadily towards the car. Ella's lips pressed together when she saw the state he was in. The press were going to have a field day. His suit was torn and dirty and he was wearing several fresh bruises too. His deathly pale skin only accentuated the fact that he hadn't shaved.

*'Buongiorno!'* Ella said loudly and brightly as he climbed in.

'Good morning, Ella.'

It was a small game that they played, one that they had partaken in since her interview. Ella, determined to show him how wonderful her Italian was, attempting to prove that just because she was Australian it didn't mean that she wasn't up for the job, had introduced herself in her very best Italian.

Santo had promptly responded in English—pulling rank and basically saying that his English was better than her Italian, which was of course right. Though, as it turned out, Ella did speak enough Italian to land the job. But when it was just the two of them, they conversed mainly in English, except for this one mutual game.

'I thought you wanted us looking smart.'

He just frowned.

'You said there were press everywhere.'

'There are,' Santo said. 'I was just warning you.'

'Here.' She handed him his coffee.

'You need to get one for Alessandro,' Santo said.

'I already did.'

'Let's go then.'

They jerked out of the forecourt. 'Why do you

have to have gears?' Ella moaned, because she always drove an automatic, though of course Santo didn't consider that real driving. Still, he didn't answer, just sat, unusually quiet, as the car moved out into the bright sunlight. Glancing over she watched him wince and, taking mild pity, Ella put her hand in her Santo Bag and handed him a pair of sunglasses. But even they didn't fully cover the purple bruise on his eye.

As the press surged, Ella inched gingerly forward, aware that one slip of her foot on Santo's accelerator could flatten the lot of them.

'Just go!' Santo cursed as they gathered for their shots and then he cursed again as Ella blasted the horn a few times and finally dispersed them.

His mood didn't improve as they drove through town. 'I hate driving in this country,' Ella muttered as she was forced to swerve and narrowly missed a Vespa. In Australia they drove on the left-hand side of the road and occasionally they even managed to follow the road rules.

Though it wasn't the traffic that was getting to Ella, nor the 6:00 a.m. wake-up call from her boss, whatever fight he had been in last night didn't account for the purple marks on his neck.

Bloody hell, she thought darkly, even in the middle of a family scandal, even as the Battaglia and Corretti families exploded, trust Santo to still be at it.

With who though?

No, Ella was not going to ask for details.

She really didn't want to know if he'd run true to form and gotten off with Taylor Carmichael, the stunning American actress who was playing the leading role in the latest film Santo was producing.

Shooting started on Monday and Santo had made it his personal mission to keep Taylor out of trouble. He had insisted that she attend yesterday's wedding to both ensure that Taylor behaved and to garner some publicity for the film. But with both their reputations, it was perhaps a forgone conclusion as to what had taken place.

It really was time to move on. If she didn't get the new job, then maybe she could head to London, or France perhaps.

Or even go home?

He asked her to stop so that he could draw out some cash to hopefully expedite getting his brother out of the lock-up and Ella closed her eyes and leant her head back on the headrest. The thought of home

brought no comfort at all. It was her mother's birthday in a few days and Ella would be expected to call.
She was gripped with sudden panic at the thought
and opened her eyes and took a couple of deep
breaths as she realised that no, she was nowhere
near ready to go home.

She watched as Santo had a few attempts at
the machine and then, with an irritated sigh, Ella
climbed out of the car and walked over to him, tapping his number in.

'What would I do without you?' There was no
endearment in his question. He turned his head for
a moment and Ella felt heat rise on her cheeks, but
then told herself that there was no challenge behind
his words. There was no way Santo could know what
she had been up to in recent days.

And, Ella consoled herself, who in her position
wouldn't be looking for another job? She was tired
of bailing him out, tired because now she'd had to
get up at some ridiculous hour on her one day off to
bail his brother out. Tired, too, of running Santo's
not-so-little black book—sending flowers and jewellery to his girlfriends, booking intimate tables in
fantastic restaurants, organising romantic weekends
and then having to calm ruffled feathers when in-

variably, inevitably, Santo upset them in his oh-so-usual way.

'How was Taylor?' She simply couldn't stop herself from asking, because it was imperative for the film publicity that Taylor had behaved herself last night.

*'Niente dichiarazione,'* Santo responded, smiling at her pursed lips. 'I am practising "no comment" for the press today. Perhaps you could practise too.'

He was so good at deflecting questions, not just about women, about everything. Always managing to shrug off things that should matter but simply didn't to Santo.

As they pulled up at the police station, Ella was relieved that there were no press waiting; at least word hadn't got out yet that Alessandro was here.

'How do you think he'll be?'

'Hungover.' Santo yawned. 'And far better off without her.'

He went to climb out and Ella, who'd assumed that she'd be sitting for half an hour, or however long it took to bail someone out, was surprised when Santo turned around and asked if she would come in with him.

'Me?' Ella checked.

'You might sweeten up the *polizia.*'

'I find that really offensive, Santo.'

'Ah, but you find so many things really offensive, Ella,' he drawled.

Ella collected Allesandro's coffee and walked towards the police station with Santo. She knew exactly what that little dig had been about—Ella was the first PA he hadn't slept with. She had made it clear, to his obvious surprise, that this was business only. To his credit he had backed off completely, but now and then there was a little dig, a tiny reference to the fact she was resistant to his charms.

Not completely, of course.

No woman could be. He was stunning to look at and incredibly sexy, but completely incorrigible. Yes, a night with the boss might be tempting at times, especially when he smiled, especially when he looked as impossibly beautiful as he did today. But it was the thought of the morning after that, for Ella, was enough to ensure she resisted.

They stepped into the station and there was a lot of talking, a lot of hand waving and the handing over of an awful lot of cash, but, surprisingly quickly, a very dishevelled Alessandro appeared. He had his share of bruises too and there were grazes over his knuckles and that oh-so-immaculate bridegroom suit was covered in dust and torn.

'Here.' Ella handed him his coffee, which was no doubt cold by now, but Alessandro drained it in one go as they walked back out of the police station. He winced at the far-too-bright morning sunlight that seemed to be magnified by the ocean, and Ella handed him a pair of sunglasses too—she always carried spares.

Ella wasn't Santo's PA for nothing!

'Thank you,' Alessandro said. Putting them on he looked at his brother, taking in the bruises and thick lip and the nasty graze on Santo's cheek. 'What happened to your face?'

Ella held her breath.

She was dying to know, but the answer served only to surprise and further confuse her.

'You did,' came Santo's wry response.

## CHAPTER TWO

'YOU DON'T REMEMBER?' Santo asked, once they were in the car and Alessandro had asked Ella to drive him to his home.

'I am trying not to.'

They were speaking in Italian, but Ella could pretty much make out all that was being said.

'I spent the whole night trying to contact you,' Santo said.

'Clearly, not the whole night,' came Alessandro's terse response. 'Who the hell did you let loose on your neck?'

Santo just laughed and offered no explanation. 'I must have rung you fifty times.'

'And forty-nine times I chose not to answer.' Alessandro withdrew into silence and Ella didn't blame him. Santo, it would seem, had not a care in the

world. He just scrolled through the endless ream of
texts on his phone as they talked, ignoring the constant buzzes to alert him to a call.

Ella drove them to the Corretti Media tower,
where Alessandro had a luxurious penthouse, but
the paparazzi were still clamouring for their shot of
the jilted groom.

'Lie down in the back if you want,' Ella suggested.
'I brought a coat for you. I'll try to get in the back
way.' But Alessandro refused her suggestion to lie
down, told her to just drop him at the front and sat
there stony faced as the cameras flashed and report-
ers shouted their questions.

'I'll come in with you,' Santo said.

'I don't need a handhold,' came Alessandro's
terse response, but Santo ignored him and when
she stopped the car both the brothers got out.

The gathered press went into a frenzy. Both were,
Ella knew, more than used to dealing with them.
There were always questions and scandal where this
family was concerned. But though there were questions that would certainly need to be answered, interviews that would have to be given and the press
to be faced, clearly, for Alessandro, it was all just
a little too soon. Ella watched as a rather personal

question was asked and Alessandro's shoulders stiffened, his hands balling into two fists. Perhaps Santo realised that his brother was very close to losing his temper again, because for once, Santo made a very sensible choice and turned his brother back towards the vehicle. Ella reached out and opened the door and Santo shoved his fuming brother into the back of the car before climbing into the front.

'Drive on,' Santo said. 'Get around the corner, and then I will drive.' He was clearly impatient by Ella's rather tentative speed and once around the corner Santo reminded her that he had asked her to pull over.

'Fine, but if you're driving I'm getting out. I can smell the whisky from here.'

For once he didn't offer a smart retort, just gestured for her to carry on, and turning the car around at the first opportunity, she drove the trio back into town.

'We can go to the hotel you are staying at,' Ella suggested to Santo. 'We can enter via the basement.'

'No,' Alessandro said. 'I'm not going to be holed up somewhere by the press. I just want away from them.'

'We could go to mine.' Ella tried to think how best

to give Alessandro privacy for a few days, though she could hardly imagine him staying at her cheap rental place. 'It's just a small villa, but it's pretty tucked away, so I'm sure that they'd never think to look for you there.'

Ella glanced in the mirror as she awaited his response, but instead of answering her, Alessandro spoke briefly to his brother, who argued with him for a moment.

But then Santo spoke. 'Take him to the harbour at Cala Marina.' Santo gave her directions. 'Alessandro wants to go to his yacht.'

Ella did as she was told, heading to the harbour where Alessandro's yacht was docked. But despite her resolve to refuse to ask for details and despite reminding herself that it was none of her business as the car ate up the miles, on this, Ella couldn't stay silent. 'Do you really think that's such a good idea?' She turned worried eyes to Santo. Ella really didn't like the idea of Alessandro alone on a yacht, given all that had happened.

'I have just been reminded that I am the younger brother.' Santo scratched at his neck and then pulled at his unbuttoned collar as if it was a little too tight.

'He insists that we take him or he shall arrange his own transport there.'

Which gave them no choice—they were hardly going to let Alessandro out on the street to make his own way. So they drove, pretty much in silence, till they neared the pretty harbour. Ella almost willed one of the brothers to start talking so she could find out just a little of what had taken place last night, but perhaps because she was there, neither spoke about family matters.

*'Dove Alessia?'* For the first time Alessandro initiated conversation, asking where his ex-fiancée was, and Ella held her breath as they pulled into the harbour.

*'Puttana,'* came Santo's crude and dismissive response, but Alessandro was insistent.

'Where is she?'

And Ella was still holding her breath when Santo answered his brother, telling him the truth in a very dismissive voice—that it would seem that Alessia and their cousin Matteo had run off together.

The expletive that came from Alessandro was perhaps merited, and unlike Santo, he was nice enough to give a brief apology to Ella for his language before leaving the car and staggering off towards his yacht.

Santo sat for a moment and watched his brother and then climbed out of the car, trying, Ella presumed, to persuade Alessandro to come back with them.

She watched them argue for a moment but the bond between the two brothers was clear. It mattered not that Alessandro had thrown a few punches at Santo last night. It didn't change anything between them. Not for the first time Ella wondered what it would be like to have a sibling, how it might feel to have someone in your corner—for how it hurt to deal with her parents alone.

But whatever Santo said to his brother, it didn't work. Alessandro shrugged him off and she watched as Santo stood for a moment, then turned around. But instead of a roll of the eyes and the slightly cocky smile Santo often wore, his face was grey as he walked back towards the car and climbed in.

They sat for a moment and watched Alessandro board his yacht.

'Do you think he'll be all right?' Ella was loath to leave.

'Of course,' Santo said. 'He's tough.'

He'd need to be tough—being jilted at the altar

with the world's cameras aimed on him, Ella thought. 'Santo, I don't know that it's right to leave him.'

'Just drive.' Again Santo dismissed her worries. 'He'll be fine.'

She couldn't believe his lack of concern, but that was Santo. He dealt with stuff as it cropped up and then moved easily on to the next thing, never worrying about the chaos he was leaving behind.

Ella rang ahead and asked housekeeping to sort out his suite and run a bath and asked for some breakfast and a lot of coffee to be sent up.

'Assuming that your company won't mind,' Ella checked, telling herself that she wasn't fishing for answers.

'She's gone.'

'Just the one?' Ella glanced over, thinking she'd get a glimpse of a smile, but Santo was just staring out of his window.

The press were still waiting but Santo didn't duck. He just sat there as they got their shots. As Ella went to indicate, to enter the hotel via the more secure route of the basement, Santo stopped her.

'The foyer will be fine—I don't need the basement.' In fact, he took off his dark glasses and pocketed them before he got out, hurling a filthy look straight in the direction of the cameras before stalking into the hotel with his head held high. Ella threw the car keys to the valet and caught up with him at the lift. As the doors closed behind them, Santo slumped against the wall for a moment, his eyes closed, and Ella was no longer just worried about Alessandro—no, she was more than a little concerned for Santo too. He was incredibly pale. Assuming that it was Alessandro who had hit him last night, then it was one very angry fist Santo would have found himself at the end of—maybe he'd been knocked out?

'Are you hurt anywhere else?'

He didn't open his eyes, just shook his head.

'Were you knocked out?' Ella checked.

'Unfortunately, no.' Green eyes opened and he gave a thin smile and she found herself staring back to a different Santo. It was as if all the arrogance had left him, as if, for once, she was seeing the man he really was and it was mesmerising. She simply could not stop staring—even as the lift doors opened—and for a moment the two of them just stood.

'What happened?' She had sworn not to ask, yet she did.

'Why?'

'I just…' She flailed for words. 'I'm concerned.'

'Sure you are!' There was an edge to his words that told her he considered her a liar. For a moment she was confused, but now wasn't the time to dwell on it. Instead they walked to his suite. Of course, he couldn't find his swipe card but, of course, she carried a spare.

As they stepped into the suite it was scandal rather than breakfast that awaited. Santo thumbed through the papers and Ella gave in and picked up one. Perhaps, she consoled herself, it was better that Alessandro was on a boat and escaping all this, for the photos and write-ups were brutal.

'Oh!' Ella let out a small crow of shock at one particular photo. There was Taylor Carmichael, the woman Santo should have been policing yesterday, the actress who he was relying on to behave, running true to form despite promises that she had changed.

'Is it any surprise?' Santo shrugged.

Probably not, Ella conceded. In fact, her only surprise was that the man in the image wasn't Santo. But did he care about nothing? Filming started tomorrow and there had been a lot of fireworks about the casting of the leading female role. Taylor's comeback after a spectacular unravelling was risky at best—a disaster for the film at worst.

And this looked like it was turning into a complete disaster.

Still, problems with the film would have to wait till tomorrow. Right now Ella had more pressing things to sort out—like six-foot-three of beaten-up, hungover male. 'Go and have a bath,' Ella said. 'I'll chase breakfast.'

'I don't want breakfast' was his inevitable response. 'I'm just going to go to bed. Thanks for all your help.'

'You have to eat something,' Ella started, and then shut up. After all, she wasn't his mother. Not that his own mother would be worrying too much—Carmela Corretti's only concerns were fashion and manicures.

'Just have a bath.' Ella settled for, 'I don't care whether or not you eat. I for one happen to be starving, so I'm chasing them.'

'Sure.'

He headed to the bathroom and after a few minutes there was a knock at the door and Ella stood as the maid set up the table.

'Thank you,' Ella said, pouring herself a coffee

and trying not to overthink who he'd been with last night. It was none of her business what Santo got up to.

She flicked through the papers, reading some of the more salacious details that had come out. They were the most complicated of families and for a while she was lost in the gossip. But later, glancing at the bedside clock, Ella realised he'd been in there ages. She thought maybe he had fallen asleep and she tried to ignore the knot of worry in her stomach, but after a moment or two she knocked.

'Breakfast is here.'

Ella stood at the door and all she could hear was silence.

'Santo...' She knocked again. 'Answer me.'

Nothing.

'Santo!' Ella tried to keep the note of panic from her voice as she thought of head injuries and hangovers and the fact that the newspaper headlines could be far worse tomorrow than they were now. She was actually terrified for him.

'Santo!' She rapped loudly. 'If you don't answer then I'm going to have to come in.'

Still nothing.

Ella tried the handle, but of course it was locked.

Heart in her mouth she ran to her bag, rummaging through it and then through her purse to find a coin. With shaking fingers, she fitted it into the slot and turned the lock.

'Santo!' she shouted and when still there was no response, Ella knew she had no choice but to go in.

# CHAPTER THREE

'SANTO...' AS SOON as she opened the door, Ella regretted it.

There were some things she simply shouldn't see and immediately Ella knew why he hadn't answered her.

Santo's modesty was covered by bubbles, his head resting on the edge of the bath. His eyes were screwed closed, and his lips were pressed together. For once Ella wasn't catching her boss doing something inappropriate—that she could deal with. What she couldn't immediately deal with was the fact that Santo Corretti, a man who charmed his way through life, who always had a smart answer for everything, who, she was sure, cared about nothing other than movies and getting laid, was lying in a bath and trying and failing not to cry.

Santo never cried.

He could not remember a single time that he had. It was an entirely new experience to him.

Not when his father, Carlo, had died alongside his uncle. Nor had there been a hint of a tear at his grandfather's death. Not even as a little boy—it was as if he'd been born knowing that tears would never work with his mother, Carmela, and any sign of weakness would only have infuriated Carlo. So instead Santo had relied solely on looks, wit and charm.

He'd just run out them today.

'Go…' He put his hand up, the word barely making it out of his lips, his shoulders shaking with the effort of holding it in. Both wished they were embarrassed for a rather more salacious reason.

'I can't just go.' And no, this wasn't in her job description, but Ella wasn't just going to leave him, so she sat on the edge of the bath and pondered the man. He was unshaven, there were bruises on his chest too and he looked battered but not just physically—he looked broken.

She had at times wondered if there were any feelings to be had in that beautiful head, but now he lay clearly shattered and she watched as he blew out a breath and then finally spoke.

'Do you really think he'll be okay?'

'It's Alessandro!' Ella said firmly. 'Which means yes—of course he'll be fine. He just needs some time.'

After a moment Santo nodded and then opened his eyes. Ella didn't want him to be so beautiful, but seeing this side of him just served to confuse her more. 'I really do think that he'll be fine.'

'It's not just Alessandro…' he admitted. 'It's the whole lot of them. You should have heard the stuff that came out last night,' Santo started, but didn't continue.

'You can tell me.'

'Because you care?' There was a strange surliness to his words and Ella frowned, but then he shrugged. 'It is family stuff—it is not for me to say.'

Ella chose not to push. She knew all about family secrets, knew there were certain things you just didn't speak about. She had lived her life keeping quiet after all.

She looked around the bathroom and wondered

how someone could make so much mess in so little time. His clothes were strewn all over the floor, the tap was still running where Santo had brushed his teeth and no, she noted he didn't replace the cap.

'It's a mess,' Santo said, only she guessed that he wasn't talking about the bathroom.

'Families often are.'

She looked at him then, met his eyes. Usually she pulled hers away, usually she could not stand to have anyone examine her soul. But she saw the green and the bloodshot and the pain in his and for a second she thought she might cry too, which she hadn't since that terrible day. As Ella sat looking at Santo she was a breath away from telling him that she knew the pain the people who should love you the most could cause, but she held on to it, just as she always had.

He did not ask.

She did not tell.

It was safer that way.

'Come on,' Ella finally said. She knew that he would hate to have been seen like this, knew that neither would mention it again.

She put her hand in the water and met his ankle, but she brushed past that and pulled out the plug.

Then standing she turned off the sink tap. But as she went to go, Santo just lay there, the water rather rapidly disappearing, and before she saw far too much of her boss Ella grabbed a towel.

'I'll avert my gaze,' Ella said, holding the towel up while trying to make a joke, but there was simply no room for jokes this morning and no room for modesty either. In the end, Santo took her hand and sort of hauled himself out of the bath as Ella did her best not to look. He tucked the towel around his hips and walked out to the suite, bypassing the breakfast that had been laid out and heading straight to bed.

'Sorry about this.'

'Oh, you will be…' Ella started and then stopped. Now really wasn't a time for their regular teasing. 'Let's just forget about it.' He gave her a slightly suspicious look, but Ella meant it. Yes, they might tease each other at times, but she wasn't going to use this. 'It never happened, Santo.'

'Thanks.' He gave a brief nod and then went back to telling her what to do. 'Can you get my phone?'

He sat on the edge of the bed as Ella went off and he could hear her loading up plates and pouring drinks. Santo really did not know what was happening to him—it was as if everything had suddenly

caught up, everything he had pushed down and ignored or suppressed was now strewn out before him
and refused to go back into its neat box. Family secrets spewing out last night had made Santo feel
physically sick. For the first time he hadn't even
been able to screw his way out of it—last night he
had removed his mouth from hers, felt her lips on his
neck and looked down at another nameless blonde
and couldn't be fagged to head to bed. Instead he
had sent her on her way and spent the night with a
bottle of whisky, trying to get hold of Alessandro.

Santo sat there searching for one good area of his
life, but even the film was in trouble now thanks to
Taylor's behaviour yesterday.

One good thing.

He looked up as Ella walked in, his very professional, somewhat aloof PA, and very annoyed suddenly, Santo climbed into bed and tossed the towel
to the floor in a very surly gesture because, apart
from the drama of his family, he'd found another
thing out yesterday.

'You're leaving?'

Ella felt a blush spread over her cheeks, and it
wasn't because he was clearly naked beneath the
sheets. There was the awful part when looking for

another job where you naturally didn't let your employer know. She had felt such horrible guilt as she'd lied about her whereabouts and, to make matters worse, Santo had been really nice about her trip to Rome to supposedly visit a doctor. He'd paid for her flight and even put her up in a luxurious hotel overnight. Ella understood now a couple of the barbs that had come her way this morning. She'd offered him the chance to speak about his family when he'd known that she was already planning to leave.

Ella walked over and actually sat on the edge of the bed and looked at his scowling face. 'I don't know for sure if I'm leaving yet,' she said.

'That trip to Rome wasn't for the doctors...' She blushed darker as he said it. 'The film industry is a tight one, Ella—people talk.'

'I don't even know if I've got the job.'

'Well, it sounds like you have. Luigi rang yesterday for your references,' Santo said. 'You'll forgive me if I don't offer my congratulations.'

And she wanted more details but, given the situation, it would be unfair to ask for them. She daren't get her hopes up either, not till Luigi contacted her. Maybe all it would be was an invite for a second interview. 'Can we talk about this later?'

'We'll talk about it now.' Santo glared at her. 'I understand you want to be a director—I get that you want some involvement—but the director I have hired for this movie comes with his own team.' He took a breath, realised that he did not want to lose her. 'When I hire for the next movie, I will make it a priority to see if whomever I hire—'

'I wanted in on this movie, Santo.' Ella looked at him. 'I love the script so much, you know that.'

'And you know how important this film is to me, Ella, even more so now.'

'Now?'

'I am not going into that, other than to say I am not taking any risks with it.'

'Unless it's a risk called Taylor Carmichael,' Ella snapped.

'And look how that risk has paid off? But I will consider you for the next one.'

'It's not just that.' Ella closed her eyes. When you were Santo's PA there was plenty of other stuff to complain about. 'I don't get a moment....' She looked at him. 'You're way more than a full-time job, Santo.'

'This was an exception. I do not ring you usually on a Sunday.'

'Santo, Sunday starts at midnight on a Saturday night, so actually, quite often, you do.'

This was her job, Santo consoled himself as he sat there, but he knew he had been pushing things this weekend. Though he would never admit it out loud, he did concede that he had been nervous about the wedding, at the two families in the same church and the reception afterwards. Spending yesterday morning with Ella had been somewhat soothing.

Today, facing his brother, he had wanted her alongside.

'You've become indispensable.'

'No,' Ella said, refusing to give in to him. Santo had a way with words and was very good at saying the right thing when he wanted his own way. 'No one is.'

'Perhaps,' Santo said, and then thought for a moment. 'We get on.'

'Not all of the time.'

'I thought we did—we have had some laughs.'

She looked at his depraved face, at a man who so easily made her laugh and had no idea what a feat that was—no idea how tender and bruised her soul had been when she had first met him. That the smile she had worn for her interview had been false on so many levels. Of course she could share that with no one and so Ella looked down, took a croissant from the plate and peeled a piece off and then popped it in her mouth, aware that he was closely watching.

'I thought you were about to feed me.'

She was glad to see the slight return to his humour.

'Not a chance.' She gave him a weak smile as he checked his phone. 'Any messages?'

'Nothing.'

She could see the worry in the set of his lips. 'I didn't realise you and Alessandro were so close.'

'We're brothers,' Santo said, as if that explained everything. 'Do you have a brother or sister?'

'Nope—just me.' He noticed the slight strain to her voice, and he should have left it, really, except he did not.

'You hardly ever speak of your family.'

'Because we hardly ever speak.'

'How come?' Santo asked, but Ella shook her head. She just wasn't going to go there with him. It was time she left the room now and so once he'd eaten a croissant and drained his coffee she took the tray and stood.

'Is there anything else I can do for you?'

'You know there is.'

Yes, his humour was back!

'Get some sleep,' Ella said and turned off the hotel phone by his bedside. Then she headed over and drew the drapes, more than a little aware that Santo was watching her. She was just too aware of him too much of the time. As she glanced down she could see the press outside the hotel, still hovering, and she knew that this wasn't going to go away any time soon.

'Okay.' She walked back over to the bed. 'I'll leave you till about two.'

'You're staying?'

'I'll do some work in the lounge.'

'Come in and check my pulse.'

'No, but I will answer your phone. Is there any comment you want me to give?'

'I'll deal with all of that.'

As she went to take his phone from the bedside he stopped her, his hand closing over hers. 'No.'

'I'll deal with the calls,' Ella said. 'Santo, that's what you pay me for. If it's Alessandro I'll bring the phone straight through to you.' She was terribly aware of his hand over hers, and more so when still it remained. She should simply have lifted her hand

and walked out the room, as she would have on any
other day, except she didn't and neither did she resist when he pulled her back to sit on the bed. With
the curtains drawn it was unlike before—dark and
more intimate and too much for her racing heart.

'Do you have to leave?'

'Santo, please…' Ella really didn't want to talk
about it now. 'I have to think about my career. Can
we…?'

'I meant, do you have to leave the room?'

'You didn't mean that.' Ella blushed as he smiled.
Usually she rebuffed any flirting easily. It was just a
little harder to do this morning and not just because
they were on a bed in a very dark room, more because she felt as if she had glimpsed today the real
Santo, the one behind the very expensive but very
shallow facade.

'I would miss you.'

'For a little while.' Ella smiled.

'There could be advantages though.…' As he
spoke, Ella's heart thumped in her chest, knew what
he was leading up to. 'Remember how you told me
you would never get involved with someone you
work with?'

'I do.'

Her second day at work, they had gone for dinner after, had sat side by side and pored through his diary, Ella taking notes, trying to be efficient but terribly aware of his beauty and trying to ignore it, just trying to work, when his hand had reached for her face.

She'd tried to emulate the hairdresser, had done everything they had said, except her curls hadn't been quite so glossy and kept escaping the hair tie. She'd felt his hand move to her cheek, his fingers capturing a lock of her hair.

'Don't.'

Refreshingly he hadn't made an excuse and neither had he apologised as he dropped contact. Instead he'd asked a question. 'Why?' His eyes had frowned a little, a curious smile on his lips at her response. No doubt it was one he wasn't used to.

'I don't have to give an answer to that.' Ella had more than met his eyes. 'But if you try anything like that again, you'll have my notice with immediate effect.'

How she rued those words now.

'We have a problem,' Santo said and she looked at him. Though it was terribly hard to think of Santo and morals at the same time, Ella realised, he did actually have some. For apart from a few stunning suggestions, apart from the odd gentle flirt, not once since that day had he put so much as a finger wrong.

She just wanted him to put that finger wrong now.

And he did.

Just one finger dusted her forearm and Santo waited for her hand to halt his, gave her every opportunity to stand, to change her mind. She'd been very clear as to her boundaries, but his breath stilled as he felt them tumble down.

Hell had been the night, and the morning pure misery, but now… He felt the tiny hairs on her arm rise beneath the pads of his fingers and the constant shiver between them deepen as her silence let him go on.

'Immediate effect…' Santo said and he wasn't checking her leaving date, more the flare of her skin to his, but she did appreciate the check-in. All she wanted now was to find out how it felt to be kissed by a man as expert and beautiful as Santo.

'I already told you—today never happened.'

He was wary to move too fast and kiss her, and anyway, there was more that his hand wanted to do. It moved up to her neck, his fingers to her cheek, and it lingered a long time on that same lock of hair, where once she had halted him, and then to lips that had never met his. He felt them, slowly explored them.

Ella sat there, her heart pounding, because she had never expected this. She had never known fingers on her lips could be so sensual. Oh, she had heard much about the man, had dreamt about him a little more than she would ever admit to, but she had just never thought of him like this.

She had never thought that he might be slow and unhurried and make her burn between her legs without even offering his mouth.

His fingers worked the flesh of her lips as if he were stroking her below, teasing and worrying the curve of her Cupid's bow. Then he slipped his finger in and she caught it loosely with her teeth and licked around it, sucked lightly on it. Her tease worked too, because Santo pulled her to him then and replaced his fingers with his tongue. It was a very deep, intimate kiss, his tongue lolling around hers. His hand was on her head, pushing her deeper towards him.

It was, Ella thought as she sank beneath his hand, as if they had kissed five hundred times before, for both knew exactly what the other wanted. She loved the noise of them, the moan he sighed into her mouth. But just as she went to end it, just when she knew she had to, his other hand found her breast and, not in the least bit tenderly, he stroked it. She succumbed to his palm and fingers for there was nothing subtle and as her body responded she was very aware that he was naked beneath the bedding and also, thanks to earlier, very aware as to how delicious the view was under there.

Just when she should leave, when she should stop this, just as her face went to move back, Santo read it. He chased her with his mouth, reached now for her hips and guided her to a stand, a stand where she was bending and kissing him. When she stopped, he did not let her retreat, because the magic of his mouth had her kneeling on the bed and the implicit message from his hands had her lying on top of him, looking down at him.

'Where were we?' He smiled. 'Oh, that's right...' and he got back to kissing. And even though it was Ella dressed and on top, she felt as if she were naked beneath, for he had completely taken her over, his hands sliding over her bottom, pressing her in. Then he moved her a fraction, till she was perfectly poised, and he lifted his hips as his hands shifted her.

It was supposed to be a kiss, but he was filthy and

indecent and just so good. It really was supposed to have been just a kiss except his fingers had undone her skirt and his hands now slid in and cupped her bottom and still he moved her.

'Santo.' She tried to halt him, had no idea the fire she'd been playing with. She'd known he'd be good, but Ella just hadn't been prepared for how good he was. In just a few minutes her body felt scalded, and in no time at all she wanted to tear at her clothes just for the relief of being naked. She was grappling for control here and fast realising that with Santo she had none.

'Come on, Ella…' He was hurrying her for a reason. He wanted her to come so that two minutes later he could, because Santo knew the second he was inside he'd explode. His hand was working the curves that had taunted him for months now and he wanted to spend the day making up for lost time. Finally there was one good thing to hold on to and hold on to it he did, squeezing and digging his fingers into her buttocks, grinding his hips up to hers. He was just lost in the reprieve from the hell she had given him, so lost that it took a second to realise that she had stopped kissing him He looked up to Ella as she lifted her head, his hands stilling as the once-mutual rhythm stopped.

'Get some sleep.' She was as breathless as he.

'Don't do that to me.' Santo grinned and pressed into her again.

'I am doing that.'

'Ella!'

'It's a kiss, Santo…' she attempted, because it had been so very much more. 'It doesn't always have to lead to something.' Except her body said otherwise, but she was not going to lose her head to him. She reminded herself why—he was a rake, and an unrepentant rake at that. 'Have you seen the state of your neck?' she sweetly said. 'I find it a bit off-putting.'

'Nothing happened last night.'

He felt her disbelieving half-laugh, felt it reverberate through him as her breasts lay heavy and warm on his chest. 'Actually, it's true. I got so bored kissing her, midway my mind wandered.' It was terrible that he could make her laugh. 'Next thing I knew she was leeched onto my neck.'

'You should pay more attention.'

She was reminded of the placement of his hands as his fingers stroked her buttocks gently and then ventured just a little further to her centre. 'Oh, I'll pay attention, miss.'

So tempting was that thought she almost conceded, but no, it was supposed to have been just a kiss and Ella needed her head, needed to think, and with Santo lying naked beneath her, it wasn't a very doable ask.

'Go to sleep.' She gave him a light kiss on the lips but did not linger. She prised her body from his and stood, did up her skirt with hands that were shaking and made no effort to tuck her blouse in, just collected the phone. But as she reached the door his voice caught her.

'Could you pass me the tissues?'

'You know what, Santo?' Ella was at the door. 'You just take things too far sometimes.'

'Sorry?' She heard the question in his voice and then he laughed. 'I want to blow my nose. It's a curious thing this crying. I've never done it before. I feel like I have a cold.'

'Liar!' Ella said, and threw him the box.

He caught it and then his words caught her again at the door. 'But if you change your mind...'

# CHAPTER FOUR

SHE WOULD NOT be changing her mind, so instead Ella headed out of the bedroom and, closing the door, poured herself a glass of grapefruit juice. She liked the tart taste on her tongue but it did not quench her, because her mouth still thrummed from his attention. The skin on her face was still alive from the drag of his jaw and there was a triangle of ache from her nipples that pointed down. The heavy bedroom door might just as well be made of paper, because it would be so easy to walk through it.

Ella was the most focused, determined person where her work was concerned, and certainly wouldn't let any man get in the way.

Not even one as drop-dead gorgeous as Santo.

Especially not one as drop-dead gorgeous as Santo.

Ella was well aware she attracted bastards—a couple of relationships had taught her that—only Santo wasn't actually one.

He never made promises he had no intention of keeping. His reputation served as enough of a warning and fool was the woman who might think he would change.

Ella wasn't a fool.

She's simply refused to give in to the want that sometimes curled inside when he was around. Her career came first, but this morning, knowing she was perhaps leaving, for a few dangerous moments she had given in.

And look at the consequences.

It was supposed to have been a kiss. She hadn't been prepared for the chemistry lab to ignite.

Ella spent the morning fielding calls, trying not to think of the man lying naked in bed just metres away, but in the end she gave in talking on the phone. She was sick of the name Taylor Carmichael, sick to her stomach about the questions being asked about Santo's family, and so she diverted all calls, except any from Alessandro. She turned on Santo's computer and, logging into the account she had on there, she checked her emails, her heart stopping for a moment when she saw that Luigi, the man who had interviewed her over a week ago, had finally replied.

She sped through the polite chatter at the beginning of the email, where he apologised for taking so long, and then she read the news she had been waiting for—in a month's time she would be junior assistant director on an upcoming film that was being shot in both Rome and Florence.

Everything seemed to stop for a moment. She had waited for this for so long—okay, it was a junior assistant director's role, which was probably more like a barista, but she had a title and she would be doing more than she was doing now. Santo was so fierce about his films, so protective of them, and she didn't really blame him for not giving her a chance.

Ella closed her eyes as her mind wandered back to the man in the bedroom.

She knew a lot about Santo's relationships—they were in days and weeks at best. A brief flash of devotion was all any woman got from Santo—a swamp of texts and phone calls, dinner, bed, breakfast, flowers, champagne. Ella paid his bills and did the bookings after all, and then, just as quickly as it all started, it would be over…and left to Ella to field phone calls and mop tears.

The hotel phone trilled. It was reception wondering what time Santo would be checking out or if he would be staying another night and Ella answered it, cold from a lack of sleep last night and stiff from sitting in the chair.

'I'm not sure.' When you were speaking on behalf of a Corretti, such answers could be given, especially as the press were no doubt nagging the desk for details.

She walked into the dark bedroom and took a moment for her eyes to accustom. Santo was deeply asleep—she could tell from the regular breathing and just the stillness in the room and the distinct lack of a smart comment from him.

'Santo?'

He rolled onto his stomach, pulled the pillow over his head.

'Santo!' She said it more firmly. 'It's two o'clock. The desk wants to know if you're checking out.'

'Did Alessandro call?'

'Nothing,' Ella said. 'Santo, it's time to get up.'

'Another hour…' came his sleepy voice, and then perhaps remembering it was Sunday after all and that he had taken up a lot of her time, he said the right thing. 'You go home.'

Then he said the wrong.

'Or—' he rolled now onto his side, a lazy smile on his sleepy mouth '—you can climb in.'

And she could go now, Ella knew. He could sort out the hotel himself. He was sober enough now to drive and she had loads to do—she was joining him on location in a couple of days and there was plenty to sort out. She turned and stood for a moment watching as he returned to sleep and then she left the bedroom.

Except it wasn't to collect her bag and leave.

Ella headed into the bathroom and stood there for a very long moment.

She trusted no one—it was absolutely safer that way. She didn't, thanks to a few months ago, even trust her own mother. And yet, in a bizarre way, she had an inkling of trust in Santo. He made no excuses and he never lied. Happily he put his hand up to claim his appalling reputation and somehow his honesty made her bold.

Because yes, Ella had wondered what it might be like to be made love to by Santo. Of course she had. After all, she had seen the most beautiful women shed hopeless tears over the man. Now, with one kiss, a little better she understood, but more than that, his kiss, his skill that had led her so close to willingness, it had made her curious.

Ella had never particularly enjoyed sex, possibly thanks to her poor choice of partners, for they had never ensured that she might, but she knew things would be different with Santo.

She just knew and, more than that, she wanted to know.

But she wouldn't cry over him.

Unlike the others Ella had no expectation to change him, knew that was never going to happen. She just wanted her sex lesson from the master, Ella told herself, wanted to go back to where his kiss had led.

It was for that reason she did as offered and changed her mind! There wasn't a romantic bone in her body—Ella knew that as she undid her blouse. She stood in the bathroom undressing and then headed into the bedroom and watched him sleeping for a moment. Then, naked, she looked at the warm bed and the man in it and, toes curling, she prepared to dive in.

She was cold, because as she joined him he told her she was.

He pulled her right into him and caught her feet between his calves and pressed his warm body to hers. For a moment she thought he had gone back to sleep, and then had a slight panic that he didn't even know who she was, because Santo was very used to not sleeping alone. He'd rung her once from a hotel bathroom, terrified to go back into the bedroom because he completely couldn't remember his date's name and had needed Ella to tell him.

She had to remember that.

'You feel better than you look,' Santo said, running warm hands over her breasts and then down to her hips, 'and you look amazing.'

Ella did not close her eyes. She would not give in to his effortless, well-used lines, would not allow herself to believe they were exclusive to her, even if he sounded as if he meant them.

'Am I dreaming, Ella?'

'No.'

'Because I won't be able to look at you if I am. This is going to be a really filthy dream....' He purred the words to her ear and she concentrated on the hands that were expert, that ran over and over her body till she was no longer cold and far more than warm. She felt the deep kiss on the back of her neck which would ensure her hair was worn down till late in the week as she was branded by Santo, and it felt good.

It felt good for Santo too.

That she had come to his bed was the most pleasant surprise. She was the strangest mix, direct at times and then so evasive, the one woman he had no idea about and yet he wanted to. 'What made you change your mind?' he persisted. 'Tell me so I know for next time.'

'There won't be a next time,' Ella said. 'Remember, we're writing off today.'

'Oh, there will be...' Santo would make sure of it. 'I've wanted you for so long.'

She squirmed as his mouth moved up and he kissed her ear. Ella tried to move away, but he clamped her down, his thigh over hers and trapping her still. His arm gripped her tight, his mouth unrelenting. It was horrible and wet, but he persisted till she found out she liked it, till her mouth was parting, till she wanted to crane her face to meet his mouth. He just kept on going and then stopped and taunted her wet, sensitive skin with words as his erection reared higher up the backs of her thighs.

'What made you change your mind?' he persisted, but still she did not answer, so he moved in with a different approach, 'I flew you to Roma.' It was wretched of him to bring it up here, horrible and mean, because he could feel her body burn in shame. 'I flew you first class and to a top hotel thinking you were going to the doctors when you were going to your interview....'

'I told you I wanted to make my own way,' she attempted. 'I was going to tell you. I thought I'd be called back for a second interview.' She stopped talking because he was kissing her neck and his fingers were pinching her nipples and none too gently either. There was this assault on her senses. He hurt a bit, but not enough, and his tongue was driving her crazy and her body wanted to turn, but still he pinned her, still he kept pausing to deliciously taunt her.

'What excuse would you have used for the second interview—would you have said you were having surgery this time?' His hand crept down. 'I was worried sick that you had to go all that way for a doctor's appointment.'

'Liar.'

'I was,' Santo insisted. 'I thought it was women's stuff, so I could not ask you.' His hand crept to a very womanly place. 'I thought you were being prodded and poked,' he said to her ear as he demonstrated and played doctor with his fingers. He was so indecent she thought she might cave there and then as intimately he explored her.

'Santo…' She didn't want her back to him. She wanted to turn to his mouth, wanted his kiss, wanted to see, but he held her firmly down. His fingers were inside, incredibly long fingers that thoroughly stroked, and if he carried on like that for much longer, Ella would be sobbing a confession of her own soon.

'Last night, with leech girl, I did consider I might be impotent.' He was licking the side of her breast, trying to get to her nipple as his hand brought her closer still.

'Please.' How could she be laughing and on the verge of coming, how could he make such a terrible topic so light?

'And now I worry that I might have *l'eiaculazione precoce*.' She was lying there, just giving in to her body for the first time and laughing, because he even made premature ejaculation sound sexy. 'So you understand when I say...' He released her then and her body, that had been desperate to turn, turned so naturally to him. It was just so wanton and readied by his hands, by his mouth, by his skin. As her mouth moved in to kiss him, he halted her, caught her chin with his hands and made sure she was looking as he spoke. 'Ella, in a moment I'm going to take you really fast,' he said. 'I mean, really fast, and then I'll spend the rest of the afternoon making up for it and doing you really slow.'

He leant over, his chest over her face, and patted the bedside table and then glanced around the room and cursed because his wallet was in his jacket in the bathroom. Then he smiled when Ella waggled a few packets she'd retrieved before coming to the bedroom.

Yes, it had been a calculated move.

'Good girl,' Santo said, thinking he'd never been more pleased to see a condom. And then, 'I'll do it...' because from the feel of her hand closing around his base and the lick on her lips as it did, it really could be over way to soon.

He dealt with things swiftly but Ella couldn't quite catch her breath as she saw firsthand the sight of

Santo fully aroused. She reached out to touch him again, but he slapped her hand away. There was the tightness of anticipation in her throat because instead of kissing her, instead of joining her, he knelt between her legs and dragged her down the vast bed, till there were no pillows beneath her.

'I have been thinking about you for a very long time, since you turned up to be interviewed,' he admitted. He looked down at her naked beneath him and then smiled as he remembered that day. 'Your Italian was shocking.'

'So why did you hire me?'

'I wanted you.' Santo grinned. 'On sight I wanted you, and you can tell me tomorrow that you find that offensive. Right now I don't care.' And no, here in his bed, Ella didn't find it in the least offensive. She was just trying to remind herself that Santo was a master with women, knew how to say exactly the right thing, except she kept forgetting, found herself falling more and more to his corrupt charm. 'But if I had known how long you would make me wait...'

Just his words, just his want as he lifted her up by her buttocks and positioned her, had the blood flood to her groin. She had always thought him sexy, but there was this animal side to him, and it was a turn-on to watch the pleasure in him. His unrivalled passion had her shivering now to his words and had Ella wondering not just why, but how, she had waited. Being with Santo was just amazing, being in the spotlight of his gaze could so easily become addictive.

'Ella…' He didn't say any more for a moment, he didn't need to. Both their eyes closed as he squeezed into her, and she moaned at the excess, and then moaned again, because once he had filled her he was still for a second. Ella was desperate for movement, and her thighs were starting to shake. Then he stroked her slowly from the inside, a movement that had her squirming in pleasure. He opened his eyes and smiled down. 'You are worth the wait.'

And did he have to say such things, did he have to be so nice? Because for a second she believed he meant them. In that moment she had this vision of her near future—of her weeping and wailing and calling and being sent straight to his voice mail and being everything she had sworn she would not, because he was heart-stoppingly amazing. He was way, way more than she had envisioned. Until now, nothing, not a single thing in her life, had ever felt this good.

'Buckle up.' Santo smiled a decadent smile.

'Sorry.'

'Cross your ankles, Ella.'

And in this, she rather liked having Santo as her boss. Ella did as she was told—locked her ankles together behind him—and he leant back into them, a small safety check before he shot her to the sky. There was no room for thoughts any more, no struggle to hold on, or anticipate regret. There was nothing other than the rapid thrust of him, the ferocity of Santo between her thighs as he jolted her out of sexual complacency, showed her how good it could be. She felt the first shudders of orgasm, felt the arch of her back in his hands, and she moaned her come as still he thrashed inside her.

'Come on, Ella...' He did not give her a moment to think, he just completely consumed her. He was holding on for dear life, when there was surely no need to, Ella thought, because she had already come, except she'd never been locked in orgasm with Santo. It was like falling through a trapdoor and then into another. He took her deeper into herself than she had ever been, deeper into them. This was supposed to be strictly sex, yet she was biting down not to shout his name. He moved her hips faster and then as his hands stilled her, as he bucked freely within, Ella was coming in a way she never had before, like lightning that strikes from the ground up. She didn't know where it began and ended. She was taut, writhing, frenzied and already crying over Santo as, satisfied by her surrender, he gave in then and pushed and pulsed within, dragging words out of Ella that made no sense even to her as she came again.

'Thank you…' The delicious assault on her senses didn't end as their bodies slowed down. He made it sound as if she'd just saved his life. He toppled onto her, was kissing her, his words dizzying. It wasn't over, it was a mere interlude. She was in his bed and going nowhere, Santo was sure of it, because finally there was one good thing today and he wasn't about to let it go.

# CHAPTER FIVE

SANTO SOON DECLARED he was starving.

'There are some pastries out there...' Ella started, but then stopped. As if Santo would make do with stale pastries and tepid fruit juice—he was already reaching for the bedside phone.

'What do you want?' There was no consulting menus with Santo, Ella already knew that. He ordered and generally got whatever came first to mind.

'I don't mind.'

Santo ordered finger food and champagne, but unable to wait, he headed out and poured some fruit juice, looking out to the press below and sticking up one finger.

He'd checked his phone—still nothing from Alessandro. He flicked on his computer, more to see if there was any breaking news on his family, but he stood quiet for a moment, reading the email she had been sent, the last thing she'd been looking at before she joined him in his bed.

That was what had changed her mind.

He'd spent a long time wondering about Ella.

Too long thinking about how they'd be in bed.

And now he knew.

Except, unusually for Santo, he wanted to know more, a lot more.

He climbed back into bed and gave her a drink. When a little while later there was a knock at the door that declared their refreshment break was about to commence, unlike Santo, Ella couldn't just lie there as supplies were brought in, so she hid in the bathroom for a few moments, much to his amusement.

'You are such a prude.' Santo grinned as she walked back into the bedroom and he held open the sheet for her to climb in. 'And soon we will work on it, but first, I apologise—I am going to have to make some phone calls.' Of course the real world was waiting and she was more than used to Santo on the phone. All too often he wandered off, or stepped into another room, but this afternoon, privacy was somewhat discarded and they ate and drank champagne as he made a couple of rather terse phone calls to various family members. From the gist of things there was a lot of fallout from last night, which Santo confirmed when he hung up on the previous call and asked her to divert all calls unless it was his brother.

'Unless it is Alessandro I'm staying out of it.' He lay back and rested his hands above his head and looked up at the ceiling, examining yesterday's events a touch more calmly now. For once he wanted to talk about it with someone who wasn't family—not, of course, that he could tell Ella everything.

'You know we are going for the contract to renovate the docklands?'

'Sort of.' Ella, who was trying to decide between the sweetest figs she had ever tasted and the last of the chocolate-covered strawberries, looked over at him. Everything was so guarded with the Correttis and yet so intertwined. The docklands they were hoping to renovate was in fact being used for filming. She knew that the Correttis were hoping to breathe new life into the area and, naturally, bring a lot of money in.

'For me,' he said as she decided on a strawberry.

Ella looked at him, aware almost that she was being tested.

She was.

She knelt over him and Santo took the food from her fingers. She watched as his teeth cracked the chocolate, as he took the last one, but at the last second he relented and pulled her head to his, let her have half. As she nibbled at the strawberry, she tasted, too, his mouth.

'I want to ring down for more strawberries.' Ella smiled as she spoke with her mouth full.

'There are figs—' he smiled '—and they are harder to separate and we don't want disturbing.' He looked at her glittering amber eyes and the pink on her cheeks that would soon be scalding again. He saw the new flare of arousal and he was about to pursue it, yet, surprising himself, he spoke. 'Salvatore, my grandfather, put it all in place before he died—that was the point of the wedding.'

'So it wasn't a love match between Alessandro and Alessia?' Ella asked. When Santo gave her a quizzical look Ella remembered she was in bed with a Corretti—and so she took it as a no!

'Battaglia has withdrawn his support.' What Santo didn't add was that Battaglia was now throwing his might behind Santo's half-brother, Angelo. There was just so much history in his family, so much feuding, and last night things had suddenly got a whole lot worse, not that he could tell her even half of it. 'Right now, all I want to concentrate on is the film.' Then he smiled over to her. 'And you.'

'I think you should save it for the film, Santo.' Ella wanted things left at the hotel checkout. She had no intention to wait till Santo got bored, yet as the conversation turned to the film, as his hands lazily wandered, as they fed each other figs with their mouths, reluctantly Ella admitted that there was no place she would rather be than here with him today.

'When did you first want to start directing?' He had dusted her breasts with chocolate powder and was now licking it off. The white sheets—like Santo, an absolute disgrace—but right now, Ella didn't care.

'Always,' Ella said.

'Always?' Santo checked. Ella thought for a moment, remembered being five or maybe six and just shutting herself in her room, closing off from the noises downstairs and making movies with her mind. Not just once, but over and over, changing the camera angle, concentrating on a scene, getting it so right. Any money she'd had went towards buying scripts, and later it was bliss to find them online. She was twenty-seven and had no experience, but she had been training for more than two decades now. 'It's what I've always wanted to do.'

'So why are you a PA?' Santo asked. 'You told me that was your passion when I interviewed you.' And he smiled as he remembered the very determined, extremely smart woman who had arrived in his office unannounced.

Then he licked around her areola till she was wet, rather sticky, and she thought she might die if he didn't take it all in his mouth. 'You told me you took great pleasure ensuring your boss's life ran seamlessly.'

'I lied.' Ella smiled. 'As one does at interviews. Being your PA is my second passion in life, Santo.'

He could hear the wry note to her voice and it should have offended him. Why then did she make him smile? 'Third,' Santo said, because he wanted her again, but Ella was still talking about the film and she was lost to his hands for a moment, sitting up in bed with the sheet loosely wrapped around her, as if hiding herself from him as she spoke about the script.

It was a beautiful movie about a soldier going

missing at war, presumed dead, and his wife turning to the soldier's best friend for comfort. Both drawing on each other in grief, resulting in her pregnancy, only to find out that her husband wasn't dead.

'It has to remain a love story,' Santo said. 'But really, there are a couple of parts where it doesn't gel for me,' Santo admitted. She loved that they could talk about movies, that they both shared this passion, because often Ella knew that she bored others with her observations and thoughts, but Santo was just as into it as her. 'I can't see how, if she loves him, she could just forget so soon.'

'She doesn't forget him though, not even for a minute.'

'If she can so easily sleep with someone else so soon after—' Santo was firm on this '—then he was not the one love of her life.' He frowned at her smile. 'What?'

'You're a fine one to talk.'

'I've never been in love,' Santo said. 'I don't even know that it exists—this love-match you speak of.' He pondered it for a moment, scanned through his family history and shook his head. Then, as he opened up a little, Santo also convinced himself he was speaking with Ella for the sake of the film, rather than for his own peace of mind.

'My nonna said she fell straight in love with my grandfather.'

'See.'

'I never said it was returned. Salvatore loved power first—like my father.' He thought a moment more. 'My uncle, Benito...I thought he loved his first wife, but...' He gave a tight shrug. 'You know...' Ella watched as, for the first time she saw him pensive. 'Whether or not true love exists, in the film it has to be believable and that is going to be the struggle, because when Taylor and Vince make love the scenes are so passionate.'

'They don't make love,' Ella corrected. 'They have sex. She's grieving so badly and he comforts her.'

'A few days after the love of her life goes missing.' Santo gave a rueful smile. 'See now why we need a good actress?'

'Oh, yes.'

He looked over to her. 'Have you ever been in love, Ella?'

'No.' She looked over to him and smiled. 'I've been in lust.'

'I've seen.'

'But really,' Ella said, 'I'm not sure I'd want to be in love. I think it makes for less than sensible decisions.'

'Such as.'

Ella shrugged. 'I don't forgive and I never forget, which is a requirement apparently.'

'Apparently?'

'Well, from what I've seen.' She wasn't going to tell him about her family. She wanted nothing to dim this day, so she spoke about more casual acquaintances. 'I've got a friend back home and I've spent more hours watching her crying over the love of her life than I have seen her smiling. I've got another who—'

'What about your parents?' Santo interrupted her, realising just how little he knew about the woman who had been in his life for some considerable time now, by Santo's standards at least.

'Oh, I've seen a whole lot of forgiving and forgetting there too.' She gave him a grim smile, but refused to elaborate. 'So, all things considered, I think I'll stick with lust.'

Santo had no problem with that.

Or just a slight one, because he actually wanted to know a little more. But Santo was fast realising as he lay there that Ella was as skilled at deflecting personal conversations as he was. To prove his point, she returned to the discussion about the script.

'Do you think he forgives her?' Ella asked about the husband's return, about the kiss that would leave the audience hopefully reeling. It was the million-dollar question, the one he wanted the audience to be asking as they walked out of the theatre.

'I wouldn't.' Santo's response was decisive.

'Why not?' Ella challenged. Talking about film she was more animated than he had ever seen her, and for Santo, long may it continue because as she spoke, as her hands moved to make certain points, more and more of her left breast was being exposed.

'How can he?' Santo said. 'It's supposed to be the love of his life.' Then he gave a rueful smile, because of course there was no such thing as love. 'Perhaps,' he said, but he honestly didn't know. Really, he did want her opinion on this. 'What about you?'

'I don't know,' Ella admitted. 'I think that's the point of it though, that it's for the viewer to decide. I can't wait to see how Taylor will play it.'

'Nor me,' Santo admitted and they were quiet for a moment, sharing a similar vision, going over it in their minds—the script and a kiss that to the viewer must seem seamless but was actually going to be incredibly complicated to film. Ella had read the script over and over. Nothing was actually said at the end. It all came down to one kiss, an incredible reunion, relief mingled with fear as his hands roamed her body, as the soldier noticed the subtle changes, as he realised the love of his life had slept with someone else a matter of days after his supposed death.

This film had to work.

It had always been important to Santo, but never more so than now. With Alessandro gone, with the family name about to be smeared over the papers, for once there was a chance to prove himself, a chance to step out of his older brother's shadow and show that he wasn't a lightweight. He was dangerously close to telling Ella that.

He actually opened his mouth to. He looked at the woman in his bed and maybe that angry fist of Alessandro's had loosened something in his head, because for a second he thought about telling her what it was like growing up with Carlo as a father, how as the second son he had just been dismissed. He had even had the boardroom closed in his face once. Not one smile of approval from his father—not one. Not that Santo needed it, but there was something to prove now.

But even as he opened his mouth to tell her that, Santo changed his mind. There were things you didn't think about, let alone discuss with another, and he looked where the sheet had slipped and her breast was exposed. There was a welcome, most pleasing distraction from his race of dark thoughts.

'I think we need to sort out a few technicalities.' Santo smiled, and reaching for the bottle he topped up her glass.

'Oh, really?'

'I'm still struggling with the ending.'

'Which is why you are paying big bucks to someone like Taylor, to carry it off...' But her voice trailed off as she realised they were no longer actually discussing the film. Instead Santo had replaced the bottle then dipped into the ice bucket and pulled out a cube. She stared, fascinated, clutching on for dear life to her champagne glass, as his fingers approached her naked breast.

'The script reads that he notices the small changes to her breast...' He watched her bite down on her lip as he ran the ice cube around her nipple.

Her free hand went to move his, to stop him, but

she wanted the full Santo experience. Instead she looked down at her nipple, tight and erect, and then, just as it was surely unbearable, she got the warm reprieve of his mouth. He sucked, gently at first and then deep, and just when it was too much, just when her body was begging for conclusion, his hand dipped back into the bucket for more ice.

'And realising that she might be pregnant—' Santo's voice was low as they worked through the script, as between words he kissed her '—his hand moves to her stomach…' And Ella's eyes screwed closed as in the film Taylor's must, but in Ella's case it was because his hand was full of ice. 'And still he kisses her,' Santo said, taking the dripping ice into his mouth and kissing her with a very cold tongue. 'Why would he still kiss her when he knows she has been unfaithful?' Santo lifted his head and asked her.

'Because when he stops kissing her, he knows they must talk and he doesn't want to know the truth.'

'Does he forgive her?' Santo asked. 'Does he end it?'

'He surely has to,' Ella said.

'Even though he loves her?' Santo checked.

'He cannot trust her,' Ella said.

'Too simple.' He was sucking on the ice and she watched the round, smoothed slivers as he ran them over her stomach.

She was so turned on, watching his fingers work the cubes down. She lifted her knees a little, blanched as he teased and intimately iced her then breathed as his tongue warmed and sucked a far more tender place than her breast.

And she was more than a willing participant. The sensations he delivered and the skill of his tongue were exquisite, and it was Ella sucking on ice cubes and passing them to him now.

For Santo, the feeling was incredible. He liked sex, and a little play prior just to be nice, but if the clock stopped now, even without coming, this was the best sex he had had. He was just fascinated by her body, by the sighs and moans from her mouth, how if he put his tongue there her fingers tightened in his hair, and if he put it there, her hands sought her thighs and still she kept passing the ice.

'I always use…' He was pressing ice into her with his tongue and she thought she might die from the pleasure.

'I know,' Ella whimpered, locked between pleasure and pain.

'I want to try...'

'Please...' She was in this very strange place, where for the first time she could voice her want, did not have to be demure, be quiet, did not have to hold back what was on her mind. She had never opened up to another before, but she handed herself over to him now, if just for a while.

He climbed up her body and she was frozen deep on the inside and frenzied with heat at the surrounds. Her body, her skin, wet and cold from their games, sought the relief of him dry and warm now on top of her and he wrapped his arms under her.

'God, Ella...' He looked down, nervous at diving in as she begged him to hurry. Santo had never expected to be tentative his first time unsheathed, and she heard his shocked moan as he entered. 'I don't like it.' They were both shaking with laughter, with shock, with adventure, and then he moved a little more. 'Actually—' he rocked deeper and harder '—I've changed my mind.'

The friction warmed her, warmed him, till they were soaked and panting, and Santo was true to his word, had never made love unsheathed, but for this he willingly broke the rule. As she warmed to him he found new pleasures—the grip of her muscles, the increasing warmth. His promise to take forever, to do her slowly, was one he wanted to keep, for all he wanted was this.

'This morning I hated the day—' he was moving so fast within her now '—and now...' She couldn't understand what he was saying, she was too locked in her own thoughts. Then he was gracing her with Italian, but her brain didn't attempt to compute, because she felt her thighs starting to shake and this flood of warmth to her groin. But more than that, she was thrashing with her own thoughts, holding back her own words,

'Santo.' She considered for a brief second that the press outside must have got in, because lights were exploding in her head as if there were a thousand cameras aimed at them. She moaned and writhed and climaxed as Santo moved faster and it was bliss to come first, to just gloat from the podium and savour as he came a delicious last.

Santo was lost, feeling her pulse around him. He forced his own torture just so that he could feel each flicker and throb, and then gave in.

Ella watched his face contort and felt the pulse

of his relief. Then, as if he might have been hit over the head, he collapsed onto her, the weight precious, the calm of sated. Santo lay there, his face in her hair that was spilled on the pillow, and he was almost nervous to look up.

It was the lack of condoms that had made it amazing, he told himself.

Or perhaps that he had wanted her for so long that made it all more intense?

'Santo?'

He went to move, assumed he was too heavy, except her hair was sliding beneath his face as she turned hers to his, and what Ella couldn't possibly know as his lips met hers was this was Santo's first kiss with meaning.

## CHAPTER SIX

THEY ENDED UP checking out at four.

In the morning!

But, ever thoughtful, Santo left a huge tip for the maid.

The press were still convinced that Alessandro was in the hotel and so, instead of heading out there with soaking wet hair from the shower, Ella took a bit of time to dry it. She stood in bra and panties and put her make-up on and turned herself back into his PA again, but with Santo watching on.

'You like make-up,' he observed, watching her rouge her cheeks.

'Do I?' Ella answered, adding mascara and then moving to her lips, but Santo wasn't paying attention. He had taken out her concealer and was now standing behind her trying to cover up the mess he'd made of her neck. He looked amazing, wearing black jeans and black shirt and, with his eye a vivid purple, he looked sulking and rough. But there was a smile on the edge of his lips as he painted her neck.

'Do you want to borrow it?' Ella heard the slight edge to her own voice and fought to check it.

'No need.' He turned her round to face him. 'I never cover up my mistakes.'

And she'd have to see them.

It hit Ella then what she'd signed up for, understood all his ex-lovers' tears that she'd mopped. She had sworn she could handle just a little bit of Santo, but standing facing him, Ella knew enough about herself to know that already she wanted more. Yes, her notice should have been with immediate effect, because four weeks was way out of Santo's attention-span range.

As his mouth moved in to kiss her, as he hoisted her body to him, she could feel him dressed but indecent on her near-naked body and the effect of him made her nervous.

'No.' She said it too sharply. It came out too tense and quickly Ella qualified. 'I've just done my make-up.'

And in the world Santo inhabited, it was an entirely appropriate response, just his wasn't. 'I could turn you around then...'

He did just that. As he started to kiss her shoulder she watched his hands sliding over her stomach in the mirror and then she looked to her own eyes and saw her sudden panic, because he was going to be impossible to get over, because forever she would remember this.

And Ella didn't do sentiment.

'You've got a movie kicking off in a couple of hours and I want to go home.' She turned and smiled and she meant it. Ella put on her skirt and blouse and her shoes and made idle chit-chat, but she could hear blood whooshing in her ears, was fluttering in mild panic and didn't want him to see, didn't want to even give him a hint that he moved her.

Santo didn't seem to notice any difference in her. It was Santo who had changed, for this time as he faced her in the lift, he was a different man going down than up. Relaxed even as he headed out, not even bothering to scowl to the media, he saw her into the car, then drove towards Ella's villa. He needed no direction as he had dropped her off a couple of times before, but she had never asked him in and neither did she now. But Santo was having none of it.

'Make me coffee.' Santo yawned, because there was another drive ahead now to get to the run-down docklands where they were filming, only Ella wasn't joining him till Tuesday. 'And if you do...' He smiled. 'I will give you today off.'

'I was already taking it off anyway!' Ella said as he followed her into her villa. She was just a touch embarrassed—it was pretty sparse, just a small one-bedroom rental. As she headed into the kitchen to put the coffee pot on the stove Santo stayed in the lounge, looking at the few books she had and noticing they were all about directing.

Noticing, too, that, apart from that, there were no real clues to her.

He was very used to checking out women's homes—it was a fleeting game he played—but there was nothing to be learned about Ella here. Maybe it shouldn't have surprised him—she was only here temporarily after all—but there wasn't even a family photo above the fireplace.

And nothing much about her in her bathroom either, Santo noticed when he excused himself for a moment and shamelessly peered into her cabinets.

He did make a mental note of her favourite scent and then smothered a smile, because he had been about to let Ella know, so she could order some, and flowers and jewellery too! Had she not been a woman she had just bedded, Ella would have been told later this morning that the works were needed for her new lover. For once, Santo wasn't feeling seedy after excess. Nope, there wasn't even the vague pang of guilt that happened all too often after an empty encounter.

'Coffee!' he heard her call from the kitchen. Santo glanced into her bedroom, saw the unmade bed and a bra on the floor. As exhausted as he was, as much as he needed to get to work, when he thought of her lying there calling him a bastard into her phone, he could easily have called to her to say to hell with the movie and that he wanted his coffee in bed.

Instead he headed back to the kitchen, watching as she poured the thick black coffee into two small cups and then sweetened them. She passed one to him and he took a grateful sip.

'For that—' he smiled '—you can turn your phone off till tomorrow.'

'And have you go crazy that I didn't pick up? I don't think so.'

'I mean it,' he said. 'Just have a day—I'll deal with

anything that comes up. Turn your phone back on when you get there tomorrow.'

'I've got some things that need to be done....'

'Nothing that cannot wait. Do them tomorrow and then drive down—maybe get there in the evening. There won't be much action on set for a couple of days. It will all be setting up and getting to know the others.'

'You're sure?' Ella checked, because Santo was a pretty demanding boss, but she really was exhausted.

'Of course I'm sure,' Santo said. He watched her face closely when he spoke next. 'Unless you need to keep your phone on in case your family ring...'

'No.'

He took another sip of his coffee. She really gave nothing at all away.

'Your mother's Italian?' he checked. 'From where?' Santo asked, though he knew already from her dialect, but he wondered if she would share.

'Sicilian.'

'And your father?'

'He's Australian.'

And her eyes warned him that she would tell him

no more than that, but he chose to ignore. 'Are they still together?'

'Why do you ask?'

'I just wondered...' Santo said. 'I was just asking about your family in the same way you asked about mine.'

And yes, Ella realised, she was being brittle and defensive when there was absolutely no need to be. It was a simple question after all. 'Yes—' she gave a tight smile '—they're still together.'

'Now,' Santo said, noticing her breathe out in relief as he changed the subject. But that soon faded when she found out to what he was changing it to. 'We need to speak about this job that you are considering taking....'

'No.' Firmly Ella shook her head. 'We've just spent the day and night in bed.'

'Which makes it a perfect time for talking.'

'For you, perhaps' was Ella's swift retort. 'I'll speak to you about this at work.'

'Ella, I don't want you taking that job.'

He didn't know how thin the ice was that he was skating on, because so many times her own father had used those very words to her mother.

'I choose where I work.'

'If you could just listen—'

'I mean it, Santo,' she interrupted. 'We will talk about this at work. You have a say in my career when we're there and that's the only place that you do.'

'You're being ridiculous.'

Not to Ella. Her mother had worked in a factory until Ella was born, but had given it up to help out in her father's shop.

Occasionally Ella could remember her mother asking her father if she could take an outside job—heaven knows they had needed the money—but her father had liked his wife close by, liked that she could speak little English, liked the lack of friends in her life.

'I don't care if you think I'm being ridiculous. I'll talk to you about this on Tuesday.'

'Can you hold off from responding to him till we've spoken though?'

'Santo!' Ella warned.

'Okay!' He wasn't at all used to being told no to anything but he conceded and gave her a very nice kiss on her mouth. 'Thank you—I never thought it possible, but you made yesterday a good one.'

'And you.' She smiled back at him, conflicted. She wanted him gone, yet she did not want to let him go, did not want him heading off to the film set without her. She could feel little snaps of doubt biting at her, because, really, Ella wasn't so sure that she could handle this. Santo was big league—no matter how much she told herself that this wasn't going to hurt, there was the sensible part that was starting to re-alise that it was.

Any day soon.

She looked into his eyes, perhaps for the last time like this, because with Santo's track records he could be in Taylor's arms tonight.

'Good luck with the first day of shooting.'

'I'll need it…' Santo rolled his eyes.

'What are you going to say to Taylor about the photos?'

'What's the point saying anything?' Santo shrugged. 'I told her to behave. I told her how much the film was relying on her to stay out of trouble. Really, it might be easier to just stitch her knees to-gether.'

Ella laughed as she said goodbye to him, but her heart wasn't in it—because even with her knees stitched together Taylor was still breathtakingly beautiful, and Ella wouldn't put it past Santo to be ringing her at midnight with an urgent call for scissors!

Except, Ella remembered, she was turning off her phone.

It was bliss to climb into bed and to know that nothing would disturb her, except she hadn't counted on her thoughts. The panic that had gripped her in the hotel bathroom was back now.

It wasn't just sex.

She lay staring up at the ceiling, still trying to tell herself that it was, that she could do this. Ella had long since guarded her heart well, so she certainly wasn't going to start holding out hope for Santo. She smiled at the very thought of him reformed, but then it faded, because even if the reformed Santo came tied up with a bow she'd never be able to trust him.

Ella slept well into late afternoon, but of course as soon as she woke she checked her phone—presuming, because she knew how he operated, there would be an awful lot of calls and endless texts from Santo. To be in his spotlight was intense.

Nothing.

She checked and checked again, trying to batten down her disappointment before it properly took hold. Surely she should be pleased he hadn't bombarded her, except…yes, the high she had been floating on was starting to disperse. Without her propping Santo up, there were no flowers arriving at her door bearing cards filled with overused sentiments. Ella even managed a wry smile as she recalled one of their recent conversations.

'What should I put?' She'd checked when he'd told her to send some flowers.

'You decide.'

He'd clearly had second thoughts about leaving this particular note to Ella, because he'd buzzed her a few minutes later. 'What did you put?'

Ella had sighed before replying. "I enjoyed our weekend. You were amazing. Santo."

'No, that's the flowers she should be sending me.' He thought for a moment. 'Don't worry about flowers, just some jewellery, sapphire.'

'She's got blue eyes then, has she?'

Yes, she knew him too well.

*Stop it, Ella,* she told herself as she set about packing for the shoot, reminding herself that she wasn't going to let Santo upset her, that she had gone into this with her eyes wide open. Then, refusing to heed Santo's advice on her career, she replied to Luigi and accepted the job and then wrote out her resignation—because whatever happened now between her and Santo, she wouldn't be working for him for much longer.

She got through the night without a single word from Santo and long into the next day, running the million errands a wild weekend in Santo Corretti's life generated. It was actually late evening by the time she finally pulled up at the boutique hotel, close to where filming would take place. The drive should have been a pleasant one—the scenery was stunning after all, the traffic light—but she passed a few signs for her mother's village, and though the area where they were filming wasn't where her mother had come from, it was closer than Ella felt comfortable with. Stepping out of her car, there was a knot of unease in her stomach. It was her mum's birthday in a few days and she'd have no choice but to ring her. If her mother found out just how close she was to her village, it would be terribly awkward not to visit her aunts.

Rude, in fact.

There were certain rules in all families, but none more so than a Sicilian one, Ella thought as she walked through the glass revolving doors.

There was a faded beauty to the hotel, a quiet elegance to it, and the staff were formal but friendly. Once checked in, Ella headed to the gated lifts, blinking as Taylor Carmichael stepped out. She was wearing huge dark glasses, and Ella gave a shy smile of greeting, but of course, Taylor had no idea she worked for Santo and naturally she was ignored.

Still, it was so exciting to glimpse such a celebrity, and to think that tomorrow she might get a chance to watch her acting and the movie Ella loved start to unfold.

Ella found her room and swiped the card but frowned as the door opened. The hotel was gorgeous, but this room was seriously stunning. Ella stood a moment. The French windows were open to a large private terrace, taking every advantage of the aquamarine sea, and surely she would ask for the rich heavy drapes to be left open at night, just to drink it all in. Ella looked at the antique furniture and huge gilded mirrors and wondered if she'd been upgraded. There were vases of fresh flowers, even champagne chilling in a bucket, and she blushed at the memory of the other night, a smile playing on her lips as she did so. Realising now that this was the work of Santo, she was touched that he had been so thoughtful. But it faded as she heard Santo talking from the bedroom and, realising the mistake, she walked over and picked up the internal phone.

'Ella...' Santo came out then. 'At last, you're here.'

'I am!' She was suddenly awkward, embarrassed that she had thought he'd ordered flowers and champagne for her room. 'There's been a mistake at reception. I think they thought I was sharing with you.' She rolled her eyes. 'I spoke in Italian when I made the booking. I must remember not to in future.'

'There's no mistake.' Santo smiled. 'I asked them to send you to here. I thought we could have dinner, talk—there has been so much happening....'

'You can't just move me in.'

'I am not just moving you in,' Santo said.

'So where's my room?' Ella asked.

'Ella, we will be working fifteen-hour days...or at least I hope that we will.'

'Sorry?'

'The director quit.'

Ella's mouth gaped open, her living arrangements temporarily forgotten.

'He quit?'

'He gave ultimatums. I do not like ultimatums.'

Ella had seen him clash with directors now and then, but to lose one on the first day of filming...it must have been a pretty spectacular row. She asked him what had happened.

'It's finished with now.' Santo shrugged. He was never one to go over the past, as always he moved easily on. 'I have been chasing around trying to think of who would be best to direct the movie, and who is available too, but I think that finally it is sorted.' He was pouring champagne and there was a small flurry in Ella's stomach as he handed her the glass that had bubbles rising in it, like the sudden hope that for Ella flared. 'I have found someone good, someone who I think shares my vision, who really is keen to bring out the very best in Taylor.' He smiled at Ella and she gave a tentative one back. 'Tomorrow we have a new director starting, Rafaele Beninato.'

'Rafaele Beninato?' He must have heard the disappointment in her voice. She simply was too upset to hide it. Because of the champagne, the smile, the conversations they had had about the movie, the visions they had shared, Ella really had, for a blind, stupid moment, thought that Santo was going to give the role to her.

'Ella…' Not only did Santo hear her disappointment, he saw the burn of her cheeks. 'You didn't think—'

'No.' She was embarrassed to admit that yes, she had thought he might consider her. After all, this was a major movie they were talking about, as if he was going to trust it to her. But then Ella was suddenly angry too, that he hadn't. 'It's that you didn't think! That you didn't even consider me for the role.'

'How could I?' He was incredulous. 'Ella, you have no experience whatsoever.'

'No!' She was beyond hurt now. They had lain in bed just yesterday, acting it out, going over scenes. But clearly, not once had it entered his head that she might make a good director.

Yes, it hurt.

'Santo, I love that movie. I have gone over and over the script. I know it inside out. I know exactly what's needed.' She put down her glass, missing the coaster, her feelings raw, because while his words made perfect sense, were completely logical, Ella wasn't thinking logically right now. 'I'm going to change the booking....' She just wanted away before she said too much, wanted to think, and she couldn't with Santo so close. Ella, who never cried, was dangerously close to doing so as she picked up the phone and asked that the booking be reverted back to the one she had made. She told the receptionist that she'd come down and get the key now.

'So you're storming out because you didn't get the part?'

'No!' Ella snapped. 'I was leaving already. That's the whole point of separate rooms, Santo—there's somewhere to go when you row!'

Ella's bags arrived then and she quickly diverted them, but there was her room key to collect and it took forever until she was finally alone. Ella attempted to gather her thoughts, but even that didn't last for long, because in no time at all, Santo was rapping on her door, refusing to budge till she let him in.

'You want it both ways.' It was Santo who was angry and aggrieved now. 'You insist that we keep work separate—you make this great song and dance as to how we cannot work and sleep together, that we are to keep things professional at work, yet when it suits you want all the favours of being my lover.'

'That's not true.'

'Yes.' Santo stood firm. 'It is true. You want it both ways,' Santo said. 'I want it only one. I am myself now and in the bedroom, but at work I make the best decisions for my movies.' She heard the passion then, the absolute single-mindedness that made him so brilliant. 'When I am at work I choose only the best for my films and I make decisions with my head only at all times, and if you think I am going to hand over a director's role because we have good sex, then you are the one who has an issue, not me.'

'I wanted that role long before yesterday.'

'And I did not consider you for that role long before yesterday too, because the fact is, Ella, you have no experience.'

'Because you won't give me any.'

'When a suitable vacancy comes up, it will be yours, but the world is not waiting for you to debut, Ella. You have to earn your stripes in the industry to be respected and not in the bedroom.'

She wanted to slap him, his words burnt so, but instead Ella stood with her face scalding, because what he was saying was true and he hadn't finished yet. 'So, to reiterate, I enjoyed our time together. I hoped to take things further today. I hoped to share a meal, to talk, to make love. But instead, because you cannot manage to separate work from the bedroom, instead we sleep alone.'

'I'm handing in my notice....'

'More fool you,' Santo said. 'Go work for Luigi, go let him dangle you the promise, and you will find out I am not such a bastard after all. And at least you enjoy sleeping with me.'

'Luigi is nothing like that,' Ella flared. 'He's a brilliant director and he's keen to have a willing assistant—'

'Hey,' Santo interrupted, 'you know when people wait while their potential employers ring for references. I often wonder why don't the potential employees do the same? Why don't they take a little while to find out what they are getting into before they jump?'

'I wish to hell I had.'

'No.' So swift was his retort. 'You knew exactly what you were getting into. As I said, I don't hide my supposed mistakes and I don't expect favours and neither do I give them for sex.' For a man who appeared to have no morals, he stood there and proved otherwise. 'For all the bastard you seem to think I am, think carefully, Ella—because your job has never depended on sleeping with me and it still doesn't. I know how to close the bedroom door and carry on with my work.'

Her back was to the wall, and not just literally, because he was right.

'How much notice are you giving?'

'Four weeks.'

'Fine,' Santo said. 'Ring the agency tomorrow for your replacement, see if you can get someone who can start ASAP so that you can train them up. And, this time, can you tell them I want someone fully fluent in Italian, please?'

How that stung but she refused to jump.

'Anything else?'

'With a lot of experience.'

'Good looking too?' Ella jeered.

'I would hope so,' Santo said without contrition. 'And preferably without too many hang-ups and is-sues.'

'You can go on your own dating sites....'

'I don't go on dating sites,' Santo said. 'I don't need to, and anyway, I don't have time,' he retorted. 'I want someone who is good at their job, who is pleasing to the eye, and someone who doesn't pin everything on what happens between the sheets.' And with that he walked out and slammed the door.

He was right.

Ella sat shaking on the bed.

Her disappointment was on a professional level but it was personal too.

It was she who couldn't separate things, but of course, with Santo, she'd never been able to.

Ella admitted it herself then—every woman he'd dated, every time he'd crooned into the phone to his latest lover as she drove, she'd had bile black and hissing in her stomach and it had felt like a personal slight.

She had known what she was getting into but had completely ignored it, just to have the refuge of work. Had chosen to keep her days busy when she should have lain on a beach and somehow healed from all that had happened with her father. When she should perhaps have curled up and hid for a while to process things, instead she'd insisted to herself she was fine and had looked for a job, had ignored what now she could not.

A hotel room was not a nice place to be gripped by panic and unlike Santo's there was no private terrace, just shuttered windows which Ella flung open and gulped in night air. She wanted to ring home, wanted to scream, wanted to run to Santo and batter down his door, for she could not stand to be alone with her thoughts.

She could not bear to remember the feel of her father's fist in her face and the screams and shouts from her mum and the feeling of being twenty-seven and feeling as if she were six.

Except right now she was doing exactly that.

Remembering every horrible moment, every terrible feeling, crying and sobbing for the first time since it happened, reliving the nightmare when she didn't want to…

…and in a hotel room alone.

# CHAPTER SEVEN

FOR THE FIRST time since she had started working for him, Ella wondered if she could face breakfast with Santo and going through his diary. They always started the week like that, and as she'd had yesterday off, it would be assumed she would meet him in the hotel restaurant at 6:00 a.m., as they did when on location.

Ella stood in front of the mirror after a very sleepless night. A cool shower had done little to reduce her swollen eyelids and the tip of her nose was bright red.

She looked like a woman who had spent the night crying.

Except she hadn't, as Santo would no doubt assume, been crying over him—it was the issues that he had alluded to that had finally made her break down.

It had been six months without tears.

Six months of telling herself that she was strong, that she would not let what her father had done affect her, would not let his fists bruise her soul.

But they had.

It wasn't just the beating that had left its mark.

It was the years that had.

Years of watching her mother suffer, years of walking on eggshells so as not to upset him, years of scrimping and saving to afford a home where she could take her mother away from him.

Ella was in danger of crying again, so she chose not to think about that awful day. Instead she attempted magic with a make-up brush, but nothing was really going to work. So, once dressed, it was Ella who donned huge sunglasses this morning and took the elevator down, fervently hoping that Santo would be polite and pretend not to notice the state of her face.

'Jesus!' He stood up as she approached the table. Of course he looked immaculate and well rested. Because it was Santo he promptly took her glasses off—he was just so bloody Italian—and wrapped her in his arms. 'Sorry, baby…'

'Stop it.'

'I went too far.' He was talking into her ear, slowing her heart that had been beating frantically all night. 'Hire someone ugly—' she felt tears fill her eyes at his attempt to help '—a man, I don't care.'

'Santo.' She pushed him off a little, took a seat. 'I wasn't crying about that.' A waiter poured her coffee and Santo sweetened it for her. She took a drink of it and wished he wasn't being so nice, because it would be so easy to again break down. 'I've got stuff going on. You were right.'

'Of course I was right,' Santo said. 'About what?'

'You know…' God, but she hated the word. 'Issues…'

And where most men would run Santo was over in a flash. He moved his chair right beside her and wrapped an arm around. 'Tell me.'

'No!' She did not want his arm, did not want a man who was so comfortable in his own skin that he could sit in a restaurant and not care who saw, nor one who thought she could discuss such things.

'I'll tell you mine.'

'No.' She was not going to let him make her smile.

'I've got hundreds of them,' Santo said, and yes, he made her smile. Then he was terribly kind. 'But right now, my main issue is you.'

'We've got to head over to the set.'

'I'll say when we go.'

'I can't talk about it.'

'You could.'

'No.' Ella shook her head. She didn't have to explain her choices to him, except she found herself trying to. 'You don't talk about things you don't want to, you don't discuss your family.'

'You know my family are...' He didn't finish and she looked over, watched his hand move to the collar of his shirt as he struggled to come up with a suitable answer, but Ella found it for him.

'You're a Corretti,' Ella said. 'So your troubles are far darker and far more serious than mine could ever be.'

'Yes.'

'I was being sarcastic, Santo.'

'I know,' he said. 'And so was I, but what I'm trying to tell you is that there is little that hasn't happened in my family. My nonno, Salvatore, started with nothing and died one of Sicily's most powerful men, so yes, there are things that I cannot talk about. His sons—my father, Carlo, and his brother, Benito…' Santo stopped then. 'You know what they say about loose lips…'

'Speaking of ships…' She went to tell him about an arrangement for the film but he stopped her.

'Don't change the subject.'

'I am changing it, Santo, because in being so open about your family and issues, you've told me precisely nothing.'

'I'm trying to let you know that you can tell me if you want to,' he said. 'And if you can't, that is fine, but you are never to spend a night like that alone again when I am a short elevator ride away.'

'Santo…' Someone was calling out to him, telling him it was time to head off, but he called over his shoulder that he would catch up with them there.

'Do you understand me?'

'Sometimes it's better to be on your own.'

'You prefer what you went through last night to making love with me?' He kissed her temple. 'Then you are mad.'

'Sex isn't the answer to everything.'

'It's a good one though,' he said. 'It works very well for me. But if you want to continue with your sex strike, still we can talk.' He stood, offered his hand. 'Come on, we can walk to the set.'

'It will take too long.'

'They can wait for me,' Santo said with all the arrogance of someone who knew that the world would. He handed her back her sunglasses as they stepped outside and he was the nicest company, pointed out villages as they walked down the hillside.

'My mum's from there,' Ella said, wondering if it was being here that had upset her and perhaps brought it all to a head. 'I've got aunts there.'

'Are you going to visit?'

'Maybe after we finish shooting.'

'Don't tell them you work for me then,' he nudged. 'They will warn you.'

'I already know your reputation.'

'Not me,' Santo said, 'my family.' He pointed yonder. 'My nonna lives over there. There is a lot of history, a lot of enemies have been made. Ours is not always a good name.' He gave her another nudge. 'Issues.' But this time it didn't make her smile and for the first time Santo knew he couldn't just joke his way out of things, that her silence was perhaps a demand for something more, something he had never given. Except he looked at her swollen lips and thought of her eyes puffy behind the glasses. If he wanted more, then Santo realised he had first to give.

'My father and his brother were killed in a warehouse fire.' He wasn't telling her any great secret. It had been the talk of Sicily then and still was at times. 'That is when my grandfather divided everything up.'

'When the warring started?'

'Oh, it started long before that,' Santo admitted. 'My father and Benito were always rivals, Salvatore saw to that.'

'You call him Salvatore?'

'I call him both,' Santo said. 'You don't really sit through business meetings saying Papà and Nonno.'

'I guess.'

'It's got worse since he divided things up. Once a year we put on an act and are civil.' He saw her frown, explained just a little bit more. 'The family gets together at my nonna's each year for her birthday—the only thing we all agree on is that we adore her, and we call a truce for one day, but after that, it's gloves off again. These next few weeks…'

Santo shook his head. He simply never went there, not even with himself, and really, there wasn't time to now. There was a movie to be made after all. Except Santo found himself standing on a hillside and looking out to the docklands and the sea beyond, thinking how black it had all seemed on Sunday, the hell he had felt in a hotel room, except Ella had been there for him, had turned that day around. He wished last night she had let him do the same, wanted her to open up to him, so for her he broke his unspoken rule.

'My grandfather played his sons off against the other. He taught them from the start that to get on you had to be ruthless.' He looked at Ella. 'So they were. When his health got worse he divided things up. Benito he put in charge of the hotel empire, and my father, Carlo, media. Now though, if we want the proposal to redevelop the docklands to go through, we need to pull together.' He gave a wry grin. 'I can't see it happening. Angelo is—'

'Angelo?'

'My half-brother.'

'You never said.'

'I never do.' He looked down the hill. 'He has bought some of the houses here. This is supposed to be our development, but now Battaglia is throwing his weight behind Angelo.'

'Because the marriage didn't go ahead?'

'Because of so many things.'

'Does it matter?' Ella ventured. 'I mean, it's just one project.'

'It matters,' Santo said, and in that he wasn't going to go into detail, wasn't about to tell her that the Corretti empire was crumbling around them. It wasn't so much that he didn't trust her—he could not bear to admit it to himself.

'Right now, I need to concentrate on this movie, but first...' He pulled her into his arms and took her glasses off again, and kissed her very nicely, strangely tenderly. It made her want to cry, because she understood perfectly now her predecessors' tears and rantings. It wasn't just the sex—Santo Corretti was the whole package. How cold and lonely would the world be after him.

And then, when his phone started begging for the producer to please arrive on set, there was no choice but to get moving.

They arrived at the docklands. It was rough and worn down, but Santo told her that with some money thrown at it, it would one day again be so beautiful. 'The town is dying,' Santo said, 'but if the tourists found it, if the people came back...' There were locals all gathered to watch the activity. 'See...' Santo said. 'That café has not been open for years, but now, today, it is. That is the sort of thing this film could do, and maybe it would have the people associate the Corretti name with what it can do in the future, not ways of old....' Then he stopped talking about family. 'Will you do one thing for me?' Santo asked before he got to work. 'Will you check out Luigi before you accept the job?'

'I've already accepted it.'

To his credit, Santo said nothing, not that he had much chance to. He was in a lot of demand and Ella took a seat and started working. Or trying to work, more often than not she found herself peering over her computer, frowning at a couple of Rafaele's suggestions, because they weren't interpretations Ella would have considered.

Still, Rafaele was the expert, Ella told herself, determined to put pride aside and to learn from him.

'Are you okay?' Ella blinked in surprise a little while later to the sight of Santo handing her a coffee.

'Better,' Ella said.

'Because if you being here is a bit much, I don't need you.' He winced. 'That came out so wrong— what I meant...'

'I know what you meant.' Ella smiled, touched that he seemed to realise that last night had been about so much more than their exchange of words. 'How's it going?'

Santo grimaced. 'Vince just lost his temper. I don't know. It's early days, I guess.'

She sipped on her coffee, but after a moment or so she decided to take him up on his offer. 'If you're sure you don't need me I might go and get some work done in the hotel.'

'Sure,' Santo said. 'I'll call if I need anything.'

It was safer to be alone right now—she simply daren't get closer to him. He'd been open, far more open about his family than Ella had expected him to be and, as nice as it had been to talk, on reflection it disarmed her. Sex she could handle—it was the rest that terrified her so. Holding that thought once back in her room Ella contacted the agency that had first sent her to Santo. She spent most of the day going through résumés as well as confirming the docking times for the ship which was going to be a huge part of the film set. Ella did a few phone and on-line interviews, until she had narrowed it down to two. Then she checked her own emails, frowning a little at the response from Luigi, who was, he said, delighted to give her this opportunity and that he was looking forward to seeing her when she came to Rome, that they must have dinner as soon as she got there.

Of course Luigi would want to take her out to dinner and go over things before filming started. It was dinner, Ella told herself as she headed down to the restaurant to have dinner herself with Santo.

'Better?' Santo checked, standing briefly as she walked over.

'Much.'

And then there was no more personal talk, because there was actually an awful lot of work to discuss, especially now that they had started shooting. They worked their way through most of it, even the rather more delicate stuff.

'Her name is Marianna Tonito.' Ella brought him up to speed on her potential replacements. 'She's worked for two movie producers and one film star, so she has loads of experience. I spoke to the agency and then I spoke to her. She seems very...' Ella struggled for the right word—knowledgeable, competent, confident, all applied, and thanks to the magic of Skype, Ella knew that Marianna was also terribly, terribly sexy. 'Suitable' was the word Ella settled for, though she knew that she was handing inevitable heartbreak over as she passed Santo the résumé, but Marianna was in fact the perfect person for this role.

'When can she start?'

'Immediately.'

Santo frowned. 'How can she be so good if she is so available?'

'I checked all that.' Ella had thought exactly the same. 'She's still working, much the same as me— actually training up her replacement now, at her boss's wife's request.'

Ella saw the slight raise of one eyebrow. 'Are there any other candidates?'

Ella handed him the second résumé. Santo tried, he really did, to keep his expression bland—so much so that Ella had to suppress a smile. 'He seems to have a lot of experience.'

'He does,' Santo said carefully. 'And perhaps things would be a little less complicated.' He glanced over to Ella, as if to check her thoughts, but she refused to give them. 'How soon can he start?'

'Paulo has already given his notice. He's in Singapore now with his current boss, but should be back

in Italy in the next couple of days, though he wants
to take two weeks off before he starts a new job.'

'Fly them both over for an interview.' He could
feel this huge sulk unfurling. He did not want her
gone. It was all so unnecessary to Santo, and certainly he did not want her working for Luigi. 'You
haven't given your notice in writing.'

She went into her huge handbag and took it out.
'I meant to give it to you last night.'

He didn't take it.

'File it.'

'Fine.'

'In the shredder.'

'I'll email you a copy before I do,' Ella said. 'Anything else?'

'I need to change the ship date.'

Ella blinked. Surely he wasn't talking about the
ship date. It had taken her forever to organise—ships
sailing into the sunrise generally did!

'I need you to make it for two days later.'

'Santo…' Ella drew a long breath. It was just the
sort of request she'd come to expect from him, just
the usual impossible ask that with one look he expected her to fix. 'There are three hundred extras
booked.'

'You think that I don't know that?' Santo responded. 'But the fact is we lost a day's filming yesterday and things haven't exactly gone well today.' She sat quiet for a moment as he voiced it. No, things hadn't gone well. All the hope and excitement that had greeted them this morning had slowly dispersed throughout the morning, and from the whispers Ella was hearing, after she had left things had gone from bad to worse. 'I think I might have made a mistake.'

He didn't actually say it, but Ella knew that he was talking about Taylor. She hadn't exactly shone today, but Ella could see it wasn't her acting that was the problem. Though it would sound like sour grapes if Ella suggested that it was the director who was the issue.

'Things might improve tomorrow,' Ella attempted. 'It was never going to be perfect the first day of filming.'

'I know. But for now just sort out the ship and the extras. We're going to need more time.'

'I'll see what I can to…' Her voice trailed off as his phone bleeped the text. She watched relief flood his face.

'Alessandro?'

'Thank God,' Santo said, reading the text. Ella

found herself wishing he'd tell her what his brother had said. She wanted more into his life and was having terrible trouble dealing with that. 'So we're done?'

Ella nodded.

'Did you want another drink?' he offered.

'No, thanks.'

'Did you want to talk?'

'We're up at five tomorrow.'

'Fine.' He was curt—it had been a hell of a day and not a particularly good last night and Santo would love to happily screw his way out of it, but he wasn't going to beg.

He didn't understand her.

But he'd tried to.

'You'd really rather be alone than be with me.'

Yes, Ella thought, because it was safer to be alone tonight. In his bed she'd be telling him she loved him or something ridiculous, which wouldn't cause a remote problem for Santo, Ella knew. He was more than used to hearing that.

It just caused a huge problem for Ella. She simply didn't want to love anyone, didn't want her heart out there in harm's way, and she was already scrambling to take it back.

''Night, Santo,' she said, because it was far safer too.

''Night, Ella.'

# CHAPTER EIGHT

SHE WAS UNABLE to get hold of Paulo for a couple of days, but when Ella did he was delighted to hear from her.

But trying to arrange an interview proved a little difficult. 'What about next Sunday?' Ella peered at the diary, then changed her mind. If they changed the shipping dates, it would be the final day of filming and there would be three hundred extras milling around and the set would be crazy. 'Let me sort out things this end and then I'll get back to you.'

'No problem.' He was just so funny and nice and keen to work for Santo, and he told Ella that he was happy now to take just one week off between jobs. 'Even no time off, but don't tell him that yet—I would love to work for Santo,' Paulo said. 'I have heard so many good things.' He laughed then and so did Ella. 'Lots of terrible things too—the whole family, really. They're a PR nightmare. I assume you've seen the papers this morning?'

'You really don't expect me to discuss that!' Ella smiled, because there were tales of infidelity and missing grooms and illegitimacies. It was Santo's mother, Carmela, who was taking up the news today. She was an exceptionally cold woman, one who had been more interested, the newspaper article read, in her designer suits than being a mother to her children. Even if Santo knew that already, he was surely reeling from the news that had just broken of his mother's most illicit affair.

She turned her attention back to Paulo. They really weren't gossiping. Ella had asked him questions about his employer, liking the fact that though Paulo chatted away, he told her nothing. 'There is an awful lot of discretion required for this role.'

'Of course.'

'Even with Santo—though you work alongside him, really, you won't have a clue half the time what is going on. He especially doesn't discuss his family.'

'I would never expect a Corretti to,' Paulo said. 'I am Sicilian, I know.'

Marianna was nowhere near as accommodating or as pleasant to speak to as Paulo.

Most annoyingly, Marianna insisted on speaking in English. God, the Italians were so good at delivering a snub when they wanted to, but Ella took it nowhere near as well as she did when it was Santo. It was even harder to pin her for an interview time than it had been with Paulo.

'I'll arrange transport for you if you can just give me a suitable date.' Ella did her best to keep her voice even. 'Santo really would like to get this organised as soon as possible, so if you could let me know when you're available, I'll try to sort things out with him.'

'I'll arrange my own transport,' Marianna said. 'You can reimburse.' Ella held on to her breath. Really, she felt rather more as if she were the one being interviewed, as if she was Marianna's assistant. She tried to remember that this was the sort of person best for the job—someone brash and confident, someone who would be able to reschedule a ship at five minutes' notice and deal with all the drama Santo generated. There was certainly no off-the-record chats with Marianna. In fact, she wanted to speak only with the man himself.

'I will look in my diary and see when I am available. Perhaps if I speak directly with Santo...'

'Santo is busy with filming at the moment,' Ella said. 'I arrange his diary.' And she heard the note of possession in her own voice and tried to stifle it. 'If we can organise a mutual time that would be great, but there are several applicants and Santo is very busy.'

'I'll be in touch.' It was Marianna who rang off.

Still, it was a minor triviality and not one she would worry Santo with, because the filming was going from bad to worse and, as the days progressed and the filming didn't, his mood darkened. The crew were putting in incredibly long hours but it was seemingly all going backwards. Still, Ella had more on her mind than Santo. It was the day she had been dreading for weeks—her mother's birthday—and later she needed to ring her.

And say what?

Ella tried not to think about it. Instead she responded to a couple of texts from Santo, who was already on set, and then sorted out some of his overnight correspondence.

The second it was 9:00 a.m., she started on the

endless phone calls to sort out the extras and ship, and then it was time to head for the set.

She could feel the tension on set as she approached.

Santo had been right to reschedule the ship scene. There was no way they would have been ready otherwise.

'Where's Vince?' someone called.

'Sulking in his trailer.' Santo scowled back.

She looked to where Rafaele was placing all the actors, and then glanced over to Santo. There was a muscle jumping in his cheek as he watched the placement. 'What the hell is he doing?'

Ella said nothing—it wasn't her place to—but how she would have loved to get in and change things. Rafaele had Vince walking along the docklands where he would come across Taylor crying and stand watching her for a long moment before making his way over.

It didn't work.

The characters weren't supposed to even like each other and it just made Vince look opportunistic, especially when Rafaele asked him to put more purpose in his stride.

'Yep...' Santo gritted. 'March over there, why

don't you…' He turned his head to Ella. 'Is Rafaele reading the same script as you and me?' Ella said nothing, just watched in silence as, yet again, the make-up team were called on to touch up Taylor's make-up.

'This is a disaster,' hissed Santo.

Again Ella said nothing.

But absolutely he was right.

Over and over they watched as Taylor cried on cue, and then, over and over, Rafaele called for her to do it again.

'It's too much,' Santo said, and Ella stayed silent, knowing Santo wasn't stressing about the pressure on Taylor. It was that there was far too much going on in the scene that was the problem. This particular scene was to be combined with a flashback of her receiving the news that her lover had died. It was supposed to portray the devastated heroine staring out to sea and breaking down as she realised her lover would never return.

'Action,' Rafaele called, and Ella watched as again Taylor broke down. Vince was being filmed too, from the rear first, watching her from a distance, then walking across the docklands towards her. It was at the end of this scene their grief and passion would ignite.

'First her face—' Santo was incensed '—then the beach, then back to her face, and now Vince.'

Santo was right. Vince was just bombarding the scene. Ella could see what was needed, could actually see it before her eyes. Taylor was acting beautifully. It was an Italian shot that was needed—an extreme close-up of her eyes with the ocean reflected in them and then turning as Vince joined her side.

God, she could see it.

'It's going to be like watching tennis,' Santo moaned.

Still Ella said nothing, just watched as a very tense Taylor flounced off. Finally Rafaele told everyone to break for lunch.

'What do you think?'

An ironic smile twisted her lips, that he had the audacity to ask her.

'Come on, Ella, say what you're thinking.'

'That I need your signature to transfer some funds for the extras....'

'I meant about this scene.'

'I'm your PA,' Ella said. 'You declined directing advice from me.'

He looked over, his expression somewhat incredulous. 'Are you still sulking about that?'

'I'm not sulking.'

'Absolutely you are.'

'Do you know what?' Ella muttered. 'Not everything goes back to you, Santo.'

'Of course it does.' It was the first smile she'd seen on him today, but it faded when he turned and saw her expression. 'That was a joke,' he said. 'So what's wrong?'

'It doesn't matter.'

'It does to me.'

Sometimes he could be so nice, just so damned nice, which was why he charmed so many, why he was so brilliant with women, Ella reminded herself.

'Are you having second thoughts about working for Luigi?' he asked as he added his signature to the paper she had brought for him to sign.

'No.' Which was an outright lie, since Ella had accepted the job she'd had five emails from her soon-to-be-boss, each one a touch more familiar. 'We need to sort out a time for your interviews with my replacement.'

'And when you no longer work for me, can we celebrate in bed?' He watched her eyes close for a second. 'Get used to it, Ella. If you think I'm a lech, you wait till you start your new job.'

'I never said you were a lech.'

'What then?'

'Let's just concentrate on work for now. Paulo can't come till next Sunday.'

'It will be the final day of filming.'

'If I can rearrange the ship.'

'You have to,' Santo said. 'We're getting nowhere.'

'Okay.' Ella sighed. 'I'm doing my best. I'll arrange for Paulo to come about four. You can do a brief interview in your trailer and then I'll take him out to dinner, while you lot all party.' She gave a tight smile, because the parties Santo threw at the end of filming were legendary, though the way this movie was going it might end up being more of a wake.

'What about the other one?'

'Marianna seems to think she should be discussing things directly with you.'

Santo merely shrugged. 'I'm a bit busy with other things to be sorting out interview times, Ella.'

'I know that. I was just letting you know. Okay, if

there's nothing more you need me for here I'll head back to the hotel.'

'Stay,' Santo suggested. 'Rafaele is going to give the crying scene a rest, thank God, and work on the final kiss.'

That, she did not want to see, because she remembered them acting it out. But more than that, she wanted to give in to him, to just give in to herself and say yes.

'I have a ship to sort out.'

'Ella…' He could not stand this. He had never wanted someone so badly. He was turned on and pissed off and he did not understand why she was so reluctant to be with him, why she didn't even seem to want to talk to him.

Santo blew out a breath called frustration. He had been nothing but nice. The sex had been great and he had kept his distance. He didn't know what he was doing wrong. Finally there was a woman his user guide manual couldn't work out and he didn't like it a bit. 'I want to talk to you,' Santo said. 'Away from here. I am going to finish at seven tonight and then I am taking you out for dinner. No work—' he made it very clear '—there is no need to bring my diary. We are going out for dinner.'

'I don't think that's necessary.'

'It's very necessary…' he started, but he didn't get to finish because his assistant came to tell him that Taylor was getting upset.

'That's all I need.' Santo rolled his eyes and then turned to Ella. 'Can you talk to her, maybe have lunch with her. You're good with people. It might calm her down.'

'That's not my job, Santo.' And she should say nothing, Ella knew it, should just walk off and be done, except she couldn't resist. 'And I don't blame her for being upset—she's done an amazing job this morning. If Rafaele didn't get his shot, it has nothing to with Taylor. If I were directing we wouldn't be wasting so much time on the crying scene. I'd zoom into an Italian shot of Taylor crying, which could be done back in the studio if it doesn't work out here, and I wouldn't have Vince walking over to her. I'd have a moment of him watching and then Taylor turning, just his hand moving towards her face….' And she was sulking—oh, yes, she was—because it should be her directing this film, and with that she walked off.

And Santo stood there, when he wanted to chase after her.

Ella was affecting him in a way no woman ever had. Since their time together she was all he had thought about—and for what?

He looked up and straight into the eyes of a pretty young actress who smiled straight back at him. If he just took her to his trailer he'd feel better in ten. He should just get over Ella in ways of old, but he was back to the wedding that never happened again—just utterly bored and unmoved by the usual temptations. He'd been working in the chocolate factory too long, perhaps, Santo realised, had possibly reached his fill, except he wasn't sure he wanted it over.

And for what?

For someone who didn't even want to talk to him?

For woman who was heading for Roma and that sleaze Luigi?

A moody, unreasonable, uptight woman who wasn't even a very good PA, Santo told himself.

So why had he hired her?

You know why, a small voice told him.

Because it wasn't for her PA skills that he wanted her around, and no, he hadn't been thinking with his head when, despite her terrible Italian, he'd kept her on.

And then he stopped thinking about Ella. Santo had no choice but to, as suddenly, albeit not completely unexpectedly, all hell broke loose on the set.

# CHAPTER NINE

IT WASN'T ALL about Santo.

Ella had been telling the truth.

Today was the day she had been dreading for weeks now.

Calling home had always proven difficult, but in the past six months it had become almost impossible.

She put it off for as long as she could. Ella completed some of Santo's banking, rang and arranged the interview with Paulo and left a message for Marianna to call her. When she could put it off no longer, Ella dialled her parents' number and prayed that she'd get the answer machine.

She didn't.

'Hi, Mum.' Ella attempted upbeat. 'Happy birthday.'

'Ella!' She could hear the strain and discomfort

in her mother's voice. No doubt she had been dreading this phone call too. There was just so little they had to say to each other. 'It's so lovely to hear from you–where are you?'

'We're on location, filming.' Ella did her best to be vague, but when her mother pressed for more information about her beloved homeland, Ella told her where she was.

'Oh!' There was silence for a moment. 'That is close to where I grew up.'

'I know.'

'Have you been to have a look at my village?'

'Not yet,' Ella said. 'I've been so busy with work and everything and the shooting is falling way behind.'

'Your aunts will be so excited to finally meet you,' Gabriella said. 'I told them so much about you, about your work in the film industry.'

'I'm not working in the film industry.' It was a very sore point. 'I'm a PA.'

'For now,' Gabriella said. 'But you don't need to tell your aunts that. You tell them how well you're doing, how good things are....' Ella could hear the veiled warning, the call to keep up the pretence, to carry on with the hopeless charade that everything was perfect. 'Or maybe it would be better for you to say nothing about work. I don't think it will be good if they know you are working for a Corretti.'

'I'm not going to lie.'

'I never ask you to lie. I just don't think they need to know everything. The Corretti name has a long history—it might not go down too well. You know how shocked I was when I found out who you were working for. That name is one that strikes fear into a lot of people and especially in my village.'

And finally, finally, there was something to talk about, a common ground they could share. Maybe her trip to Italy was worth it, because at last there was a mutual link. 'That family is dangerous,' her mother warned.

'I think things are very different now.'

'There are no changes. I saw on the news that the wedding between the Corretti and Battaglia families didn't go ahead.' Ella smiled, because since she had been a little girl her mother always had the Italian radio on. The one thing Ella had been able to do for her mother, to make her life a little more pleasurable, was to get satellite television so that she could watch the Italian news, which Gabriella did, all of the time. 'I remember only too well Salvatore's sons...'

'Carlo and Benito?'

*'Morto!'* her mum said. 'I still remember the night they died. My sister rang and I turned on the news.... Don't you remember?' And a memory unfurled then. Ella would have been about twenty. She could see her mother standing by the television screen, shouting, a huge warehouse fire being shown on the news. It had meant nothing to Ella at the time, but it meant so much more now. She listened more carefully than she had back then as her mother spoke of that night. 'It was no accident, whatever anyone says.'

'They were killed?' Ella felt a shiver run down her spine.

'Who knows?' Gabriella said. 'They have a lot of enemies. Some people said it could have been an insurance scam that went wrong. These are the people you are dealing with—you should remember that at all times.'

'Santo is nothing like that,' Ella said.

'Please,' her mother scoffed. 'He is Carlo's son. He could be no other way. Carlo was obsessed with power, with money, with women—he could not stay faithful to his wife for even five minutes. Oh, but he was a charmer too.' Maybe Santo did take after his father after all. 'Salvatore was the worst.'

'Did he cheat too?'

'Who knows?' Gabriella said again. 'He was just pure bad—the Battaglia family too. How they ever slept at night with their consciences…' Gabriella said. 'Their wives were as bad too. Lording over everyone as if they were royalty, holding their fancy dinner parties. Your aunt worked in the kitchen of Salvatore's wife, Teresa, once for a dinner party. Their money was filthy—you ask your aunts. They will tell you—oh, the stories you will hear.…' Then her voice cracked as a huge pang of homesickness hit. Gabriella missed her sisters so very much, but it wasn't just them. She missed her home, her village and her history too. 'I wish I could speak with them. I mean, I know we speak on the phone but I want to see them. I wish I could be there when you all meet. I want to show you my village.…'

'Mum…' Ella's voice was thick with unshed tears. 'Why don't you come over?'

'Please, Ella, you know it is not possible.'

'Just for a holiday. I will pay your airfare…' But Ella stopped then. She was just repeating herself and, given it was her mother's birthday, Ella didn't pursue it further. She didn't want to upset her today.

'I'll go and visit everyone soon and give them all your love.'

'Let me know when you go, so I can ring them and tell them to expect you.'

'Okay.' Ella could not manage upbeat even a single second longer. 'I really do have to get to work now. I love you, Mum.'

'I love you too, Ella. Do you want to speak with your—'

It was Ella who hung up.

She was actually shaking with anger as she did so. That her mother could even suggest that she speak with her father after all that had gone on, that still she was supposed to pretend that terrible day had never happened.

Yet it had.

She could not break down again, but she could no longer pretend to forget either. She looked into the mirror, lifted her hair and saw the pink scar. The scar was proof that that day had happened. It was even there when she smiled. Those lovely white teeth had come at the most terrible price. Ella could still remember spitting her own teeth into her hand, but worse than that was the memory of the betrayal— that her mother could have forgiven him and stayed.

That she could watch as her own daughter was beaten and, instead of calling the police, had stood there sobbing and screaming. Instead of calling for an ambulance, she had handed Ella ice packs and told the story to give to the dentist, to the doctor. Had told Ella that if she didn't want to make it worse for her mother, then she must tell everyone that she fell.

Ella needed to get out, to walk, to run. It was the reason she opened her door, for she would never have opened the door to Santo in this state. She wasn't crying, but she was still shaking in anger, still holding in a scream that wanted to come out.

'Ella?'

She brushed past him, but he caught her wrist.

'Please, Santo.' She was having great trouble keeping her voice from shouting. 'I was just about to go for a walk.'

'Later...' He simply could not let her walk off like this. He could see how upset she was.

'I just need to get out for a while.'

'Of course you do.' Santo was very practical. 'We all go a bit stir-crazy in the hotel after a few days. I'll take you for a drive. I could use one too.' He was not going to argue about this. He had come to visit

Ella for rather more pressing reasons than a drive, but for once, work could wait.

They drove, in silence at first, around the winding streets, but Santo drove the powerful car with far more finesse than Ella and it was actually nice to sit back and stare at the scenery.

'It's beautiful.' Ella looked at the dotted beige buildings built into the hills and then they turned into a village. Another one, Santo explained, that was run-down and in much need of the new lease of life the redevelopment might bring.

'There is only one café now,' he explained, slowing the car down. Ella peered up a long set of steps. 'Do you want to stop for a drink?'

Ella shook her head.

'There are only a couple of shops....' She was starting to understand more and more the difference this movie could make. It was such a stunning part of the country. There were just picture-perfect views everywhere. Yet so many, like her mother, had left. She blinked and turned her head as she passed vaguely familiar buildings, recognising some of them from the photos her mother spent a long time reminiscing over.

'This is my mother's village.'

'I know.' Santo turned and smiled. 'You could drop in on your aunts now.'

'I don't think so.' Ella gave a tight smile.

'Probably a good call,' Santo said. 'Your mother would never hear the last of it if you arrived with a Corretti in tow.'

'Slow down a moment.' He did so. 'I think that's the baker's that my mother used to work at before she moved.'

'Does she work now?'

'No,' Ella said. 'She worked in a factory till she had me, then gave it up to help out in my father's shop.' She peered into the window as Santo slowly passed. 'It's nice to see it.' It really was. There were a few people walking, and some women sitting in the front of their gardens talking. And it was actually nice to see it for the first time with Santo rather than alone. She took a breath. 'Could we get that coffee?'

'Sure.' He turned the car around on a very narrow road with a very steep descent on one side. Only that wasn't what had the sweat beading on Ella's forehead. She should take a moment to touch up her make-up. She was supposed to look nice at all times, but she wasn't actually working, Ella realised.

This was very personal indeed.

They walked along the narrow pavement. Even the street was cobbled—it was like stepping back in history. They stopped outside a tiny church.

'My mum gets so upset when anyone gets married. She's told me all about the church. She says the parties afterwards are amazing....'

'The whole street comes out,' Santo said. 'Tables are set up for the reception.'

'It's just so different from anything I'm used to,' Ella said. 'Not just here, the whole of Italy. Everything's so much newer in Australia, even the old buildings aren't comparatively old.' She looked around at the relatively unchanged architecture, could completely understand how her mother missed it, how Gabriella could still picture it so well, because it was just as it appeared in the photos. 'Nothing's changed,' Ella said.

'Of course it has,' Santo responded. 'The changes just don't show.'

They climbed the narrow steps to a café and certainly they turned heads when they walked in. Ella was quite sure it was because Santo was a Corretti, and that it had nothing to do with the fact he was possibly the most beautiful man in the world.

The whole place fell silent and they were shepherded to a seat.

'Are they scared of you?' Ella asked in a low voice. 'Or angry?'

'Both,' Santo said. 'I hope soon they will be neither.'

He ordered—coffee and crêpes that were filled with gelato. It was just so nice to be away from set. The locals were starting to talk amongst themselves again, and yes, the gelato was as good as her mother described.

'It's nice to be out, thanks for this.'

'No problem.'

'How come you're not on set?'

He just shrugged—those reasons could wait. For now Santo just wanted to talk about her. 'Your mother's never been back?'

'Nope.'

'One day, maybe?'

Ella didn't answer.

Even when they were back in the car, when he tried to work out just what it was that had upset her so much today, still Ella spoke about work.

'I spoke with Paulo and arranged his interview

and I left a message for Marianna. Paulo sounds really good, he's just not able to start yet.'

'Which is a problem,' Santo admitted. 'I need someone who can start as soon as possible.' He had, Ella realised, stopped trying to dissuade her from leaving. 'What about Marianna?'

'The truth?' Ella checked. It was nice to be chatting, nice to be driving and away from everything, and just so very nice to be with Santo.

'The truth,' Santo confirmed.

'She's awful,' Ella said. 'She's incredibly confident, treated me like I was her secretary, wanted to only deal directly with you. She refused to give an inch when I tried to pin her for a time to come in for an interview.' Ella rolled her eyes. 'To sum up, I think she'll be perfect for the job.'

'I thought I already had perfect.'

He glanced over and reluctantly she smiled. 'No, we both know that you didn't.' Maybe it was because Santo was so open and honest, that in this, Ella found that she was able to be. 'I'm not tough enough.'

'I don't always like tough.'

'I'm not…' She didn't really know how to say it, how to admit just how much it all had hurt her. 'I don't think Marianna will sulk if you don't send her flowers.'

'So you were sulking.'

'Yes.'

'What else is Marianna good at?'

'Multi-tasking apparently.' She looked out of the window at the ocean and the beauty of the day and hated her melancholy, hated that she hadn't been able to play by the rules and happily tumble in bed with him without adding her heart to the equation. 'She'd probably be taking dictation now and giving you a quick hand-job as she did so.' Ella turned to the sound of his laughter, realised she was smiling now too, because that was how he made her feel. Yes, it was so good to get out.

He pulled the car over and he just smiled as she sat there blushing, as the best lover in the world, as the man she had so foolishly thought she could bear to lose, cupped her face.

'I walked into a storm that morning—I lost my director, I had stuff going on with my family, I had my brother out at sea.'

'I know, I know.'

'But when I knew you were arriving I did arrange flowers,' Santo said. 'I had them sent to the room, the same room that you took one look at and left. And I organised dinner—I really wanted to tell you how much our time together had meant, how I was looking forward to seeing you, how it killed not ring—' He looked at her for the longest time. 'Who hurt you?' He saw her rapid blink. 'Is there an ex-husband?' He saw her frown.

'Of course not.'

'What do you mean "of course"?' Santo said. 'I know nothing about you, Ella. What I do know I could write on a Post-it note. I know your parents are together, that there are no brothers or sisters, that your mother is from here.' He saw the well of tears in the bottom of her eyes. 'That the sex was like nothing I have ever known, but I don't know you....'

'You're my boss, you don't need—'

'I'm your lover!' He almost shouted it. 'Get it into your head.'

'For how long though…' She hated the neediness, but it was the truth, because he was telling her to open up to him, to give him more than sex, and she was terrified to.

'Who knows?' He was completely honest. 'But if we can't talk, then not for much longer.'

'You don't talk about the stuff that troubles you.'

'I've tried more than you,' Santo said.

'Santo, I don't tell anyone...' She was close to panic now. 'I don't share myself with anyone and I'm not going to start pouring my heart out to you.'

'You will.' The view was more stunning than the ocean behind him—his eyes so intense, the passion blazing—and she was there in his spotlight now. He would strip her bare and she was petrified, not just of it ending, but of the togetherness too. She could simply not envisage sharing herself so completely with another, of trusting another. 'Tell and kiss.' She could feel the warmth of his skin so close and she teased his translation, just as he did to her.

'It's kiss and tell.'

'No.' His eyes were open. Santo had made up his mind and he moved back and started the engine. 'It's tell and kiss.' And as he drove off, as always he made her smile. He took her hand and placed it in his lap. 'Though, of course, I don't mind a woman who can multi-task.'

'Ha, ha...' She took back her hand.

They had been out for a couple of hours and he knew no more than he had when she had opened her hotel door.

'What was it like?' He turned to her question. 'I

mean, back there, in the café. People were nervous just to see you....'

'That is because I would rarely go there, but here...' He nodded ahead. 'They are more used to us. This is where my nonna lives.'

'But what was it like?'

It was Santo who couldn't answer. He could see his grandparents' house, huge and imposing and the keeper of so many secrets.

'Have you seen today's papers?' He didn't wait for her response, he knew that she had. 'There is far more to come. Always it is about power—that is how it is, that is how you are taught—but sometimes you just want to walk in a café and have coffee.' Ella nodded. 'That is why I like being on set—I am just Santo there. Of course, there are a few awkward looks today, given what has been said in the newspapers about my mother. I just have to wear it. Battaglia is determined to crush us and will stop at nothing—so now he makes sure that every piece of filth he can find ends up in the papers.' He looked at Ella. 'There is a lot of filth.'

There was, Santo knew that, but there was a lot of good too, and somehow he wanted to show her that. But there was something he, too, had been putting off for a while, something that might be easier with Ella by his side.

'Now,' Santo said, 'I take you where I have taken no woman before.' He glanced over to see her wide-eyed reaction. 'My nonna's.'

'Do you think that's a good idea?'

'Probably not.' Santo shrugged. 'She will have us married off in her mind the moment we walk in there, but I really ought to visit her. She will be very upset with all that is going on in the family and she is worried about Alessandro too, as well as mourning her husband. She never really got over losing her sons....' He was pensive for a moment. 'You know, for all that the cousins do not get on, for all the arguments, the one thing that unites us is our love for her—she is a good woman.' Perhaps Ella's silence spoke volumes, for Santo turned his head in instant defence. 'She is.'

'Of course,' came Ella guarded response. Salvatore Corretti's reputation was legendary, and if Ella knew a little of what had gone on to get there, then absolutely his wife must have known a whole lot more.

'Her family hated that she married him,' Santo

explained a little, 'but she loved him, and turned a blind eye to all that he got up to.'

Ella bit down on her lip in an effort not to voice her thoughts.

'Sometimes it is easier to, perhaps…' Santo said.

'Or simply more convenient.' Ella could not stay silent on this. 'I'm sorry, Santo. I'm trying not to judge your nonna—I haven't met her after all—but I don't buy that turn a blind eye excuse.'

'And I am not asking you to.' He saw her tense profile. 'I'm just letting you know, before we go in there, that these past years have been very hard on her. These are exceptionally difficult times, so just…' He shook his head. 'It doesn't matter.'

As they approached Ella was both nervous and excited to be meeting such a legend. It was like being invited backstage and the chance to meet the matriarch of this family was just too good to pass up. But as they walked towards the house she could see Santo's strained face.

'I'm not going to say anything that might offend her.'

'I know you wouldn't,' Santo said, or he would never have brought here.

# CHAPTER TEN

A MAID LET them in, but rather than standing and waiting in the hall, Santo took Ella's hand and they walked straight through, Santo calling out to announce he was here.

'Santo!' There was a crow of surprise as Teresa heard them and they were in the large lounge before she was even standing. There was a flurry of kisses and introductions. Teresa was dressed from head to toe in black, and from the candle burning by a bible on a table, it was clear she was deep in mourning. But there was absolute pleasure on the old woman's face as she greeted her grandson. There was no denying the bond was a genuine one and that Teresa was so pleased to see him.

'It is lovely to meet you,' Teresa said to Ella. 'Such

a nice surprise—you will forgive me if my English is not very good.' She smiled. 'And you are to correct me if I forget and speak in Italian,' she added to Santo. 'My mind is everywhere at the moment.'

'Don't worry,' Santo said. 'Anyway, Ella's mother is from here, so she speaks a little Italian.' He smiled and so, too, did Ella.

'He is teasing you, yes?' Teresa checked and then answered her own question. 'Of course he is.'

Santo brought such a smile to her weary face. He was incredibly good with women—all women—because he didn't mind a bit when she cried a little when they spoke of Salvatore. 'The house, it is too quiet,' she said, 'but then I tell myself at least he is not dealing with all this, at least he died thinking that the families would unite.'

'It will sort,' Santo said, but Teresa shook her head.

'I am not so sure that it will. Have you heard from Alessandro?'

'He is okay.' Santo was so gentle with her. 'I saw him the morning after and he has texted me a couple of times. He just needs time.'

'And the rest of the family? Have you seen Luca?'

'I am staying out of it as much as I can for now.'

Santo was firm. He certainly didn't want to discuss the scandals that were going on with his nonna. 'The better we do with this film, the better it will be for the family, for everyone. The locals are watching the filming. The docklands are busy, for the first time in a long time. This is what I need to give my attention to now.'

'But even that is having problems!' Teresa kept her eyes on everything, Ella realised. 'That actress…' Teresa screwed up her nose. 'I saw the photos—she should be ashamed.'

'It does take two.' Santo grinned.

'So, how is she doing?' Teresa asked and the smile wavered on Santo's face.

'Taylor's a very good actress,' Ella spoke then. 'Well, she's got a lot of potential, if she had the right person directing to bring it out.'

'Ella thinks she should be directing.' Santo's voice was wry, but he was glad for the change in conversation, because it was clear Teresa was getting more and more upset. The challenges the family faced were not going to be easily fixed and he hated that she was sitting alone and fretting.

'You have a problem with a female director?' Teresa teased.

'Oh, I have no issues with Ella being a woman.' Santo grinned but then his phone went. 'Excuse me, I have to take this.'

As he went outside to take the call, Teresa poured them two small glasses of limoncello. It was tart and lovely and tasted just like her mother made and she told Teresa the same.

'There are many recipes, but this is the local one. Your mother would make it the same way. Have you been to visit where she lived yet?'

'Santo took me there on the way here,' Ella said. 'I am going to visit my aunts when we finish shooting.'

'And your mother, does she love Australia? I have heard so many good things about it.'

And Ella sat quiet for a moment, sipped on her limoncello and answered carefully. 'It's a beautiful country,' Ella said, 'but my mother misses home an awful lot.'

'Of course,' Teresa said. 'But she is happy with her choice?'

And she looked at Ella for a very long time. There was a moment, a long one, and one Ella decided where it would be prudent to play by very old rules. It was, Ella told herself, a practice run for her aunties. 'Very happy,' Ella said and returned Teresa's smile, looking up in relief when Santo came in.

'Take Ella and show her the winery,' Teresa said. 'Choose something nice for dinner tonight.'

'You have to get back, don't you?' Santo said to Ella. It was nice that he offered the choice as to whether they stay longer, but Ella knew it would be rude to leave now, knew from her mother what was silently expected.

'No.' Ella smiled. 'I've got everything done. Dinner would be lovely.'

'She seems to like you.' They were walking in the grounds, through the vines and out to the winery. She'd have loved to take a photo, to tell her mum she was here, but she wasn't sure that that suggestion would be particularly welcomed.

'You're quiet,' she commented, because Santo rarely was.

'It feels different to be here and know he isn't.'

'Sorry...' Ella could have kicked herself for her own insensitivity. 'I didn't think.'

'No!' Santo shook his head. 'I am not upset.'

'I do understand that whatever has gone on, still he was your grandparent.'

'It's not fond memories I'm having, Ella.' Santo

said no more than that. They walked into the cool dark winery and she wondered if here he might try something, but instead Santo spent an awful long time choosing the wine.

'This one,' he said. 'This was from the year you were born.'

'I didn't know you knew the year I was born.'

'I read your résumé.' He gave her a smile and walked over, lifted his hand to her hair, just wondered about her, really. 'You know I always wanted to have sex in here.'

He was just so direct.

'With your grandmother waiting in the house?'

'That doesn't come into my fantasy.'

'Well, it's a bit off-putting in mine,' Ella said. She was terribly wary of him, trying to keep things light when she felt anything but, trying to keep her head on during a most difficult of days.

'I miss you.' He watched her frown.

'You don't know me.'

'That's what I miss.'

He didn't even try to kiss her, did nothing other than take her hand and walk back to the house. She just couldn't read his mood.

The food was heavenly—fennel salad dripping

in the best olive oil Ella had tasted, and a huge la-
sagne, but the Sicilian way, stuffed with Italian sau-
sage and cheeses.

Santo sat at the table, chatted and spoke and
smiled in all the right places, and she tried to fathom
him, but couldn't. He looked up and caught her staring, and smiled till she blushed as he stared back
and he pressed his foot to her leg just once, but it
wasn't Santo.

It was like watching an actor play his part.

'Do you remember my birthday?' Teresa smiled
and recounted tales of supposed happier times, but
Ella watched a muscle flicker in Santo's cheek as
Teresa mentioned Benito's children and asked after
Luca and Gio, though she was wise enough perhaps
to not mention Matteo. 'And that time Lia hid and
we could not find her for hours. You were so young
then. Grace was still alive.'

'Grace?'

'Lia's mum,' Santo explained. 'Benito was married before Simona.' He was so much more open
here, but then so was Teresa, Ella realised. She must
assume, given that Santo had brought her here, that
they were serious.

'She lived with us,' Teresa explained. 'When

Grace died.' And she smiled over to Santo, and Ella watched as there was just a brief pause before Santo duly smiled back, not that Teresa noticed. She turned her attention to Ella.

'Will you tell your mother that you ate with me?' Her eyes twinkled.

'I can't wait to tell her.' Ella laughed, because she'd been sitting there thinking just that. For the first time in a very long time, she actually missed her mother, wished that today was something they could have properly shared.

'She will be shocked, and she will warn you about me, but also she will love to know!' Teresa promised, and it was as if she had met her mother—she just knew what she was like. 'She will want every single detail,' Teresa said as the maid brought in a huge tray of sweet canelloni, 'but even as you give her the details she will tell you that you should not have come!'

'Then she'll ask me to tell her about your furniture.'

He watched as the two women sat laughing, and thank God he'd brought Ella with him, because Santo wasn't sure he could have got through this visit alone, and certainly not as well. Memories were

churning. The happy birthdays his nonna all too fre-
quently regaled were not quite as perfect, if Santo
remembered correctly.

And he was quite sure he did.

Surprisingly it was Santo who declined coffee.

He just wanted out.

Even as they left, Teresa was plying her with bot-
tles of olive oil and limoncello and, even as they
climbed in the car, offering them to come back in
for coffee.

'We really have to go,' Santo said. 'We need to
get back to the Olympic Village.'

Thankfully his little dig went straight over Teresa's head.

'That wasn't funny,' Ella said, her cheeks scalding as he started up the car.

'I thought it was.' Santo smirked. 'You know, I
think sex actually enhances performance.'

'I'll draft a letter to the IOC for you,' Ella said
tartly. 'I'm sure they'll welcome your thoughts.'

'Do you?' She turned and saw that his expression
was serious. 'Can you talk to me? Can you tell me
why you were so upset when I came to your room
this afternoon?'

And he'd shared so much with her today that

maybe she could. There was this argument raging but it was dimming. Quite simply, with Santo she wanted to share—she just didn't know how. 'It's my mum's birthday today,' Ella admitted. 'I'd just called her when you came to my room.' Santo said nothing. 'I find it really hard to talk to her.'

'You don't get on?'

'I don't agree with some of her choices,' Ella said and then amended, 'I don't agree with a lot of her choices.'

She said nothing more for a while, and neither did Santo. He was waiting for her to talk to him and she tried to a couple of times, opened her mouth to speak, then closed it again. It was twenty-seven years of silence that she was fighting to break and it was especially difficult to break that silence to a man.

Except Santo was like no man she had ever met and maybe she was starting to actually trust him, maybe it was time that she opened up. As they drove in to the hotel and the valet approached, just as he went to open her door, Ella spoke.

'My father is an alcoholic.'

As she went to climb out of the car he caught her

wrist and gently pulled her back. 'For that you get a kiss.'

He ignored the open doors, the people standing in the foyer, the valet waiting to take his keys. Instead, as promised, he gave her a kiss for telling, and she was crying as he did so, because she'd never actually said those words before. Then his tongue was on her cheeks, taking her tears. It was a very private, very thorough kiss, in a very public place, but right now, neither cared a fraction.

'Let's get inside,' Santo said.

Once they were out, he took her hand and they walked towards the hotel. Clearly he had to let it go, ought to let go, for they were about to step into the revolving door, but it was as if they were glued together, as if neither could bear to be apart, not even for a second, and they walked into the door together.

'He beats her.' She just said it out loud in a tiny space and, oblivious of onlookers, not caring that no one could now get in or out of the hotel, as promised, he rewarded her with his mouth, just pulled her right into him. They were the only two people left in the world. He could have taken her there had he wanted to. There was just this slow unfurling of her heart as he held and kissed her, and in that moment, Ella truly thought she could tell him anything. For the first time in her life, she trusted another with her heart.

'Now,' Santo said, 'I take you to bed and then after—' because there would be after '—if you want to, we can talk some more.'

Ella, weak from admission, was grateful for the chance of a reprieve from her confessions. As he pushed the glass door, as they walked through the entrance, all she wanted was his bed, his warmth, the shield of him that for far too long she had denied.

'Santo Corretti...'

It felt as if she were being rapidly brought out of an anaesthetic, the antidote to surrender shooting through her veins, as a stunning woman walked towards them and the safe, warm feeling she had, so briefly, sampled was suddenly threatened. The bubble of bliss burst, and his arm, around her, squeezed suddenly tense shoulders.

'I am Marianna...' She smiled warmly to Santo, but it turned black when she greeted Ella. 'Your replacement.'

'Now is not a good time.' Santo was extremely curt. 'I do not do impromptu interviews. You can arrange a time with Ella for tomorrow.'

'No...' Ella just wanted it over and done with. She could hardly blame Marianna for jumping on a plane to convince the boss personally—hadn't Ella done exactly the same? 'You two go ahead, I need to...' She didn't even try to come up with an excuse. 'Tomorrow you are busy with filming. It might be better if we can sort this all out tonight.'

Ella ignored Santo as he tried to call her back. Instead she pulled back the gate to the lift and headed to her room, horribly unsettled at the turn of events, but possibly glad for them.

She had been so close to telling everything, to opening up and pouring out her heart.

But for what?

She was leaving, moving to Rome in a few short weeks—what hope was there for them anyway? Santo couldn't even manage longevity in a normal relationship, a long-distance one was surely an impossible ask.

Ella needed to think. She had sworn to never cry over him, to not give this playboy her heart, and she had just come dangerously close to doing so. She opened the door to her room and there was a huge bunch of flowers waiting there. They brought a very watery smile to her lips. Santo had been on and off the phone for a lot of the afternoon, and though she was touched at his thoughtfulness, as she opened the attached card, Ella braced herself for more of his endearments, reminded herself that Santo was a stunning flirter, yet she found herself frowning as she read the card.

You will be amazing.
See why I had to sleep with you before I told you?
Santo xxx
P.S. You're fired.

She didn't understand his cryptic message, but knew this evening she had been played, that, all day, sex had been on his agenda, that it had been an absolute certainty for Santo that the day would end in his bed.

And, had it not been for Marianna, it would have.

She poured herself some limoncello from the bottle Teresa had given her, tried to tell herself that she must calm down, tried to work out what his message meant. Not liking where her thoughts were leading, that once in bed he'd take away the problem of her working for him, no doubt, right now, he was giving Marianna the job.

How bloody convenient for him.

'Ella...' She had known that he would come to her room, that Santo would have to offer a rapid explanation for his message, and she was very tight-lipped as she opened the door. 'You got the flowers....' There was an attempt at a joke, when Ella really wasn't in the mood for one. 'Now do you see why I need a PA? Even flowers I manage to screw up.'

'So you were going to fire me, after you slept with me.'

'No, no, you have it all wrong.'

'I was a dead certainty, was I?'

'Yes.' He made no apology about it. 'I was certain that tonight I was going to make love to you.'

'So, how was Marianna?'

'She was everything that you said she was. Ella, please, will you just listen?'

'You don't want me to hang around and train her up?'

'Ella...'

She didn't let him get a word in.

'Because it shouldn't take long—I've streamlined the process....'

'Really!' Santo's raised an eyebrow. He actually rather liked her angry. 'How so?'

'Well, you're a full-time job, but not a very complicated one. She watched his tongue roll in his cheek. 'I'll just hand her the Santo Bag.'

'The Santo Bag?'

'It contains all the essentials.'

And she took the huge bag she'd been carrying around and adding to for four months now, and tipped the contents onto his bed.

'New white shirt, grey tie, black tie…' She glanced over and there was a very unrepentant smile curving on his lips. 'You do seem to attend an inordinate amount of funerals.'

'The company I keep,' Santo said, because actors lived and played hard as well, 'and I have a complicated family too.'

'Headache pills,' Ella said. 'And sunglasses.'

Santo said nothing.

'Condoms—you tend to run out an awful lot.' Tears pricked at her eyes as she remembered a frantic 3:00 a.m. phone call from her boss, and she was so blisteringly angry with him, so completely furious with herself for loving him. Loathing him too, for all he had, however unwittingly, put her heart through, because it had killed to see him with others.

'We shoot in strange locations.' But he wasn't smiling now, realising now the depth of her hurt, because until last week there hadn't been any hint that she even liked him.

'First aid kit and those amazing gel Band-Aids...' She heard his breathing come angry and hard as she reminded him of one time. 'Great for carpet burn.'

'I get the message, Ella.'

'Oh, I haven't finished yet. Antiseptic...' she continued. 'Great for scratches.'

'You were jealous.' He was angry with himself for not seeing it, angry with her too, for all she had put herself through. 'All that time...'

'Jealous!' She snorted. 'I'm not jealous, Santo, I'm sick of it. You don't need a PA following you around—you need a school nurse!'

And she hated him for smiling then, hated the stealth of his approach. Yes, she was jealous, had, even though she'd denied it, been hot, spitting jealous and even worse than that, now he knew.

'Do you know what you need?'

He picked a condom up from the bed and then he tossed it. 'Oh, that's right, we don't use them.'

'Of all the arrogant—' He hushed her with his mouth, pushed her against the wall with a kiss so violent there was a clash of enamel and she tried to push him off.

'You do need it,' Santo said, refusing to release her, his hands pushing up her skirt. 'You need a quick reminder of how good we are. And then we're going to talk.'

'When you fire me?' she spat out.

'When I hire you.' He reclaimed her mouth as he tore at her panties and—love him or loathe him, she didn't know—all Ella knew was that she was kissing him back. She'd never had angry sex before, had never been caught in a row that came with pure passion. At the return of her kiss he lifted her and she found that he was backing her into another wall, his mouth still on hers as he spoke. 'I was going to offer you a job....'

'As what? Your on-set tart?'

Right now she'd take it. She was kissing him back and grappling with his zipper. 'I hate you, Santo,' she told him. 'I hate that you planned this.'

'You love it.'

He lifted her onto him, and she hated more the legs that so willingly wrapped around him, but then, he'd taken off that shackle. This was no threat to her job. As of now, she didn't work for him, and she found herself feeling surprisingly free.

'You love it, more than you want to admit to it.' He was inside her and she was grinding down. 'You are the most uptight woman I know,' Santo said, 'except in the bedroom.' She was starting to come and trying to hold on to it. 'Guess what?' He was battering into her, not just her sex but her head. 'I accept that...' He went to say something more, but gave in. She could hear the neighbours banging on the wall as Santo switched to rapid Italian, heard her own moans and shouts as they locked into oblivion. He was right, she loved it. She was just petrified of loving him.

'I have to change rooms.' She was leaning on him, stunned and a bit dizzy, never wanting to face her neighbours again, but Santo lifted her chin to face him.

'There's something I came to tell you this afternoon.' Ella looked up at him. 'I fired Rafaele.'

He was an absolute gentleman. He took her shredded panties and put them in the bin, retrieved a wayward shoe and even smoothed her skirt for her as she processed the news. It was huge to fire a director mid-shoot and she didn't dare hope, didn't dare dream. He tucked in his shirt and did everything up, a strange attempt to separate this from the bedroom, except she could feel him trickling between her thighs.

'Ella, I have given a lot of thought as to his replacement and I think you would make an amazing director.'

'Santo.' She ran a tongue over her lip, a lip swollen from passion and the bruising crush of his kiss. 'I don't know what to say. Is it because you can't get anyone else?'

'I have three people who can fly out tonight.' He scuppered that argument with a flick of his wrist.

'Then is it because...' She couldn't even bring herself to say it. 'Santo, you're right. I should never have considered you doing me a favour just because we slept with each other.'

'It has nothing to do with sex.' He was almost stern as he said it. 'I would never hire for that reason, never. A director's role is too important. I am only hiring you because I now think you are right for the role. I have given it some serious thought and have come to the conclusion that you would be fantastic—you understand the movie inside out. You have seen the disaster Rafaele has made...'

Ella nodded.

'And you know what the movie needs.'

'Taylor would never agree.'

'She already has,' Santo said. 'There was a lot of trouble on set today. Things turned very nasty and, you're right, it is not her acting that is at fault. I spoke to her at length. That is when I told her your suggestions and how passionate you are about this film. She is happy to work with you.'

'Really?'

'Fresh vision is always good,' Santo said. 'So here is your chance.'

She was terrified, because his earlier argument had been right. She hadn't earned her stripes. She hadn't even been an assistant. If she took this role Ella would be stepping straight into the big league and she told him that.

'You can do it,' Santo said. 'I have every faith that you can handle this, but it's the last professional handhold I will give you, Ella. We will be fighting tomorrow on set. I am not going to hold back just because it is you—and if I don't think you are doing well...' Then he paused. She didn't need to be told.

Ella knew only too well how he operated. 'But when we are off set...' He waited and he watched as she shook her head. 'Ella, I promise you that whatever happens between us on a personal level I will not bring it to work.'

'I can't.' She couldn't, but she knew more explanation was needed. Santo had offered her the biggest break professionally, and also emotionally. She had never opened up more with another, and she needed to do so now. 'I only slept with you when I knew I had the other job.'

'I know,' Santo said. He had no issues with truths. 'You left your email open on my computer.'

'My mum used to work for my father.'

'You are not your mother.'

'I know that,' Ella said.

'And this is very different...'

'I know, but I swore a long time ago that my career would always come first, that I would never jeopardise it for a man, any man. I've broken way too many of my own rules lately but this really is a big chance. It's not a PA job that I don't particularly want that I'm risking now. I can't go back on my promise to myself just because it's you.'

And she waited for his argument, for him to attempt to dissuade, but it never came. 'I accept that.' And only now did she understand the true meaning of his earlier words, that he had known from the start what her rules would be.

'It's a couple of weeks,' Ella said. 'I need to concentrate properly on the film.'

'Then do,' Santo said. 'But understand this, Ella—you don't get to pick and choose.'

'Sorry?'

'Till filming is over you are in or out.'

Ella just looked at him, wasn't entirely sure she understood what he was saying.

'You don't get to dip in when you choose to,' Santo clarified. 'So what is it to be—in or out.'

And for Ella, there could only be one answer. 'Out.'

'Fine.' He headed for the door. 'Good luck. As my note said—you'll be amazing.'

## CHAPTER ELEVEN

SANTO BLINKED IN surprise when he walked on the set this morning, not because Ella was there. He'd known she'd be early. More it was an Ella he had never seen.

She was wearing a faded denim skirt and espadrilles and a halter neck top. The hair that was usually groomed was hanging loose as it did in the bedroom. As she smiled at him, Santo saw she was wearing absolutely no make-up.

'Is this director Ella?' he asked as she walked over to him.

'No, this is Ella.'

And it was a bit of a fist to the gut, that all the clothes and the make-up had been the part she had played for him, and just confirmed that Santo didn't know her at all.

'The ship is all organised.' Marianna came over and spoke in Italian with Santo as Ella half listened, translating easily. Yes, Marianna was a far more efficient PA. She had achieved in a few hours what Ella had been struggling with for days. 'So everyone will be in place for 5:00 a.m. and it sails at 3:00 p.m. the following day.'

*'Eccellente.'* He glanced over to Ella. 'We have to be finished by then.'

'We will be.'

Santo nodded and turned back to Marianna, telling her to organise a party that final night for the crew. That was the one part of the job Ella had loved doing. Santo knew how to throw a good party and Ella had enjoyed organising them. She mentioned a couple of contacts she had to Marianna.

'I can run through things this evening,' Ella offered. 'I'm sorry, I really haven't been much help handing over.'

'No need,' Marianna said. 'I have my own contacts. Anyway, I'll speak with Santo if I need to know anything. I prefer to find out things firsthand.' She went to head off and then changed her mind.

'Actually, I need his spare car keys, his diary, that sort of thing....'

Ella was terribly aware of Santo's smirk as she went in her bag and handed over a few items.

'You forgot the sunglasses,' Santo said.

'So I did,' Ella responded tartly, her cheeks burning as she handed them over.

'Headache tablets,' he prompted.

'No need,' Marianna chimed in. 'I have some on me.'

Ella's bag was soon considerably emptier as she handed over a shirt and a couple of ties too.

'I think that's everything,' Ella said.

'Sure?' Santo checked, enjoying her discomfort.

'I'm sure Marianna is prepared for every eventuality.' Ella smiled sweetly and then turned her attention back to what was important, what would remain.

Work.

Except she wanted to share it with him.

To start with, Ella was incredibly nervous. It seemed wrong to be giving directions to someone as skilled as Taylor, but overriding her nerves was the rising thrill that Taylor seemed to completely understand her.

'You're not happy as such,' Ella said, trying not to be too rude about Rafaele's interpretation. 'It's more that you're carefree. Yes, you know he's leaving tomorrow, but for now you have no idea what's to come.' She looked through the viewfinder, watched Taylor walking along the beach with her lover who would soon go missing, watched the shot of her life before it changed for ever, and any nerves Ella had died then, because she could do this.

All those endless nights of her childhood spent locked in her room making movies with her mind reaped the rewards today as finally a scene came to life, and there were actually tears in her eyes as Ella watched it unfold.

And Santo watched her grow before his eyes too.

'Vince, from now on you're not going to be watching her.' Ella got back to the heart of the script. Rafaele had interpreted it that Vince came upon Taylor crying, but over and over Ella had read it and pictured it differently. Now she brought it to life. 'You need to be here first, thinking about your friend, then you see Taylor arrive. Remember that till this point you've never really liked her. You've always thought that she was using him, but watching her cry, you see for the first time how much she loves him—it is that that moves you.'

'Right.' The sulking Vince actually smiled because, till now, Rafaele had made his character look nothing other than a man taking advantage of a vulnerable woman.

'That's why you go over,' Ella said to Vince. 'You realise that she knows how you feel, that you both miss him. And, Taylor...' Ella said. 'When he turns around, you're defensive. You're used to him making sarcastic comments. He's already accused you of crocodile tears, but it is his empathy that is going to have you two heading off to the beach.'

'Got it.'

'And we're not going to do the full-on crying scene yet...' Santo watched as Taylor breathed out in relief. The past few days had been draining at best. 'Just a few tears. What I want to get is your expression when Vince joins you.'

Taylor was brilliant. For the first time since filming had started Santo could breathe. Just having Vince there first changed everything, shifted the whole dynamics. It was something he wouldn't have thought of and he told Ella the same as they headed back to the hotel.

'We've got more done today than we have all week.'

She was glowing inside at the praise, on a high from finally doing the job she loved and knowing that she was doing it well.

'I'm starving,' Santo said. It was 10:00 p.m. and they had been too busy working to stop and take advantage of the catering. Now, all Ella wanted to do was to order something from room service, or... She looked over to Santo as they walked through the foyer. Perhaps they could have dinner and talk about the scenes tomorrow, or perhaps—Ella took a deep breath—they could simply talk.

'So am I.' She was beyond conflicted, wavering as to the choice she had earlier made. Santo would do nothing to jeopardise this film over something that might happen between them. And he was right—she was not her mother. She was so much stronger than that. 'Maybe we could...' She paused as his phone rang, waited while he took the call.

'Sorry about that.' His expression was grim when he came off the phone. 'Right, I'll see you in the morning. We start at six.'

'Sure.' Ella took a deep breath. 'I might get something to eat in the restaurant, if they're still taking orders.'

'Of course they are,' Santo said. 'I told them we would not be finished filming till late. They are being very good—they understand the odd hours.' His phone bleeped again, and his teeth gritted. 'Enjoy your dinner.' He dismissed her and, now she had said where she was going, Ella had no choice but to head into the restaurant. She told herself she was a working woman and there was nothing to be embarrassed about asking for a table for one, but all she felt was awkward. There was Vince, but he was engrossed in conversation with another of the actors and it was clear there was some serious flirting going on. Just when Ella had ordered, just when she had decided it wasn't so bad after all, in walked Santo, still talking on his phone. She smiled as he walked towards her, but the smile disappeared when he returned it and then promptly walked past her.

Ella couldn't believe he'd take things that literally, would have them sit alone rather than share a meal, but as Marianna came in, Ella realised that Santo had no intention to eat alone.

It was work, Ella told herself as she twisted pasta around her fork and tried not to hear their talk and laughter. It was exactly the same as she and Santo had done, in many hotels on many occasions, she told herself.

But did it take a bottle of wine to go through his diary?

It really was a hell of her own making, Ella told herself over and over through the coming days.

On a shoot it was a small closed world, but not even that could filter out the whispers and rumours that abounded about the Correttis. Ella watched as Santo read a newspaper, one that announced that the cousins were firmly divided, that Carlo's children were having nothing to do with Benito's, and that they were going to offer a counterproposal against Santo's half-brother, Angelo, who had the full weight of Battaglia behind him. Ella knew it must be killing him, knew the effect that it would be having on Teresa too.

Yet, unless it was relevant to the movie, Santo gave her not so much as a word as to what was going on in his life.

His usually smiling face was closed now, his eyes constantly hidden behind dark glasses, but Ella could see the tension in his lips, could hear the impatience in his words as he endlessly spoke on the phone. She loathed that at one point, as they were discussing the next scene, Marianna came over and asked if she could have a word with him.

'In private...' Marianna said and then switched to Italian. *'Familia.'*

Ella watched as Marianna drew him aside, watched as Santo's features paled and his fingers moved to his neck, pulling at the top he was wearing as he did when rarely he was anxious. Then he reached for his phone.

'Is everything okay?' she asked at the first opportunity. They were back at the hotel and heading up to their rooms, but instead of pressing the button for her room, Ella tried to speak with him.

'Of course,' Santo said. 'It went well today. The whole crew seems happier.'

'I meant...' She took a deep breath. 'With you? Have you heard from Alessandro?'

'Ella, I thought we agreed that we were talking only about work.'

'Santo, I know that something's wrong.'

'And?' He glared. 'As I said, you can't pick and choose what bits of me you have. You want professional, then here I am. You are the one who said we can't be both. Now, did you want to speak about the movie?'

'No.'

'Then if you'll excuse me, I am going to get ready to go to dinner.' The lift was at his floor and Santo stepped out, but Ella followed him.

'Santo, please,' Ella said. 'I made a mistake. I thought if we just concentrated on work till after shooting, then it would be better for the movie.'

'And now you've changed your mind?'

'Yes.'

'And will you change it again tomorrow?' Santo said nastily. 'Will you go back on your sex strike, because this is not a nice game, Ella.'

'I'm not trying to play games.'

'I have done everything you ask of me. I have never pushed you to do anything that you don't want to do, but you signed out of this, Ella. I know things have been bad for you, but right now things are bad for me. That's fine, I'll wear it. I can deal with tough times—though it could have been a hell of a lot better with your support. But you were the one who chose separate rooms and not to be there. So now, if you will excuse me, I would like some dinner.'

'Can I join you then?'

'I already have company tonight,' Santo said.

'Marianna?'

'Of course.' He shrugged. 'I have more to sort out than just this film at the moment.' And she was determined not to go there, to just say nothing, but the words blazed from her eyes and, without hesitation, Santo answered them.

'What?' He wasn't Sicilian for nothing. His words were harsh and direct. 'Is she too good-looking for me to eat with?' Santo demanded. 'If I hire only ugly people will you trust me then?' He looked at her for a long time. 'You know, I don't think you ever will.'

'Do you blame me?' She just stood there. 'I've seen you in action, I know better than anyone....'

'No.' He walked right up to her face. 'Don't try to turn this on me. The fact that you will never trust me has nothing to do with me or my reputation, because you haven't even given us a chance, not one. The fact is you don't want to trust.' Santo said. 'We could be stuck on a desert island and there would still be a problem.'

He could see tears in her eyes and the burn on her cheeks as his words hit home, because he was right. It wasn't Santo with some irredeemable past that was halting her. Ella didn't actually know if she was capable of a full-blown relationship, did not know how to love and be fully, properly, completely loved back.

'You deny us even a chance.'

'No.'

'Yes,' Santo said. 'You made it very clear right from the start that you wanted no relationship with me. You set the tone, so don't blame me for meeting it. Don't blame me for respecting the distance that you insisted upon.' He raised his finger, to make a point in the way that every Italian man did. He watched her flinch, watched her head snap to the left, and his breathing came harder. 'So,' he said. 'You think now that I would hit you?'

'No.'

'Yes.' He shook his head in disgust. 'I will not take the blame for him—I will not take the shame for him. You are as trapped as your mother,' Santo said. 'You might be on the other side of the world to him, but really, you have never left home.'

Santo could not have been more insulted.

'I go now and eat with a grown-up.'

# CHAPTER TWELVE

SANTO WAS RIGHT.

Sort of.

Ella lay on her bed and rather than denying his words, rather than defending herself to herself, instead she saw the hurt in his eyes, the absolute offence taken by Santo, and she didn't blame him a bit.

It wasn't that she didn't want to trust him, more that Ella simply didn't know how to, had found it far safer to hide behind her career and excuses rather than take a chance with a relationship.

It didn't feel such a safe place now. It felt empty, and worse, it felt selfish. Ella knew that she hadn't been there for Santo, hadn't shared in the tough times with him, and because of that, she might have blown their slim chance.

Why the hell had she had to go and fall in love with Santo though? Of all the billions of people on the globe, how had someone with major trust issues ended up with a man as wickedly bad as Santo? Ella even gave a wry smile to the heavens at the cruel lesson they had sent her, but then jumped when her phone rang. Now she wasn't Santo's PA, it was unusually quiet, but she jolted again when she heard who it was.

'Mum?' It was the first time her mother had rung her since she had started off on her travels. 'Is everything okay?'

'Everything is fine,' Gabriella said. 'Well, the same,' she corrected. 'But I waited till your father was asleep so that I could speak to you.'

'Has something happened?'

'I miss you,' Gabriella said. 'It seems strange to know that you are there. What have you been doing?'

And Ella told her—not about the promotion, more the news her mother would be stunned to hear.

'You ate dinner with Teresa Corretti? Ella, you must be careful.' She sounded terrified. 'Do not tell your aunts.'

'Mum, she's a lovely lady and I don't think their

name is all bad now. All the locals are watching the filming and seem really excited—'

'What did you eat?' Gabriella interrupted and it was actually a nice conversation. She told her about the food, and yes, her mother asked about the furniture. 'She gave me some olive oil to send you.'

'She gave you that for me?'

'She said you would miss it.'

'I do.'

There was a very long silence and then Gabriella revealed the real reason she had rung.

'Ella, I am so sorry.'

'Mum…' She was about to tell her to stop, but wasn't that what she scorned her mother for, for not talking about things, for just closing off?

'I should never have asked you to cover up for him, but I was scared. If we told the police, what would happen afterwards? You were right to get away and you are right to not want to speak with him. I will never ask you to again.'

'Thank you.'

How she'd needed to hear her mother say sorry and they spoke some more, cried some more. As Ella hung up on her mother, she knew that there was someone she had to say sorry to herself.

Properly though.

Except he was at dinner, and it really would be poor form to disturb, so Ella texted instead, asked if she could speak with him, that it didn't matter what time.

Ella wasn't surprised when he didn't answer.

She'd hurt him, offended him, and she knew that Santo was incredibly proud.

## CHAPTER THIRTEEN

HE WAS SCOWLING and completely unapproachable on set the next morning, arms crossed. He was talking with Luca, one of his cousins, and the conversation didn't look as if it was pretty, but Ella tried to focus on Taylor.

'We're going to zoom in to a close-up,' Ella said to Taylor. 'Just go for it, but anything we can't get today, we'll get in the studio. I'm not going to be asking you to do this over and over. Just give it all you've got now.'

As Taylor headed off for a touch-up of hair and make-up, she glanced over to the dark brooding shadow of Santo. Luca was nowhere to be seen now. The cameras were all set up and ready and, even if she was dreading it, even if this might prove the most embarrassing moment of her life, still she had to face him—had to tell Santo that it wasn't a game she'd been playing, that she'd just not been able to stick to a playboy's rules.

She walked over to him, and even with dark glasses on, she could feel his eyes telling her to back off. He was leaning on a trailer, arms folded, and he said nothing as she walked over.

'I'm sorry.' God, it was a very hard thing to say when you absolutely meant it. 'I am so sorry. I know how much I insulted you yesterday. I know that you would never hit me.'

Still he said nothing. It was like talking to a cardboard cut-out of him because his face never moved, his body was still. The effusive, expressive Santo was lost to her now and she wanted him back.

'I spoke to my mum last night and I realised you are right. I have been holding back.' Ella took a deep breath. 'I've liked you for a very long time,' she admitted. 'A lot, and yes, I was jealous even if I didn't want to admit that I was. And because I know that you don't do long-term, I knew that by sleeping with you I'd be pretty much writing my own resignation. I knew that I wouldn't be able to work alongside you if you were with someone else.' She wished he would speak but, when he did, she wished that he hadn't.

'You assume so much.'

Santo looked at her from behind his dark glasses. Not once had she even hinted that his lifestyle bothered her—irritated her, maybe. He had heard the barbs. He thought of the cards he had had her dictate to the florist. Except there had been none in recent months, for the familiar, well-used lines had stopped coming so readily. Jewellery was a far easier option with a quick, simple line about matching her eyes...

And Ella had written them.

'It was a lot more than sex to me and I didn't want you to know how I felt, but now you do.'

'Taylor's taking her place.'

'Santo...'

'Get to work, Ella.'

She was shaking as she walked away from him. She had told him everything and he had given her nothing back.

Not everything.

Ella knew she hadn't been completely open with him—but how? She wasn't about to play the sympathy card. She'd declined the chance to talk to him

on too many occasions. It wasn't exactly fair to demand that right back now.

'Ready?' Ella checked in with her leading lady.

'You want to take my place?' Taylor asked when
she saw Ella's brimming eyes.

'Right now, I probably could,' Ella admitted, 'except it wouldn't be acting.'

'If I get this right you can buy me a drink tonight,'
Taylor offered. 'And I'll lend you an ear.'

Taylor did get it right.

Whatever place Taylor took her head to, she was
in agony and it was a privilege to watch. To witness
her pure pain. There was no question that Vince
would be drawn to her. Absolutely the viewer would
understand why the characters would make love on
the beach a few minutes later. Ella almost wanted to
tell Taylor to stop, to breathe, because even though
Taylor was hardly making a noise, it was clear she
was broken.

Her eyes were screwed closed against tears that
squeezed out, her lips were pressed tight and there
was this river of pain building. She was locked in
hell, just as Santo had been that morning where she
had found him crying in the bath.

It hit her then.

She remembered the tears that Santo had shed that morning, the hell he had been in, all they had shared. It had been, she was sure now, far more than sex for him too, and she'd just walked away from him.

The one time Santo had needed another, had been himself with another, she'd closed off.

Frantic, she looked away from Taylor for a second, and over to Santo, but he just stood there, his arms folded, watching the action, watching Taylor, as she now must.

Taylor's blue eyes were open. She was choking in tears. Then, even though they already had the shots, she repeated it just in case, turned her head to Vince, blanched as if she expected criticism and then her face moved in for his kiss. And what a kiss it would be, because now Ella knew for sure that this movie would work.

'Cut.'

The second Ella said it Taylor burst out laughing, from the high and the elation of a perfect scene.

'That was amazing!' Ella enthused. 'Just brilliant.' And she told Taylor the same again later when she bought her a drink, shy to be sitting and talking with someone as famous as Taylor Carmichael.

'You'd better get used to it,' Taylor said when Ella

admitted how nervous she was to be talking to her off set. 'If this film does well, you're going to be known soon. You'll have scripts arriving…'

'I haven't really thought about after,' Ella admitted. 'I'm just trying to concentrate on getting this right. I know there won't be an opportunity like this again.' Her voice trailed off for a moment. 'I've been so focused on work I've forgotten what's important.'

'We all do it at times,' Taylor said. 'Santo will understand that.' Ella burnt red that what was going on was so obvious to everyone, but then it turned to guilt as Taylor continued. 'But things are pretty hellish for the Correttis at the moment.' She was direct without being indiscreet and Ella caught her eye. Taylor would know only too well what was going on at the moment, that compromising photo that surprisingly hadn't contained Santo had still had the scandal of the Corretti name attached to it! 'Maybe it's time to forget about work for a while,' Taylor suggested.

It was.

Ella finished up her drink and thanked Taylor again for her amazing work today and then headed to the lift, not to the safety of her room, but the danger of his, for she wanted to say sorry again. She wanted to explain, and properly this time, why she had flinched when he had raised his hand. And it had nothing to do with playing the sympathy card. It was about telling the truth and admitting just why she hadn't felt able to give them a proper chance. Ella took a deep breath and knocked on his suite door.

Silence, and then as she knocked again, it opened to her dread—the stunning Marianna, dressed in a hotel bathrobe, her lacy bra on clear show. She barely blinked when she saw that it was Ella.

'*Scusi,*' she said. 'I thought you were room service.' She gave a smile. 'Santo is just in the shower.'

And Ella said nothing.

'Ah, here it is now...' Marianna said as a large ice bucket and bottle of champagne was delivered to the room and a large table of food was wheeled in. All covered, of course, but Ella could guess as to what lay beneath and it didn't take much guesswork to know what she was interrupting.

'By the bed,' Marianna ordered.

Just as Santo liked it.

'Did you need him for anything in particular?'

'Nothing that won't keep,' Ella said and walked more than a little numb back to her room, waiting for the pain to hit, waiting, as she secretly always had been, to find out how it felt to have a heart broken by Santo.

# CHAPTER FOURTEEN

ELLA WAS ON set at six, still numb, still waiting for the damn to burst as she braced herself to see a postcoital Santo, knowing that she had to somehow remain professional and not make any reference to what had happened between the sheets.

As she'd insisted on.

*'Dove Santo?'*

It was the word on everyone's lips and in the end Ella rang him, but it went straight to voice mail. So she rang the hotel and asked to be put through to his room, determined to keep the bitterness out of her voice if Marianna answered.

She didn't.

Signor Corretti, it would seem, had checked out.

'Marianna Tonito?' Ella enquired.

She had checked out too.

And then her phone bleeped a text from him.

Something important came up. Know the film will be okay in your hands. Marianna has left my diary for you. I know you have a lot to deal with, but can you make sure there is champagne for after-party?

Er, no, Ella corrected herself. This was how it felt like to have a heart broken by Santo, except the numb feeling remained. The sky didn't fall in, the damn didn't burst and Ella found out, to her infinite surprise, that she was actually incredibly strong.

'Something came up...' Ella told the assembled set. 'I've no idea when he'll be back but we're going to just carry on without Santo.' And so, too, must she. 'We'll be fine.'

Because he gave them no choice but to be fine.

Was nothing at all important to him?

'Come on.' Ella looked at her watch. They'd wasted enough time this morning already and she was not throwing her career and the career of others away over a man, even one as drop-dead gorgeous as Santo. Yes, Ella found out she could put a broken heart on hold, because, over the next few days there were plenty of dramas, tears and tantrums, just none from Ella. She dealt with them all. She had no choice but to—there was a ship coming in and three hundred extras and she dealt with all that too. And yes, she even ordered the champagne.

'Last day of shooting tomorrow,' Ella told everyone. 'I want us all here at four.'

The town was buzzing. The restaurants were open for all the extras. There was just such a high all around and Ella did her best to match it, just could not give in yet. She took a picture of the busy streets and one of the ship and thought of sending them to her mother, thought of ringing her tonight. She so badly wanted to know more about the dangerous Corretti men and the women who loved them, but Ella knew it might hurt a little more than she could bear right now, that she had to make this through without tears. She would have, Ella was sure of it, had there not been a certain someone waiting for her back at the hotel.

## CHAPTER FIFTEEN

'TERESA CORRETTI IS here,' the desk told her, clearly anxious that someone so revered had arrived unannounced. 'I explained that Santo was not here, but she has waited to speak with you.'

'Thank you.'

Ella looked over and, sure enough, there was Teresa. Ella forced a smile. 'I'm sorry, Santo isn't here....'

'I was aware of that.' Teresa kissed her on both cheeks. 'I came to see you.'

'Oh.'

'Come, we go through...I believe there is a nice bar lounge.'

Ella was more than a little taken back, and perhaps so, too, were the bar lounge staff. A woman dressed in black was a rare sight in here, and that it was the Corretti matriarch made it double so.

Teresa ordered them both a drink and made polite chatter as they waited for them to arrive, asking after her mother and if she had told her about her visit.

'I did.' Ella smiled. 'She didn't even pretend not to be fascinated.'

'How is the filming going?'

'Very well.' Ella struggled to keep the edge from her voice as their drinks were served. It wasn't Teresa's fault that her grandson had walked off midshoot.

"You are the first woman Santo has brought to visit.' Ella fought with the blush that was spreading on her cheeks, not sure how to tell this elegant woman that she had already been royally dumped.

'Actually...' Ella was supremely uncomfortable. 'It's really not that serious between Santo and me.'

'Really?' Teresa frowned. 'I thought there was a lot of affection between the two of you.'

Ella could feel her grip tighten on the glass in her hand. Really, she couldn't say to this elderly lady that her grandson was an exceptionally affectionate man, with many.

'My grandson is very complicated,' Teresa said.

'Of all my grandchildren he is the one that…' She gave a helpless gesture. 'Even as a child he smiled and laughed, was the happy one, but his heart was black and closed.'

'Santo?' Ella checked.

'Santo.' Teresa nodded. 'He is the same now. He laughs, he is wild, but he lets no one close. Always there are women, yet you are the only one he has brought to see me.'

'Signora Corretti.' She just didn't know how to handle this. 'I don't think Santo was introducing us. I mean, I don't think he was bringing me to visit you in the old-fashioned sense.' She just couldn't do this any more. 'I think things are over between Santo and me.'

'You think?'

And she thought of Marianna, and how he could just up and leave. Even if Ella had somehow engineered it, manifested it almost, for she had offered him on a plate such an irresistible temptation, it killed he had so readily taken the bait.

'I know,' Ella said. 'There are some things you just can't forgive.' And she wasn't going to discuss his sex life with his nonna, but when you loved a man like Santo there were so many other reasons to be cross. 'He was supposed to care about this film. It was the most important thing to him, to this village, to the family name. But without a second thought he just walked off....' Then Ella begged, more for herself than the movie, but it saved a little face. 'Do you know where he is?' she demanded, 'What suddenly came up?' She was starting to cry and didn't want to. 'Who he's with?'

'These are not questions that we ask in my family.'

No, they were so bloody corrupt, so powerful, they made their own rules and didn't care who they mowed over in the process.

'It's a movie...' Teresa shrugged. 'You can forgive if you want to.'

'Maybe you can.' She looked at the older woman, who she actually adored, which was why she could be honest, rather than rude. Both knew they weren't talking movies. 'I never could.'

And it was a nice thing to know, to know she had boundaries, that no matter how much she might love him, that she wouldn't simply turn a blind eye. That knowledge was enough to halt Ella's tears, to smile and chat some more with Teresa.

To know she would get on with her life.

'I have to get back,' Teresa said a long while later,

when Ella was drooping and doing her best not to show it. 'Or we could have a coffee...'

Ella went to shake her head, but though she might not be like her mother, she had been brought up to abide certain rules.

'That would be lovely.'

'Perhaps—' Teresa smiled '—we have an amaro... good for digestion.'

She had to be up long before the dawn but Ella obliged, joining Teresa in sipping the herbal syrupy drink, listening as she reminisced about Salvatore. 'I talk too much,' Teresa apologised.

'It's been lovely to talk,' Ella said.

'You are a good girl,' Teresa said as they walked out to the hotel where her driver was patiently waiting. 'You looked after me well tonight. It has been nice to be out.'

'I've enjoyed it too.'

She had, Ella realised, even if she was beyond exhausted, finding only the time to set her alarm before falling into bed, too zonked to think about Santo, too exhausted to think about the movie they would be wrapping up tomorrow.

# CHAPTER SIXTEEN

SHE WOKE UP missing him though.

The final day of filming and Ella looked out from her hotel window. A stunning moon glittered off the water. She looked at the ship Santo had been so pedantic about and he hadn't even hung around to see it.

No, this was how it felt to have a heart broken by Santo. She was starting to feel it now, not just the hurt but the little flare of anger towards herself for her handling of things. But she plunged her heart back into deep storage and dressed in her favourite denim skirt and halter top and then deliberately, as if serving herself a warning, applied some mascara and not the waterproof kind either.

She could cry it all off tonight when it was over,

could take a bottle of his blasted champagne that she'd ordered up to her room and drink it warm if she so chose.

She so didn't want ice.

It was the promise of that that got her through, because watching the final scene, with the ship behind them, watching the returning husband's hands roam Taylor's body and remembering Santo's hands doing the same to hers, had her biting on her lip, willing the scene to be over, for this day to be over so she could say she had made it through filming.

Oh, there would be some studio stuff, but the bulk of it was done, or it would be a few seconds from now.

She watched husband and wife kiss, and as his hands explored her body, the infidelity was revealed. The whole set was in tears, even Ella. The ocean was just glimmering the ship, the extras all in harmony, and as the camera zoomed further in, Ella looked through her viewfinder. It could not be more perfect until she felt someone standing beside her, knew without turning her head that Santo had returned. And it could not be less perfect now because Santo was by her side and so badly she wanted him, despite everything, still she did and Ella was determined not to look around.

'Call cut.'

'Not yet.'

'Please,' Santo said, 'then I can take you back to the trailer.'

He had to be joking.

'I need to speak with you.'

'I'm kind of busy right now....'

But she called cut, because it was over, and there were cheers and applause from the crew as they wrapped up. Ella wiped her eyes with a tissue, saw the black streaks and let out a wry laugh. For all her effort not to cry over him, now she had to face him looking like a panda.

'Those tears aren't for you.'

'I know,' Santo said. 'I was watching you.'

She wished he wouldn't. Ella tried to keep her mind on work—she couldn't bring herself to look at him. 'It's all gone well. I need to go and congratulate—'

'Not right now. I need you to come with me.'

She turned and looked and it was like the first morning she had slept with him. His left eye was black, and there was a small cut above his lip, but this time she absolutely did not want to know the details. She wanted as far out of Santo's personal life as possible.

'There is something I need to tell you,' Santo said, 'something you may feel...' His usually excellent English faltered. 'You may feel that I have over-stepped the mark.'

Ella closed her eyes. Really, she had thought it something she could never forgive, and yet, in some masochistic streak, she had ensured Santo had his perfect choice of woman working for him, while she had sulked and hidden. Now she had to pay the price for dangling temptation in front of so read-ily tempted eyes. She had made a stupid move in a very grown-up game with a very liberal man, and now she couldn't really stand here and protest that he had taken the bait.

No, this wasn't a conversation they could have here. They were being handed glasses of champagne and the party was starting. Ella followed him to his trailer, dreading this conversation, but preparing herself to face it.

'I never really intended for it to happen,' Santo said. 'It was an impulse thing....'

And she tried to play the grown-up game, to shrug

it off, to say she understood, except tears were welling in Ella's eyes and there was a burn in her gut. No, she couldn't do it.

'If a man deceives me once, shame on him. If he deceives me twice, shame on me.'

She said the old Italian proverb that Santo must know off by heart, for it had been surely cussed to him many times. On this occasion he did not correct her Italian, and Ella spoke on. 'You know, everything I love about you is the part I hate too.'

He frowned.

'I'm not going to forgive you.' It was who she was. 'I know that sounds really unsophisticated, but maybe that's who I am. I can't forgive....' She closed her eyes, because she had withdrawn so rapidly that she had practically hand-passed him to someone else. 'I never expected you to take this as seriously as me.'

'Oh, I take this very seriously.'

'I know about Marianna.'

'Marianna?' Santo frowned. 'Marianna's gone.'

'Of course she is, because she slept with you.' He had to see her point. 'That's why I can't mix the two.'

'Ella, I think it is crazy that we do not sleep together. It has been driving me crazy, but I respect it.

But Marianna…' He shook his head. 'Do you really think I took it all so lightly?' His hands moved in exasperation. 'I had to fire her, she came on to me.' He looked at her nonplussed face. 'I came out of the shower and…' He gave a tight shrug. 'You do not need detail but there was champagne and too much lace and suggestion…' He gave her the smile that melted, the smile that could well shoot her straight back to his bed. 'Nothing happened—we did not even kiss.' He gave a small yikes look. 'I fear I have lost my prowess unless she comes with much baggage and is more focused on camera angles than me.'

'You didn't sleep with Marianna.…'

'I told you not.' Santo never lied. Ella realised it then. Never once did he try to cover up his mistakes. 'She tried, but I could not even be bothered to. Not even a stirring…' He actually seemed to think about it for a moment. 'Maybe a teeny one…' He held his thumb and forefinger up. He was just so honest Ella actually smiled and that was all it took for him to move straight in for the kill. 'I've missed you so much.' He pulled her into him, buried his head in her hair. 'I want you so much.'

'Santo—' she struggled '—you can't just disappear and then come back as if nothing's happened.'

'I can...' He was at her top, undoing the straps, just so impatient. 'You'll forgive me soon, but first I have to have you.'

'No.'

'I have to...' he moaned. He was peeling off her top now. 'Ella, please, it's been too long.'

'Where the hell have you been?' She looked at his battered face. 'Santo?'

'You don't need to know now.'

'I do,' Ella begged. 'I need to know what's been going on. I'm sorry I shut you out. I'm sorry I wasn't there for you while you've been having problems. I was so locked into me, into looking out for me, that I forgot all you're going through.'

'And...' Santo pushed her to go on, unhooking her bra as he did so and burying his face in her breasts.

'I was wrong,' Ella admitted.

'Why?'

He sucked her nipple. 'Why?' he growled.

'Because...' she flailed.

'Because I need you to be there for me,' Santo said. He took down her skirt and pushed her onto the bed and then undressed himself with Santo haste. 'The same way I need to be there for you.'

'Where have you been, Santo?'

He was kissing her all over and then he paused.

'Can I tell you after?'

She lay there squirming and not just with indecision.

'Do you really have to know now?'

And she looked up at him, looked at the want and the passion that needed matching, not questions and answers.

'No.'

'Say it again.'

'No.'

'No what?'

'No, right now I don't need to know where you've been.'

'Because?' He parted her legs, and she lay there naked and beneath him. And just like their first time it was Santo completely in control. He dragged out of her the truth, her answer, one she didn't know till now. 'Are you turning a blind eye, Ella?' Santo asked.

'No.'

'Which means?'

Yes, what did it mean? Ella asked herself. If she didn't need to know where he'd been, if she didn't require immediate explanation... 'That I trust you.'

And surely he should reward her with his naked length, but he was a bastard, a good one though, because he made her wait, made her say it first.

'Which means?' Santo demanded.

'That I love you.'

'Right answer,' and she got her reward then. She loved him—she'd always known it, had just held back on it. It actually didn't matter in that moment if he loved her or not too, because it didn't change things, and she learned more in those blissful moments than she could learn in lifetime.

She loved him, like it or not, returned or not, quite simply she did. Ella stopped fighting it then, just gave into the bliss of being back in his arms as he took her to a place that only Santo could.

After, she covered herself with a sheet, as she always did, Santo noted, and he turned to her. 'You love me?' He grinned.

'Fool that I am.'

'I am very lovable.'

'So your nonna told me.'

Santo laughed, but it faded as she squealed when, mortified, Ella dived under the sheets as the trailer door opened.

'I didn't see a thing,' came a vaguely familiar

voice, one that sounded not in the least embarrassed at what he had found. 'I'll come back....' She was just burning with shame beneath the sheets. 'I was told the interview—'

'Paulo?' She heard Santo speak, could not believe he was prolonging the agony. 'How soon can you start?'

'Is "now" the right answer?'

Clearly it was, though Ella thought she might die as the conversation continued. Did Santo have to be quite so comfortable with sex? But then again, Ella realised, Santo's PAs saw an awful lot, so Paulo might just as well get used to it.

'I need you to sort out a selection of rings,' she heard Santo say. 'Engagement rings,' he clarified as her heart stood still.

'Is there anything in particular you have in mind?'

'Her eyes are amber,' Santo said, 'but she would think that I was being superficial—'

'As well as cheap,' Paulo said.

'I know.' And she listened as Santo pretended he had come up with an idea, as if he hadn't planned every second of this. He was a step ahead of her all of the time. 'A diamond,' Santo said, 'as big as an ice cube, the shape of an ice cube....'

'Princess cut,' Paulo said. 'Leave it with me.' From beneath the sheet she heard Paulo move for the door. 'And don't worry, Ella,' Paulo called out, 'you don't have to take me out for dinner.'

'He seems good,' Santo said as he pulled back the sheet. 'And I can't see myself ever fancying him. Still...' He smiled. 'You know what they say—never say never.'

'You're incorrigible.'

'Only with words,' Santo said. 'And from now on, those words are only to you.' She looked up at him. 'I'm done,' he said. 'I'm through. I will have Paulo cancel my condom order from my shopping list and, if you will have me, I am exclusively yours.'

It wasn't the most romantic proposal but they were the nicest words she had ever heard.

'I will never hurt you,' Santo said.

'I know.'

She did.

'I mean it, Ella. I want to marry you as soon as Paulo can arrange.'

'We'll just slip away...' She couldn't believe they were actually discussing a wedding, their wedding.

'No.' Santo shook his head. 'We will do this properly. A good Sicilian wedding.'

'How!' Ella asked. 'We've no idea where your brother is, and my parents would never come.'

'Hey,' Santo broke in. 'I thought you said that you trusted me.'

And she remembered then how much she did. 'Teresa came and saw me.' Ella turned to him. 'She told me some of the stuff that's going on in your family. I'm sorry I haven't been there for you.'

'You're here now,' Santo said. 'And you can make up for lost time—believe me when I say that there is plenty more to come.'

'I'm sorry your family is such a mess.' She ran a finger over his bruises.

'So is yours,' Santo pointed out. 'Your father likes to use his fists....'

Ella didn't want to talk about that now and she went to tell him that, but Santo spoke first.

'I promise you though, I didn't hit him back.' He saw her eyes widen in realisation, an appalled look on her face as she realised that the bruises he wore came from her own stuffed-up family. 'I went to ask your father for permission to marry you and I saw firsthand how it was.'

'Santo!' She was panicking, appalled at what must have taken place, what her mother was going through at this very moment. As she went to rise from the bed, he grabbed her, pinned her down with his weight.

'Your mum's here,' Santo said. 'She is staying for a couple of nights with my nonna and then we will take her to meet with her sisters.'

It was too much to take in. 'She left.'

'She was scared to, but yes. She came back on the plane with me,' Santo said. 'You have to understand our ways. It is the same for my grandmother—they are loyal, their vows are more important than themselves.'

'How though?' Ella asked. 'She wouldn't leave for me. How did you convince her?'

'I spoke to my nonna.' He looked at Ella. 'I wanted to better understand…I wanted to know what best to say when I spoke to your mother.'

'How would she know?' Ella didn't get it. Yes, the two women were similar, both very locked in ways of old, but their lives were completely different. She looked to Santo and saw that for once he was struggling with words, not avoiding talking and not deflecting, just breaking a lifetime of silence. Ella knew how hard that could be.

'Salvatore beat her.' Santo's lips were white as

he said it, curling in disgust at what his own blood had done.

'She told you?'

'Never.' Santo shook his head. 'That is one reason she liked you. You played by family rules. You say things are fine, you stay for dinner, you do what a good Sicilian girl should, but I have told her that that ends now. There will be no silence on certain subjects and my nonna agrees. She had held her secret for too long.'

'How did you know?'

'That birthday party she was talking about. I was listening at a door—I did a lot of that—and I heard my father confront him, said what he had seen all those years ago.'

'What did Salvatore say?'

'That is was just once.' Santo looked at her. 'That is no excuse.' Ella just lay there. 'No one else knows this, not even Benito, and I have told my nonna I will not repeat...except to you. It is her story to tell if she feels she needs to.'

'Why wouldn't he have told Benito?'

'To spare him perhaps?' Santo shrugged. 'They were rivals, but at the end of the day they were still brothers.'

She couldn't believe he would go and speak with his nonna, that he would confront so boldly a shame from the past, just to better help her, and she told him the same.

'Of course I would,' Santo said. 'I will always stand by you as in the coming months you will stand by me as my family tears itself to shreds.'

'They might not,' Ella said. 'There must be some bond there—you're related.'

'The worst enemies to have,' Santo said. 'Because they never go away. But at times they prove to be the best allies too. My nonna said that despite all he had done, your mother would be scared for your father too.'

'I'm scared for him,' Ella admitted, for though she loathed all he had done, the thought of him alone and suffering did not bring comfort when once she had thought that it would. 'I'm scared for him too.'

'You don't have to be,' Santo said. 'I have arranged a nurse daily, a housekeeper. He will be looked after, but not by your mother. I promised your mother all these things to get her to leave, and I did not hit your father back, but had I known what I do now, I might not have managed such restraint. I spoke at length with your mother. It is a long flight from Sydney to here.' He watched the colour spread across her cheeks and the tears pool and then fall from her eyes.

'He beat you.'

'Once.'

It was a pale defence of her parents and his expression struggled not to move.

'I left home as soon as I could and I got a place and enough money. Then a few months ago I went back to get her....'

'How badly did he beat you?'

And he insisted on details—he did not believe her mother's version, he only believed in her—and so she told him. She pulled back her head and showed him the scar and that capped expensive smile, and his face never moved a fraction. 'I should have gone to the police—pressed charges. But I knew that it would only make things worse for her. I just could not believe she would stay after what he did to me.'

'She does not think you can forgive her.'

'I'm trying to.'

'I will try then too,' Santo said. 'I will never show her my anger, but...' He swallowed it down. 'She's here now. I said that we needed tonight and we will go over tomorrow.'

'That's not very Sicilian.' Ella smiled.

'I know.' He grinned back, but then he was serious. 'You will work through it with your mother, I am sure.'

'We're already starting to. I almost rang her last night....'

'Why do you think you were sitting drinking in a bar with my nonna?'

She turned and grinned in quiet surprise.

'You sent her!'

'Of course! Surely you know that the Correttis are very good at arranging decoys. We were so worried you might ring home and get your father, so Teresa suggested we make sure that you were too tired to even think of ringing home.'

Santo climbed from the bed. 'And now,' he told her, 'we have an after-party to go to. I have been around long enough to disappear and be forgiven, but your career is still new.'

Even in that, he was looking out for her. Ella looked over to him, to the man she could not wait to marry, to the man she could not wait to spend the rest of her life with. His eyes met hers and they told her he loved her just the same. There was time for one more kiss before they headed out to the party and then Santo suddenly remembered something.

'I haven't told you I love you.'

'I think you just did.'

'Well, to be certain.' He pulled her back to his arms. 'I love you,' he said. 'And I have never said that to another. I love you so much that I will spend the rest of my life proving to you that, though you had every reason to be wary of me, you were so right to trust me.'

And Ella answered with a truth of her own. 'You already have.'

## EPILOGUE

THE REFORMED SANTO didn't come wrapped in a bow.

But, as was the Sicilian way, there was a huge white bow on the church in her mother's village to show that there was a wedding about to take place.

'Even in my dreams,' Gabriella said as they walked along the dark cobbled streets lit by flaming torches towards the church, 'I never thought I would see this.'

'Where your daughter marries a Corretti?'

'I still cannot believe it!' Gabriella smiled. 'But no, that I would see you married in my church, with my sisters there....'

Together Santo and Paulo had worked wonders. Yes, they had wanted quick and discreet—the family was too fractured to make for a pleasing wedding and there was still a twist of pain for Ella when she thought of her father who, through his choices, would not be here for this day—but for Santo there were certain traditions that he would not cast aside.

Still, if it was her mother's dream wedding, it was going to be a small one. Teresa would be there, and her aunts, and she had two tiny nieces as flower girls, though it didn't matter to Ella. As the church doors opened, all she wanted to see was her groom.

'Oh!' The church was packed, all heads turning and smiling.

'Your soon-to-be husband has been sweet talking the locals. They are all happy to see me back and want to welcome, too, my daughter.'

And no doubt they were all delighted to have a Corretti just a little beholden to them, Ella thought as she walked towards her ex-reprobate and soon-to-be husband. He looked at her very pale green dress, which had once been her aunt's, and he smiled.

'I wondered how you would get around that!' Santo said as he greeted his bride, but in English, which the priest did not speak.

'It's for fertility,' Ella said, because in old Sicilian tradition, a green dress was sometimes worn and certain traditions worked best at times. They had known for all of three days that there was no trouble in the fertility department and they were brimming with excitement at their secret news.

It was the most wonderful service. He smiled as she made her vows in Italian. Santo was actually nervous for once as he made his, Ella knew, because his fingers moved to his neck as if to loosen his collar. But she knew when he gave them that they came from the heart.

And now they were married.

'We stay here,' Santo explained as they waited in a small house close to the church. 'Now they set up for the party.' He pulled her onto his knee. 'And we behave.'

'Of course.'

And he told her about the house he had seen in Palermo, but first they were going to go and lie on that beach as she should have done ages ago.

'But then I wouldn't have met you.'

The Sicilians did know how to throw a good party. The streets were lined with tables. There was food and more food, and speeches and then more food, but there was talking and laughter too. Ella looked over to her mother, chatting with Teresa, and she could never, even in her wildest, dreamt of this moment either.

'We dance now,' Santo said.

And she had thought the wedding would just be a formality, but being held in his arms, maybe Ella did have a few romantic bones in her body, for it was the best night of her life and she looked up at him and never wanted to change him.

'I love you.' She said it so easily now. 'Never change.'

'Only for good,' Santo answered in all seriousness. 'But not too good...' he added. 'I have chosen three scripts to take on our honeymoon.' Ella frowned as they danced their first dance. She really didn't want to talk about work.

'One, a hostage situation,' he whispered in her ear. 'There is a lot of dialogue, they talk a lot....' She was starting to smile.

'One, a romance,' Santo whispered. She smothered that smile in his chest, so grateful for the imagination that had saved her as a child, as she made a new movie in her mind. 'God, I love our work so much,' Santo said to her ear. 'We are never going to be bored.'

No, with Santo, you could never, ever be bored.

'And the third?' Ella asked, her stomach folding over on itself in want as she gazed up to him.

'A western.' Santo's face was deadpan as he looked down to her, watched her start to laugh in his arms as to the visions that conjured up.

And happiness was infectious.

The party smiled and starting tapping spoons on their glasses for the lovely bride and groom to seal it with a kiss.

'It's tradition,' Santo said. 'You have no choice but to kiss me.'

No, no choice at all, but it was for more than tradition when her lips met his then.

It was simply for love.

\* \* \* \* \*

*Read on for an exclusive interview*
*with Carol Marinelli!*

## *BEHIND THE SCENES*
## *OF SICILY'S CORRETTI DYNASTY*

### *with Carol Marinelli*

**It's such a huge world to create—an entire Sicilian dynasty. Did you discuss parts of it with the other writers?**

There is generally a huge flurry of discussions at the start. Then we all seem to go off into our own worlds to write our own stories and come back for fine-tuning.

**How does being part of the continuity differ from when you are writing your own stories?**

My own stories are tiny seeds that I grow, but when I am a part of a continuity I am given flowered seedlings and lots of them. I am usually a bit of a hermit when I write—being in a continuity forces you not to be.

**What was the biggest challenge? And what did you most enjoy about it?**

One of my biggest challenges was writing an epilogue for a book that was first in a series with many secrets still to be revealed that I couldn't reveal. What did I enjoy? The moment when I worked out how to do it—I had so much fun researching, which can be a major procrastination tool, but when I found out that Sicilian brides used to wear green it all started to slot into place.

**As you wrote your hero and heroine, was there anything about them that surprised you?**

Their love of ice! More seriously, my hero really surprised me and, in turn, my heroine too. There was a pivotal scene at the beginning of the book that I struggled with and kept trying to dilute and, after a *lot* of rewriting and trying to change him, I ended up going back to my original vision of that scene.

**What was your favourite part of creating the world of Sicily's most famous dynasty?**

I love writing about complex family ties. A Sicilian dynasty was like a moth to flame for me—though I knew it would burn.

**If you could have given your heroine one piece of advice before the opening pages of the book, what would it be?**

I don't think I would have—people make their own mistakes and find their own happy endings.

**What was your hero's biggest secret?**

His whole life was a secret—and he was unearthing that fact.

**What does your hero love most about your heroine?**

He shares her imagination.

**What does your heroine love most about your hero?**

He shares her imagination, too.

**'I have a feeling that whatever I do, I will always be in the wrong.'**

Taylor felt a flicker of sympathy. 'I know that feeling.'

'I'm sure you do. You, Taylor Carmichael, are one big walking wrong.' His gaze lingered on her mouth. 'So tell me what else is on your list of banned substances.'

'Men like you.'

'Is that right?' His eyes on hers, he lowered the champagne bottle back into the fountain. Somehow, without her even noticing how he'd done it, he'd moved closer to her. His dark head was between her and the sun and all she could see was those wicked eyes tempting her towards the dark side.

'What are you doing?'

'Testing a theory.' His mouth moved closer to hers and suddenly she struggled to breathe.

'What theory?'

'I want to know whether two wrongs make a right.' His smile was the last thing she saw before he kissed her.

# An Invitation to Sin

## SARAH MORGAN

First published in Great Britain 2013
Mills & Boon, an imprint of Harlequin (UK) Limited,
Eton House, 18-24 Paradise Road, Richmond, Surrey TW9 1SR

THE CORRETTIS: SINS © Harlequin Enterprises II B.V./S.à.r.l. 2013

*An Invitation to Sin* © Harlequin Books S.A. 2013

Special thanks and acknowledgement are given to Sarah Morgan for her contribution to the Sicily's Corretti Dynasty series

ISBN: 978 0 263 90615 8

53-0513

Harlequin (UK) policy is to use papers that are natural, renewable and recyclable products and made from wood grown in sustainable forests. The logging and manufacturing processes conform to the legal environmental regulations of the country of origin.

Printed and bound
by CPI Group (UK) Ltd, Croydon, CR0 4YY

For my editor, Lucy Gilmour, with thanks.
Of all the things we shared over the years,
winning the RITA® was the best. xx

# CHAPTER ONE

'ZACH? WHERE THE hell are you? You'd better not bail on me because I don't think I can do this without you. Any moment now I'm going to give in and eat carbs and that is going to be the end of this dress. When you get this message, call me.' The phone almost slipped from her sweaty palm and Taylor gripped it tightly. It was just a wedding. Just a bunch of people she didn't care about and who certainly didn't care about her. It shouldn't be enough to put her in this much of a state. She was only here because the producer of her latest film had insisted on it.

She tried to take a deep breath but the dress wouldn't allow her chest to expand. The designer had sewn her into it and then told her to send a text when she needed a bathroom break.

The Sicilian heat scalded her bare back and Taylor rolled her eyes at the absurdity of the situation. It was too hot to be sewn into anything and she'd kill before she allowed someone in the bathroom with her, which basically meant she couldn't eat or drink. Not that she ate much anyway. The discipline instilled by her mother at a young age had never left her. She was used to feeling hungry but lately the cravings had got worse and she knew it made her irritable. She was likely to snap someone's head off and if that happened she was going to make sure the head belonged to the member of the Corretti family responsible for her current discomfort.

She'd wondered if he'd had done it on purpose. This film was his baby. He'd probably briefed the designer to make sure no man could remove her dress and ruin her big comeback.

Zach was going to laugh when he saw her. She'd lived in jeans for so long and he'd never seen this side of her.

She'd stayed away from this for so long she'd forgotten how much she hated it. She hated the falseness, the agendas hidden behind air kissing and polished smiles.

Resisting the childlike temptation to bite her nails, she glanced at her slick manicure and was depressed to see her hand shaking.

She didn't dare hold a glass of champagne. She'd spill her drink on her dress. Or, worse, on someone else's dress and she knew how that would be interpreted.

Irritated with herself for caring what people thought, she dropped the phone into her bag.

It was pathetic to be reacting like this about something so trivial. The past couple of years had taught her what mattered in life. There were people out there with real problems and hers were all of her own making and all in the past.

She'd made bad decisions. Trusted people when she shouldn't have done, but she was a different person now. Given time, she'd prove it.

And that was what today was all about, of course.

She was supposed to prove it.

No mistakes. No spilled drinks, however innocent the reason.

It didn't matter if someone threw oil on the path in front of her, she wasn't allowed to slip.

This was the price she had to pay if she wanted her acting career back—and she wanted it desperately. Desperately enough to star in the publicity circus that was part of the job. This was the price she had to pay for doing what she loved.

The thought had her dragging her phone out of her bag again. 'Hey, Zach?' Her voice shook. 'Just letting you know that the women here are really hot. Even you can't fail to get laid so hurry up before you miss your chance. And if that isn't enough to get you here then I can tell you that I can't pee unless someone removes the stitches from my dress. You are going to laugh yourself sick when you see me. Call, will you?'

She was frightened by how much she needed him here.

Zach was the one who had encouraged her to follow her dream and return to acting, but some dreams came with nightmares attached. If she couldn't cope with this, how was she going to be able to cope with the attention of being back on a film set? She missed acting, but she didn't miss this.

'Taylor!' Santo Corretti, head of the film production company who was reputed to have slept with every single leading lady of his past five films, strode towards her across the perfectly manicured grass. 'You're late.'

'I was being sewn into the dress you chose.' She didn't mention that she'd been outside for half an hour trying to summon the courage to walk through the gates. That was too embarrassing to admit to anyone. She was terrified he'd see through her perfectly groomed exterior to the shivering wreck beneath. 'In my experience the paparazzi are all the keener if you make them wait and work for it.'

'Just remember you're here to promote my film, not yourself. I want publicity and when I say publicity I mean good publicity. I don't want anyone raking up your past.'

There it was. Just two minutes into a conversation and already the topic was her 'past.'

There was no escaping it. Her mistakes had been played out so publicly they were branded into her so that now it was the first thing people saw, including him.

Her stomach growled a reminder that it was empty. 'In a wedding packed full of various members of the

Corretti dynasty, I'm sure the press will have plenty of alternative headline options.' A different version of Taylor might have found him attractive but these days she avoided trouble instead of seeking it out. And she especially avoided the type of trouble that came shaped like a man. She'd learned that lesson and she'd learned it well.

'Are you blushing?' His eyes raked her face. 'Taylor Carmichael, wild child and sex kitten, able to blush when the situation demands it. I'll take that as a sign of your acting abilities. And I approve. The public loves vulnerability. They might even be prepared to excuse your shocking past.'

'My past is no one's business but my own.' But it was stuck to her, like a dirty mark she couldn't rub out. 'So who do you want me to charm first?'

'Weren't you bringing someone?' His eyes scanned the immediate area and Taylor managed to turn clenched teeth into a smile.

'My friend Zach, but he's been held up.' And she was going to kill him.

'Just remember your job today is to mingle with the people who matter, not nurture your love life.'

'Zach isn't—' She stopped in mid-sentence, wishing she'd stayed silent but already he was nodding approval.

'Good, because your messy love life has no place on my film set.'

'My love life isn't messy.' She could have told him her love life was non-existent but she didn't.

'There are two reasons this film is going to pull in a big audience. The first is because it's my film—' his smile was cool '—and the second is because you're starring in it, Taylor Carmichael. People are going to pack out movie theatres to see your big comeback because you're a train wreck and everyone loves ogling a train wreck. If I'm right about you, they'll leave knowing you can act. Don't screw up.'

Despite the heat, she shivered.

This was what she hated. The press intrusion and studios who believed they owned her, not just on set, but in every area of her life. As a young star it had almost broken her, but she wasn't that naive girl any more.

There was no way she'd let that happen to her again.

There was no way she'd screw it up or let them screw her.

They could fix their damn camera lenses to her ass and they still wouldn't be able to catch her misbehaving. She was going to be so perfect the press would die of boredom. She was going to rub that dirty mark off her image until she shone like silver in sunshine.

'So who is the most important person here today? Give me a brief.' Brisk and professional, she was all business despite the fact the dress was all Hollywood. 'Who am I supposed to impress?'

'All of them. Every guest at the wedding is waiting

for the chance to talk to you. Taylor Carmichael, finally back from exile. Everyone wants to know the details. The grapevine is buzzing.'

'You've made sure of it.'

'You're my biggest asset and I know how to use my assets. Don't give them details. No interviews until I say so.'

'No problem.' She'd pushed her past into a drawer and locked it and she hadn't opened that drawer for years. The thought that others might be trying to uncover her secrets made her feel sick and his next words didn't help dispel that feeling.

'They'll be persistent. After all, you're the girl who fired her own mother.'

'I fired my manager. The fact that she was my mother had nothing to do with it.' But it should have done. It shouldn't have been that easy to get rid of a mother, should it?

'People have a morbid fascination with the way you crashed your own life.'

'Thanks.' The pain rose and she pushed it down again, alone with it as she was always alone.

'So what have you been doing the past few years?'

Taylor watched as a bee hovered over a flower and then carefully landed on the fragile petals. 'I was keeping a low profile.'

His eyes narrowed at her evasive answer. 'Just as

long as that profile isn't going to suddenly pop up and hurt my movie.'

'It won't.' She shifted her weight to ease the pain in her feet. She'd forgotten how uncomfortable stilettos were. Still, at least it took her mind off her growling stomach. 'You can relax. If there is any scandal attached to your movie, it won't come from me.'

'It's your first public appearance since you disappeared.' His tone was hard. 'Everyone is waiting for you to slip up, you know that, don't you?'

'Then I predict they're going to have a very boring time.'

'No drinking.'

'Is that why you had me sewn into the dress? So I can't use the bathroom?'

'The dress shows your body. Your body is one of your assets.'

There had to be some benefit for being permanently starving. 'And there was me hoping you wanted my acting skills.' The bitterness leaked into her voice and he narrowed his eyes.

'I do, but I'm not so naive as to think your looks don't help. It's all about the film, Carmichael. Don't answer any questions about the past. You are the Mona Lisa. All they get is an enigmatic smile.'

'I can tell you now there is no way Mona would have smiled if she were sewn into her dress. If she were forced to wear what I'm wearing she would have been the Moaning Lisa. And now we've established the ground rules, point me towards hell.'

'Wait. You didn't answer my question—' He caught her arm. 'What have you been doing with yourself for the past two years? You just disappeared. Were you in rehab or something?'

Rehab.

Of course they would think that. It never occurred to anyone that there could be any other explanation for her absence.

'Sorry,' Taylor murmured, disengaging her arm from his grip, 'I'm absolutely not permitted to talk about my past. Your rules.'

'You're a beautiful woman. There won't be any shortage of men interested, not in you but in the potential to make some money from selling a story. You screwed that up before.'

The pain was so intense he might as well have punched her. 'I was young. Trusting. I'm not any more. And as for men—' Taylor managed a careless shrug '—I can assure you there isn't a man out there hot enough to tempt me.'

Luca Corretti downed another glass of champagne to numb the boredom of behaving well.

For the past twenty-four hours he'd driven under the speed limit for the first time in his life, declined seven party invitations and made it to bed before dawn. The fact that he hadn't been alone at the time didn't count. As far as the outside world was concerned, his behaviour had been impeccable. The only thing he hadn't done in his quest for instant respectability was kissed a baby and even he wasn't prepared to descend to those levels of hypocrisy just to impress the board of directors who'd decided his lifestyle wasn't compatible with running another chunk of the family business. Apparently business flare counted for nothing, he thought savagely, wondering whether he could get away with swapping the champagne for whisky.

And now, to add insult to injury, he was expected to sit through his cousin's wedding.

Was he the only person who hated weddings? All that happy-ever-after crap that everyone knew was a temporary illusion. Or maybe it was a delusion. Luca didn't know and he didn't intend to find out. He was going to be out of here at the first opportunity, preferably with the brunette bridesmaid he'd spotted on his way in.

'Luca! I've been looking everywhere for you. Where have you been?'

Before he could react, Luca was enveloped in soft bosom and a choking cloud of perfume. At any other time he would have thought it wasn't a bad way to die, but he was conscious that heads were turning and, when heads turned, disapproval was bound to follow. It irritated him that he had to care. 'Where have I been?' He disentangled himself. 'Avoiding you, Penny.'

'My name's Portia.'

'Seriously? No wonder I didn't remember it.'

She giggled. 'You are a wicked, wicked man.'

'So people keep telling me.' Luca put down his empty glass, trying to think of a method of stress reduction that didn't involve sex or alcohol.

Portia lowered her eyelashes. 'About last night—'

Aware that his one indiscretion was about to be made public, Luca removed the drink from her hand and swapped it for orange juice. 'Last night? I have no idea what you're talking about. Last night I went to bed with a book.'

She gave a snort of laughter. 'Well, you certainly turned my pages. I'll never forget it. How could I?' Her eyes on his mouth, she leaned towards him. 'You were amazing. It's never been like that for me before. You're a genius.'

'So I keep telling the board,' Luca said in a flat drawl. 'Unfortunately my opinion doesn't seem to count. For some reason they seem to think activity in the bedroom saps my mental abilities so for the time being I have to prove I can keep my pants zipped.'

'We could be discreet. Leave the wedding.'

'I love weddings and I love my cousin,' Luca said immediately. 'I couldn't possibly leave until he's married...married—' what the hell was her name? '—the woman of his dreams.'

'You love weddings? Honestly?'

'Weddings never fail to make me cry,' Luca said truthfully. 'The thought of two people promising to love each other for ever makes me want to break down and sob like a baby.'

'Oh. I had no idea you were so romantic.' Her eyes misted. 'And I'm so pleased that all those rumours that you hate your cousins are wrong. You're nowhere near as bad as everyone says.'

'Bad?' Luca adopted his hurt expression. 'I'm a saint compared to some people.' He hoped she didn't ask him to name someone as bad as him because he knew he'd struggle.

'You're quite a softie—' she stroked his arm with her fingertips '—except in the one area that counts.' She'd moved closer to him again and Luca stood up, cursing his lack of thought in picking up a guest at the wedding.

What he'd taken to be a few moments of fun, she'd taken to be a future.

Now he had to shake her off before the Corretti board gave him another black mark.

Unfortunately Portia didn't want to be shaken anywhere. 'Will I see you tonight, after the wedding?'

'The definition of a one-night stand, *angelo mia*, is that it lasts one night.'

'You were keen enough last night.' She pouted. 'What's wrong? Don't you like me in this dress?' The words robbed him of breath.

*Do I look good, Luca? Do I look better than her? Will he love me if I wear this?*

'Luca?'

He dragged himself out of the black pit of his past and stared into Portia's over-made-up eyes. 'You look great,' he said flatly, relieved when one of the wedding guests shrieked a greeting and Portia was reluctantly dragged away.

Relieved by his narrow escape, he was momentarily distracted by a sheet of blonde hair that hung down the back of a woman standing on the far side of the terrace. People were pressing close, all desperate to get a piece of her, and he shifted slightly to see who she was.

When she finally turned her head, he felt a flash of surprise.

Taylor Carmichael. Well, well.

It cheered him up to know that there was one person present whose reputation was as bad as his.

According to the media, she'd done it all—drink, drugs and partying. And then she'd disappeared for a couple of years. He wondered what she'd been doing with herself and decided it was probably something disreputable. She was one of the few people at this wedding who could make him look saintly. Almost.

Luca watched her across the room and remembered reading that his cousin Santo had recruited her to play the lead in his latest film.

She had the most incredible body. Thinking that all

that blonde hair would look good spread over his pillow, he took a step towards her and then remembered that members of the board were watching his every move and waiting for him to step out of line.

Exercising a restraint he didn't know he possessed, Luca turned away and engaged a suited man in a conversation about the economy.

If Taylor had been able to take a big enough breath, she would have screamed.

'You poor thing,' the woman said in a voice sweet enough to rot teeth. 'This wedding must be so stressful for you.'

'Why would it be stressful?' Taylor kept her smile in place and wished Zach would show up. She was going to need someone to lend her a jacket when her stupid dress split. 'It's the perfect opportunity to meet interesting people.' *Unfortunately you're not one of them.*

'But so much temptation for someone like you.' The woman eyed the glass of water in Taylor's hand. 'I suppose you don't dare even take a sip of champagne in case you undo all the good work and lose control. It must be impossibly hard given the circle you move in.'

'It isn't hard.'

'What stops you drinking?'

The knowledge that she couldn't pee without the assistance of a seamstress. 'I'm going to be filming twelve hours a day. My focus is on my work.' And she couldn't wait. She knew that once she was playing that role, she'd be lost in it. Acting was all she wanted to do. And not just because it meant she could escape the empty, meaningless circus of her life.

Another woman pressed closer. 'I can't believe you're back in circulation. You just vanished off the face of the earth. You have to tell us whether those stories about you were true.'

They circled her like wolves waiting to pounce on a carcass. And she was the carcass.

Taylor laughed inwardly. Given the amount of weight she'd lost in preparation for this part, she almost *was* a carcass.

The moment filming was over she was going to rush to the nearest Dunkin' Donuts and indulge her carb fantasy but until then she had to play the game.

She couldn't keep this up for much longer. She was going to punch someone, split her dress and end up naked.

Exhausted, Taylor pressed a button on her phone and made it ring. 'Oh, excuse me—' with an apologetic smile, she pulled it out of her bag '—I just have to take this call. So good to meet you. I'll see you inside the chapel in a little while!' *And I hope you both choke on a canapé.*

Phone held to her ear, talking to herself in a bright tone, she walked to the edge of the terrace, aware of Santo's eyes watching her every move.

As far as she was concerned, he could watch all he liked. She wasn't going to slip up.

She could do this. All she needed was a quick breather and then she'd sit somewhere at the back of the church, away from all the intrusive questions.

Bypassing the groups of people gathered on the terrace, she glanced around her to find somewhere less populated. Spying the English garden and, beyond that, the maze, she increased her pace. Perfect. What better place than a maze to find shade and peace?

The high hedges gave much-needed protection from the burning Sicilian heat and the curious stares of the other guests. Taylor slipped off her shoes, moaning with relief as the soft grass cooled her throbbing feet. Breathing deeply, she listened to the sound of the birds. Live in the moment, wasn't that what Zach had taught her? Block everything else out. It's all about now.

Slowly, her pulse rate slowed. The knot in her stomach eased, leaving only the hunger pangs that had been her constant companion since she'd signed up for the role. She was just congratulating herself on being back in control when she turned a corner and walked straight into a man.

'*Cristo*, can't you take a hint?' Hard hands gripped her and kept her on her feet but his tone was ice cold and Taylor stared at him, disorientated.

'What hint?' She recognised him instantly. Luca Corretti, billionaire playboy, occasionally described as Sicily's biggest tourist attraction and absolutely the last man in the world she would have chosen to be alone with given her current objective of staying out of trouble.

'*Mi dispiace, chicca.*' His smile was disturbingly attractive. 'I thought you were someone else.'

'Well, I'm not,' Taylor said coldly, 'so if you'd just let go of me, I can carry on walking and you can carry on hiding or whatever it is you're doing.'

'I'm dodging my past.'

Him too? 'I would have thought that was an ambitious objective for someone with your reputation.'

'Actually, I was talking about my immediate past. Last night.' His smile held no hint of apology. 'And you're not exactly in a position to judge, are you, Taylor Carmichael? Your past is every bit as dirty as mine.'

His use of her name made her insides lurch. 'You know who I am.'

'Of course. I've even seen you semi-naked.' Those eyes gleamed dangerously. 'That movie about the teenage runaway? God, you were sexy.'

Why did he have to pick that movie? She'd made over twenty films, but he'd picked the one she'd filmed at the very lowest point of her life.

She felt cold and hot at the same time. 'That was a long time ago.'

'But you have the same incredible legs....' His voice was a soft, sexy purr and his eyes dropped to her breasts. 'And other parts of you. I remember envying the director—what was his name? Rafaele. He got to see you on and off set, lucky bastard.'

Taylor felt as if someone was choking her. 'I don't want to talk about him.'

'Why not? So you dumped him and he sold his story to the press.' Luca gave a dismissive shrug. 'Who cares?'

She'd cared.

And she still cared.

She had no choice. The moment she'd accepted the film role, the texts had started. Just like before. It didn't matter how many times she changed her number, he always managed to track her down. His threats had been part of her life for nine years. Occasionally he went quiet, only to re-emerge when she'd started to hope it had all gone away and he'd finally become bored with tormenting her.

The dress was squeezing her like a boa constrictor trapping its prey. Taylor couldn't breathe. She tried desperately to change the subject. 'So what does your immediate past look like? Blonde? Brunette? You'd better tell me so that I can give her a wide berth. I'm not in the mood for dealing with an angry, jealous woman.'

'Me neither. Why the hell do you think I'm hiding in here?' He gave an exaggerated shudder and glanced up at the green wall of the maze. 'I'm hoping the Corretti board don't have security cameras planted round the grounds. I'm supposed to be behaving myself.'

Despite her stress, she found herself wanting to smile. 'This is what you're like when you're behaving yourself?'

'I'm positively restrained and it's killing me. Especially right this moment.' His eyes lingered on her mouth with blatant interest. 'I might be about to fall from the wagon. Or roll in the back of the wagon. You and me. Together. Now there's an interesting thought.'

Taylor felt her heart beat faster.

Against her will, her eyes moved to his mouth too. Firm, sensual and very masculine. There was no doubt in her mind that Luca Corretti would be a skilled kisser. If rumour were correct, he'd certainly had enough practice.

Appalled by her own thoughts, she turned her head away and took a step backwards. 'It's a thought that doesn't interest me in the slightest. I'll leave you to hide. I hope your past doesn't catch up with you.'

'Me too. I don't suppose you saw her on your way in?'

'I didn't see anyone. What does she look like?'

'Desperate?'

She choked back a laugh. 'You spent the night with her?'

'Not the whole night, obviously.' He looked so horrified by the suggestion that this time she did laugh.

'Have you ever spent the whole night with a woman?'

'*Cristo*, no! My mantra is "Until dawn us do part."'

My longest commitment so far is six hours and I was bored by the end of that. You?'

It was uncomfortable to remember the number of times she'd thought a man was serious about her only to discover he was only interested in selling her out to the press. It had been a harsh training ground for independence. 'I'm not big on romantic commitment.'

He groaned. 'You should not have told me that.'

'Why?'

'Because that makes you my perfect woman.' That sexy mouth slanted into a charismatic smile. 'Just don't tell me you're addicted to sex and fast cars or I'm doomed.'

Silence stretched between them. They were standing in the dappled shade of the maze but the heat was stifling and oppressive.

Their eyes met and held.

His head lowered towards hers.

And suddenly they heard voices.

Appalled by how close they'd come to kissing, she glanced at him only to find him doubled up with laughter.

Taylor was torn between laughter and panic. The last thing she needed was to be caught with Luca Corretti. No one would believe it was an innocent encounter.

'Stop panicking, *angelo mia*, I'll rescue you.' Putting his finger to his lips, Luca took her hand in his and forced her to sprint with him deeper into the maze. 'I am the expert at the great escape. No one knows more about running from women than I do.'

'What are you doing? I don't want to be caught running away with you. And don't pull me—this dress has no give in it.' She tugged at her hand but he held it firmly, turned another corner and she gave a little gasp because there, in a shaded glade, was a pretty fountain and by the fountain was an open bottle of champagne.

'No glasses, I'm afraid.' With a wicked, sexy smile he released her hand and retrieved the bottle. 'We'll have to slum it.'

Weak with relief that they'd avoided detection, Taylor shook her head in disbelief as she watched him. 'How did you—?'

'How did I get it here?' Those wide shoulders lifted in a careless shrug. 'I imported it here under cover of darkness in case of emergencies. This definitely constitutes an emergency. Judging from the look on your face earlier, your need is as great as mine. I'm always willing to help out a fellow sinner in need. Sit down. Make yourself comfortable. Take a dip in the cool water.'

Taylor looked wistfully at the fountain. 'I wish I could. This dress is the most uncomfortable thing I've ever worn but sadly it isn't designed to allow sitting.'

'So take it off.'

'Even if I wanted to, I couldn't. They've sewn me into it.' She caught his look of astonishment and glared. 'Don't ask.'

'All right—' there was laughter in his eyes '—but if you want my opinion I'd say you've been stitched up, *angelo mia.*'

'Very funny.'

'I like the idea that you're sewn into your dress. It could be erotic.' He prowled around her, his eyes on her body. 'So what do they expect you to do if you need to have wild, animal sex?'

'I'm not going to need that.'

He scanned her dress. 'This is your punishment for not picking something from the House of Corretti. Our clothes would make you feel seductive and feminine. We don't have to sew our women into their dresses for them to look good. The dress becomes part of the woman.'

She'd forgotten that he ran the fashion house but it explained his effortlessly stylish appearance. Even with his shirt collar open and strands of dark hair falling over his forehead, he looked spectacular.

'I didn't pick this dress.' Heat and hunger made her irritable. 'I wore what your cousin told me to wear.'

'He'd never pick anything from my company,' Luca drawled, 'it might signify approval and God forbid the rivalry between us should ever die. That fabric isn't allowing your body to breathe. I could help you with that.'

'Nice try.'

'I've got moves that would make you weep.'

'I'm sure you make women weep a lot, but I'm not a crier.'

'I like you more and more. You could bathe naked in the fountain.' He reached for the chilled bottle of champagne. 'Or I could roll this over your skin.'

Her skin was prickling with the heat and she made a sound that was half laugh, half groan. 'Now you're torturing me. Talk about something else, before I melt.' Taylor knew she should walk away but she decided it was safer to wait a few minutes until the people they'd overheard were safely back among the guests. Just five minutes, she promised herself. Five minutes. 'So who is this woman you're running from?'

'I have no idea. Apparently her name is Portia but that was news to me.'

Taylor lifted her hair away from her neck to try and cool herself down. 'You're terrible.'

'Not terrible enough to induce her to dump me, sadly. She was alarmingly difficult to shift.'

'Some women find bad boys attractive.'

'And from what I've heard, you know a lot about that.'

'Do you often listen to gossip?'

'All the time. Gossip makes me laugh.' The cork flew out of the bottle with a pop. 'So tell me the truth, Taylor Carmichael? How do you like your men? Well-done, medium or rare?'

'Rare.' Sticky and uncomfortable from the heat and

the conversation she squirmed, wishing she could dip her toes in the water. 'So rare I can't remember when I last touched one.'

'So I'm looking at a desperate woman.'

'You're looking at a controlled woman. I'm no longer a slave to my impulses.'

'That sounds like the tag line for a good bondage movie. Slave to Her Impulses. The sequel could be Slave to His Impulses. I might be willing to star in that for a price providing you were the leading lady.' That mocking smile touched the corners of his mouth and he tipped champagne into a glass and held it out to her. 'Drink. It will help numb the boredom of the wedding.'

Hating the fact that she was even tempted, Taylor reluctantly shook her head. 'No, thanks. Champagne is on my list of banned substances, particularly on an empty stomach.'

'Personally I have a taste for banned substances.' Shrugging, he tilted his head and drank, the sun glinting off his dark hair.

Just for a moment, because he wasn't looking at her, she looked at him. At those slanting cheekbones, that nose, the olive skin—

It was so long since she'd looked at a man and found him attractive, the spasm of sexual awareness shocked her.

She reminded herself that Luca Corretti was probably the most dangerous man she could possibly have

found herself with. 'I thought you were trying to behave yourself.'

'This is me behaving myself.' He took another
mouthful of champagne and she laughed in spite of
herself, sensing a kindred spirit. A part of her long
buried stirred to life.

'So both of us are making a superhuman effort to
behave. What's your excuse?'

'I have to prove myself capable of taking charge of
another chunk of the family business.' Underneath the
light, careless tone there was an edge of steel and it
surprised her because she didn't associate him with
responsibility.

That thought was followed instantaneously by guilt.
She was judging him as others judged her, based on
nothing but gossip. She was better than that.

'But you already run a business. I read that you'd
turned the House of Corretti around.'

'I have a flare for figures.'

'Especially when those figures belong to models?'

He laughed. 'Something like that. Unfortunately
trebling the profits of Corretti isn't enough for them.'

She had to stop herself reaching for the champagne
in his hand. Because she wasn't able to get out of her
dress, she'd avoided drinking and now her throat was
parched from the heat. 'But why do you want to med-
dle in other parts of the business?'

'Sibling rivalry.'

'But you're all members of the same family. Surely that qualifies you for a seat on the board.'

'The qualifications for a seat on the board seem to be old age and sexual inactivity.' He suppressed a yawn. 'I suppose that's why they call it a "bored." Needless to say I'm bombing out big-time. I have a feeling that whatever I do, I will always be in the wrong.'

Taylor felt a flicker of sympathy. 'I know that feeling.'

'I'm sure you do. You, Taylor Carmichael, are one, big walking wrong.' His gaze lingered on her mouth. 'So tell me what else is on your list of banned substances.'

'Men like you.'

'Is that right?' His eyes on hers, he lowered the champagne bottle back into the fountain. Somehow, without her even noticing how he'd done it, he'd moved closer to her. His dark head was between her and the sun and all she could see was those wicked eyes tempting her towards the dark side.

'What are you doing?'

'Testing a theory.' His mouth moved closer to hers and suddenly she struggled to breathe.

'What theory?'

'I want to know whether two wrongs make a right.' His smile was the last thing she saw before he kissed her.

# CHAPTER TWO

WHAT THE HELL was she doing?

Taylor opened her eyes and found herself staring into two dark, slumberous pools of molten male hunger.

As his mouth moved skilfully on hers, desire punched low in her belly and then spread through her body with a speed that shocked her. One minute she was thinking, the next minute she was kissing him back, gripped by a deep, visceral emotion she couldn't even name.

He seduced her mouth with lazy expertise, his tongue teasing hers with a delicious skill that weakened her legs with frightening speed.

Her stomach twisted. Her body melted. She wanted to stretch luxuriously into the warmth of that hand resting high on her bare thigh.

Her bare thigh?

Horrified, she tried to pull back but her body was

weakened by pleasure. 'My dress—' The words were swallowed by the heat of his mouth. 'Luca—'

'I agree. The dress has to come off.'

'No.' She was laughing and appalled at the same time, her hand covering his as she stopped him sliding the fabric upwards. 'You've ripped the stitches.'

'No, you ripped the stitches,' he purred, 'when you wrapped your leg around me.'

'You pulled my leg round you—we shouldn't be doing this. I don't want to be doing this.'

'Tell that to your pulse rate. It's revving like the engine of my Ferrari.'

'I thought you were trying to prove to the board you're responsible?'

'I'll use a condom. Does that count?'

Appalled by how much she wanted to laugh, Taylor locked her hand in the front of his shirt, feeling hard male muscle against the backs of her fingers. 'I don't think that's what they have in mind. You don't want to take this risk and neither do I. We have to get back to the wedding before the bride comes.'

'If I have my way you'll come before the bride.' Laughing wickedly, he delivered a slow, sensual kiss to the corner of her mouth. 'Some things are worth taking a risk for and you, Taylor Carmichael, are definitely one of those. You are sexy enough to make me forget all about being good—' his hand was buried in her hair and his mouth was on her neck '—and it really turns me on to know that underneath your icy, composed exterior you are still a bad, bad girl.'

Taylor closed her eyes but that simply intensified the crazy swirl of feelings so she opened them again. 'You're wrong. That isn't who I am.' It couldn't be. 'I don't want this.'

'You're crushing me, *dolcezza*.' He was kissing her jaw and she could hear the smile in his voice. 'Think of my poor, delicate ego.'

Nothing about him was delicate. Not the powerful shoulders, nor the rock-hard biceps. He was all muscle and masculinity and Taylor was so desperate for him her whole body ached. 'I don't want you.'

'Yes, you do. You want me as much as I want you but you're determined to deny your true self.'

'I'm not denying anything.' Panicking, she shoved at his chest. 'Enough! Damn it, Luca—get away from me.' In the past two years she hadn't even looked at a man and suddenly here she was, pressed against the hardness of him, her body melting against the heat of his. The chemistry was off the scale and it terrified her. Of all the men she could have found herself with, he was the most dangerous of his species. 'I'm not that person any more. I've changed.'

'That person? What person? You mean the woman who embraced her life without apology?'

'The woman who screwed up her life by trusting men like you,' Taylor snapped, 'and I'm not doing it again so stay away. I mean it, Luca. If you want to live up to your reputation then go ahead, but I'm not going to let you take me down with you.'

'Why are you so ashamed of yourself?'

'I'm not ashamed—' she spoke so quickly she stumbled over the words '—but I've grown up.'

'Grown-ups accept their mistakes instead of running from them.'

Hers haunted her.

The threatening messages never ended.

Her heart was pumping as she backed away from him. 'Good luck with your future. I hope you manage to convince the board to trust you before you give in to the worst part of yourself and blow it completely.'

'Ah, but that's the difference between us, *angelo mia*.' Reaching for the bottle of champagne again, he leaned his hips against the fountain, effortlessly sophisticated and insanely sexy. 'I consider it to be the best part of myself. The fact that no one else appreciates it is their problem, not mine.'

For a brief moment she felt a flash of envy that he was so indifferent to what people thought and then the urgency of her situation propelled her into action and she jammed her feet into her shoes, the movement parting the seam of her dress as far as the waist. Gripping it with her hand, she held the two sides together and hurried through the shadowed corridors of the maze, grateful for the high hedges that concealed her from prying eyes.

If a photographer had been hiding in the maze, or even another guest—one of Luca's disgruntled women—it would have looked awful and no amount of explaining would have worked.

She would have ruined everything before she'd even started filming.

The thought of how close she'd come to doing just that made her feel sick.

Weak with relief that her reputation was still intact, she pulled her phone out of her bag and texted the designer one-handed.

Ready to be sewn back into my dress. Meet me by the maze.

Luca let her go, that exercise in self-restraint costing him dearly in terms of physical discomfort. He shifted slightly and decided he didn't dare leave the maze until his hormones had settled down.

Lifting the champagne to his lips, he paused as he spotted a woman approaching down another green-lined tunnel.

'Luca, there you are!'

Cursing under his breath, he lowered the bottle of champagne. 'Paula!'

'It's Portia.'

'That's what I said. The maze distorts sound.'

Her eyes were a little less warm than they'd been earlier. 'Were you hiding from me?'

'I didn't trust myself around you,' Luca said smoothly. With the taste of Taylor still on his lips, he felt no inclination to take her up on her less than subtle invitation. 'Last night should not have happened. You're a beautiful woman but I need to behave myself.'

Her eyes narrowed and she stared down the path where Taylor had recently disappeared. 'Really? So you're telling me women are off the agenda today?'

Something in her tone made Luca wonder if she'd seen Taylor but he decided that wasn't possible. No one could have sneaked up on them without him noticing.

'Sadly, yes. What we shared was very special—' he pulled out one of his stock phrases '—but I can't risk anything else at this point which is killing me because last night was one of the best of my life.'

'All right. If that's the way it has to be then so be it.' She looked at him for a long moment, as if she were working something out. 'You're never going to forget me, Luca Corretti.'

'Of course I'm not.'

'And you'll never again forget my name.'

'It's your own fault for being beautiful—I take one look at your face and my memory goes.'

Three minutes, Luca thought idly, glancing to the

place he'd last seen Taylor and missing the jealous glint in the woman's eye. That was how long it would take him to forget her.

Forty-eight hours later Taylor sat in the back of a limo as she was driven to the docklands for filming to begin. She'd spent the entire previous day locked in her hotel room checking every online newspaper and gossip column for pictures, terrified that her momentary lapse with Luca might have been captured on camera. When she realised she'd got away with it she'd been weak with relief.

From now on she was going to keep well away from men like Luca Corretti.

Never again would she do something that gave a man power over her.

But even as she thought that, she knew that her response hadn't been driven by stupidity but by a raw attraction so strong nothing could have prepared her for it.

And it wasn't just his physical appeal that had caused her downfall, it had been something else. Something layered beneath the surface of masculine perfection. An honesty that presented a stark contrast to the atmosphere of falseness that had hovered over the wedding. Yes, that was it. Luca Corretti embraced everything he was. He took what he wanted without explanation or apology and that was—she struggled to describe it—refreshing.

She felt a twinge of envy and dismissed it instantly. She didn't want to be like Luca, a slave to her emotions. Her life had been so much happier since she'd been in control.

'We'll be there in ten minutes, Miss Carmichael.'

The voice of her driver came through the intercom and excitement buzzed through her. She couldn't wait to be back on a film set. She was going to throw herself into her work and forget about her narrow escape. And forget about Luca.

Blocking out disturbing memories of that kiss, Taylor leaned her head back against the seat, finally able to think back to the wedding and laugh. What a crazy day. She still couldn't believe that Luca's brother Matteo had run off with the bride before she'd made it as far as the altar. Bad behaviour was obviously in the DNA, but she was grateful for that because all the attention that had been focused on her had immediately switched to the Corretti family.

She shook her head at the irony of it.

And Santo Corretti had been worried about her causing a scandal.

As the car approached the docklands area, she noticed the pack of photographers pressed against the security fence and her heart sank.

There were so many of them, no doubt all waiting

for her to screw up on her first day and give them a nice juicy headline.

Was it going to be like this all the time?

Her phone buzzed with a text and she checked it quickly, her heart rate doubling when she saw it was from Rafaele.

New phone. New number. And still he had no trouble contacting her.

She hesitated and then opened the text.

Good luck today. Enjoy Sicily.

Flinging the phone back in her bag, she rubbed her forehead with fingers that shook. She felt as if she'd been dipped in iced water. He wasn't wishing her luck, he was telling her that he knew exactly what she was doing and where she was doing it.

She was never going to be rid of him. Never.

Knowing that she couldn't afford to think of him now, she took a deep breath as the car slowed and shut off all those parts of herself she no longer showed to the world. Maybe everyone at the wedding had been fake, but she was the biggest fake of all. No one saw the real Taylor. She hadn't even been sure she could access the real Taylor any more until that moment in the maze with Luca.

Pushing that thought aside, she stepped out of the

car, telling herself that the media attention would die down after the first day of filming.

Her confidence lasted as long as it took her to notice the black expression on the director's face. She'd assumed he was meeting her in person out of courtesy and respect for her position on the movie, but one look at his face told her that was a false assumption.

It was a struggle to keep her smile steady. 'Sorry about the media circus. Hopefully they'll lose interest soon enough.'

'Why would they lose interest when you are a never-ending source of juicy stories?' His voice was cold. 'Your brief was to create interest in the movie, not in your personal life. The moment Santo told me he wanted you on the project I knew it would be a disaster.'

'Oh.' Shaken by that unwelcome news, Taylor spun a few more layers of protection between her feelings and the world and kept it professional. 'I'd like to think you'd judge me on my performance now, not on something that happened years ago.'

'The whole world is judging you on your performance at the Corretti wedding.' His face was scarlet with anger and for the first time Taylor noticed the newspaper clutched in his hand.

'The wedding never happened, but even I couldn't be blamed for that, surely?' Confused, she eyed the newspaper. Did people even still buy those things? If she ever wanted to glance at headlines she just used her phone. 'If you're worried about the fact the wedding didn't go ahead, then don't be. I'm sure Santo Corretti will deal with it. The publicity might even be good for the film.'

His mouth opened and closed. '"Good" that the movie-going public see you as a man-stealer?'

She looked at him blankly. 'A what?'

'Just in case you were too drunk to know what you were doing, you can read it for yourself.'

Taylor almost lost her balance as he thrust the paper at her. 'I don't drink. And I remember everything.' An image of Luca's handsome face floated into her head and she pushed it away as she fumbled with the newspaper.

'Portia Bateman.' He enunciated every syllable. 'Are you going to tell me that name doesn't mean anything to you?'

'Yes, that's exactly what I'm going to tell you because it doesn't. I've never heard of Portia Bateman.' Taylor's mind was working in slow motion. Her fingers were clumsy as she unfolded the offending paper. 'In fact, I don't know a single person called Portia—' The words stuck in her mouth as a snippet of conversation rose in her mind.

*So who is this woman you're hiding from?*

*Apparently her name is Portia.*

Driven by a horrible, awful suspicion, she shook her head. 'Oh, no, no, she can't have done that. I checked.

I looked...' She muttered the words to herself but the director was watching her keenly.

'So you do know someone called Portia.'

'No, I don't! I've never even met her. She's just someone he...' She scanned the piece, saw the photograph of a tearful blonde woman under the caption *Exclusive—Taylor Carmichael Stole My Man*. And there beneath the caption was a photograph of her and Luca. His bronzed hand was plastered against her bare thigh and they were kissing. Not just kissing. Devouring each other. Passion was painted into every line of the photo and she stared at it in dismay.

Her fingers gripped the paper.

The sounds faded around her.

Dizziness washed over her.

She'd congratulated herself on the fact that no paparazzi had caught her moment of indiscretion. She'd forgotten that since the advent of camera phones, everyone was a photographer. And this one had hit the jackpot.

Bathed in horror, Taylor closed her eyes. This couldn't be happening to her. It just couldn't be. She couldn't think through the panic. 'Why did she wait a day to publish this?'

'She says she offered Luca Corretti the chance to buy the photograph but he just laughed and told her to go ahead and sell whatever story she wanted to print. So she did. She sold her story to the highest bidder.'

He'd laughed?

Taylor felt cold.

What had she done?

The answer to that was nothing, but no one looking at this photograph was going to believe that. She'd dropped her guard for a few moments, that was all, and this was the result.

Keeping her expression neutral, she handed the newspaper back to the glowering director. She wanted to wake up and start the day again. She wanted to wind the clock back. She wanted to never have gone to that damn wedding. Most of all she wanted to kick Luca Corretti in a place that would ensure he'd never seduce a woman again.

'I understand your concerns and I realise that the story looks bad, but I'm asking you to trust me. This piece isn't—' how on earth could she even begin to justify it in a way that would change his expression from sour to sympathetic? '—accurate. Please judge me on my acting ability, not the media circus that follows me.'

'You think that pack of journalists are interested in your acting ability? Your movie comeback is over before it began. Santo Corretti is on his way here now and I can tell you he is not amused. After that wedding fiasco he isn't in the best of moods as it is and this project means a lot to him. He doesn't want it hijacked by your never-ending need to grab the headlines.'

He wasn't interested in an explanation, Taylor

thought numbly. The truth wasn't going to help and a small part of her couldn't even blame him for that because the picture did look incriminating. It had just been a kiss. Other people kissed all the time and did a whole lot worse and no one knew or cared. She slipped for one moment and the evidence was plastered everywhere and she had her mother to thank for that. She'd ensured the media had been fed a steady diet of Taylor Carmichael from the first moment she'd stuck her child in front of the camera.

Taylor wondered if Luca had even seen the pictures.

He'd probably laugh, she thought bitterly. It wasn't his naked thigh that was up there for the world to see. It wasn't his career that was ruined. Even if the board refused to give him more responsibility, he still had the fashion house. And anyway, he didn't appear to care what the world thought of him. In fact, he seemed to behave in a way designed to invite and encourage salacious headlines.

'I can tell you that Luca Corretti isn't involved with that woman. It's a kiss and tell. He rejected her and she's getting her revenge.'

'So you're trying to tell me that picture is Photoshopped?'

'No, but—'

'It's not you he's kissing?'

'Yes, it's me, but—'

'It's not your dress that's ripped?'

'The dress isn't ripped. The stitches came undone.' Feeling like a fox with a pack of hungry hounds snapping at her heels, Taylor gritted her teeth. 'They sewed me into it which I knew was a stupid idea right from the start.'

The director looked disgusted. 'This story is everywhere. Tell me how I'm supposed to deal with this. How am I supposed to focus on making this movie when every single person on my set is looking at the bare thigh of my leading lady and sniggering? Just being this close to you is making me feel dirty.'

*The whole world is going to know you're dirty, Taylor.*

Her breathing grew shallow.

Anger burst free inside her. This was all Luca's fault. Because he didn't care what people thought of him, he'd exposed her. He'd stripped her, almost literally, with no thought to the consequences. If he hadn't been so careless with that Portia woman's feelings, this would never have happened.

'The press have embellished this to make it look bad, but it isn't how it seems.'

'The truth doesn't even matter.' The director made a hand gesture to signify two minutes to someone over her shoulder. 'I can't work in this circus. You're off the movie.'

Those words turned Taylor's limbs to water. 'What? No!' Composure deserted her. She wanted to act. More than anything else she wanted to act. It was all she wanted to do.

'You can't do that. You can't get rid of me because of what the media say. You can't give them that much power and control. I need to speak to Luca. Give me a chance to sort this out.'

But he'd already moved on. People were shouting things at him and his eyes were on the phone in his hand as he read a text. 'You can't sort this out. Wherever you go, trouble follows. It's always about you and never about the film. You're finished.'

Furious at the injustice of it, Taylor straightened her shoulders. 'That's Santo Corretti's decision, not yours.'

'Fine. He can tell you himself.' Standing back, the director gestured towards the low, expensive sports car that had just parked behind her.

Taylor closed her eyes. This was a nightmare. She had to do something but nothing she said was going to rub out that picture of Luca with his hand on her thigh.

She forced herself to stand still as Santo strode towards her, his face black as the sky before a storm.

Judging from the little she'd read about the aborted wedding, he'd had a worse weekend than she had.

'It isn't how it seems,' she said, trying and failing to keep the desperation out of her voice. Part of her hated herself for having to try and excuse herself but she was willing to do anything to keep the part. 'She's one of his exes and she obviously followed him and spied on him.'

'And what were you and Luca doing together in the first place?'

'I was—' She broke off, suddenly furious with Luca. If he'd just paid the woman they wouldn't be in this mess. Her mind raced ahead. She'd make him pay in another way. 'We were meeting each other. You told me I couldn't have a relationship, so we were trying to be discreet.'

'Luca is never discreet. He does exactly what he wants to do with whomever he wishes to do it. He doesn't care.'

'But I do, and he respected that. He understands what the press are like and he wanted to protect me.'

Santo shot her a look of undiluted incredulity. 'Your date at the wedding was some guy called Zach. I heard you on the phone.'

'And you heard me tell you that Zach isn't my boy-friend,' she said truthfully. 'He's just a friend.' And by that she meant that he was allowed one layer closer to the real her than most people.

The truth was she trusted no one.

'So you were using him to cover the fact that you're with Luca? You're trying to convince me that you and my cousin are an item?'

'That's exactly what I'm telling you.'

'My cousin isn't capable of a relationship.'

'I think he was as surprised by how quickly our re-lationship developed as I was. After what you said to me, I made him promise to keep it a secret. I couldn't change the way we felt about each other, but I thought I could stop you finding out. There is nothing sleazy about that kiss.' Making a last-ditch attempt to halt the free fall of her career, she shot a look at the director. 'It was two people sharing a special moment and that woman exploited that. We love each other. Now can we move on?'

'Love?' The director started to laugh. 'You expect us to believe that nonsense? Today it's Luca Corretti— who will it be tomorrow?' Perhaps if he hadn't sounded so contemptuous, she wouldn't have said it but she was so upset at his implication that she was unlovable, the words fell out of her mouth.

'It won't be anyone tomorrow,' Taylor heard herself say, 'because I'm in love with Luca and he's in love with me. We're getting married.' People used her all the time. Why shouldn't she use someone else for a change? And since this was all Luca's fault, he was the lucky candidate. 'We didn't want to say anything on Saturday and draw attention away from the bride and bridegroom.' She couldn't for the life of her remember their names. 'We were trying to be unselfish which is why we sneaked a quiet few minutes together.' For a few seconds she had the satisfaction of seeing the pair of them silenced. She held her breath, knowing that they were never going to believe her. Never.

Santo was the first to break the silence. 'If my cousin were engaged, I would have heard.'

'It's a secret.' So much of a secret that even Luca didn't know about it. Her insides clenched as she realised the enormity of what she'd done. 'No one knew but us. And because we're keeping it a secret, obviously we had to be discreet.' She snapped her mouth shut before she could trip over her own tangle of lies. 'And now I'd be grateful if neither of you would mention it again. As far as the media is concerned, I'm single. That's what you wanted, isn't it?'

The director let out a stream of profanities and raised the palms of his hands. 'I can't work with this. If you want me on this project, I demand another actress.'

Santo stood in silence, a frown on his brow.

Taylor felt sick. So that was it. It was all over. She was just about to slide back into her car and hide her humiliation behind tinted glass when Santo spoke.

'Taylor stays on this project.'

The director's eyes narrowed. 'If she stays, I go.'

'Then go.' With a total absence of sympathy, Santo nodded his head at Taylor. 'We'll talk to the press and then get on with the job we're here to do.'

'You just fired the director.' Stunned by his unexpected support, Taylor could hardly speak. 'And yesterday you told me to be discreet and not say anything to the press.'

'That was when I thought you were likely to stir up

a scandal. Taylor Carmichael engaged to Luca Corretti isn't scandal, it's news. It will stop the media focusing on your past and it will shift attention away from my family's wedding fiasco. Don't look so shocked—' he placed the flat of his hand on her bag and guided her towards the press pack '—you've finally done something right. Relax, you still have a job.'

There were only two thoughts in her head. The first was that when Santo found out the truth, he'd fire her anyway, and the second was that Luca Corretti was going to kill her.

# CHAPTER THREE

'I'VE BEEN CALLED before the board, no doubt to answer for my sins. This promises to be a gripping meeting, Jeannie, the general tone of which will be that I'm a very bad boy who can't possibly be trusted with the company even though my brother has just very inconveniently gone AWOL and another of my disgruntled cousins is trying to take over our flagship hotel.' Hiding his bitterness beneath layers of boredom, Luca leaned back and put his feet on his desk, earning himself a reproving look from his long-suffering PA.

'You could try not to be so shocking all the time.'

'Where would be the fun in that?'

'I'm just saying it might help if you were more...' She hesitated and he lifted an eyebrow to prompt her.

'More?'

'More conventional.'

'Conventional?' Just saying the word made Luca

shudder. 'In the fashion business that word is death. And talking of death, whose idea was it to put lilies in my office? Get rid of them. They remind me of funerals.'

She put a strong cup of coffee in front of him and glanced at the extravagant display of fresh flowers that dominated the centre of the table he used for internal meetings. 'I'll have them changed. Gianni is having a meltdown. He wants to know if you've approved the location for the fashion shoot? The agency is driving him mad. He wanted me to remind you the theme is nautical, using unexpected twists on classic elements.'

Luca rolled his eyes. 'Roughly translated from designer-speak to normal language, that means the sea, yes?'

'The agency wants to use your yacht but Gianni wants something more edgy.'

'I don't want them on my yacht. It's my bolt hole from press madness.'

'Talking of press madness, they've been calling all morning about your latest—' she cleared her throat '—indiscretion. Is there anything you want me to say to them?'

'Yes. You can tell them to mind their own business.' Irritated, Luca swung his legs off the desk. 'Don't look so shocked about it. You've worked for me for ten years. I know nothing shocks you.'

'I just get upset when I read bad things about you.' Jeannie's voice was fierce and Luca frowned slightly.

'Don't let it bother you. I don't.'

'That's why I let it bother me. One of us has to care, and it doesn't seem to be you. I could strangle that Portia woman with my bare hands. How dare she tell those terrible lies.'

'Ah, yes, Portia. I underestimated her.' He wondered how Taylor was coping with the publicity and then shrugged it off. If anyone was capable of dealing with a media feeding frenzy, it was Taylor Carmichael. Her past was almost as messy as his. 'The lawyers are dealing with it. I'm not worried.'

'I'm worried enough for both of us. Between you and your brother, you keep the media going—'

'Talking of my brother, I don't suppose anyone has heard from him since he ran off with the bride?' Shaking with laughter, Luca checked his phone for messages while Jeannie gave a despairing shake of her head.

'It isn't funny! What about poor Alessandro?'

'"Poor" Alessandro had a narrow escape. He's been saved from a miserable marriage followed by an expensive divorce. He should be celebrating his good fortune.'

'You don't really think that.'

'I try to think about marriage as little as possible.'

'Your parents were married for years.'

Luca stilled. If there was one thing worse than thinking of marriage in general then it was thinking of his parents' marriage. 'Did I miss the memo about introducing boring topics into office conversation?'

'Sorry.' Jeannie flushed. 'But where do you think Matteo is?'

Luca shrugged. 'Holed up somewhere enjoying wild honeymoon sex with his cousin's almost-bride, I suppose, which makes it all the more galling that the board are proving so intransigent. They need a Corretti to run the company in his absence to stop that snake Angelo getting his claws on the company. They should be embracing me.'

'Judging from the pictures of you and Taylor Carmichael, they probably think there's been more than enough embracing.'

Taylor Carmichael.

He could still feel the silk of her hair against his fingers and the soft slide of her tongue against his mouth. In those few moments before she'd pushed him away, they'd created enough heat and energy to power a small country. The blaze of sexual chemistry had shocked him as much as her, the only difference was that he hadn't wanted to fight it.

Before he could respond to Jeannie, the phone on his desk rang and she leaned across to answer it.

'Signor Corretti's office—no, he is currently out of the office....Which rumour?' She paused, her calm professionalism visibly disintegrating as she listened to the person on the other end of the phone. She lifted shocked eyes to Luca. 'No, I don't have any comment to make….Yes, I'll tell him you rang.' Her hand shook as she replaced the phone and it immediately rang again. Luca clamped his hand over hers as she reached for it.

'Leave it—it's just the press wanting more details on that kiss. Don't feed the frenzy.'

'They didn't want details of the kiss.' Jeannie looked at him nervously. 'You're not the sort of guy who would shoot the messenger, are you?'

His radar for trouble on full alert, Luca released her hand and leaned back in his chair. 'That,' he drawled slowly, 'depends on the message.'

She swallowed hard. 'They want to know when you'll release a statement on your engagement.'

'I'm sure when he said that no one was to disturb him, he didn't mean me.' Taylor shot a dazzling smile at the security guard who was left blinded.

'Well, er, he hasn't mentioned you as such, Miss Carmichael—'

'Of course he hasn't. We agreed not to speak about each other.' She stepped closer and lowered her eyelashes just enough to ensure he wouldn't be able to think about anything but her all day. 'If he talked about me, our relationship wouldn't be a secret, would it?'

'I suppose not.' Sweating, he slid a finger around his collar. 'Knowing Mr Corretti, I'm sure he'll be only too pleased to see a beautiful woman walking into his office.'

'Good.' Striding into the express elevator before he could change his mind, Taylor hit a button and closed the doors. Safely inside, she switched off her megawatt smile and checked her reflection in the mirror.

She was going to kill the bastard.

First she was going to rip his elegant suit from his perfect body and then she was going to injure him in places that would ensure he'd remember her for ever.

It had proved difficult to persuade Santo to give her a few hours off from filming, but in the end he'd decided that they'd be more productive if they dealt with the media first.

Taylor hadn't revealed that the only person she was going to be 'dealing with' was Luca.

The doors opened and Taylor stepped out into a contemporary office space like no other she'd seen. The walls were lined with photographs. Famous models in various poses pouted at her, their razor-sharp cheekbones accentuated by the powerful beam of sunlight pouring from an atrium above. It was a shrine to beauty and elegance.

The wide glass reception desk was unoccupied and she looked through the open door beyond and saw Luca Corretti at the same moment he saw her.

Their eyes locked.

Just for a moment she was back in the maze with

his hand pressed to her bare thigh but then she remembered that was the reason she was here and her temper spurted.

'Well, well—' his sarcastic drawl carried across the open space between them '—it's my fiancée. What an unexpected pleasure, *angelo mia*.'

'In the circumstances, how could I stay away?' Head held high, in full battle mode, Taylor stalked across the marble floor and into his office wondering how on earth they were going to unpick this mess.

She was going to kill him and how was she going to explain that to the press?

'Leave us, Jeannie,' Luca ordered in a silky tone. 'It's not every day a man gets engaged. I need to savour the moment. I might even indulge in desk sex so better not come in without knocking.'

The woman sent him a troubled look and then retreated from the office and closed the door behind her.

Taylor went straight into attack mode. 'How dare you? How dare you play with my life just because you don't care about yours! You should have paid that woman.'

'If I paid every woman who threatened to take stories of me to the press I'd be broke.'

'Maybe you should stop seducing women and then the problem would go away!' She paced the length of his office, her attention caught by yet more black-and-white photographs on the walls. 'You have photographs of women everywhere. You just can't help yourself, can you?'

'I run a fashion house. What do you expect?' He looked effortlessly sophisticated in a suit designed to accentuate his physique and dark good looks. 'Is that jealousy I hear in your voice?'

'Don't be ridiculous. I couldn't care less whose picture you have on your wall or who you kiss.'

'Really? Isn't that rather a liberal attitude for someone who only recently decided I was the only man in the world for her?'

Livid by his flippant response, she glared at him. 'Right now the only thing standing between you and death is the fact that I don't want more negative headlines.'

Dark brows rose above eyes that glinted with mockery. 'So much passion so early in our relationship. Not that I'm complaining. I love a woman who isn't afraid to show emotion.'

'Damn you, Luca, are you ever serious? Do you know how hard I've worked over the past few years to get people to take me seriously? This was a fresh start and then you—you...' Her hands curled into fists and she turned away from him, hating the loss of control. Hating the attraction she felt towards him. Hating him.

'And then I—what?'

'You know what! You—you kissed me. You had your

hand on my—' Just thinking of the photograph made her close her eyes in horror. 'It looked as if we'd—'

'Do you ever finish your sentences? You're like a walking crossword and I'm too lazy to fill in the blanks.'

'I'm—I'm just so mad with you.'

'Don't worry about it. I'm sure it will be good for you to express honest emotion once in a while.'

'Don't mess with me, Luca.' Furious, she stabbed her finger into his chest and then wished she hadn't because all she felt was muscle. 'Be careful. I haven't eaten carbs for three months and I'm always danger-ous when I'm hungry.'

'For what it's worth, I'm mad with you too, and my diet is fine. My taste has never run to women who sup-press their real selves. And now let's get to the point.' The snap of his voice raised the tension in the room several more notches. 'Why the hell did you announce that we're engaged?'

'Because, thanks to you, I was about to be fired from the job I haven't even started yet!'

That drew a frown from him. 'Why would you be fired?'

'Because the director refused to work with someone with my reputation.'

He looked bemused. 'That's crazy. So you like sex and you're not afraid to show it. What's wrong with that?'

Her cheeks burned. 'What's wrong is that I want the focus to be on my skills as an actress, not on my ability to make a fool of myself with a man.'

She'd done that before and she'd lived with the mistake ever since.

He'd left another message on her phone but this time she hadn't even opened it.

It was a relief to be in Sicily, far from California.

Far from *him*.

Luca was watching her curiously. 'So you are afraid to show it. You really need to get over that. Who you choose to kiss in your own time is no one's business but your own.'

She felt like telling him it wasn't that simple. That a kiss could be used and used again. 'I didn't choose to kiss you. You grabbed me.'

'I don't remember you struggling.' He was maddeningly cool. 'It takes two people to make a kiss look like that, *tesoro*.'

'I never would have started it.'

'But you finished it.' His voice was low and threaded through with a sensuality she found off-the-scale disturbing. 'Don't be too hard on yourself. It was an understandable slip.'

'You're so full of—'

'Now, now, Miss Carmichael—' he placed his fingers over her lips '—you don't want to give the press another quote, do you? I'm sure they have a lens trained at this office even as you shriek.'

'You're finding this funny. I don't even know why you did it—why did you do it? Why the hell did you kiss me?'

He gave a careless shrug. 'You were there.'

'That's all it takes for you to kiss a woman? She just has to be there?'

'Unlike you, I don't try and deny my true nature.'

'Nice to know you're discriminating.'

'Have you played Katerina?' One dark eyebrow lifted. '*Taming of the Shrew?* Because you'd be a natural. Do I need to remind you that you kissed me back?'

'I was stressed out. I hadn't eaten for two days.'

He smiled. 'So that was why you were so hungry for me.'

'Don't flatter yourself.'

'Why not? A moment ago you were telling the world you intend to spend the rest of your life with me.'

'I didn't know what else to say.' Taylor paced over to the window of his office, her heels tapping on the floor. 'I don't need all the adverse publicity right now. It was a spur of the moment thing. I didn't even think people would believe me, but they did. Apparently people are captivated by the thought of us together.'

'Of course they are. I'm the man who has publicly said on numerous occasions that he never intends to settle down and you're the wild child with a bad attitude.

It's a match made in hell. How can the public not be fascinated? If you'd kept quiet the story would have died by tomorrow. As it is, you've ensured it's kept alive.'

'Stories don't die.' The words tumbled out of her mouth along with years of anxiety and pressure. 'They never die. Sometimes they lie dormant and that's even worse because you have no idea when they're going to explode in your face.'

He stared at her in bemusement. 'I have no idea what the hell you are talking about.'

Of course he didn't. And she had no intention of enlightening him. 'This is all your fault.'

'You kissed me back.'

'I wasn't talking about that, I was talking about the fact that you treated that woman badly and she sold her story to the press! If you were more sensitive, this wouldn't have happened.'

'You kissed me back.' His voice was dangerously soft and suddenly her mouth was dry and her heart was thundering.

'Or if you'd just paid her—'

'You kissed me back.'

'Yes, all right, I kissed you back!' Her head full of images she didn't want to see, her voice rose. 'But I wasn't thinking at the time.'

'I know. You were stripped down to the most basic version of yourself. The real you. I like that version much better, by the way.'

'Well, I don't,' Taylor snapped. 'I've left that version behind.'

'You might want to look in the maze. I'm sure I had my hands on that version yesterday.'

And that version of her wanted to grab him and haul his mouth back against hers. That version wanted to rip at his clothes and explore those parts of his body she hadn't already explored. That version was burning up with sexual awareness and a need so strong it took her breath away.

That version was driving her mad and had to be buried.

Just to be sure she couldn't be tempted to follow her instincts, she kept her hands locked behind her back. 'This is a joke to you, isn't it?'

'Surprisingly enough, no. There is nothing amusing about marriage or anything that goes with it.' The phone on his desk rang and then immediately stopped as his PA intercepted it from her office. 'That is about the seventieth call I've had from journalists on my private line since you so kindly announced our engagement a few hours ago. It's not working out for me. It's time we broke it off.'

'No!' Anger turned to desperation. Trying to ignore the chemistry, Taylor lifted her fingers to her temple and forced herself to breathe. 'Please. You have no idea how badly I want this job.'

His gaze was cool and unsympathetic. 'Buy cheaper

shoes or, better still, wear one of the thousands of pairs you already own.'

She lowered her hand slowly. 'You think this is about shoes? About money?'

'What is it about then?'

It was about acting, but it didn't occur to anyone that she loved her job. They thought it was all about the publicity and that was her mother's fault. She'd made a name for herself as the pushiest parent in Hollywood and Taylor's reputation had suffered as a result.

Not just her reputation.

Her decision making.

'I want to be taken seriously as an actress, that's all you need to know.' She'd learned the hard way to guard the private side of her life and she did it with the tenacity of a warrior. 'I need this job to go well.'

'And for that I'm expected to marry you?'

'No, not marry me. But I thought maybe we could keep the whole engagement pretence up, just until filming is finished.'

'You thought wrong. So far we've been engaged for about ten minutes and that's ten minutes too long as far as I'm concerned.'

The thought of having to walk out there and admit that she'd fabricated the engagement pushed her close to the edge of panic. 'You travel a lot,' she said desperately, 'we wouldn't need to see each other much.

Just the odd photograph of us looking happy together would do it.'

'It wouldn't do it for me. I have no desire to tie myself to one woman, fictitious or not. It would cramp my style.' He glanced at the expensive watch on his wrist. 'I'm late to a board meeting. When I come out of that meeting I'll be behaving like a single guy so unless you want the next headlines to say I'm cheating on you, I suggest you break the news to them fast.'

'I just told them we were engaged.'

'Your problem, not mine. Tell them you came to my office and found me with another woman. Tell them anything you like—unlike you I have no problem having the real me presented to the world. But by the time I come out of my meeting I want calls asking me for a comment on how I feel about being dumped and if that doesn't happen then I'll be making a statement about dumping you. Your choice, *dolcezza*.'

With that he strode out of the room and left her standing there.

Women.

Unsettled by the depth of the chemistry and even more upset by overexposure to the word *engaged*, Luca strode towards the boardroom like a man trying to escape the hangman's noose.

He genuinely couldn't understand why anyone would choose to get married. The thought of committing to one woman for the rest of his life made him break out in a rash. Where was the pleasure in tying yourself to one woman? He could cope with female insecurity for the duration of a photo shoot, or even a single night of passion—providing it wasn't the whole night—but the thought of a lifetime of ego stroking made him contemplate entering a monastery. Or maybe not a monastery, he mused as he was momentarily distracted by the chairman's pretty executive assistant, but certainly a place where marriage was banned.

She blushed prettily. 'The board is waiting for you, Luca.'

Boring old fossils, Luca thought, suppressing a yawn. They needed blasting into the twenty-first century and he was perfectly happy to be the one to do it if only they'd let him but there was no chance of that.

As he entered the room, he estimated that the meeting would take four minutes. One minute for them to stare at him gravely and comment on how his appalling behaviour left a stain on the Corretti name and the company as a whole, another minute while they told him he wasn't going to have a seat on the main board and a further two minutes while he gave them an uncensored, unvarnished account of what he thought of them. That part promised to be entertaining.

Prepared to make full use of his two minutes, it threw him to see the chairman rise to his feet, tears in his eyes.

Tears?

Luca executed a perfect emergency stop. He was used to women crying over him, but men crying over him? That was taking things a step too far.

'Luca…' Hands outstretched, the man who had been a close friend of his grandfather's walked round the table towards him.

Preferring all physical contact to come from the opposite sex, Luca backed away hastily, crashing into a chair in the process. 'No need for the drama. I'm the sort of guy who prefers the truth without embellishment.'

'I'm not going to lie to you, we didn't see this coming.'

'Didn't see what coming?'

'Your engagement.'

The word felt as if someone was rubbing sandpaper over raw skin. 'Ah, yes. About that—'

Bursting into a stream of Italian, the man hugged him and Luca stood rigid in that embrace, thinking that if becoming engaged triggered so much uncontrollable emotion in people then he was doubly relieved he'd chosen never to do it. 'Look, there's something I need to—'

'It changes everything.'

'Marriage? Yes, I know, that's why I've never—' Luca broke off, horrified as the older man took his face in his hands.

'If you're responsible enough to take that step then you're responsible enough to have a seat at this table.'

'*Scusi?*'

'We're voting you in as Matteo's successor at least until the fuss dies down and he returns. Angelo thinks he can just walk in here and take over our hotel—we'll show him a united front. You're a family man, now. A true, loyal Corretti.'

Biting back the observation that the words *loyal* and *Corretti* went together about as well as *lion* and *baby gazelle*, Luca extracted himself carefully from the man's grip, thanking his lucky stars that he hadn't actually been kissed. 'So what you're telling me,' he said slowly, 'is that my track record with the House of Corretti meant nothing to you but now that I'm engaged, I'm suddenly fit to run the hotel group?'

'Running a hotel group takes more than brain power.' One of the other directors spoke up. 'It takes dedication. You have to demonstrate responsibility not just to your employees, but to your shareholders. We saw no evidence of that in your life, but it seems we were wrong. Not only that, but you've proved yourself capable of discretion. You and Taylor Carmichael are both high-profile people and yet somehow and we can't imagine how—' he beamed approvingly '—you have managed to keep this relationship a secret until now. Frankly, this has come as a shock to us, Luca.'

'It came as a shock to me too,' Luca confessed with perfect honesty. 'I didn't see it coming.'

'So what are your plans?'

Plans? He'd planned to kill the engagement rumours and move on with his life, unrestricted, but now he was rethinking fast. Being engaged seemed to have afforded him a status within the board that impressive profits and innovative thinking had failed to produce.

If that was what it took to prove to this bunch of dinosaurs that he could add value to their company, then maybe it was worth considering.

He tested the water. 'The wedding itself isn't going to happen for a while.'

That statement was met by more beams of approval.

Encouraged, Luca elaborated. 'And right now we're both so busy we're not managing to see much of each other.'

Approval turned to sympathy and Luca decided that maybe he could be the first engaged man on the planet who never actually saw his 'fiancée.' Pondering on that thought, he decided that the situation could actually be turned to his advantage. All he had to do in return for the responsibility he wanted was resist the urge to throw himself under the wheels of a passing car every time someone said the word *engaged*.

As his mind gradually emerged from the vice-like panic that came from thinking about weddings, he re-

alised that Taylor Carmichael was probably already an-
nouncing to the world that she'd dumped him.

Knowing he had to act quickly, Luca spread his
hands and smiled at the board. 'I just came here today
to share the happy news, but I'm afraid I can't stay. Gut-
ted though I am not to spend more time with you, I'm
sure you understand. It's Taylor's first day of filming
down at the docklands and I want to just go over there
and be supportive, because—because—' never having
been supportive before, he floundered for a plausible
reason for his actions '—because that's what engaged
people do.' Truthfully he had absolutely no idea what
engaged people did. All he knew was that he had nothing in common with them. 'I want to be there for her.'

Fortunately the board seemed impressed. 'Of course.
After Matteo's behaviour at the wedding that demon-
stration of loyalty is just what the public need to see.
Who would have thought you would be the one to add
sobriety to the Corretti family name.'

Sobriety?

Luca recoiled in alarm. He was prepared to live behind a facade of respectability just to prove to these old
codgers that he could do more for the company than
a whole boardroom full of men in suits, but being accused of sobriety made him wonder if it was worth it.

'Go.' Visibly moved, the chairman waved his hand
towards the door. 'We'll have a meeting of the hotel
executive committee tomorrow evening and we look

forward to hearing your ideas for boosting the hotel business then. Bring your fiancée!'

Biting back the comment that his ideas would have been the same whether he were engaged or not, Luca left the room not sure if he were in the frying pan or the fire.

Whichever, there was no doubt in his mind that he needed to get to the docklands where filming was taking place before Taylor ruined everything. He'd tell her he was willing to go along with this whole engagement thing just as long as it got him a seat on the main board.

How hard could it be?

# CHAPTER FOUR

'WHEN ARE YOU getting married?'

'Tell us how you met Luca Corretti.'

'Why didn't you attend the wedding together?'

Journalists pressed around her, trapping her with a volley of questions until Taylor wanted to scream at them to leave her alone but she couldn't react because there, at the edge of the pack, watching her with a warning in his eyes was Santo Corretti.

He hadn't said a word but she'd got the message.

If she didn't handle this well, she was off the film.

He wouldn't save her.

And how could she handle it well? Thanks to Luca's refusal to play along with her, there was nothing to handle. As soon as she told them there was no engagement, it would be over.

The day was turning into a bad dream.

She'd already ordered herself a taxi and in the meantime she was stalling, waiting for it to arrive. Once she told them the truth she'd be on her own. She had no illusions about that. She needed an escape route.

And once she was safely away from here, she'd rethink her life. She didn't have much choice, did she? Her past was a constant roadblock to her dream of being taken seriously as an actress. Maybe she should give up on film and work in theatre instead. Maybe she could fly to England and base herself there. They had Stratford on Avon and The Globe.

Swallowing down the lump in her throat, she told herself that the first thing she was going to do when she was safely away from here was eat something. The second was to give that Portia woman Luca's home address and all his personal details. They deserved each other.

The loud roar of an engine made heads turn.

Taylor's heart beat faster. So this was it. 'I have something to tell you—'

But the journalists weren't looking at her. They were staring at a red Ferrari hurtling towards them at a terrifying speed.

At any other time the car would have made her drool, but right now the only car she was interested in was her taxi and this definitely wasn't it.

She felt a flash of panic. Already some of the journalists were turning back to her, waiting for her to finish her sentence. It was too late to back down. She was going to have to go ahead and tell them the truth about

Luca. Santo Corretti would be so disgusted he'd leave her to it. She was going to have to elbow her way out of this mob alone and just hope the taxi showed up before she was ripped to pieces.

The sports car showed no sign of slowing and she saw several journalists mutter to one another in alarm before taking a few precautionary steps backwards.

Just when it appeared the driver was going to mow them down he hit the brakes, sending a cloud of dust rising upwards. And Taylor simply stared because there, seated behind the wheel, his eyes hidden by a pair of dark glasses that made him look insanely attractive, was Luca Corretti.

A female journalist standing nearby reached into her bag for lipgloss and Taylor felt the anger start to boil inside her.

This was all his fault.

Not only had he created this whole situation with his careless lack of concern for other people, but he'd refused to go along with her plan to bail them both out. And now he had the nerve to turn up here to make sure she'd confessed to her crime in public.

Her anger grew as he vaulted from the car and strolled towards the journalists with indolent grace. 'So maybe I broke the speed limit just a little bit—' playing to the crowd, he gave a wicked smile that held no trace of regret or apology '—but some things are worth rushing for and a beautiful woman is one of those.'

Furious that he could be so relaxed when her life was in shreds, Taylor elbowed her way through the journalists, who retreated in fascination, their professional sensors telling them that they were about to witness something worth writing about.

Taylor didn't care. She was off the film anyway. How much worse could it get?

'Luca Corretti, you are the most—'

His hands cupped her face and his mouth covered hers. His kiss was hot, explicit and devastating, and when he finally lifted his dark head enough for her to speak, the only sound she was capable of was a moan. Because there was no way she was moaning in public, she stayed silent.

'Sorry, *tesoro*, you were saying?' Slumberous dark eyes looked down at her. 'You wanted to tell me that you missed me, no? That I am the sexiest man in the world? The most clever? The most amusing?' Sliding his arm around her shoulders, he turned to face the journalists, his smile disarming. 'She is struck dumb.'

A ripple of laughter spread across the crowd.

Taylor was so shaken by that kiss, she couldn't focus. All she wanted to do was lock her hands in that glossy dark hair, pull his head down to her and kiss him again. And again—

'Luca—'

*'Mi dispiace...'* Turning towards her, he leaned his forehead against hers and smiled that smile that made

women forget how to put one leg in front of the other to walk away. 'Forgive me for not making it here on time. I am a rat. A total bastard. I don't deserve you.'

She stared at him, eyes locked with his, hypnotised by the sheer power of the chemistry. It wrapped itself around her like metal bands, holding her trapped.

A sea of excited questions washed up against the wall of their own private sexual cocoon.

'So it really is true?' A female journalist thrust a microphone towards them. 'Luca, you always said you weren't the marrying kind. What's changed?'

Taylor wanted to ask the same question. 'Yes,' she muttered through clenched teeth, 'do tell us what changed.' But relief spread through her, taking with it her anger.

He was going to play along. For now, she was safe and that was all that mattered. They could work out the detail later.

His fingers stroked her face gently. 'I realised there is nothing I want more than to be engaged to Taylor.'

Another journalist stepped closer. 'You've just broken a million women's hearts.'

'I'm only interested in one woman's heart.' He leaned closer to her, his mouth by her ear. 'How long am I supposed to keep this up?'

She went from wanting to punch him to wanting to laugh out loud and not just because she was relieved he'd decided to go along with her plan. She stood on tiptoe and brushed her lips along the dark shadow of his jaw. 'Mess this up and I'll sentence you to death by a thousand Portias.'

'Portia?' His tone was innocent. 'I've never met anyone called Portia.'

To the watching journalists it looked like a romantic exchange and she heard someone sigh wistfully.

'All right, that's enough romance for one day,' Luca murmured under his breath, easing away from her and addressing the crowd. 'All this attention is very distracting for my...fiancée.'

Taylor wondered if she was the only one who noticed he stumbled over the word. 'Yes. I need to get on with my job. So if there are no more questions—'

'Tell us about the proposal. And why aren't you wearing a ring?'

Taylor froze. Deprived of sleep, her brain failed to think of a response but Luca pushed his hand into his pocket and there, dangling from his fingers and sparkling in the Sicilian sunshine, was a huge diamond ring.

'I chose an extra big one,' he drawled, 'to hold her in place so she can't run away when I misbehave. And also so that when she's angry with me she can throw it and knock me unconscious. I've been keeping it with me because we hadn't exactly planned to go public with this today.'

Wondering where he'd managed to find such an incredible ring at such short notice, Taylor allowed him to slip it onto the appropriate finger and smiled her most romantic smile while the female journalists gazed on with envy and greed.

'Taylor, can you tell me in a single word how you felt when he gave you that ring?'

That was easy enough. 'It was a moment beyond words. I was speechless.'

'And that was the best possible response because speechless is how I prefer my women.' At his most shocking, Luca kept her hand tightly in his and ploughed his way through the flock of press back to his Ferrari. 'And now if you'll excuse us, we are going to seek some privacy to do, er, to do those things engaged people do. Santo, when you find a director with balls, call us.'

She was still on the film.

Weak with relief, Taylor closed her eyes, leaned her head against the passenger seat and let the wind blow through her hair. Beneath her she felt the power of the engine and smiled. The car was a glorious, sinful expression of luxury and speed and part of her just wanted to push him aside, grab the wheel and slam her foot to the floor. She wanted to swing round tight hairpin bends and drive the car to the edge in every sense of the word.

But Taylor Carmichael didn't do things like that.

Not any more.

Taylor Carmichael behaved herself at all times.

Taylor Carmichael was never, ever going to be caught out again.

She opened her eyes feeling light-headed. Somehow, she was still on the film. Unfortunately she was also with Luca Corretti, a man as capable of extinguishing her good fortune as he was at nurturing it. 'Where are we going?'

'Somewhere away from all those people who seem determined to share in our special, private moment.' He shifted gears smoothly. The engine roared and they overtook car after car as they sped along the coast road.

Taylor, who normally hated being driven, wondered why she didn't feel nervous. 'So why the change of heart? I thought you didn't want to be engaged.'

'I don't. But I don't mind pretending to be engaged for as long as it suits me. I gained instant respectability. The board cried over my instant transformation.'

'They cried? Really?' The wind whipped her hair around her face and she anchored it with her hand, exhilarated by the speed, a smile on her lips. 'That's almost funny.'

'I agree.' Leaning on his horn as he executed a death-defying acceleration to pass another car, he threw her a slanting smile that made her think of nothing but sex. 'Who would have thought it? We appear to share a sense of humour. And a love of speed.'

Unsettled at the thought of having anything in common with him, Taylor frowned. 'We'll be sharing an ambulance if you don't slow down.'

'Oh, come on—' his eyes were back on the road '—you're a woman who was built to go fast.'

'I hate driving fast.'

'No, you don't. You love it.'

'You're reckless.' She told herself it was the speed of the car not the wicked curve of his mouth that made her heart beat a little bit faster.

'Has it ever occurred to you that it's the other drivers who are going too slowly? There should be a sign— Dithering Is Dangerous. And you should know that fast is my default speed for everything except sex.'

'I don't need to know that.' She'd been trying not to think about sex but it was impossible around this man. Everything about him screamed masculinity, even the way he handled the car. She looked away quickly, trying to forget the sheer animal passion they'd unleashed together. And that had been just a single kiss. Her brief moment of relief turned to dread as she realised that her desperate, impulsive attempt to protect her position on the film had placed her in a position where she was going to have to spend time with this man. This man who tempted her more than any other. Despite the baking sun her skin felt suddenly cold. 'I already know enough and I think you are the most infuriating man I've ever met.'

'No, you don't.' His voice was a soft, masculine purr.

'I make you laugh and we understand each other, *dolcezza*, because we are so alike.'

It felt as if someone were squeezing her throat. 'I'm nothing like you. And you drive me mad.'

'You just think that because you're hungry. A hungry woman is always irritable. When did you last eat?'

'Eat? I don't want to eat.' She just wanted to get out of the car. She wanted to wind the clock back and find another way of extracting herself from this mess.

She didn't do this. She didn't put herself in the way of temptation.

'Of course you want to eat. You're permanently starving but for some reason you suppress every appetite you ever experience.' Without warning, he took a right turn, roared into a small village and cut the engine, oblivious to the stares he earned from the locals. 'Wait here.'

He disappeared for a few moments and then reappeared and dropped a bag onto her lap. 'Never let it be said I don't know what a woman really wants.'

The smell made her stomach rumble and Taylor opened the bag curiously. 'A cheeseburger? You think that's what a woman really wants?'

He leaned towards her and for a terrifying, breathless moment she thought he was going to kiss her again but he simply smiled that maddening smile that made her stomach curl. 'I'm good at understanding a woman's hidden desires, *dolcezza*.'

Pride kept her still in her seat. 'Evidently not, because I have no desire for a cheeseburger.' Her stomach growled loudly and his smile widened as he pulled back from her and started the engine.

'I'll leave you to argue with your stomach about that one. But while you're engaged to me, you'll eat carbs. Otherwise one of us will kill the other and that is not going to produce the headlines you're hoping for.' Eyes in the mirror, he executed a perfect U-turn and rejoined the main highway while Taylor stared at the cheeseburger, remembering the time she'd sneaked out with friends for a burger and been caught by her mother. She'd been twelve years old, excited by her first-ever invitation to join a group of girls and feeling almost normal for the first time in her life, when her mother had come storming into the restaurant and dragged it out of her hand, demanding to know why she was so determined to ruin her career.

Taylor closed the bag and gripped the top so that she wasn't tempted, but the smell wouldn't leave her alone.

Her mouth watered. Her stomach mewed.

She made an impatient sound. The day was turning from a bad dream into a nightmare. 'You're cruel, you know that, don't you?'

'Just eat it and spare me the drama.'

'I can't.' Her fingers tightened on the bag. 'It's on the forbidden list.'

'*Scusi?*'

'The forbidden list. The list of things I can't do.'

'You're seriously telling me you have a list of things you can't do?'

'I don't expect you to understand,' Taylor snapped, 'but I can't eat this. For a start my character in the movie is supposed to be slender.'

'Your character will be found strangled by her infuriated fiancée if you don't eat something substantial soon.' He pulled back onto the coast road. 'Tell me more about this forbidden list. I think I might have one too.'

'You? You have to be kidding.'

'Well, I have a list—the difference is that mine is called my priority list. What else is on yours?'

Spending time with men like him.

'Everything that is bad for me and will wreck my career.'

'So it's also called the boring list. I suggest you flip that list and do everything on it, starting with eating food that's bad for you and tastes good. Open that bag and feed the real you. Go on. You know you want to.'

She did want to. She wanted to so badly.

Oh, hell, why not?

Tired and starving hungry, Taylor gave in to temptation. It wasn't as if one hamburger was going to kill her.

Trying to block out the sound of her mother saying 'think of your career' she closed her eyes and took a bite. Flavour exploded in her mouth. She moaned. 'I think that might be the best thing I've ever tasted.

Find a bin, quickly. I have to throw it away before I'm tempted to take another bite.'

'Take another bite. And then another. When your stomach is full and you're not behaving like a she-wolf stalking her prey, we'll talk.'

Flavour slicing through her willpower, Taylor took another bite. 'OK, you win. When filming is over I'm going to buy a truckload of these. How do I ask for it in Italian?'

'You ask for *pane con la milza*.'

'*Pane con la milza*. That's Italian for cheeseburger?' She took another mouthful and chewed slowly, savouring every moment. 'I know that *pane* means "bread," and *con* means "with." So *milza* must be—what? Beef? Ham?'

'Spleen.'

Taylor stopped chewing. 'Pardon?'

'*Milza* means "spleen."'

At the point of swallowing, she choked. 'I'm eating a spleen burger? You fed me spleen burger?'

'Your translation is less than elegant but yes, the meat is spleen. *Pane con la milza* is a delicacy, particularly around Palermo. My grandmother used to make it in her kitchen when I was a little boy.'

She dropped the rest of the 'burger' in the bag and put it on the floor of his car. 'Pull over. Now.'

'Why?'

'I'm going to throw up.'

'Throw up in my Ferrari and this engagement is off. Nothing is worth that. *Cristo*, Taylor, stop behaving like a wimpy female.' He flung her an impatient look before fixing his eyes on the road again. 'What is that phrase you use? Put your big-girl pants on. But not literally—I prefer you in something more revealing. A thong works for me. Does that phrase exist? Put your sexy-girl thong on? Whatever—show some guts.'

'Thanks to you I just ate guts.'

'And even as we speak the nutrition will be flowing into your starved veins. Your starved body should be thanking me.'

'You have a problem with my body? That's odd because it certainly didn't seem that way when you were ripping my clothes off a few days ago.' She had the satisfaction of seeing his hands tighten on the wheel.

'I didn't see enough of it to judge.'

The atmosphere in the car had shifted dangerously and she wished she'd kept the conversation on the topic of food. Wiping her fingers on a napkin, she shuddered. 'Do not ever mention this particular meal again. I do not want to even think about the fact I just ate a— never mind.'

'I never would have thought you were squeamish. Meat is meat.'

'I don't often eat meat and when I do I like to know what I'm eating before I eat it. Now I understand why all your relationships have been short. I don't think I can even *pretend* to love you enough to marry you. You drive me crazy.'

'Anyone choosing to get married has to be crazy, so I don't see that as a problem.' He slowed the car, waiting as a pair of electric gates opened slowly, and then accelerated along a drive bordered by tall cypress trees.

'Where are we?' She threw a glance at his profile, wondering why he was so firmly against marriage. She decided it was probably because he lived his life surrounded by gorgeous women.

'We're somewhere exclusive where we can be assured of privacy.' The tyres crunched over gravel as he pulled up outside a beautiful building built from honey-coloured stone.

A woman appeared from nowhere. 'Luca!' She burst into a stream of fluent Italian and Luca replied in the same language. Taylor glanced around her, trying to ignore the fact that hearing him speak in that beautiful, lilting language made her tummy tighten.

Impatient with herself, she reminded herself that any time her self-control weakened around him she just needed to think of him feeding her a spleen burger. Most of all she needed to remember that there was nothing romantic about this situation.

Which suited her just fine.

Never again was she trusting a man. Or any other person for that matter. She was using Luca Corretti, just as he was using her.

Having reminded herself of that, it was doubly unsettling when the woman walked across to her and took her hands, her eyes filling.

Taylor suppressed her natural impulse to back away. 'Er, *bueno*, er...' She glanced hopelessly at Luca, who rolled his eyes.

'That's Spanish. What are you trying to say?'

Taylor felt her face turn scarlet with embarrassment. 'I'm trying to be friendly and say hello.'

'If it's after midday you can just say *buona sera*. This is Geovana. She speaks some English, although she might not be familiar with "spleen burger."'

'You have no idea how relieved I am to hear that.'

Geovana's hands tightened on hers. 'Welcome.'

Touched by the warmth shown to her, Taylor looked at Luca. 'How do I say "I'm pleased to be here" in Italian?'

*'I amarlo così tanto la sua folle.'*

She repeated it slowly and was stunned when Geovana flung her arms round her and hugged her tightly. Unused to being hugged, Taylor held herself rigid. 'Oh! This is...nice and...welcoming.' Most of all it was unfamiliar. She frowned slightly, feeling something inside her unravel. Geovana was warm and plump and... motherly. Taylor swallowed. Her own mother had seen her as a meal ticket, as a means to live out her own dreams, not as a daughter to be hugged. Their conversations had only ever been about how Taylor could do more, be more, never about who she was or what she wanted, and it had never, ever been about affection. They'd parted ways when Taylor was seventeen and hadn't spoken since.

When Geovana finally released her only to kiss her on both cheeks, Taylor felt confused, raw and vulnerable.

'She likes you,' Luca said in a flat drawl, 'that's a compliment. Come on, I'll show you to our bedroom suite.'

*Our* bedroom? She decided to ignore that until they were alone. 'Doesn't she usually like your girlfriends?'

'She's never met any of them.' Taking her hand, Luca strode into the house as if he owned it, crossed the beautiful, light-filled entrance hall and up a curved staircase.

'Why hasn't she met any of them?' Taylor tugged at her hand but he didn't release her. His fingers were cool and strong. 'I assumed this hotel is one of your regular sex hideouts. Or do you smuggle your women in and out through the window?' She tugged at her hand, harder this time, and this time he released her.

Relief flowed through her and she promised herself that from now on she'd keep a physical distance from him. No touching. She had enough problems without adding to them.

'This isn't a hotel.' He pushed open a door and walked into a room that took her breath away. Through the open French doors the view stretched across a garden to a vineyard and, beyond that, in the distance, the towering peak of Mount Etna.

Taylor decided she'd never seen a more perfect view in her life. 'Wow. You have an eye for beauty, I'll give you that. It's stunning. And so private.' Reluctantly, she dragged her eyes from the view to look at him. 'If this isn't a hotel, then what is it?'

'It's my home.' He shrugged off his jacket and removed his tie. 'And I don't bring women here, so don't get too comfortable. Strictly speaking I should have blindfolded you before I brought you to my private lair.'

'Why don't you bring women here?'

'Because my home is a place to relax and women are exhausting.' He strolled across the sunlit room and placed his cufflinks in a dish on the nightstand, 'From their uncanny ability to misinterpret everything a man says or does, to their endless demands for reassurance, including such well-loved phrases as "Does this dress make me look fat?" and—every man's favourite—"What are you thinking?"'

'Yeah, that must be a tough one for a guy like you who never bothers thinking. If you had bothered to think you wouldn't have messed up so badly with Portia.' She used sarcasm to cover up the way he made her feel. It wasn't just the sexual chemistry that terrified her, it was the buzz she had from talking to him.

'I didn't mess up with Portia. That relationship

ended precisely when I intended it to. I consider that to be a success.'

'But if you'd ended it more thoughtfully we wouldn't be in this position.'

'In what position? Suddenly we're both respectable. It's a miracle.' With a complete lack of self-consciousness he undid the rest of the buttons of his shirt, allowing it to fall open. His trousers rode low on his lean hips, revealing toned, male abs, and Taylor averted her eyes, ignoring the dangerous curl of warmth that spread through her body.

'Thanks, but I can live without the striptease.'

'Is it bothering you?'

Exasperation mingled with a much more dangerous emotion. 'No, it isn't bothering me. But I'm the sort of person who needs personal space. We should have stayed at my hotel.' The glimpse had been brief, but the image of his bronzed, fit body was seared onto her brain. 'I have a suite with two rooms.'

'I can't stand hotels.'

'And yet you want to run the family business?'

'That's different.' He shrugged, his tone bored. 'That's just about proving a point. And if we're going to be engaged then I need space too. I'm not good at being trapped with a woman.'

But now they were both trapped and he was looking at her, assessing her with that lazy, sexy stare that was so much a part of him until she felt as if her skin might catch fire.

Desperately, she steered the subject onto safer ground. 'So tell me about Geovana.' She thought about the warmth the other woman had shown her. 'Why did she hug me so tightly? When I said I was pleased to be here, she almost strangled me.'

'That's because you didn't say you were pleased to be here. You said you were so in love with me it's driving you crazy.'

She gaped at him. 'I said what you told me to say.'

'Yes. And you were remarkably fluent. Very impressive for a non-Italian speaker.'

Mouth tightening, she tapped her foot on the floor. 'I suppose you think that's really funny. Like teaching a toddler to use rude words.'

'Since I don't intend to ever marry, that's an experience I'm not going to be in a position to comment on but strangely enough I didn't do it to be funny. I did it because we're supposed to be engaged. You're not the only one who can act a part when required.'

'That's why she hugged me? Because I told her I was crazy about you?'

'So it would seem.' A ghost of a smile touched his mouth. 'Today is probably the happiest day of her life. Geovana had given up on seeing me bring a woman home.'

'Because no woman would put up with you.' But part

of her wondered whether there was a deeper reason for his aversion to marriage. Her instincts told her there was more to it than simply a love of a playboy lifestyle. 'Have you known her a long time?'

'Since I was five years old.'

Taylor felt a twinge of envy at the warmth of his relationship with the woman.

She didn't have anyone in her life she was close to. No one she could trust as Luca clearly trusted Geovana. It was obvious that the older woman adored him.

'How did you meet her?' She asked the question as they walked up the stairs towards the bedroom.

'She was our nanny until my mother fired her in a fit of jealousy.'

'You had a nanny?' She bit her tongue. Of course he'd had a nanny. He came from a rich family. He hadn't been used as the breadwinner by an ambitious mother while he was still in nappies. 'Did your mother work?'

'It was a full-time job trying to keep my father happy.'

She was about to question that statement when he started to unbuckle his belt. 'Whoa. Rewind. I do not need to see you naked. This engagement is fake, remember?'

'There is no way I'll forget that, *dolcezza*. Just make sure you don't.'

'Oh, please—there is no way I'll forget that.'

'Don't be so sure. Every woman I meet thinks she's

going to be the one to change my ways and drag me to the altar.'

Turning her back on him, Taylor paced around the room, noticing the art on the walls and the beautiful stylish touches. There were no photographs. Nothing personal. 'You are known for living the high life. We are going to have to work extra hard to convince people this is real. Even pretending is giving you a hunted look. I'm going to have to teach you to act.'

'I can act. I don't need your help.'

'And I may not need yours if Santo doesn't manage to replace the director.' Battling a rush of insecurity, Taylor walked through the French doors onto the pretty balcony with its glorious views of the Sicilian countryside. 'It's gorgeous. Are you sure the press won't find us here?'

'Of course I'm not sure. They can find us anywhere, that's their job.' He seemed completely indifferent to the possibility and she felt her own pulse rate quicken as she walked back into the bedroom.

'Don't you care?'

'Why would I?'

'It's an invasion of privacy.'

'I've never seen the need to hide what I do.' He removed his shirt and dropped it onto the bed. The flex of hard, honed muscle across his wide shoulders had her staring, and because this was the day where nothing was going her way that was the moment he turned and caught her.

'Enjoying the view?'

'Not particularly. And I have no idea why you're undressing.'

'Purely for your entertainment, *dolcezza*.' Sending her a sexy smile, he unclipped his watch. 'And for the entertainment of any photographers who happen to have long lenses trained on my bedroom. I'd hate to disappoint them. Oh—and because I intend to take a shower.'

'Photographers?' Horrified, she looked from him to the long windows that offered a view into the distance. 'Can this house be seen from the road?'

'I have no idea. I suppose we'll find out now you're staying here.'

'I'm not staying here...' She stumbled over the words in her panic, tripping over her bag as she backed to the door and opened it. 'If the press could be watching, I can't stay. I have to go somewhere I know I can't be photographed—I have to—'

'You have to calm down.' Luca strode over to her and pushed the door shut with the flat of his hand, saying something to her in Italian. '*Cristo*, Taylor, why all the drama? You're not on set now.'

'I hate being photographed.'

'Yes, I'm starting to get that part. Even I'm not that obtuse.' His keen gaze was fixed on her face. 'What I don't get is why. You're an actress. You're photographed all the time. It's part of the job.'

'And I accept it when I'm out filming, or at a premiere or even when I'm out having fun because I know I can never go anywhere without being recognised any more, but I have to know I'm safe when I'm at h-home. I don't want to be photographed when I—think I'm alone.' She was stammering. 'I deserve that. Doesn't everyone deserve that?'

'Yes, I suppose so, if that's what they want. And now are you going to tell me what happened?'

Her stomach felt as if someone had tied a knot in it. 'What do you mean?'

'No one freaks out like that without a reason. So tell me the reason. What happened?'

'Nothing happened.' She had no intention of talking about it, especially not to him. She'd learned the hard way that no one could be trusted. Thinking back to how naive she'd been at seventeen made her want to curl up in embarrassment but at least she'd learned the lesson. 'I'm a private person, that's all. There's nothing wrong with that.'

'Except that, like most celebrities, the press considers you public property.'

His choice of phrase triggered something inside her. 'I'm a person, not property. I am not anyone's meal ticket!'

'Taylor—'

'Enough, OK? I don't even know why we're talking about this. I just hate the press, that's all you need to know. I don't want to stay somewhere they can see me! If they're pushing a camera in my face, I want to know about it.' Shocked to discover just how much emotion was still simmering deep inside her, Taylor reached for the door handle but his hand covered hers.

'*Cristo*, you're shaking.'

'No, I'm not.'

'You are the most confusing woman I've ever met,' he breathed. 'Ballsy one minute and fragile the next.'

'I'm not fragile.'

There was a long pause. 'I'll brief my security team. I'll make sure this place is like a fortress. The only photographs those bastards get will be the ones we want them to take. Us doing engagement stuff—whatever that is. Talking of which, we'd better find out what we're supposed to do.' He released her and strolled across the bedroom as if nothing had happened, leaving Taylor shaken. It unsettled her to know she was nowhere near as in control as she liked to think she was.

Pulling herself together, she looked at him. 'What are you doing now?'

He keyed something into his phone. 'Given that you and I are clueless, I'm doing a search for the typical behaviour of engaged people. There has to be a website. It's probably called getmeoutofhere.com. Or possibly killmenow.org.' The remark was typical of him and for some reason that normality helped relax her.

'We're not just engaged, we're newly engaged.'

'And the significance of that is…?'

'The first glow of excitement has yet to wear off. We have to be supersickly.'

'No worries. The thought of being engaged makes me feel more sickly than you can possibly imagine.'

'And you fed me spleen burger. Need I say more?'

'No, but you're a woman so no doubt you will anyway. If you want to sit down, sit on the bed. It can't be seen from the window unless they have a lens shaped like a periscope.' It was the only reference he made to her sudden loss of control. 'Here you are. Ten habits of engaged couples. Can you believe someone researched that and then wrote about it? What a total waste of a life.'

Taylor glanced from the window to the bed and decided to follow his advice. She slid off her shoes and sat cross-legged on the end of the bed. 'Go on. Read it out.'

He was staring at her legs. 'What are you doing?'

'Relaxing. I do yoga. It's good for the core and helps keep me flexible.'

'Flexible?' His voice slightly rough, Luca lifted his gaze from her legs to her face, his phone forgotten. 'How flexible?'

The temperature in the room shot up and suddenly

all she could think of was the way his mouth had felt on hers.

'Flexible enough to make sure that when we're seen in public you're looking very tired.' Unable to resist teasing him, she wrapped one leg behind her neck and his brows rose.

'That position has amazing possibilities but there's no way I'd look tired in public. I have endless stamina. Maybe you'll be the one who is looking tired, *tesoro*, from my male demands.'

Her heart thudded a little harder. 'I've been working with a trainer for months in preparation for this role. I can cope with any physical demands you care to throw my way.'

'Is that a challenge?'

'Absolutely not.' Taylor swallowed and allowed her leg to slide back into its original position. 'So what advice does your website offer?'

His eyes lingered on hers and then eventually he looked back at the screen. 'Touching.'

'Pardon?'

'According to this, newly engaged couples touch all the time. They can't bear to be next to each other and not feel each other. Does that mean I have permission to stroke your breasts in public? Maybe this won't be so bad after all.'

'Public. Of course. We have to be seen in public.' Taylor pushed away thoughts of his hands on her breasts. 'We need to be seen, otherwise no one is going to believe this is real. We should go out for dinner or something.'

'What's the point of that? You don't eat anything.'

'All the better. People will assume my love for you is putting me off my food.'

'Just as long as you don't expect me to be off my food too, because I have no intention of starving myself for the role.' He scanned the screen, his expression comical. '*Cristo*, is there anything good about being engaged?'

'Why ask me? I've never been engaged before either. Nor do I want to be.'

'No?' His gaze lifted to hers. 'Then that makes us a perfect pair. So what happened to you to put you off relationships?'

Her heart thudded a little bit faster. 'Life.'

'You mean a man.'

Would a real man take advantage of a vulnerable girl? Would a real man cynically manipulate someone's feelings for his own benefit? She felt the panic stir deep inside her and squashed it down. 'Well, he had a penis, if that's what you mean. But apart from that no, I wouldn't call him a man.' The words tasted like acid in her mouth and they must have sounded the same way because he lowered his phone, his dark gaze suddenly sharp.

'Is this guy the reason you hate the press? What did he do?'

Why on earth had she started this conversation? Especially with a man as shallow and superficial as Luca Corretti. She was surprised he'd even asked the question. What did he know about loneliness? Or vulnerability, come to that. He came from a huge family. He had no idea what it was like to have no one. He would never in a million years understand what had happened to her.

'It isn't relevant.'

'I'm your fiancé. If you have something in your past that had that big an impact on you, I need to know about it.'

'No, you don't.' She felt the panic rise from deep inside her and block her throat. 'My past is none of your business.'

'For someone who claims this is in the "past" you look pretty stressed out.'

'It's being with you that makes me stressed out. And what about you?' She turned it back on him. 'Anything in your past I need to know about?'

'Nothing at all.' He deflected her question with ease. 'My life is an open book.'

No one's life was an open book, she knew that now. There were hidden corners, areas of darkness, a graveyard of secrets.

She wondered what his were.

While she was musing on the comment he'd made about his mother, he strode across the room, picked up the phone and spoke in Italian. 'I'm taking you out to dinner. My team will book us a table at Da Giovanni. It's very elegant. And high-profile. You can push a lettuce leaf around your plate and gaze at me adoringly.'

'You'll have to gaze at me adoringly too.'

'I can do that as long as you don't get confused and start thinking it's real.'

'When I grab a gun and shoot myself through the head you'll know I'm starting to think our relationship is real,' she told him in a cool tone. 'Until then, you're safe. Unfortunately I don't have any faith that you are capable of even acting the part of a man in love, so concentrate because I'm going to give you some hints.'

'I've already told you I don't need an acting lesson.'

She ignored that. 'The best way to convincingly play emotion is to conjure up the feeling. So if I'm playing someone sad, I try and remember a time when I was sad.'

'I've never been engaged so I can't conjure up the horror that went with it.'

'Very funny, but not helpful. Tonight you have to look as if I'm the only woman in the world for you. Is there any chance you can do that?'

'Are all the other women in the world dead? I suppose if that were the case, I might be relieved to be shackled to you. You're not bad once you're fed.'

Taylor clenched her jaw. 'This is a nightmare. You

are never going to be able to act as if you're engaged. It isn't in your nature.'

'Watch me prove you wrong. I can act. I can dredge emotions from deep inside me or wherever it is emotions are stored. You want happiness, right? I can do happiness as long as I'm not expected to associate it with relationships.'

Taylor breathed slowly. 'All right, let's try this another way. What is the happiest moment you can remember?'

He didn't hesitate. 'The day they delivered my Ferrari.'

'Fine! Tonight, you are going to look at me as if I'm your Ferrari.'

'Do I get to put your top down?'

'You are infuriating!' So why did she want to laugh? 'This was such a bad idea. You'll blow it and this will be the shortest engagement on record.'

'I am not going to blow it. I love my Ferrari. I love my Ferrari.' He muttered the words under his breath and shot her a glance. 'Perhaps I'd better dress you in red, just so that there's a similarity.'

Taylor shook her head in despair. 'And on that note, I have to go back to my hotel. I can't go out to dinner in the same clothes I've been wearing all day, and anyway, if we're going to stay here I need to pack up my things and move them here.'

'One of the advantages of being engaged to the head

of a fashion house is that clothes aren't a problem.' He sent a quick message on his phone. 'If we're going to be seen together, you might as well showcase something from Corretti.'

'So now you're using me for free publicity?'

'Of course I'm using you. That's what this is all about. I'm using you. You're using me.'

*Of course I'm using you.*

Taylor ignored the uneasy feeling in her stomach. She told herself this was different. Yes, she'd been used before but Luca was right—this time she was using him too.

And that made this different from all the times people had used her before.

# CHAPTER FIVE

LUCA DREW UP in a no-parking zone in front of the pretty waterside restaurant.

'You can't park here.' Taylor turned her head, the sun glinting on her sleek, shiny hair. She'd twisted it skilfully into an elaborate confection on the back of her head and fastened it with a jewelled pin that made her look very much the movie star. 'It says no parking.'

'Do you always obey rules?' The artist in Luca admired the perfect lines of her jaw and cheekbones, those beautiful cat-like eyes and the hint of a pout on that kissable mouth. 'That dress looks good on you.'

'I know. That's why I picked it.' Her cool, confident response threw him.

Raised by a woman who had needed constant reassurance and working in an industry defined by its dedication to narcissism, he was conditioned to offer praise and reassurance. These days it fell from his lips unprompted, but Taylor appeared to have no need for his approval. Presented with a choice of dresses, she'd selected one instantly, without hesitation or consultation. The only help she'd needed from him was fastening the zip.

'Of course you'd look better out of that dress.'

'I try not to trigger horrible headlines.'

'Really? I try and trigger horrible headlines on a daily basis. If I don't read at least one bad thing about myself every day I take a long look at my behaviour and try harder to be shocking.'

Her response to that was to roll her eyes but he could see she was holding back laughter and he hid his own smile because he didn't want her to know she made him laugh.

She held everything back, he thought, remembering the way she'd tried to resist the explosive chemistry in the maze. Always up for a challenge, he wondered how hard he'd have to push before that control cracked.

She glanced towards the restaurant. 'Isn't this place a bit obvious? I would have chosen somewhere more discreet. That would have been my normal behaviour.'

'But not mine, *dolcezza*.' He flipped her chin gently with the tip of his finger. 'You're with me and I refuse to slink around like a criminal. You're living by my list now and your idea of forbidden is my idea of compulsory. Get used to it.'

'If we're a couple then my list is as important and valid as yours.'

'Not if it contains things like "don't speed" and "never park in a no-parking zone." The idea of marriage isn't to die of boredom.' Reaching across, he unfastened her seat belt, the backs of his fingers brushing against the softness of her breasts as he released the strap. The punch of desire was so powerful he sucked in a breath at the exact moment Taylor flattened herself to the seat.

'Hey, don't push your luck.'

'We're engaged. That means my luck ran out a long time ago. And what is the point of an engagement if you can't touch? Or is it simply to leave an enormous hole in a guy's bank account and set one lucky jeweller up for early retirement?' Gripped by a flash of instantaneous lust, Luca found himself looking at her mouth and that mouth was so smooth, so feminine, it seemed like a terrible waste not to just go ahead and kiss it. Never one to deny himself, he did just that.

Fire and flame licked around the edges of his nerve endings. Within seconds he was rock hard. What had started as exploration shifted to something so primal and basic that he forgot everything except the urge to strip her naked and get his hands on her glorious body. He wanted to drive into her and watch all those restrictions she placed on herself unravel.

His tongue was in her mouth, tangling with hers, when she shoved at his chest.

'This is an engagement, not a one-night stand. You don't have to cram the entire relationship into six hours.' She was out of the car so quickly she almost stumbled and Luca stared after her for a moment, his mind temporarily wiped. She was as jumpy as a kangaroo on a trampoline and yet she was the one who had lectured him on playing his part properly. How the hell was he expected to play his part when she was running away from him? He didn't claim to be an expert on being engaged but was willing to bet sprinting in the opposite direction during a kiss counted as less than convincing behaviour.

He chose to ignore the tiny part of his brain that was telling him the kiss had nothing to do with role play.

Infuriated that she wasn't putting more effort into it, he sprang from the car. 'Taylor!' Aware someone might be listening, he clenched his jaw and forced himself back into fiancé mode. It was as ill-fitting as a second-hand suit. *'Mi amore—'* He'd never said those words to anyone before and even knowing that they weren't genuine didn't make it any easier. 'Where are you going?'

There was a brief pause and then she spun on her heel and gave him an easy smile that probably seemed genuine to all but him. 'I was leaving you to park the car.'

He sensed her tension but didn't understand it. Hell,

he was breaking his neck here to act like the devoted fiancé. 'It's parked.'

'You call that parked?' One eyebrow raised, she looked at the Ferrari. 'You can't seriously intend to leave it there.'

'They're lucky I choose to park my car outside their restaurant. People will pause, admire it and then want to dine in their restaurant to catch a glimpse of the man who owns such a cool car.'

'Or the woman.'

'This is a man's car, *tesoro*.'

'So defined by the idiot driving it?' Those beautiful green eyes narrowed in challenge and he was pleased to have broken through that seemingly impenetrable wall of control.

He decided to push a little harder. 'There is no way you'd be able to drive it. This baby has a six-point-three-litre V-12 engine with four valves per cylinder—' he glanced lovingly at the car '—and it hovers on the borders of legal. It can shift from car to beast in less than four seconds.'

'A bit like its owner.' Without waiting for him she strolled into the restaurant, those long bare legs drawing more admiring glances than the Ferrari.

She looked good and she knew it. He was fast discovering there was no greater aphrodisiac than a woman aware of her own appeal.

His own gaze fixed on those legs, Luca tried to cool

the heat burning inside him and decided she and the
car had more in common than she ever would have
admitted. Both were high maintenance and both were
eye-catching.

As he caught up with her he took her hand in his.

Her eyes widened. 'What are you doing?'

'Playing the part of your devoted lover,' he drawled
softly, 'only my leading lady appears to have forgotten her lines. If I have to be engaged, then at least let it
be to the woman who yesterday had her legs wrapped
round me in the maze. Don't give me this bland, va-
nilla version.'

She blinked. Frowned slightly. 'This is who I am.'

'If I thought that for a moment this engagement
would be off. I'd die of boredom before we hit our
first anniversary and you'd burst from suppressing all
that emotion.'

'Signor Corretti!' A man approached them and Luca
felt Taylor tug at her hand, trying to free herself.

He tightened his grip and greeted the owner in Italian. 'I need a table.'

'Somewhere private?'

Distracted by Taylor's glossy lips, Luca lost concen-
tration. 'Of course.'

'No, not private.' Taylor flashed her eyes, trying to
transmit a message, but he was too busy deciding if
those eyes were green or blue to translate the unspoken communication.

'I don't want an audience.'

'But I do.' She slid her arms around his neck and gave him a feline smile. 'Don't you want to show off our love to the world, honey?'

Luca, who had never been called 'honey' in his life, remembered belatedly that the purpose of being here was to be seen. 'You're an exhibitionist, *angelo mia.*'

'Says the man who just parked a red Ferrari in a no-parking zone.' Laughing, she trailed a purple fingernail across his cheek and he turned his head and caught her finger gently in his teeth.

Clearing his throat subtly, the owner of the restaurant beamed at them. 'I have a table by the water. So romantic and, on that topic, may I offer our congratulations. We are all delighted by your news.'

Determined to demonstrate that he could play his part as well as her and remembering what she'd said about conjuring up the emotions from deep inside her, Luca tried to imagine how it would feel to be engaged. Deciding that 'freaked out' wasn't going to help his performance, he swiftly ditched that advice and instead thought about the article he'd read. 'I am happy, excited and can't bear to be parted from her even for a moment.'

Smiling at an astonished Giovanni, Taylor urged Luca towards a prime table situated at the edge of the water. 'Your performance was terrible,' she hissed in an undertone. 'You should have let me give you acting lessons.'

'I don't need acting lessons.'

'You sounded as if you were reading from an autocue.'

'An autocue might be a good idea. I'm definitely not fluent in the language of love.' Luca sat down at the table and ordered champagne.

'Yes, about that.' She paused as the waiter fussed around them, waiting until they were on their own to finish her sentence. 'From now on, I don't want you to touch me.'

'*Scusi?* Are we or are we not supposed to be engaged?'

'We are, but I'm not into public displays of affection.' She kept her eyes down, adjusting her cutlery while Luca stared at her in disbelief.

'I'm Sicilian. We're an emotional, physical race.'

'Then hold it in.' Her eyes lifted to his and he saw something there he didn't expect to see.

Panic?

For a moment he was baffled by it, then he remembered the way she'd responded to him in the maze. 'Ah—now I understand. Enjoying sex is on your forbidden list too, and you are finding it hard to resist me, no?'

'No.' She answered just a little too quickly and then covered her glass to stop the waiter pouring champagne. 'Just water, please.'

Luca rolled his eyes and removed her glass, handing it to the waiter. 'Fill it up. She needs help to relax.'

'I do not need help to relax. I'm already relaxed.'

He waited for the waiter to leave them alone. 'I've seen steel cables more relaxed than you. You're such a sexual woman, and you hate that about yourself, don't you? You're trying to lock that part of yourself away and pretend to be something you're not.'

'I do eat. I drink if I want to, and our relationship is not about sex so that's irrelevant.'

'Let's hope no one was lip-reading when you said that.' He lowered his voice. 'Trust me, if we're engaged, there's going to be food and champagne and, most of all, sex. Lots of hot, steamy, very dirty sex so if you want this to appear genuine you'd better stop suppressing that side of yourself.'

Her cheeks turned pink as the waiter approached with her water.

'Thank you so much.' She gave a smile that turned the poor man into a gibbering wreck and Luca gave an amused smile.

'You're all promise and no follow-through.'

'I can follow through when it suits me.'

'And when is that? When you explode from holding it all in?'

Her fingers tightened on her glass. 'I'm not holding anything in.'

'You are suppressing so much, *dolcezza*, that when

you finally blow the aftershocks are going to be felt back in your homeland. Don't worry. I'll be there to drag you from the rubble.'

She smiled. 'Do you think about anything but sex?'

'You're upset that I understand you so well.'

'You don't understand me at all.'

'No? Let's do a Taylor Carmichael 101.' He put his glass down and leaned forward in his chair. 'You long to let yourself go. I saw the way you reacted to my car in the first few minutes before you remembered you weren't supposed to enjoy fast cars. You long to drink champagne, but you daren't in case you drink a bit too much and lose control.'

'Is that the best you can do?'

'I haven't finished. You can't go anywhere without first looking to see where the photographers are hidden. You know they're part of the job but for some reason they make you nervous.'

She reached out slender fingers and took an olive. 'Are you done?'

'Not yet.' It was only because he was looking that he saw her fingers shake slightly. 'You don't trust anyone any more. You've locked yourself away. You won't tell me why so I'm guessing it's something you're ashamed of. Something you regret.' He watched as the colour drained from her cheeks.

Her breathing grew shallow and she looked away quickly. 'You talk nonsense.'

'I scored a direct hit,' Luca said softly. 'Now drink some champagne or the headlines tomorrow will be that you're already pregnant and that's the reason we're marrying. Neither of us wants that.'

After a moment's hesitation she picked up the slender champagne glass. 'To our future.'

'To lots of legal sex.' He glanced up as the waiter approached. 'Don't bother giving my beloved a menu, Pietro, I'll order for both of us. It will be a good test of how well I know her.'

To give her credit, Taylor kept her smile in place. 'But, sweetheart, you know I like to order for myself.'

'I know you do, my little cabbage, but I'm a macho Sicilian male and apart from that inherent trait that drives me to protect you from all things including menus written only in Italian, I'm suspicious of your ordering skills. You'll order the wrong thing.'

'I order what I want to eat, light of my life.' Her eyes gleamed. 'How can that be wrong?'

'You order what you think you're supposed to eat, kitten paws. That's not the same thing at all. A romantic meal out is about feeding the senses.' Enjoying himself, he watched her across the flickering flame of the candle, wishing they were alone so that they could laugh properly and enjoy their food without the audience. 'I refuse to order you a lettuce leaf. It would be criminal.' He proceeded to order in Italian while Taylor drummed long, manicured fingernails on the tablecloth.

Only once the waiter had left, did she speak. 'I can't believe you ordered for me. Dare I ask which unusual part of the anatomy I'm likely to find myself eating this time?'

Sending her a wicked look that brought colour to her cheeks, Luca raised his glass. 'To us! I'm much better at this than you are, by the way. If you like, I can arrange for you to have acting lessons.'

There was a brief pause and then she put her napkin down slowly. 'There's something I have to say to you, Luca, and perhaps this isn't the place but I need to say it so badly....' It was a voice he hadn't heard her use before. Soft, sultry and so richly feminine that the hairs on the back of his neck stood up. She reached across the table and took his hands in hers. 'I've never felt like this before. I'd given up on love. And then I met you and—and I didn't expect...' Her voice faltered and she looked puzzled, almost humbled.

The vulnerability on her face shocked him.

He knew she was acting, but the emotion in her eyes was so genuine he felt an involuntary flicker of panic. She was giving him 'The Look' and The Look was something he'd avoided all his life. He made a point of ending relationships before The Look was even a tiny germ in a woman's brain.

He tried to respond but his tongue was stuck to the roof of his mouth.

Her face was soft, transformed by love. 'I never

thought this would happen. I never thought it was possible to feel love like this and then I met you and—' her breathing was fractured '—and you're everything to me. That's what I wanted to say. I love you. I've never said those words to a man before but I'm saying them now. I'm trusting you with my heart.' The look in her eyes was so adoring his muscles clenched in terror. She was so convincing he couldn't shake the uneasy feeling that crept up his spine.

'*Cristo*, Taylor, you're giving me chills.'

As the waiter murmured something incoherent and melted away, the soft look in her eyes morphed into something harder and more brittle. 'Don't ever call me "kitten paws" again and don't tell me I need acting lessons or the next thing you'll be eating between two slices of bread will be a certain supersensitive part of your anatomy.' As Luca shuddered, another waiter placed food in front of them and Taylor gave an appreciative sniff. 'Mmm. I can see wedded bliss is going to do nothing for my waistline.'

'Eat, *tesoro*. You can go back on your stupid starvation diet tomorrow.'

'I might not need to if the director can't be replaced.'

To another man her insecurity might not have been visible beneath the layers of polish and poise, but Luca had been raised by a woman whose insecurities had been welded into her skin.

*Of course you're beautiful, Mama. Of course he loves you. The other women don't mean anything.*

Unsettled by the emergence of that unwanted memory, he drained his glass and allowed it to be filled again. Why was he thinking about that now when he hadn't thought about it for years? 'He'll be replaced.'

'How do you know?'

'Because I know my cousin. He has many faults, but failing isn't one of them. He's too competitive. Now stop worrying.'

'Aren't you worried about your brother?'

Luca shrugged. 'Why would I be worried?'

'He ran off with your cousin's bride-to-be!'

'That's his problem, not mine. Now try this—it's delicious.' He spooned caponata onto her plate and watched as she dissected it with her fork. 'What are you doing?'

'Looking for its spleen.'

'It's vegetable, *dolcezza*. Vegetables don't have spleens.'

'This dish is vegetarian? You promise?' Cautiously she tasted a small amount and moaned. 'It's delicious.'

He watched as her eyes closed and she savoured the flavours. Her tongue licked at a tiny drop of oil on her lips. She was the most sensual woman he'd met and yet she suppressed it ruthlessly. 'Locally grown food and good olive oil. It doesn't come any better.'

'I don't want to know that it's cooked in oil. So are

all Sicilian kids raised on this? Did your mother make this for you when you were small?'

Mention of his mother wiped his own appetite coming after his own thoughts on that topic. 'No. My mother wasn't the hearth and home type. She had other priorities.' He reached for his glass and changed the subject. 'Did yours cook for you?'

'No. My mother wasn't the hearth and home type either.' The poise didn't slip, but he heard something in her voice. The same dark undertones that coloured his own.

*Her too?*

They had more in common than either of them could have imagined.

'So what type was she?' He surprised himself by asking the question because normally he had no interest in delving beneath the surface of the person he was with and maybe he surprised her too, because she didn't answer immediately.

'The ambitious type. She had big plans for me.'

'She didn't want you to be an actress?'

'It was all she wanted.' She kept her eyes down so that all he could see was the dark fan of her lashes as she concentrated on her food. 'She was determined I would achieve what she hadn't and determined I would be the one to save the family fortunes. She was a single parent and money was tight. When I was a newborn she signed me up for work. I appeared in a daytime soap as someone's baby, then I played toddlers and so it went on. I worked right through my childhood. I didn't go to school—I had tutors on the set.'

'And you hated it?'

'No.' She stabbed her knife through a piece of asparagus. 'I was living every kid's dream.'

'Is that what she told you?'

Her eyes lifted to his and just for a moment he saw a little girl, lost and friendless. Then the look was gone. 'I had the most amazing experiences. I've travelled to places most people only dream about. Our house was always full of famous people.'

'So if it was so fantastic why did you fire her?'

Her face was white, her fingers shaking as she reached for her champagne. 'She was my manager and I decided she didn't have my best interests at heart.'

She was back in control, her insecurities masked by the poised smile she'd perfected. It was as if that unguarded moment had never happened.

'What about your father?'

'My father played no part in my life until he sold his story to the press when I was seventeen.' Lifting her glass, she took a sip. 'Are we done talking about me? Because the journalists outside the restaurant are beginning to create an obstruction. It isn't fair on the other diners. They have a right to eat their meal in peace. We should probably skip dessert and leave.'

Luca turned his head and felt a flash of shock as he

registered the size of the press pack. '*Cristo*, is it always like this?'

'No. Sometimes it's really bad. Today is a quiet day.' Calm, she rose to her feet. 'Shall we go?'

Taylor walked through the tables, acknowledging greetings with a polite smile, hiding her dismay at the number of journalists hovering in wait.

Maybe it was tiredness, maybe it was vulnerability caused by the fact that he'd forced her to talk about things she didn't normally talk about. Maybe it was worry about the film part, but suddenly her control slipped and she stopped dead.

Luca took her hand. 'Ready? We need to look like two people in love as we walk out of this restaurant.'

'I hate them.' She blurted the words out before she could stop herself and he turned with a frown on his face. 'I can't face them.'

'Taylor—'

'They're like hunters, looking for weakness. When they find it they savage you.'

And they'd find hers.

It was only a matter of time before they exposed the one thing she dreaded them exposing. The threat of it had hung over her for so long she could no longer remember how it felt to live without it. It was a constant surprise to her that it hadn't come out before now.

Luca pulled her into the curve of his arm and Taylor gasped.

'What are you doing?'

'You give them too much power over you,' he said softly, his lips in her hair so that no one watching could lip-read or overhear his words. 'Rule number one, be who you really are. It's far more uncomfortable living a lie than living the truth. Rule number two, never let the enemy know your weakness. Now we're going to go out there and you're going to smile or not, whichever you prefer, but you're not going to show them that they scare you, *capisci*?'

His body pressed against hers, hard and powerful, and she realised that he hadn't been pawing her but protecting her. The way he'd angled his body had prevented the press from seeing her sudden panic.

Thrown to discover he was capable of sensitivity, she swallowed. 'I have no idea what *capisci* means but I assume it's some unspeakable part of an animal that you probably just fed me.'

The corners of his mouth flickered into a smile. 'Lift your chin. The first rule of hiding something is not to look as if you're hiding it.'

'I'm not hiding anything.'

'You're hiding more secrets than MI5, *tesoro*, but now is not the time to talk about them. Now smile that perfect smile you've perfected—the one that tells the world everything is good in your life even when it sucks.'

Taylor smiled obediently and he took her hand firmly in his and led her across the vine-covered terrace, down some steps and onto the street.

His hand tightened on hers. 'You are thinking only of me,' he murmured, 'you're not interested in them because you're so in love with me.'

She just had time to mutter 'in your dreams' before they were mobbed.

'Luca, Luca! Can we get a picture of you together?'

'When is the wedding?'

'When did you first meet Taylor?'

There was no such thing as privacy, Taylor thought numbly. There was no question they wouldn't ask. No secret that they wouldn't unearth and expose. They had no limits.

She thought of what they didn't know and turned cold.

It would come out. It always came out.

She hadn't realised she'd stopped walking until she felt Luca's arm tighten round her. 'You've already had more than enough pictures of us together.' He spoke in that lazy drawl that made it sound as if he didn't have a care in the world. 'The wedding will be when we decide it will be and you will most certainly not be invited. Now go and bother someone else.' Gently but firmly he nudged her forward, deflecting the barrage of intrusive questions with casual charm as he guided her to the car.

She envied the ease with which he dealt with them and she left him to do just that and was just about to climb into the passenger seat when he threw her the keys.

'You're driving.'

'You can't be serious?'

'You've had one mouthful of champagne. I intend to take advantage of that. Not to mention the fact that you could barely keep your hands off the wheel earlier. Admit it, you're longing to take this baby for a spin.'

'One car is exactly the same as another to me.'

He smiled. 'Right.'

It drove her mad that he knew her so well after five minutes in her company. 'I'm not a speed merchant like you.'

That maddening smile widened. 'Of course you're not.'

Since her act was obviously wasted on him, Taylor slid behind the wheel, promising herself that she wasn't going to drive fast. No way. She was going to prove that a car like this could be driven sedately. She was going to prove he was wrong about her.

Luca stretched out his legs and rolled his eyes. 'Any time in the next century would be good.'

'I'm taking my time.'

'And while you're taking your time, they're snapping away,' he murmured under his breath. 'Snap, snap, snappety snap. Unless you want tomorrow's headlines to be Taylor Carmichael Forgets How to Drive, I suggest you make a move.'

Horrified by that prospect, Taylor pressed her foot down and the car roared and sprang forward like a racehorse out of the starting gate. 'Oh, I love this.' The words burst from her spontaneously and he smiled.

'So drive it. I presume you have no objection to speed on this occasion, my little petal? Let's lose them, shall we?' With a wolfish smile, Luca put his hand on her thigh and pressed her foot to the floor.

Taylor gasped and heads turned as the engine of the supercar screamed. The paparazzi jumped out of the way and she flinched back in her seat.

'Did I kill anyone?'

He glanced over his shoulder. 'Sadly, no. But if you slam it into reverse now and spin the wheel to the right you might just get lucky.'

'You're terrible.' She gave a snort of laughter and accelerated away, the power making her moan with pleasure. 'I've never driven anything like this before.'

'I can tell. Speed up. If they're going to chase us at least give them something to chase.'

'You're an exhibitionist.'

'This from a woman who ripped her dress at a celebrity wedding.'

'You ripped the dress.'

'And great fun it was too. I'm partial to naked thigh, particularly when it's wrapped around me.'

She felt a rush of relief as they left the photographers behind and she had to admit that the car was sublime. There was something illicit and wickedly good about the power she now controlled. 'Are they following us?'

Tilting his handsome head, he glanced in the rear-view mirror. 'Strangely enough, no. Clearly they think we're off to have boring almost-married sex which no longer makes us worth following.'

'I wish.' She changed gear smoothly and he raised an eyebrow.

'You wish we were having almost-married sex?'

'No! I meant that I wish they thought we're not worth following.' Flustered by the way he made her feel, she shifted gear slightly too early and saw him wince.

'Premature gear-change, *dolcezza*. Keep her hanging on until she's desperate—then you give her what she wants.'

She felt her cheeks burn. 'Is everything about sex to you?'

'This car is all about sex and you know it.'

Taylor kept her eyes fixed on the road. She was trying really hard not to think about sex around this man. Quickly, she changed the subject. 'Thank you for what you did back there.'

'You mean when I chipped your frozen, terrified carcass off the ground? Want to tell me what that sudden panic attack was all about?'

No.

'It wasn't a panic attack.' Ahead of her the setting sun dipped low on the horizon, touching the sea and sending slivers of red across the darkening surface while the soft evening breeze whispered across her face and whipped at her hair.

It was a blissful, perfect moment and Taylor wished she could freeze time and keep things this simple for ever but that wasn't life, was it?

She was aware of Luca watching her, his expression veiled by thick dark lashes. 'You were scared.'

'Journalists do that to me.' Her hair tangled in front of her face and she pushed it away, hating the fact that her fingers were still shaking. She had so much to hide and deep down she knew it was only a matter of time before it all came out. And when it did… 'They wrecked my life.' And they'd wreck it again without a moment of hesitation.

'You mean they wrote stuff about you. You're too sensitive.'

'They wrote about private things. Things that were none of their business. And they lie—' The wind dried her lips and she licked at them. 'Do you honestly not care when they do that?'

'No. If people want to write about me they can go ahead. But I'm not ashamed of who I am. Unlike you.'

'I'm not ashamed! I'm—' She kept her eyes on the road. 'Private. People change. I'm not the same person I was at ten, or seventeen or even twenty-four, so I don't want to have to stare at that version of me when I switch on my computer or open a magazine. And yes, there are things I wish I hadn't done. Things I'd do differently if I had my time again.' Things she regretted deeply.

Her past lurked out there like a beast in the shadows and she knew it was going to pounce. Suddenly she wished she could keep driving into the sunset. Vanish and live a different life.

On impulse, she pulled in by the side of the road and stared at the view. 'It's so beautiful.'

'Sicily is the most beautiful island in the world. That's why I try and spend as much time here as I can.'

The phone in her bag pinged to signify a message, disturbing the moment, and Taylor reached across him eagerly and pulled it out of her bag. 'With luck this will be good news on the director situation.'

But it wasn't and her excitement turned to sick panic as she read the words on the screen.

Her hands grew clammy and her phone almost slid from her fingers.

She wanted to hurl it off the cliff, as if that simple gesture might cut her off from her past and keep her safe. But she knew there was no point. Whatever she did, her past would always haunt her. He would always haunt her.

'Trouble?' Luca was watching her and she tried desperately to pull herself together.

'No.' She shut off her phone and slipped it back into her bag.

'For an actress, you're a terrible liar.'

She knew she wasn't a terrible liar but she was fast discovering that Luca Corretti, for all his reputation as a shallow playboy, was sharp as a razor. 'I'm not lying. Just tired. I wish the press would disappear.'

'You care too much about what people think.'

'You have no idea what it's like.' The lump in her throat appeared from nowhere. 'No idea what it's like having cameras filming your every move from your first step to your first boyfriend. No idea what it's like to be betrayed by the people closest to you—people who are supposed to care about you and love you—and no idea how it feels to wake up and realise the only person in the world you can trust is yourself.' Her outburst shocked her almost as much as it clearly shocked him.

Taylor sat there, wondering how to pull back the words and recover the situation. She was usually so good at hiding her feelings but from the first moment she'd met Luca Corretti those feelings had been perilously close to the surface.

'Sorry.' Her voice was husky. 'Ignore me. It's been a difficult few days for me and today has been the most difficult of all.'

'Why are you apologising? For once, you were honest about your feelings.' Luca stared straight ahead, sunglasses hiding his eyes. Then he turned to look at her and when he spoke there was no trace of his usual humour. 'We should go. Do you want me to drive?'

'No.' She was grateful to him for not delving further but of course he wouldn't, would he? That sort of confession probably came under the heading of 'emotional depth' and Luca Corretti was a man who avoided 'emotional depth' at all costs.

He was no doubt already trying to find ways to ease himself out of their 'fake' engagement because who would want to be engaged to someone as messed up as her?

It took another ten minutes to get back to Luca's house and, as the car purred through the security gates, she spotted cameras and two security guards.

'You say you're not worried about the press but you have very high-level security.'

'That's to protect me from all the women I've upset. And all the ones I haven't yet upset, but probably will in the future.' He was back to his normal self, his tone smooth and bored, and was relieved he clearly didn't intend to question her further about her past.

'I would have thought you needed an army for that.'

'Fortunately for me I now have a fiancée.' The tyres crunched on the gravel and he sprang from the car and opened the door for her in an old-fashioned gesture that surprised her. 'I hate the word, but the institution might prove more useful than I could ever have imagined.'

'So now you're using me as a female defence system?'

'Something like that.' He relieved her of the car keys. 'You drive well for a woman.'

'That is so patronising. If I'd known you were going to say something like that I would have wrapped your precious Ferrari round a lamppost.'

The banter felt so much more comfortable than confidences but just being with him unsettled her. She was used to spending her time around ridiculously attractive men—men who spent their days working on their physique, men who spent a considerable time in front of the mirror, none of whom tempted her. Luca was different. He was spectacularly handsome, that was true, his Sicilian bloodline evident in his darkly brooding features and his volatile personality, but for her the attraction lay deeper. She was drawn to his self-confidence, his lack of pretentiousness and, most of all, his innate honesty. Luca Corretti didn't waste time putting a barrier between himself and the world and if they came too close, he simply shrugged.

As his arm brushed against hers she felt sensation flutter across her skin and float through her body. She was tall but he was significantly taller, much taller than her current leading man, who needed heel lifts and clever camera angles to increase his height. Luca needed no such help.

It was only as he closed the bedroom door behind them that she realised they hadn't discussed this part of their arrangement.

'Where am I sleeping?'

'In my bed, where all good fiancée's sleep.'

Keeping her expression in place she dropped her purse on the soft white sofa. She realised that she was exhausted. She hadn't slept well since hearing the film role was hers and now wouldn't sleep until she knew she hadn't lost it. 'I will sleep in your bed, but not if you're in it.'

'Sleeping apart is not one of the habits of happily engaged couples.'

'Unless you're expecting hoards of slavering women to break into your room tonight, I assume we're not going to have an audience for the next part of our deception?'

'We might. It would strengthen our story if Geovana deserves to hear you moaning with pleasure as she walks past the door.'

'I'm not a moaner.'

He smiled as he undid the buttons of his shirt. 'You'd moan if you were with me, *bellissima*.'

'Sure of yourself, aren't you?'

'I've never subscribed to the benefits of false modesty. I can have you moaning in under thirty seconds. Want to try it out? Practice the scene?'

Her heart was pounding. 'I don't need to practice. I'm a one-take wonder. And the only way I'd moan is if it was written into the script.' Her mouth dried as he shrugged off the shirt, revealing bronzed shoulders and muscles that could have featured in an action movie. The hardness of his physique contrasted with the effortless elegance of his clothes and she clenched her jaw and dismissed the thought that he was better looking than any of the actors she'd worked with.

'Admit it.' Fully aware of her scrutiny, he dropped the shirt over the back of the nearest chair. 'You can't stop thinking about that kiss.'

'What kiss?'

He smiled. 'How does it feel to spend your life pretending to be someone you're not? Uncomfortable? Frustrating?'

'I'm not pretending. This is who I am.'

The smile faded and this time when he looked at her there was no sign of the flippant playboy. 'No. You present the world with a plastic, perfect version of yourself. No flaws. You show the person you think the world wants to see, not the real you. Maybe that's what some men want, but not me.' The hardness of his tone surprised her and she took a step backwards, wondering what had triggered that response.

'But this isn't real so what you want is of no relevance.'

'If I'm expected to spend time with you then it's going to be with the real you. The real you is the woman who was with me in the maze. That woman interests me extremely. Any chance she could come out and play?' His tone had lightened again but it was too late because already there was an electric tension in the atmosphere.

She was so aware of him, almost blinded by the raw sexuality that radiated from every throbbing, muscular inch of his powerful frame. From that silky dark hair to those moody black eyes, he was all man. And the most dangerous thing of all was that, somehow, he knew her. Not the public her that she'd created, but the real her. 'That woman is a figment of your imagination.'

'You had your hands on me. My imagination had nothing to do with it.'

'You had your hands on me first.'

'I never said it wasn't mutual.' Those eyes were dark as night, seeing everything she was hiding.

'It isn't mutual.'

'Sweetheart, you should know that I have a highly competitive nature and you're tempting me to prove it.'

'No.' She looked away from him, trying to snap the connection. Trying to pull together the torn threads of her protection. 'It was just a kiss. A badly timed kiss as it turns out.'

'Maybe not. We're here because of that kiss.'

'Precisely!'

Without warning he slid his hand behind her neck and drew her towards him. 'Once again we see things differently. You see this as a bad thing, but because of this situation I finally have the board listening to me and you—'

'I'm on a film that currently has no director.' His mouth was so close to hers she was afraid to breathe. 'How is that good?'

His phone buzzed and he paused, his eyes locked on hers.

For a moment she thought he was going to ignore it and then he let his hand drop. Instantly she stepped backwards, creating distance, and he gave her a mocking smile as he drew his phone out of his pocket and read the message. Dark brows rose. 'Apparently you do have a director.'

'We do?' Taylor's heart was pounding in her chest. 'He found someone? Who?'

'Rafaele Beninato.'

Just hearing the name made her feel sick.

'Are you sure?' It was her worst nightmare and the irony was that if she hadn't been caught in the maze with Luca, it wouldn't have happened. The first director would still be in place. But Rafaele had found a way to infiltrate her life, as he always had.

'His name is familiar. Didn't you and he have a thing once?'

'I—yes. But it was a long time ago.' She'd been seventeen years old and had been thrown out of the house by her mother. She'd been young, vulnerable and desperately lonely. A perfect target for a calculating opportunist like Rafaele. How had he got himself on the movie? He must have been stalking Santo Corretti as well as her.

Whatever the reason, her relationship with trouble had stopped being long distance and was suddenly right up close.

Luca glanced up from his phone. 'Bit old for you, isn't he?'

She was struggling to think. 'Is this the part where we talk about our past relationships?'

He looked at her steadily and then slowly put his phone down. 'I'll assume from your defensive response he was one of the ones who let you down. Is it going to be difficult to work with him?'

'I'm a professional,' Taylor croaked. 'I'll work with anyone I'm expected to work with. No problem. I'm just pleased to have a new director.'

'Are you sure?' His tone was deceptively casual. 'Because I can rough him up a little if you like. I'm your fiancé after all.'

She gave a choked laugh. Was it pathetic of her to wish, just for a minute, that their engagement was real and for once in her life she had someone who cared enough to offer support? 'If you rough him up we'll be minus a director again. And I want to act. I must do this film.' Not just because the complexity of the role would finally earn her a reputation as a serious actress, but also because she didn't want to give Rafaele the slightest reason to use what he had against her.

Luca stared down at her for a long moment. 'All right. But he'd better not step out of line. I've met him a couple of times. The guy gives me the creeps. They want you on set at eight tomorrow morning to start filming the docklands scenes. He said he texted you but you switched your phone off.'

She hadn't wanted to see another text from Rafaele. In the past she'd blocked him and changed her phone but he always managed to find a way to contact her.

'I like to relax when I'm off set.' She didn't confess that she never relaxed because lurking in the back of her mind was the knowledge that her secrets could be revealed at any time.

Secrets that Rafaele knew.

And now he was back in her life.

Luca glanced at his watch. 'I'll drop you on set with a large fuss and dance and then pick you up later. And Randy Rafaele had better keep his hands to himself.'

He was seriously proposing that they spend the night together? In the same room?

Suddenly she realised that she had more immediate problems than Rafaele and that problem was six foot two of insanely sexy man.

'They have a trailer for me,' Taylor stammered. 'I should stay there. It's usually pretty luxurious.'

'There is no way I'm spending the night in a trailer for anyone, however luxurious.' Luca's appalled expression was almost comical. 'I'm strictly a five-star guy.'

'I wasn't inviting you to stay with me. I was suggesting we don't spend the night together.'

An incredulous dark eyebrow rose. 'People are no doubt struggling to believe I'm engaged. If we don't spend the night together the whole thing is blown. We'll stay here and I'll drive you. That's much more romantic. What's the film about anyway? I probably ought to know what my beloved is spending her day doing.'

Her gaze skidded round the room. If he wouldn't sleep on the couch then she would. There was no way she was sharing the bed with this man. No way.

'The heroine's husband was missing in Iraq, presumed killed. She goes to bed with his friend, gets pregnant and then the husband turns up alive. It's a film about forgiveness, I suppose. It's a very emotional role.'

Luca shuddered. 'Chick flick. Don't invite me to the premiere.'

'No chance of that. Do you have another room I can use? I need to read through the script if I'm filming first thing tomorrow. It's part of my routine and I don't want to keep you awake.'

'My routine is to have hot sex the night before a big meeting and I definitely do want to keep you awake.'

His smile was slow and lazy, his gaze unapologetically sexual as he focused on her mouth.

She felt her limbs weaken. He was gorgeous. Too gorgeous. 'You're winding me up.'

'Maybe I'm not.' Dark eyes grazed hers from under long, sinfully thick lashes. 'Maybe I think you and I would be explosive together, Taylor Carmichael. Maybe I think we might as well take advantage of this situation.'

'Yeah, right—and tomorrow you'd sell the story to the press.'

'I'd never do that.' His voice was suddenly cold. 'Anything the press printed wouldn't have come from me.'

She thought about Portia and realised he suffered from the same problem. 'Doesn't it upset you? When women talk to the press about you—doesn't that make you mad?'

'No, because I haven't the slightest interest in what the general public think of me.'

'So what *do* you care about, Luca Corretti? There must be something.'

'I care about living my life the way I want to live it. I'm not a people pleaser—' his eyes mocked her gently '—except in bed. That's the one place I'm willing to make an exception to my rule.'

'Then go ahead. I'm not stopping you. If you can

find a woman brainless enough to have sex with you then call her. I'd rather sleep in the spare room anyway.'

'No, you wouldn't. Admit it, Carmichael—you're tempted.'

'I'm so not tempted.'

'Yes, you are. But you won't give in to it—' his hand cupped her face and he stroked her cheek with his thumb '—because you're scared to death of being yourself with anyone any more. You are so busy holding yourself back you've almost forgotten how to live.'

Her heart was pounding.

He was supposed to be a shallow playboy so how did he manage to read her so well?

'I know this will come as a shock to you, but the fact that I don't want to rip your clothes is because I just don't find you attractive.' His response to that was to laugh and she pulled away from him. 'You are so arrogant. You just can't imagine there is a woman who doesn't want you, can you?'

'I'm sure somewhere in the universe there may be a woman who doesn't want me—it just doesn't happen to be you. But we'll see how long that self-control of yours lasts when it's really tested, *dolcezza*. You can sleep in the bed tonight. I'll take the sofa.'

And with that he walked into the bathroom leaving her fuming, confused and more desperate for a man than she could ever remember feeling in her life before.

# CHAPTER SIX

THE SET WAS heaving with people when Luca dropped Taylor off the next morning.

He'd been intending to leave immediately, but he took one look at her white face and parked his car in a no-parking zone.

'Are you going to be all right?'

She turned her head to look at him, her expression blank, the dark shadows under her eyes telling him she'd lain awake for most of the night. 'Pardon?'

And Luca realised the reason she hadn't responded to a single word he'd said during the journey was because she hadn't heard him.

And the cause of her distress lurked at the edge of the set like a lion waiting for an injured impala to leave the safety of the herd and limp into the open.

Rafaele.

Luca knew the director was going to take one look at her pale face and see a potential victim.

With a soft curse, he unclipped his seat belt and she looked at him in confusion.

'What are you doing? You're going to be late for your meeting.'

Luca stroked her pale cheek with the backs of his fingers. 'I hope the make-up department on this film is good because you look like hell, Carmichael. Shame you're not making a vampire movie.'

'Make-up…?' She gasped and scrabbled for her bag. 'How could I have forgotten make-up?'

Because she'd been distracted. Scared.

Luca tapped his fingers on the wheel and thought quickly. 'I suppose I should apologise.'

'For what?'

'It's my fault you couldn't sleep last night. You should have just taken me up on my offer, *dolcezza*, instead of lying awake desperate for me.'

'Desperate for you?' Her voice rose slightly. 'You think I was desperate for you?'

'I know you were. You should have just admitted how you felt. There's no shame in finding me irresistible. It happens.'

'Not to me.' Two streaks of angry colour highlighted her cheekbones and Luca smiled and sprang from the car.

'*Bene*. Forget the make-up. You don't need it and he doesn't need to see you putting it on. You're ready.'

'Ready for what? Ready to kill you? You make me so mad I could—I could—'

'You could thank me. Two minutes ago you were the colour of mozzarella. Now you look human. Anger is instant blusher. So is sexual arousal, by the way, but I'll save that trick for when we're alone. And by "ready" I mean ready to face him.' Sliding his hand around her waist, he hauled her against him and lowered his voice. 'Never go up against a man like Rafaele showing you're afraid. Go out there and fight.'

Her eyes were wide. 'You made me angry on purpose?'

'*Sì*. Making a woman want to kill me is my special gift. It ensures they don't exceed their sell-by date.'

She made a sound between a sob and curled her fingers into the front of his shirt. 'You're—you're—'

'I'm perfect. Now smile—' he kissed the top of her head '—we have company. Not the company I would have chosen, but such is life. Ah, Rafaele, I saw you admiring my car. Work hard and maybe one day you'll be able to afford one.'

Rafaele ignored Luca and looked straight at Taylor. It was like an eagle spotting a vole.

To give her credit, Taylor managed to look relaxed as she greeted him. 'Rafaele.'

'*Querida*. We have so much to catch up on.' The

sentence was loaded with subtext and Luca frowned slightly and was about to intervene when Taylor stepped forward.

'My name is Taylor.' Her voice was steady and strong. 'And we don't have anything to catch up on.'

'And soon she'll be Taylor Corretti,' Luca said coldly, 'so you might want to bear that in mind before you call her *"querida"* or anything else that implies intimacy. I don't tolerate other men hitting on my woman. Unlike the wimp in your movie, I don't forgive or forget.' He draped a possessive arm around her shoulders, his eyes fixed on the older man's face in blatant challenge. He thought of Taylor as she must have been at seventeen and then looked at the man standing in front of him and decided he didn't like what he saw.

Rafaele stepped forward, eyes narrowed. 'I read about the engagement. I see her taste in men hasn't improved over the years.'

'I disagree.' Luca delivered his coolest smile. 'Any time you want to treat yourself to a suit that fits properly, just give me a call. Well-cut quality fabric can transform even the most unfortunate of body shapes. I'm sure we can do something for you.' He could sense Taylor's tension. And something more. Nerves. This man made her nervous.

Clearly her history with Rafaele upset her deeply and it was obvious the director knew it and used it.

'I hope all this personal stuff isn't going to distract

you from your work. This is a challenging role for someone like you.' With every carefully chosen word he chipped away at the woman Taylor had become, exposing the vulnerability underneath.

Luca, who loathed bullies, resisted the urge to rearrange the other man's features. 'Taylor is the most talented actress of her generation. When you worked with her she was hampered by bad direction.'

Rafaele's lips curled. 'Taylor always responded well to direction.'

Luca stepped forward but Taylor's hand gripped his arm.

'I can handle this. I just want to do my job.'

'Good—' Rafaele gestured to one of the crew '—because today we're filming the scene where you discover the husband you thought was dead, is alive.'

'Obviously going to be a laugh a minute,' Luca drawled, turning her away from Rafaele and towards him. 'I'll leave you to it, *tesoro*, and pick you up at the end of the day. The board want evidence that you're real so we're going to a drinks reception at the hotel. Not my favourite way to spend an evening. I'd much rather be alone with you.' Before she could say anything, he cupped her face in his hands and kissed her slowly and deliberately on the mouth. The kiss was for the benefit of Rafaele but the moment their mouths met they were lost in it, the passion raw and elemental. He kissed her hungrily and she kissed him back, their surroundings forgotten, everything forgotten until the blare of a car horn cut through the sexual storm. Luca lifted his head, disorientated.

He stared down into her shocked blue eyes, saw his own confusion reflected right back at him and released her instantly. 'I should get to work....'

'Me too.' Her voice was husky and Luca, unsettled by how badly he wanted to kiss her again, backed towards the car and crashed into Rafaele, who made his frustration known.

'Look where you're going!'

Luca was too shaken to bother responding. Instead he slid behind the wheel of his Ferrari and started the engine, instantly comforted by the throaty roar. At least something in his life felt familiar which was more than could be said for his feelings.

He couldn't remember a time when he'd been so out of control with a woman. When had he ever before lost track of time or place? Never.

Pulling onto the road that led to the office, he told himself that he'd got a little carried away with his role. After all, she'd questioned his acting ability, so it was only natural that he would try and prove how wrong she was, wasn't it? He was as competitive as the next guy and any suggestion that he might not be convincing in his role as 'fiancé' was guaranteed to result in a performance worthy of Hollywood.

Having justified his behaviour to his satisfaction and

confident that he had the situation completely under control, Luca relaxed.

He'd helped her deal with that slimy bastard Rafaele and she, in turn, could turn on her charm for the board.

So far their plan was working magnificently.

'So, Taylor, I admit we never saw this happening. Luca has never shown any degree of responsibility in anything he does. He's chosen to live his life on the fringe of this family.' The air on the sunlit terrace of the Corretti flagship hotel was thick with cigarette smoke and disapproval of Luca.

Taylor, who knew exactly how it felt to feel disconnected from the family you'd been born into, disliked the pompous chairman on sight. 'I'm confused.' She smiled her most feminine smile and had the satisfaction of seeing him blink, dazed. 'You say Luca has no sense of responsibility and yet he's built a staggeringly successful business worth a fortune.'

'Luca appears more interested in the models he employs than he is in taking business seriously.'

'I disagree. Luca is a man who works hard but also plays hard. He appreciates beauty. To be able to achieve the level of success he has achieved and yet still have fun seems to me to indicate a man who appreciates the importance of work-life balance.'

'Your defence of him is to your credit.'

'But should a man need defending from his own

family?' Taylor was beginning to understand why they drove Luca mad. She glanced up and saw him surrounded by members of the hotel management team. He didn't even bother to conceal his boredom and she hid a smile because she sensed he went out of his way to live up to his terrible reputation.

And suddenly she realised what a clever strategy that was. Because he didn't appear to hide anything, no one looked deeper. No one suspected there was anything more to expose, which gave him an extraordinary level of privacy.

He lifted his head and caught her eye.

Just for a moment they looked at each other and the sexual charge was so powerful she felt the punch of it from across the room.

Her stomach tightened as she remembered the way it felt to kiss him and be kissed by him.

Turning away quickly she reminded herself that a kiss, even an exceptionally skilled kiss, wasn't trust. A kiss was a type of sensual manipulation. Trust was something different.

And trust was an indulgence she didn't allow herself.

Extracting himself from the group of grey-suited businessmen, Luca joined her.

The chairman smiled. 'You'll be pleased to hear your fiancée was defending you vigorously. We were discussing your addiction to beautiful women.'

Feeling Luca's tension, Taylor slid her arm through his. 'I'm thrilled Luca appreciates beauty.'

'Many women would be jealous.'

'Perhaps. But not me. We're with each other through choice. Love cannot be bound and held captive. It has to be freely given.'

Luca was looking at her strangely but he didn't say anything and the chairman beckoned to an overweight man in a suit. 'Taylor, this is Nico Gipetti, manager of our flagship hotel. You're his idol so he's been hoping for an introduction.'

Nico Gipetti's face turned scarlet up to his ears as he shook her hand vigorously. 'I love your work.' Having stammered his way through a stream of compliments, he turned to Luca. 'Any news from Matteo?'

'Not a sound.' Luca was looking at her mouth. 'But I suppose that isn't so surprising in the circumstances.'

The manager's features tightened in disapproval. 'What does he think he's doing?'

'I should think right now he's probably smashing his way through all ten commandments,' Luca murmured and then winced when Taylor drove her elbow into his ribs.

'What Luca means,' she said swiftly, 'is that he's probably keeping a low profile out of sensitivity to Alessandro's feelings.'

'So you have no idea when he will be back?'

Luca suppressed a yawn. 'No, but while he's away I

intend to increase your profits by an indecent amount
so I suggest you all relax and let me get on with it. I
work much better alone.'

And why was that? Taylor studied him thoughtfully,
wondering why he was so determined to keep himself
apart, both in work and in play.

'It's a difficult time for the market,' Nico snapped.
'What makes you think you can do what we can't? You
know nothing about the hotel business.'

'And that is precisely why I will make it a success.'
Luca paused to study the cut of the suit of a man walking past, a perusal that ended in a disbelieving shake
of his head. 'I don't come weighed down with precon-
ceived ideas, nor am I working from a palette of ideas
that have been used a million times before by both
yourselves and the competition.'

The chairman joined in the conversation. 'Perhaps
this is a good time to give us some detail. I'm sure
Nico is interested to hear how you intend to add value
to the brand.'

'That's easy. Your occupancy is down because you
have no appreciation of style or beauty,' Luca said
bluntly and Taylor almost laughed at the shock on their
faces.

She loved his honesty. He didn't care what people
thought, which meant he wasn't afraid to speak the
truth. Working in a profession where people rarely told

the truth, she found it a refreshing change to be with someone who spoke his mind.

Sadly Nico didn't agree. 'Perhaps we should talk in Italian so that we don't bore Taylor with our business.'

Luca scooped up two glasses of champagne from a pretty waitress with a wink and a smile. 'Taylor doesn't speak Italian—' he handed her a glass '—and unlike you, Nico, I have no problem with my fiancée expressing an opinion. I'd like her to be part of the conversation.'

They put him down at every turn and yet he was bigger than all of them, she thought. He had an innate confidence, a powerful belief in himself that resisted all their attempts to diminish him. They tried to make him look small and yet each time they knocked him down he rose higher, towering above them in every way.

She felt a flash of pride and then wondered why she would feel pride in a man who wasn't hers.

Unsettled, she sipped her champagne and asked the question no one else seemed interested in asking. 'So do you have a plan for the hotels, Luca?'

Luca didn't hesitate. 'We're going to refurbish the top six from the latest Corretti Home collection. Out with bland, hotel uniformity and in with style and originality. Instead of guests walking away with white waffle dressing gowns they could purchase from any retail outlet, they come away with ideas for decorating their own homes and recreating luxury in their everyday lives. They leave not just rested, but inspired.'

Nico spluttered over his drink. 'The Corretti name is already a strong brand. We don't need your help with that.'

Luca smiled. 'By the time I've finished Corretti won't be a brand, it will be a lifestyle.'

There was a stunned silence.

Nico hadn't touched his drink. 'You're assuming people would want your lifestyle.'

'How could they not?' Luca slid his arm round Taylor, who smiled up at him in full-on adoring-fiancée mode, but this time the act was easy because her admiration was genuine.

'So you're giving people the message that if they stay in a Corretti hotel, they soak up some of the Corretti style—that's a totally brilliant idea.'

A faint frown touched his forehead. *'Grazie, bellissima.'* He hesitated and then lowered his head and kissed her gently. 'And now I think about it, you'd be perfect to front the campaign I have planned. Corretti Hotels—First Choice for Taylor Carmichael, Movie Star.'

'I'd have to stay in it first, just to check it has my approval.'

His smile was intimate. 'Once the hotel has been refurbished, we'll christen the Presidential Suite.'

Her gaze collided with his. Her stomach twisted.

The chemistry between them rocketed off the scale. Through the thick, lazy heat of sexual awareness she heard the chairman clear his throat.

'It seems Luca has extravagant plans for the business, but what about the two of you?' He beamed at them. 'You're just so perfect for each other. It occurred to us that a Corretti wedding would focus attention away from Matteo's untimely elopement.'

'Was it untimely?' Still looking at Taylor, Luca raised his eyebrows. 'I thought the timing was perfect.'

Taylor, still shaken by the depth of the physical connection between them, decided that goading the board was a sport to him.

'What Luca means,' she said quickly, 'is that there is never a good time for such a thing to happen.'

'Perhaps not.' The chairman didn't look convinced. 'But there is no doubt that your wedding would divert attention and give the press something positive to think about. You should marry without delay.'

It was a suggestion she hadn't anticipated and Taylor felt Luca's arm tighten around her.

'A rushed wedding would lead people to assume Taylor was pregnant and none of us want that.'

The chairman's smile faded. 'You don't want to be pregnant?'

'Of course she wants to be pregnant.' Luca's gaze drifted over the heads of the people around them. 'But not before we're married.'

The chairman relaxed slightly. 'The press is full of pictures of your romantic dinner together last night. Love has transformed you, Luca. A big family is exactly what you need. I assume Taylor will be giving up her career once you're married?'

Taylor choked on her champagne and Luca thumped her on the back.

'Taylor can't wait to have children,' he said smoothly as he gave her time to compose herself. 'To the world she's this fantastic, glamorous movie star but underneath all she wants is to walk barefoot round my kitchen, cooking my dinner and nursing my babies. She's a real earth-mother type, aren't you, *angelo mia*?'

Taylor had the feeling he was enjoying himself hugely. 'Babies—' she played along '—I can't wait. We've agreed on at least six, haven't we, Luca?'

'Six?' It was his turn to be startled. 'Of course, *bellissima*. I'm all too happy to make as many babies as you would like as long as you're sure you can cope with them while I'm away on business. Which might be often.' His sensual mouth flickered at the corners and she found herself looking at that mouth and thinking of the way he kissed.

'We'll travel with you, my heart.'

'*Bene!* I'll be working on my laptop while six adorable little children, all dressed in Corretti Bambino crawl all over you wanting you to read to them, play with them and tuck them in at night.'

The image he painted was so vivid she couldn't breathe. It was supposed to be a private joke but Taylor didn't feel like laughing. How would it feel, she wondered, to have a family like that? A family that supported one another? It wasn't a life she'd ever imagined for herself. Whenever she looked into her future she saw herself alone because any alternative scenario involved trust, and she knew she wasn't capable of that.

Sadness squeezed her chest, as unexpected as it was painful.

The chairman patted Luca on the shoulder. 'We'll leave you two young things to mingle.' Smiling benignly, he drew Nico away and Luca and Taylor were left alone in the crowd.

Realising that some response was expected from her, she gave a wan smile. 'I didn't realise you had a Corretti Bambino range.'

'We don't, but I'm just realising what an opportunity we're missing. I've finally found a use for children—I can use them to increase my profits. And the idea has potential to be expanded into the hotel group—a range of clothes to give guests the chance to make sure their child co-ordinates perfectly with their hotel suite. If we do it well, they won't even know the children are there.'

She knew she was supposed to laugh. She knew he was being outrageous on purpose, but the lump in her throat was wedged so securely she didn't trust herself to speak and the feelings were so unexpected she had no idea how to deal with them.

Registering her lack of response, his smile faded and he tilted his head slightly. 'You're furious with me? I was joking, *tesoro*. I know you wouldn't want all that barefoot and pregnant in the kitchen stuff, but it was what they needed to hear.'

'Yes.' Her voice husky and she changed the subject quickly. 'Your family seems about as supportive as mine. Why do you want to work with them when you already have your own successful business?'

'Because they think I can't do it.' Luca removed her empty glass from her hand and gave it to a waitress. 'I have a congenital urge to prove everyone around me wrong. And I'm a Corretti. We were born competitive.' As he talked, Taylor felt herself relax and decided she was just tired. Everyone had strange thoughts when they were tired, didn't they?

'But you're not just Corretti, are you? You're Marco Sparacino's grandson.'

'Have you been looking me up?'

'Maybe.'

'*Non importa*. I looked you up too.'

'I'm boring, but your grandfather was a fashion legend. Right up there with Chanel and Dior. I read his autobiography, *A Life in Colour*. It was fascinating. What was it like growing up with him?'

'It was hell. He used to criticise what we were wearing. It drove my mother insane. No matter how she dressed, he used to tell her what she should be doing differently. It made her deeply insecure and she grew up thinking every problem could be solved if you were wearing the right thing.' There was an edge to his voice that made her want to delve deeper but it wasn't the right time or the right place, with people pressing in on them from all sides.

'I've seen photos of your mother. She's always so elegant.'

Luca's fingers tightened on the stem of his glass. 'Appearance was—still is—important to her.'

'The daughter of Marco Sparacino—how could it not be? So how did you handle him? I can't imagine you did what you were told.'

'I got so fed up with my grandfather telling me I was wearing the wrong thing that I once turned up to a lunch stark naked.' Luca drained his glass. 'When he bawled me out I told him there was no point in getting dressed because he always told me to get changed anyway. He never criticised me after that.'

Taylor laughed. 'I can imagine you saying that. How old were you?'

'Nine, I think. I don't remember. All I remember was learning that pleasing people is a thankless task and you're much better off pleasing yourself.'

'But you made him proud. You've turned Corretti

into something that people associate with luxury and elegance.'

'When I took over, the focus was on couture. I persuaded them to take a more integrated business model. We expanded into ready-to-wear and accessories and then we launched Corretti Home. Furniture, lighting, bed linen...' He gave a mocking smile. 'You can date in your Corretti dress and then go home and have sex on your luxurious Corretti sofa wrapped up in Corretti sheets.'

'Is that your tag line? Corretti—Bedlinen for Better Sex?'

'Not officially but I think it's possibly an improvement on the one we picked for the campaign. Thank you, by the way—' his tone was casual '—you were brilliant tonight. I haven't had a chance to ask how it went today on set. Did Rafaele behave himself?'

'It went well.' She chose not to divulge just how awful the day had been but Luca's gaze was steady on her face and she had a feeling he knew.

'If he steps out of line, tell me.'

'He's my problem.'

'You're my fiancée.'

Her stomach curled and knotted. And that, she thought, was turning out to be more complicated than she'd ever imagined.

A week later, exhausted after days of filming with Rafaele and sleepless nights in Luca's bedroom, Taylor slid a pair of dark glasses onto her nose, took a deep breath and left her trailer. Blinded by a storm of camera flashes she struggled to keep the smile in place and it came as a relief to see the red blaze of Luca's Ferrari. He was leaning against the bonnet, talking into his phone.

'No, I haven't heard from my brother. No, I don't have any comment on his behaviour,' he drawled, grabbing Taylor's hand and hauling her against him. 'I'm the last person to comment on anyone's behaviour.... I don't have a comment on my own either because frankly it's none of your business.' He hung up and pulled her into him. '*Cristo*, you're sexy. How was your day?'

'Exhausting. I filmed the scene where my husband appears from the dead and discovers I'm carrying his best friend's baby.' And she'd worked harder than she'd ever worked in order to make sure no criticism could be levelled at her but still the director had managed to make her feel inferior with his constant sniping. He'd made her redo each scene repeatedly even though she knew it had been perfect the first time. He'd wanted her to lose her temper and she'd been determined to hang on to control even if it killed her.

'What you need is to chill or, better still, get hot and naked with someone and that someone is me.'

She found herself looking into sultry, sexy eyes fringed with impossibly thick, dark lashes and wishing she could do just that. And then she found herself wishing she could turn off her senses because she didn't want to feel this way.

Spending so much time in his company was creating a level of tension she hadn't thought possible. He was supposed to be a solution to a problem, instead of which he was becoming the problem.

Her instinctive response was to pull back but she was expected to play her part so when he flattened his hand against her back and drew her against him, she lifted her mouth to his. She'd intended it to be a brief kiss but his hands came up to her face and he kissed her slowly and hungrily. And because he was so good at this, because he somehow knew everything there was to know about exactly the right way to kiss her, she didn't even try to fight it.

Seduced by the heat of his mouth and the skill of his kiss, Taylor felt will power drain from her like rain water down the gutter. If it had been up to her she never would have stopped. Who would choose to end something so perfect? And in the end he was the one who slowly lifted his head and broke the connection.

Dizzy with it, Taylor looked up at him, expecting to see mockery, but he wasn't laughing.

And she wasn't laughing either.

'Let's get out of here.' It was the most serious she'd ever heard him and suddenly she was relieved she'd thought about this earlier before he'd fused her brain with the skill of his mouth.

'I've already planned tonight. I have a surprise for you—tickets for the opera in Palermo.' The idea had come to her halfway through the day when she'd been desperate to do something that allowed them to be 'seen' together, but still gave her privacy from the public. What better place than a dark box high above the auditorium? And it had the added benefit that she'd be saved from intimate conversation.

She had no idea if he even liked opera and no opportunity to ask him with the journalists surrounding them. One of them pushed against her in an attempt to elbow the competition out of the way and Taylor would have stumbled but a strong arm came round her waist. Holding her safe in the protective circle of his arm, Luca snapped something in Italian that Taylor didn't understand. Whatever it was that he said turned the man several shades paler and he backed away, giving them space, hands raised in a gesture of apology.

'Get in the car, *dolcezza*.' Luca was calm and in control. 'I'll get you out of here.'

Grateful to him, Taylor slid into the Ferrari thinking how much easier it was to handle the press when he was with her. He wore the Corretti power as lightly and elegantly as his immaculate suits but there was strength and steel under the casual sophistication and she knew the press found him intimidating. They treated him with a degree of caution they never afforded to her.

'Thank you.'

He didn't have to ask what she was thanking him for. 'I'm starting to understand why you're so scared of the press. They never leave you alone.' He was frowning as he weaved through the heavy Palermo traffic. 'Has it always been like that?'

'Yes. Right from the beginning. I had a mother who knew how to give them exactly what they wanted. She was the master at drawing media attention and using it.'

'Just what you want when you're an awkward adolescent.'

'It's got worse since then. I've come to accept I'll never shake them off. My dream is to go out and for no one to recognise me. Once, just once, I'd love to live life like a normal person, not having to worry about who is pointing a camera and how what I do will be interpreted. Can you imagine that?' She gave a short, desperate laugh because she knew it was never going to happen.

'What would you do? If you could go out and not be recognised—what would you do?'

'I don't know. Just go to a concert or something and stand in the crowd. Blend in. But seeing as that isn't going to happen, I choose to do things that give me some privacy. Do you even like opera? It seemed like a good idea but now I'm not sure.'

'I'm Sicilian. I love opera.'

She relaxed slightly. Even the most persistent observer was unlikely to interrupt the opera to ask them questions about their relationship, and the bonus was that they wouldn't be able to talk. He wouldn't be able to make some sharp comment that showed how easily he saw through to the person she really was.

He already knew far too much about her.

An evening at the opera should be perfect.

Except that it didn't turn out that way.

She'd thought that the dark would protect them from prying eyes, but it turned out she was wrong about that too.

Seated close together in the privacy of a box, his leg brushed against hers and she immediately ceased to focus on anything that was happening on the stage. She was aware of heads turning towards them in the darkness and felt a brief flicker of frustration that even here, in the protected atmosphere of the opera theatre, they couldn't escape the scrutiny of the public.

But that irritation gave way to deeper, darker concerns. Like the fact that although their engagement might be fake there was nothing fake about the sexual tension simmering between them. It was raw, hot and real and becoming harder to ignore with each burning look they exchanged. And the intensity of the feeling confused her. He was insanely handsome, of course, but she'd met enough handsome men during the course of her career to be immune to the combination of perfectly proportioned features and a powerful physique. No, the connection came from something deeper. Something she saw beneath the surface layers of eye-catching masculinity. And whatever it was that drew her, drew her now as they sat close together, thigh pressed against thigh in the dark intimacy of the opera house.

As drama unfolded on the stage beneath them, so drama unfolded in the box.

She was aware of every beat of her heart. Aware of *him* and when Luca's hand covered hers she knew she ought to pull hers way but she didn't. Couldn't. So instead of ending it there she laced her fingers with his and he drew her hand onto his thigh. It was a subtle, sensual dance between man and woman. Her gaze was fixed on the stage but she saw nothing, heard nothing, felt nothing except the strength of his fingers on hers and the hard muscle of his thigh under her palm. Heat traced her skin, desire knotted low in her pelvis and she opened her eyes because closing them left the world to her imagination and that was a dangerous place to be right now.

She'd promised herself no more relationships. She'd trained herself to ignore that wild, passionate part of herself that had got her into trouble in the past. She'd decided there would be no more unguarded moments where she trusted a man only to wake up the next morning and discover the personal had become public.

But this—this was more temptation than she knew how to deal with.

She'd chosen to wear a floor-length dress but that

proved to be no barrier because somehow his hand was on her bare thigh, his long skilled fingers tantalisingly close to that part of her. She clamped her thighs together but the movement didn't dislodge his hand and she felt his fingers stroke inside her panties and her face burned in the darkness because she knew he'd find her already aroused. She turned her head and was scorched by the dark heat in his eyes. Her breathing was shallow and so was his and he held her gaze as his fingers slid deeper, exploring her with erotic precision and unapologetic intimacy until not moving took all her willpower. But she couldn't move or make a sound because that would have risked drawing the attention of the audience away from the performance onstage and so she was forced to stay totally still and silent. And he took ruthless advantage, relentless in his delivery of pleasure as he explored the slick heat of her, creating sensation so wickedly good she was forced to clamp her jaws closed to hold back the sound.

She wanted him to stop. She didn't want him to stop. She didn't know what she wanted but he knew and he took her there, with nothing but his fingers and the intensity of his hot, dark gaze that held hers all the way through the pulsing shock waves of her climax.

On stage the soprano was singing her way to the grave but here, in the shaded darkness of the box, it was all about life and passion.

Shattered and trembling, Taylor stared at him. He

leaned in, bringing his mouth close to hers. His kiss was slow, lingering, deliberate. Personal. Less of an assault and more a promise and she realised there was no way this was over. His hand was still between her legs. Her hand was in his lap and he was painfully aroused, rock hard under her warm palm.

Time passed. She had no idea how much time until applause washed around her. For a terrible moment she thought they were clapping for her and then realised that the singing had stopped. The opera had finished. And she was expected to stand up and act as if nothing had happened.

It was Luca who gently eased away from her and smoothed her dress before the lights came up and she was grateful for the dress because it concealed how much her legs were shaking. She wasn't sure she was capable of walking, but he took her arm calmly and somehow she managed to walk out of the box, through the crowd, as if the passion had all been on the stage and not between the two of them.

There were stares, of course, but she was used to that.

What she wasn't used to was feeling so out of control.

Taylor kept her head down as they walked, ignoring the demands of the press to know when they were getting married, afraid to look at him because she had no idea what was in her eyes.

Flashbulbs blinded her as Luca accelerated away in the Ferrari and she was so relieved by the burst of speed that left everyone else far behind she didn't even snipe at him.

She didn't speak.

He didn't speak.

But the tension throbbed between them like a living force, thickening the air until it was almost impossible to breathe, the atmosphere sexually charged and the heat almost unbearable.

Their restraint lasted until they closed the bedroom door and then they both moved. Together. At the same time, mouths fused, hands desperate, tearing at fabric, sliding over skin, greedy for each other and determined to feed the hunger.

His jacket hit the floor.

Her dress slithered after it.

Her hands ripped at his shirt, exposing wide shoulders and hard male muscle, and she felt that muscle flex as he lifted her easily and flattened her against the wall. Her eyes closed. His mouth was hot on her neck and on the exposed curve of her breasts. He dragged down the lace of her bra and fastened his mouth over her nipple, the skilled flick of his tongue dragging a gasp from her. It was a relief to be able to let the sound escape.

She wound her leg around his hips and felt him shift slightly as he loosened his belt. Desperate, he fumbled for something and then his trousers hit the floor with the rest of their clothes and she felt the silken hardness of him against her thigh.

'*Ti voglio tanto*—I want you.' Switching between languages, Luca stumbled over the words, his hand behind her neck as he brought his mouth down on hers and captured her lips in a raw, explicit kiss that sent shock waves of sensation rocketing through her body.

'Me too—me too...' She was barely coherent as she closed her hand round the thick length of him, heard him groan and say something in Italian she didn't understand and then his hands were under her bottom and he was lifting her, supporting her weight with his arms as he pressed her back against the wall and entered her with a single hard thrust that joined them completely. The feel of him deep inside her was so shockingly good she cried out. No silence for her this time as the hot, hard heat of him consumed her and no silence from him either as he released a raw, primitive groan that originated somewhere deep in his throat.

She was already so wet from the erotic torment of their silent foreplay at the opera her body welcomed his, clamping round the silken strength of him, testing his control. She knew a brief moment of relief that he'd used a condom and then sanity left her and there was only the madness they created together.

'*Cristo*—' His voice unsteady, he thrust deeper even though deeper didn't seem possible because he was already part of her and they moved together, fast, hard, desperate as they let the feelings burn through them. Neither of them tried to stop it. Neither of them pretended this wasn't what they wanted, because both knew it was. It was what they'd wanted from that first moment in the maze. It was wild, but they didn't care. It was crazy, but they didn't care about that either. They cared about nothing except the moment and when the moment came, when he drove her to another climax, she pulled him over with her, her body tightening around his, sharing each pulse, each thrust, each explosion of sensation as they tumbled together over the edge and into ecstasy.

# CHAPTER SEVEN

LUCA WOKE IN a panic.

The reason came back to him before he opened his eyes.

He'd spent the night with a woman.

The whole night.

In his bed. In his home, where he never brought anyone.

Admittedly, more than half the night had been spent having sex. Wild, abandoned, selfishly indulgent sex. After the first time when they'd barely made it through the door they'd graduated to the rug on the floor, his luxurious shower and finally the bed where each had exhausted the other until they'd fallen asleep wrapped around each other.

Wrapped around each other...

Drenched in panic, he was about to spring from the bed when he realised it was empty and that Taylor was stumbling round the room, snatching up her clothes like a woman running for her life.

Distracted by the urgency in her movements, Luca forgot his own panic and absorbed hers. 'Is Etna erupting and we have just minutes to escape? Should I call the emergency services?'

'Go back to sleep.' Dragging open a drawer, she locked her hand around the first item of clothing she encountered. Dressed only in her panties with her trademark hair clouded and tangled from a night of wild sex, she was still the hottest woman he'd ever seen.

Realising that for the first time in his life he was witnessing a woman who was even more panicked about relationships than he was, Luca relaxed slightly.

She pulled on the T-shirt without bothering with a bra, a decision Luca supported wholeheartedly.

'This is like a strip in reverse but it's surprisingly erotic.' His own panic fading, he hooked his hands behind his head and watched as she yanked on jeans in such haste she almost fell. 'Where exactly are you going in this much of a hurry? This is Sicily. No one rushes in Sicily. You're not on New York time now, *dolcezza*.' But he knew her frantic rush to get dressed and escape had nothing to do with a desire to get to work and everything to do with her need to escape from a situation that terrified her. It would have terrified him too, except that she was panicking enough for both of them.

'I'm going out—' she snapped the words and zipped

her jeans so violently he flinched '—out…somewhere. Anywhere.'

She dressed with no thought and yet she looked effortlessly stunning. It occurred to him that women would break down and cry if they knew how little effort Taylor Carmichael put into looking as good as she did. She was thought of as an actress but she could just as easily have modelled, especially now with her expression as moody as Etna on a bad day and her hair pouring over her shoulders in wild disarray.

There was something oddly vulnerable about her panic and, because he understood it, he took pity on her. 'There's no need to run. I'm not about to declare undying love and try and put a gold band on your finger. You're probably safer with me than any other man alive.'

'This isn't about you.' She bent down to retrieve her shoes, the movement so fluid and graceful he immediately wanted to haul her back to bed.

'So why are you running?'

She came upright and scooped her hair away from her face, her eyes fierce. 'Because I don't do this. I—I just can't.'

'Do what? Stay and eat breakfast? Because that's all that's on offer.'

'I don't eat breakfast.' Her foot shot out and she kicked at the pile of clothes they'd torn off each other the night before, searching for something. 'And I can't do this whole morning-after touchy-feely crap. It's not me. Damn—have you seen my watch? I was wearing it last night.'

'It lacerated my back at one stage so now it's by the bed. And I don't do touchy-feely either.' His words didn't appear to penetrate because she glared at him as she strode across the room and snatched up her watch.

'Do you know how many years I've stopped myself doing this?'

'Quite a few if your wild response last night was anything to go by. Next time you might want to shorten your periods of abstinence. Your she-wolf act could kill a regular guy. I think I have teeth marks in my shoulder.'

The look she shot him speared right through him. 'So I suppose now you think you're a sex god.'

Luca discovered he was enjoying himself. 'You moaned, *dolcezza*. Despite everything you said, you definitely moaned.'

'So? It's a long time since I had sex.' Head down, she jammed her feet into her shoes. 'Don't read anything into it.'

'So you're saying any man would have made you moan?'

If looks could have killed he would have been a rotting corpse. 'I thought you didn't enjoy morning-after conversations.'

'Funnily enough I'm enjoying this one.' It was the

first time a woman had been more scared than him. 'Admit it—last night was the hottest sex you've ever had.'

'God, why do guys need so much praise? Just shut up and let me dress in peace. I have to go.'

Luca smiled. 'All of this excess energy is wasted because you're running from a man who isn't chasing you, *tesoro*.'

'Don't call me that.' She spoke between her teeth. 'When we're on our own, there is no need to pretend we're anything other than—'

'Two people who share explosive chemistry in bed?'

'Not that either.'

'I fully understand your aversion to relationships. I'm having more trouble understanding your panic about a night of incredible sex. Is this because you lost control?'

'I did not lose control.'

'I enjoyed the opera by the way. I had no idea the whole experience could be so…passionate. I love to hear you moaning, but silent sex was surprisingly erotic.'

Her look was fierce. 'You took advantage.'

'I didn't hear you complaining either then or last night. You definitely moaned. And you dug your fingers in my back.'

'Are you finished?'

'For now. But only because we need to eat before we expend more energy.'

'We won't be expending more energy. This was a one-time thing. We're going to forget this happened.'

He should have been relieved to hear that from a woman. The fact that he wasn't surprised him. 'Fine by me. But any time you want me to make you moan again, just tap me on the shoulder. My skills are at your disposal.' He saw her eyes flash.

'I can live perfectly well without your skills.'

'Are you sure? Because it seemed to me that you were pretty desperate there for a while.'

'I was not desperate.' Without looking at him she slung her bag over her shoulder and made for the door. 'I'll call a taxi.'

Realising that she was serious, Luca sighed and sprang from the bed. 'And spend tomorrow reading that we had our first row? You need to calm down and breathe. Give me five minutes in the shower and I'll drop you on my way to work as usual.'

'Not today.'

'Yes, today. Taylor—' he hauled her round and gave her a little shake, frowning slightly as he stared into eyes wide with fear '—this was just sex. Incredible sex, admittedly, but just sex. Sex followed by a lift to work.' He said it slowly, as if he were speaking to a terrified child. 'That's all it is, so don't allow the messed-up part of yourself to ruin everything we're doing here. You were the one who got us into this but we're in it now and we're staying in it for as long as it suits us.'

* * *

She wasn't messed up. She'd made mistakes and she'd learned from them and one of the things she'd learned was not to trust people. It was a simple rule and she'd had no trouble living her life by it. Until now.

She told herself that sex wasn't trust but she knew it wasn't as simple as that. What she shared with Luca was more than just sex. He got inside her head. He saw who she was.

And yes, she'd moaned.

Appalled with herself, Taylor paced the length of the bedroom and then back again. She could hear the shower running and she turned her head, wrestling with an almost painful urge to throw caution to the wind and join him there.

*Admit it—last night was the hottest sex you've ever had.*

'No!' She covered her ears with her hands to block out the sound of the water because hearing the water made her think of the man and thinking of the man made her think of his body and how it had felt to be with him.

When that didn't work she snatched up her bag in desperation and left the room.

Down in the kitchen she found Geovana removing warm brioche from the oven. The scent was another assault on her already overloaded, overindulged senses.

Her stomach rumbled. 'Could I make myself some

coffee, please?' She muttered the words in English and vowed to learn more of the language while she was filming here. 'Strong, black. Americano.'

Geovana smiled and responded in Italian.

Taylor caught one word that she translated as *breakfast* and shook her head. 'I don't eat breakfast.' But Geovana either didn't understand her or chose to ignore her because she loaded a plate with fresh, glossy brioche and placed it on the scrubbed, antique table in front of Taylor.

Her mouth watered. It was as if everything in this house was designed to tempt her self-control. She felt herself weaken. 'That smells so good but I really can't—'

*'Granita.'* Geovana placed a glass filled with frosted sorbet in front of her and gestured that Taylor should eat the brioche with the *granita.* Unable to find a way of refusing without offending, Taylor broke off a piece of the soft, warm roll and ate as instructed, intending to take only a nibble.

'Oh, that's so good....' She closed her eyes briefly, enjoying the flavour and the novelty of starting her day with food. She was so used to disciplining herself not to eat that she'd forgotten the pleasure of breakfast.

'Sex and food in one day. You really have fallen off the wagon.' Luca strolled into the room looking maddeningly fresh and relaxed while Taylor averted her gaze. He was the biggest temptation of all.

'I came down for coffee and—' She broke off as he kissed her and then stole a corner of her brioche. 'Don't do that!'

'Kiss you or steal your food?'

Judging from the way Geovana beamed at them both, she was thrilled by the scene of morning-after domesticity and Taylor was trapped by the story they'd spun.

Luca spoke in Italian to Geovana and helped himself to coffee and brioche while watching Taylor. 'You don't like breakfast?'

'Of course I like breakfast. It's my favourite meal if you must know. Crispy bacon and a short stack.' Her stomach growled. 'I ran away from home once just so that I could eat it.'

'You had to run away from home to eat breakfast?'

'My mother decided that if I was allowed to embrace my appetites I soon wouldn't have a career.'

'So that's when you stopped eating.'

'I didn't stop eating but I learned to control myself.' *Until I met you.*

'But having to control yourself for every minute of every day is exhausting. Eventually your natural impulses escape.'

'No, they don't, because I hold them in.' Except she hadn't held them in the night before. She knew it. He knew it.

Taylor found herself looking at him across the table and thinking about the night before and maybe he felt it because his gaze lifted to hers and in that single split second she knew he was thinking about the same thing. Dropping her gaze, she focused on her breakfast, feeling intensely vulnerable. Not because they'd had sex, but because she'd been herself. It had been real.

And he knew it.

'I need to make a move.' She stood up suddenly and gave Geovana a faltering smile. 'Thank you. *Grazie...*' She stumbled over the word, embarrassed that her Italian was so limited. 'That was the most delicious breakfast.'

Draining his coffee, Luca rose to his feet, kissed Geovana lightly on both cheeks and walked to the door. 'I'll give you a lift.'

She would have preferred to drive herself but she knew that to have admitted that would have triggered questions she didn't want to answer so instead she followed him into the car, her heart sinking at the thought of another day of filming. She wanted to lose herself in the role but with Rafaele hovering in her line of vision it was impossible.

'So what's the history between you and Rafaele?' Luca accelerated down the long, tree-lined drive. 'You dumped him. Why the antagonism?'

'I'm sure your world is populated by disgruntled exes.'

'That's all that's going on here?'

She almost told him the truth but stopped herself in

time, alarmed by the impulse to confide. She'd learned never to confide. Never to trust. She knew better than anyone that today's confession was tomorrow's headline so she kept her answer suitably bland. 'He isn't an easy man to please. He's very critical.' And he'd threatened her, but of course only she knew that. Only she knew what he was holding over her.

'These photographs are boring.' Luca scanned the images of a pretty girl standing on the sand with the sea behind her. 'It's like an advert for butter, not clothes. She's too wholesome. That girl has never had wild dirty sex in her life. Where's the edge? At the very least you should have stuck a huge shark in the water. We need something more contemporary and modern.'

'She is modern.'

'She looks like the girl next door.' It didn't help that he'd just had a night of raunchy sex with a woman he suspected might be half she-wolf. He turned away and stared out of the window of his office, thinking about Taylor.

She hadn't had much sleep the night before and she was expected to put in a twelve-hour day on the set with a director known for his childish temper tantrums and out of control drinking habit.

A director who was clearly still festering over the fact Taylor had once dumped him.

Making a snap decision, he picked up his car keys.

'I'm taking my fiancée—' he frowned slightly as he realised he'd managed to say the word without stumbling
'—my fiancée for lunch. We'll meet again tomorrow
to talk about the campaign.'

Wondering why no one else shared his vision for the
new collection, he strode to the car and drove to the
docklands where filming was taking place.

As a Corretti and Taylor's fiancé, he was allowed
through the security cordon without question and he
was about to ask someone where he could find Taylor
when he saw her stroll through the abandoned docklands buildings, her hair flowing over an impossibly
thin dress that floated around her slender frame. And
he knew instantly that this was the image he wanted
for his campaign. The contrast between decaying urban
and floral femininity was exactly the look he wanted.
Gianni had wanted a marine theme—docklands could
be classed as 'marine.'

He was reaching for his phone to call Gianni and
break the good news that he'd found the perfect setting,
when he saw Rafaele striding towards Taylor.

Just looking at the way he walked made Luca clench
his jaw. It was more of a swagger than a walk.

The man was a bully, a chauvinist and an idiot.

He watched, assuming they were about to have a
conversation, and froze as he saw the other man grab
her arm, spin her round and pin her roughly against the
dilapidated wall of one of the old docklands buildings.

Taylor struggled frantically, her fists pummelling his chest as he trapped her against the wall. She was twisting and turning like a madwoman and when Rafaele locked his hand in her hair, Luca felt a rush of rage.

Pumped up and furious, he abandoned his car, vaulted over the fence that surrounded the area being used for filming and sprinted towards her even as the director grabbed her face and kissed her.

Luca launched himself at the other man with an angry growl, hauling him off Taylor as if he were a savage dog and delivering a solid punch to the side of his face. The director almost stumbled but then came back at Luca with a grunt. Within seconds both of them were rolling in the dust but Luca, younger and infinitely fitter, instantly had the advantage and he pinned the other man's arm behind his back and pressed his face into the dirt.

'Don't ever touch her again.' The blood in his veins pulsed with fury and he realised how close he was to the edge. Closer than he'd ever been in his life before. 'You threaten her, you look at her in the wrong way, and I'll come after you, *capisci*?'

'Luca?' From somewhere in the distance Taylor's voice penetrated the mist of anger. 'What are you doing?'

'I'm doing what someone else should have done the moment he touched you.' Springing back to his feet, he nursed his throbbing hand. 'I'm protecting you from him. Where the hell is everyone anyway?' He glanced round and saw people emerge from the fringes of the set, openmouthed and speechless.

'I was demonstrating a scene, you idiot.' The director stumbled to his feet, rubbing his bruised jaw with his palm. 'She kept getting it wrong.'

'If she was getting it wrong then it must have been because your direction sucked,' Luca said coldly, seriously tempted to knock him flat again.

'You shouldn't be on my set.' The other man stood there, covered in dust and fuming. 'I don't care if the producer is your cousin. You can't barge in here and disrupt filming.'

Dealing with a suspicion that he might have overreacted just slightly, Luca turned his attention to Taylor.

Her hair was mussed up and wild, her face as pale as an Arctic winter, her slender frame impossibly fragile in the flimsy dress.

He spent his days dealing with women who were considered the most beautiful in the world but in that moment he knew he'd never seen a woman more beautiful than Taylor.

And suddenly he knew. He didn't just want the docklands for his advert, he wanted Taylor. 'This is it.'

'This is what?' Rafaele snapped the words but Luca ignored him.

'This is the place.' Luca glanced around him, wondering why he hadn't thought of it before. 'It will be the perfect backdrop for the new Corretti collection.'

'Luca…' This time it was Taylor who stammered his name and Luca strode over to her and smoothed her tangled hair away from her face, worried by how exhausted she looked.

'I want to do the shoot here and I want you to model the clothes. We can link it with the film. It will be great publicity for both sides of the business. I'll talk to Santo.'

'Luca, you just punched Rafaele. And your suit…' She gave him a strange look. 'You're covered in dirt.'

Surprised, he glanced down at himself and realised he hadn't given a single thought to his appearance when he'd jumped the gates and wrestled in the dirt. 'There's a price to everything,' he drawled lightly. 'I wanted to stop him hurting you.'

'But it was part of the film. This is my work.' Her eyes skidded to the director and Luca felt a rush of emotion he couldn't interpret as he saw the look they exchanged.

It was a look of two people who knew each other. Knew each other well.

'You were struggling.'

'That was the part I was playing. My character is very conflicted about seeing her husband again.'

'You looked scared. Not the character, you. You were afraid of him.'

There was a few seconds of silence and then desperate eyes met his. 'I don't need you running to my rescue, Luca. What were you thinking?'

It wasn't what he'd expected her to say.

He'd expected gratitude, even silent gratitude. He hadn't expected criticism and he certainly hadn't expected that question.

What had he been thinking? Just for a moment his brain froze. 'I'm your fiancé.' He was relieved as the answer came to him. Yes, that was why he'd reacted in such an extreme way. He'd got so deeply into the role that he was actually starting to feel the way a fiancé should feel. What did they call it? Method acting or something. 'When I see you in trouble I'm going to try and protect you, and yes, I'm a touch possessive. Don't expect me to apologise for that. I'm Sicilian. We don't hand our women over to other men without a fight. If that isn't what you want from a relationship then maybe you're with the wrong guy.'

Her shock mirrored his own.

What the hell was he saying?

He didn't want the relationship to end. And anyway, how could you end something that wasn't real in the first place?

Freaked out by a nagging voice that told him he'd totally lost the plot this time, Luca turned on his heel and strode away.

\* \* \*

'Luca wait. Wait!' Taylor sprinted after him, ignoring the sick feeling in her stomach that was her barometer of trouble. She knew a bucket load of it waited for her back on set but right now she had other things on her mind. Like Luca's extreme reaction.

She'd never seen him anything but relaxed. Even when he was driving too fast or drinking too much she had the sense that every action he took was deliberate, but this...

He'd been out of control, and if she needed confirmation of that then all she had to do was look at his suit.

Luca Corretti was never anything less than immaculate and yet his perfectly tailored suit was marked from his scuffle on the ground and there was a small tear in the leg of his trousers, no doubt caused when he'd jumped the fence. Jumped the fence to protect her.

Her heart was racing like a horse leading the field in the derby. All day she'd tried to block out memories of the night before but she thought about it now, her mind and her body remembering the intensity, the intimacy, everything they'd shared.

'Don't walk away—don't—' She caught up with him by the gate and grabbed his arm, releasing him immediately as he shook her off. 'Just...wait, will you? We need to talk.'

He stopped walking but his face was cold. Colder

than she'd ever seen it. 'You just made it clear I'm not welcome on the set.'

'Because we're in the middle of filming, but—' She glanced over her shoulder quickly and his face blackened.

'So are you going to tell me what is going on between you and that guy? I mean, what's really going on?'

Taylor's mouth dried and her heart bumped hard against her ribs. 'Nothing.'

'This is me you're talking to.' His voice was thickened with emotion as he closed the gap between them. 'Last night we shared everything. Last night you were honest. Don't ever hide who you are from me.'

Was she the only one who thought this conversation was crazy? 'Last night was...' What was it? Taylor shoved her fingers through her hair, not knowing how to begin to unravel the emotions at play here. Not knowing which questions to ask or which answers she wanted to hear. Glancing over her shoulder, she checked no one was close enough to overhear them. 'Is this you acting? Because I don't know what's real and what isn't any more.'

There was a long pulsing silence.

Luca stared at her. Something flickered across his face. 'You were scared.'

She took a step backwards, shaken that he'd seen that when no one else had. 'I was acting.'

'No, that was real. You were scared.' He pushed and

pushed, cracking open the shell she'd put around herself, seeing right through to the truth. 'I know you were scared and as long as he scares you, I'll be there to protect you.'

That statement ripped away another layer of her protection. 'Why?' The word was barely a whisper and it was a long time before he answered.

'Because I'm your fiancé.'

Taylor looked away quickly, horrified to realise she'd hoped for a different answer. 'You were...very convincing. Unfortunately you've also upset another director.'

And she knew just what that could cost her.

Rafaele was the wrong man to upset.

And suddenly fury mingled with despair. She'd been walking on eggshells trying not to upset him and now Luca had made things worse. 'Did you have to go to those lengths? You humiliated him. You made him look like a fool.'

'He did that with no help from me.' Luca was unrepentant. 'Why was he kissing you anyway?'

'Because he was demonstrating a scene.' She rubbed her fingers over her aching forehead, feeling crushed by the situation. 'If he walks out too, Santo will freak.'

'I hope he does walk. I don't like the way he looks at you.'

Slowly she dropped her hand to her side. 'You mean the fake part of you that is "engaged" to me doesn't like the way he looks at me? I think you just might have blown my film career by acting out a part we created in order to protect my film career.' She looked away from him because looking at him made her think of the night before and they were both in enough trouble. 'And what about you? You agreed to this to make yourself respectable. Does your board approve of a man fighting over his woman?'

'Of course. They're Sicilian.' But he was frowning, as if something she'd said had given him pause for thought. 'I don't want to have blown your career. I'll talk to Santo.'

'No! You've done more than enough. I'll sort it out.'

Luca caught her arm. 'Tell me why you're scared of him.' His tone was low and urgent. 'Why do you care what that guy thinks of you?'

Her mouth was dry. 'Because he has…power.'

'Power? You mean over your performance?'

No, she didn't mean that.

'I just don't want more bad headlines.' That much was the truth. 'I just want to act.'

Luca stared at her for a long moment and then lifted his hand and brushed her cheek gently, his expression inscrutable. '*Mi dispiace.* I'm sorry if I made things difficult for you. That wasn't my intention. Go and finish filming that scene. There's something I need to do.'

Determined to make up for his momentary loss of control, which had clearly made things awkward for her, Luca spent the afternoon on the phone. By the

time he drove back to the docklands to collect Taylor
he was feeling particularly pleased with his plan so it
spoiled the moment slightly to see her waiting for him,
white-faced and tense.

'Your cousin fired Rafaele.'

Luca wondered why she thought that came under the
heading of 'bad news.' 'Good. For once he and I are in
agreement on something.'

'Rafaele is going to be furious.'

'And we care about that because…?' When she didn't
answer, he sighed. 'Get in the car.'

'I'm starting to think this project is doomed.' She
slid into the car next to him and closed her eyes but her
phone rang immediately.

Luca tensed. 'Is that him?'

'No.' She relaxed. 'It's just Zach. I'll call him back
later.'

'Zach? Who the hell is Zach?'

'Just a friend.'

'I thought you didn't have friends. I thought there
was no one you trusted.'

'I trust Zach more than I trust most people, but that
isn't saying much.' She dropped the phone back into
her bag. 'What a day.'

Luca forced himself not to ask all the questions he
was burning to ask about Zach. 'Does Santo have a replacement yet?'

'Well, that's the odd thing…' She pushed her hair

out of her eyes. 'He's given the job to his PA, Ella. I've talked to her loads of times. She's crazy about everything to do with movie making which is why she's working for Santo but I never knew she wanted to direct. He's giving her the chance.'

'I'm sure she'll be brilliant. I'll even let her kiss you—in fact, I'll hang around in case she does.' Noticing movement out of the corner of his eye, he leaned forward and kissed her himself. 'Press approaching downwind. Look pleased to see me.'

Her lips were soft and sweet under his and he took his time, kissing her slowly and deliberately until she pulled back with a frown. 'OK, enough already.'

Luca, who was unsettled to discover he'd had nowhere near enough of her, reached into the back of the car and put a baseball cap on her head.

'Ugh—you'll ruin my hair!' She lifted her hand to remove it but he stopped her.

'Wear it,' he ordered softly. 'Put on your sunglasses. And for once in your life, don't argue with me.'

She was still staring at him when one journalist, braver than the others, approached the car. 'Taylor, do you have a statement on the fact that Rafaele has been replaced as director?'

'No, she doesn't.' Luca settled his own sunglasses over his eyes, started the engine and rammed the car into gear but the journalist persisted.

'Any plans for tonight? Where will the two of you be spending the evening?'

'In bed.' With a dangerous smile, Luca pulled away and Taylor groaned.

'Thanks so much. Now the headline will be Taylor Carmichael, Sex Addict. Couldn't you have said something else? You could have told them we're going out to dinner. Why would you let them think we're going home to bed?'

'Because that's what I want them to think. I don't want them to follow us.'

'They always follow us. And you don't care.'

'Tonight, I care.'

'Why?'

'Because tonight, Cinderella Carmichael,' he drawled, 'I'm making your dreams come true.'

'My dream is to get on with my life without being bothered and you've just—'

'I've just made that happen.' Glancing in the rear-view mirror, he took a sharp right and ducked into the private underground car park reserved for the executive team of the hotel.

He parked the Ferrari next to a battered, ancient car.

'What on earth…?'

'Move.'

And she did. But being Taylor she didn't do it without demanding answers.

'Where are we and what are you—?' She broke off

and stared at the couple that had just climbed out of the battered, ancient car parked next to them.

'Give her your jacket, your sunglasses and the baseball cap.'

'But—'

'*Accidenti*, do you ever do anything without arguing? You are enough to drive a man to an early grave.'

'I'd haunt you.' Visibly confused, she pulled off the hat, the glasses and her jacket and handed it to the woman, who immediately put them on.

Luca narrowed his eyes. 'Not bad. From the back she could be you.'

'I know. It's seriously freaky. How did you do it?'

'I found a Taylor Carmichael double. She earns her living being you so she owes you a few favours.' He took off his own jacket and sunglasses and handed them to the man. 'Remember what I said. Straight home. Follow my security guards. You don't stop. Don't look at anyone. And drive too fast—that's what I'd do. You're sure you can handle the car?'

The man nodded and Luca sighed and reluctantly handed over the keys to his precious Ferrari. 'This had better be worth it. Is everything in the back?'

'Just as you instructed.'

'Then go.'

The couple drove off in the Ferrari and Luca yanked open the door of the battered car. '*Maledezione*, is this piece of junk even roadworthy? I've owned toothbrushes with more impressive engineering.' He hauled a bag out of the back of the car and thrust it at her. 'Put this on. And do it quickly before someone drives into this garage.'

Taylor opened the bag gingerly. 'A wig?'

Busy pulling on his own wig, Luca ignored her. 'I hope you appreciate the lengths I'm going to for you. Do I look hot as a blond?'

She glanced at him and gave a choked laugh. 'You look...unbelievably weird. The hair doesn't match the suit.'

'The suit! I have to get rid of the suit.' Reluctantly, Luca stripped off the exquisite Italian suit he'd changed into following his altercation with Rafaele. 'I can't believe I'm doing this for you.'

'Why are you doing this for me?'

'Because you said it's what you want more than anything and I wanted to make that happen for you. I wanted you to have fun.' His eyes met hers and he saw the shock there and he knew she was seeing the same thing in his eyes because the only fun he was usually interested in having with a woman involved getting naked. '*Cristo*, you ask too many questions. Can't you just enjoy an evening out without dissecting it?'

'Thank you.' She whispered the words and there was a sheen of something that looked scarily like tears in her eyes as she stepped towards him and pressed her lips to his. 'No one has ever done anything like this for me before. You've made me feel really special.'

Luca jerked back, rocked by emotions he hadn't expected and had no idea how to deal with.

Maybe this had been a bad idea.

He had no problem with making a woman feel special as long as it was only for a short time, but he didn't want to make one feel so special she decided to stick around. 'Really special' sounded suspiciously like a warning alarm that in normal circumstances would have had him running. But he couldn't run because he was the one who'd arranged this.

'I'm not surprised no one has done it before. The wig itches and the car is unlikely to make it out of the car park.' Unsettled by his own feelings, which he had no intention of analysing, he took refuge in humour. 'Get dressed.'

Checking that there was no one in the small car park, she shimmied out of her trousers and Luca set his teeth. He wondered if he were the only one thinking about sex all the time. He couldn't look at her without wanting to strip her naked.

'I said get dressed, not undressed.'

'One comes before the other.'

He dragged his gaze from her long, slim legs. 'You're doing it on purpose.'

'Doing what on purpose?'

'Driving me crazy.'

'Am I driving you crazy?' She lifted her arms and removed her top in a graceful movement, exposing her lean fit body. She was sexy and she knew it.

Taylor Carmichael didn't need anyone to reassure her. She made her own choices and was confident in herself.

'What would you do if I said I didn't like what you were wearing?' The question fell from his lips before he could stop it and she raised her eyebrows.

'You don't like me in my underwear?'

'That wasn't what I meant.' He wished he hadn't spoken and truthfully he could hardly concentrate. He was so hard his brain had ceased to function on any level above basic.

She looked at him thoughtfully. 'To answer your question, if you told me you didn't like what I was wearing I'd probably just take it off. Is that what you want?' Her fingers toyed with the lacy edge of her panties and his mouth dried.

'No, *Cristo*, don't take any more off. Put something on. Fast.'

'But you said you didn't like what I was wearing.'

'That wasn't...' His flesh throbbed and his mind blurred. 'Never mind. Just get dressed.'

'Maybe I won't.' She stepped closer and slid her arms round his neck. 'Maybe I'll tease you just a little bit longer. I still owe you for the opera.' Her mouth was a breath away from his and Luca felt his control unravel.

'Taylor—'

'Is there a problem?' Her lips curved slowly as she covered him with the flat of her hand. 'Because I could probably fix that.'

The skilled stroke of her fingers made him groan.

Her confidence in herself was as sexy as her body.

He'd grown up with a woman who needed constant reassurance and worked with women who were body obsessed.

He'd never met anyone like Taylor.

'I thought you were careful not to be caught doing naughty stuff in public.'

'We're not in public. We're in your private, high-tech garage with just your car as witness. And anyway, you're talking about Taylor Carmichael and thanks to you she's currently driving back to your palazzo. Which means we're alone.' Her hand slid slowly down his shaft and he groaned and hauled her against him.

'This wasn't part of my plan.'

'It's always good to be flexible. And talking of flexible…' She curved her bare leg around his thigh and he gave in to it and pressed her back against the car, breathing hard.

He looked deep into her eyes and then his hands were in her hair and he was kissing her and she was kissing him and it was exactly as it had been the night before. Exactly as he'd remembered it. The intense chemistry, the desperation, the clawing need that made him ignore the fact that his relationship with this woman wasn't following the usual pattern.

It was the wrong place, the wrong time and not part of his plan but his hand slid low and found the wet warmth of her and he heard her moan against his mouth.

A loud crash in the distance had them both pulling apart.

Frozen, they stared at each other and then Luca gave a soft curse. He would have taken her right there. Right then and not paused to think about the sense of it.

'Oops.' A strange smile on her face, she eased away from him and finished dressing in a flash. 'Maybe this isn't such a good place after all.'

'We could go back to the house.' His mind was a blur, his body rock hard.

'No. You've arranged a secret night out for me. No one has ever done this for me before. I want to do it.' She grabbed the bag and tugged on a pair of floral shorts. 'These clothes are hideous. Who chose them?'

'Someone with no taste whatsoever.' But it made no difference, he realised. Whatever she was wearing, she was the hottest woman he'd ever met. Trying to think cold thoughts, he changed into jeans and slid into the car, ducking his head so that he didn't bang it on the roof.

'Do you really think we won't be recognised?'

'I sincerely hope not or my reputation as the head of a fashion house is for ever destroyed. I would rather shoot myself than have someone think I chose to wear this. Come on. Let's do this.' Making an effort not to look at her, Luca turned the key in the ignition, rolling his eyes as the engine coughed and spluttered. 'Believe me, even if the clothes don't convince people, this car is a perfect disguise. Everyone who knows me also knows I wouldn't be seen dead driving this piece of garbage.'

Still laughing, Taylor was pushing stray wisps of hair into the wig. 'Do you like me as a redhead?'

In the process of reversing the temperamental car out of the garage, Luca allowed himself a brief glance. 'You look surprisingly cute given that you're dressed in something that should be banned by the fashion police.'

She pushed her feet into a pair of running shoes. 'Are you going to tell me where we're going?'

'No. It's a surprise. And turn your phone off just in case some nosy journalist is tracking you.'

Her eyes widened slightly but she turned it off. 'You're a very surprising person.'

'Surprising how?' He winced as the car bumped over the uneven road.

'Doing this for me. I thought you only ever did things for yourself.'

'I am doing this for myself. I want to have fun and you're no fun when you think people are watching your every move. Tonight you can be yourself. That's if we ever get there.' He pushed the accelerator but the car chugged along at the same pace. 'I'm starting to think that it might be quicker to walk. What is under the bonnet? I think someone forgot to install an engine.'

She clutched the seat as they bounced along. 'It must be killing you to drive something that doesn't go over ten kilometres an hour.'

'Next time I'll hire a donkey. It will be faster. How are you doing with that disguise? Have you tucked away all your hair?'

'I'm one hundred per cent redhead.'

Luca turned his head. *But still beautiful.* 'Scrub the make-up off.'

'You just kissed off the only make-up I was wearing. Where exactly are we going?'

'To a charity concert at the Teatro Greco at Taormina.' He could taste her lipstick. Taste her mouth. Distracted, he crunched the gears and winced. He hadn't had trouble driving since he was a teenager. 'You said you wanted to go to a concert, stand in the crowd and not be recognised. That's what we're doing.'

'I—seriously?' She sounded doubtful. 'I read about it and the lineup is fantastic but we'll be recognised.'

'No, we won't because we're not in the VIP seats, *angelo mia.* We are in with the crowd just as you requested. You are no longer Taylor Carmichael. Tonight, you are Teresa, a good Sicilian girl from a strict Catholic family—'

'You're kidding, right?'

'And I am Tomas, the son of a local farmer who is

hoping to get lucky.' Luca flattened his foot to the floor to try and overtake a tractor but nothing happened and he rolled his eyes and made a mental note never to complain about his Ferrari again. 'We are sneaking you away from your strict parents, who would beat you if they knew you were out with me.'

'You're enjoying this, aren't you?'

Luca discovered that he was. 'Maybe I'm into role play. Think you can play the role of a virgin from Catholic school who has never been alone with a boy before?'

'Sure.' There was a shimmer of humour in her voice. 'Pull over and take your clothes off.'

'Shouldn't you be shy and nervous?'

'No. If I were a virgin from Catholic school who has never been alone with a boy before, I'd be desperate. So pull over and get your clothes off, Tomas.'

'If I pull over we'll never get the car started again, especially not on this hill.' Luca shifted gears as he drove up towards Taormina. 'How do you feel about pushing?' He winced as the car juddered over a bump. 'On second thought, forget that. You don't eat enough carbohydrate to have the strength to push a pen across a desk let alone a car up a road like this.'

'Are you questioning my strength? Because that probably isn't wise. I can take you, Corretti.'

'I wish you would. I've been desperate since last night and that encounter in the car park hasn't helped.'

Ignoring the instantaneous reaction of his body, he kept his eyes on the road. 'Any time you want a repeat performance just leap on me and rip my clothes off. No prior warning needed.'

'I'm a good Catholic girl. I have no idea what you mean.' But she was laughing and he was laughing too, as the car shuddered to a halt by the side of the road.

'Let's walk from here. It will be faster and probably a lot safer. You do have the strength to walk, don't you? Ouch.' He winced as her fist made contact with his arm. 'What a hot, spirited little thing you are, Teresa.'

'Don't make me hurt you, Tomas.' Still smiling, she slid her arm through his and Luca frowned slightly and opened his mouth to remind her that they didn't need to play the role of an engaged couple tonight but she seemed more relaxed than he'd ever seen her so he closed his mouth and drew her against him as they joined the noisy, friendly crowd moving towards the arena.

He felt her tension as they were surrounded by people and then felt that same tension seep from her as she realised that no one had even given them a single glance.

They didn't expect to see her and so they didn't see her.

And the disguise was good.

'So, Teresa—' he pulled her forward to the area in front of the stage where a group was already performing '—what does a girl like you normally get up to on a Saturday night?'

She blinked innocently. 'Normally I'm milking the goats, Tomas. And what do you normally do when you're not dressing in jeans that are a crime against fashion?'

*Normally he was sleeping with some woman he never intended to see again.*

Luca was slowly absorbing that fact when the crowd surged forward.

Instinctively he reached for Taylor, intending to protect her from the crush of people, but she was already dancing, arms in the air, joining in with everyone around her as the group on the stage revved the audience into a state of excitement.

As the sun set, darkness fell over Mount Etna and coloured lights played over the crowd and the atmosphere turned from excited to electric.

And still Taylor danced and it was the sexiest, most erotic thing he'd ever seen.

She moved with unconscious grace and sensuality, in perfect time to the music, thinking of nothing but the moment. It was the first time he'd seen her out in public and not looking over her shoulder.

'You're a real wild child, Teresa.' But she couldn't hear him over the music so he scooped her face into his hands and kissed her and she kissed him back, smiling against his mouth, happier than he'd ever seen her.

The chemistry was instantaneous and mutual.

Her arms locked around his neck and they kissed, oblivious to the crowd around them.

If someone hadn't bumped against them hard, they might never have stopped kissing and Luca released her suddenly, wondering what he was doing and she was obviously wondering the same thing because her smile faltered.

'Thank you for this—' she glanced at the crowd and the stage '—and for arranging something you knew would make me happy. You've gone to so much trouble and, well, you've surprised me, Luca Corretti.'

He'd surprised himself. He didn't go out of his way to make a woman happy because a happy woman was a woman who wanted to stick around and he'd never wanted that.

But seeing Taylor having fun had given him a high like no other.

They stared at each other. He brushed her hair away from her face and she caught his hand and gave him a warning look.

'Don't mess with my hair, Tomas. Took me hours to get it looking like this.'

He'd forgotten about the wig. All his attention had been on her and suddenly he wanted to be on his own with her. 'Let's get out of here.'

'No wait—' she shouted above the noise, her voice

pleading '—can we just stay for the fireworks? I love fireworks.'

He intended to talk her out of it but then he saw her face as she gazed up at the sky, as enchanted as a child as silver exploded against black, showering the night sky with a thousand stars.

They stayed until the light from the last fireworks had died away and then mingled with the crowd as they made their way back to their car.

'That was amazing.' She lifted her hand to remove the wig but he stopped her.

'Leave it on until we're home.'

'I'm not ready to go home. I'm not ready for this to end, Tomas.' Her eyes sparkled, alive and excited, and the rush of attraction almost knocked him flat.

'I think if your father could see you now he'd have a heart attack. What exactly do you have in mind, Teresa?'

She curled her fingers into the front of his shirt and pulled him towards her. 'I want to go to the beach.' Her voice was low. 'I want to go swimming.'

'Swimming?' Luca stared down at that full mouth and knew he was in trouble. 'Did you bring a costume?'

'No.' Her smile was all woman. 'But that doesn't matter because what I want more than anything is to swim naked.'

# CHAPTER EIGHT

SHE COULDN'T REMEMBER ever having so much fun. She felt light, happy and…free.

Here in the car, protected by the darkness and the disguise he'd given her, she was no longer the Taylor Carmichael she'd created. She was the girl she'd left behind years ago. The girl her mother had disciplined into another version of herself.

The girl she'd forgotten.

'Tonight was the most fun I've had in ages. Thank you.'

She put her hand on his thigh. Felt hard, male muscle tense under her fingers.

'Carry on like that and you won't be a virgin for much longer, Teresa.'

'Is that a promise?' She slid her hand higher and heard his breathing change.

'I chose the wrong disguise for you. You couldn't

pass for a good Catholic girl if I dressed you in a nun's habit.'

'How far is the beach?'

'Too far. I need cold water.' They were close to home and he pulled off the main road and they bumped and bounced down a rough track while she soaked up the dizziness of freedom.

'I can't get used to the fact that no one is following us.'

'If they do, they'll lose a tyre on this road and it will serve them right.' He switched off the engine and they sat for a moment, listening to the hiss of the sea as it hit the sand and the soft, rhythmic sound of the cicadas as they sang in the night.

The full moon cast a silvery light over the water and she decided she'd never been anywhere more romantic in her life.

'Come on.' She was first out of the car, pulling her T-shirt over her head as she ran down the sandy path that led to the beach. She heard him behind her and they hit the sand at the same time, kicking off shoes and stripping off the rest of their clothes. 'Cover your eyes, Tomas.'

'Why would I do that when the view is so good? I may be a simple farmer but I'm not stupid.' Without shifting his gaze from her he stepped out of his jeans. 'No wonder your father has kept you locked up, Teresa. You're a danger to mankind.'

Taylor undid her bra. 'I have a lot to pack into one night before you send me back.'

She dropped the bra on top of the rest of her clothes.

'I could be wrong but I get the distinct impression you really are thinking of swimming naked.'

'If I arrive home with my clothes wet my father will be suspicious.'

'True.' His eyes gleamed. 'In that case you'd better remove everything, Teresa.'

'Way ahead of you.' She dangled her panties from her fingers and saw his gaze darken but as he reached to haul her against him she dodged backwards and sprinted towards the sea, gasping as the cold water closed over her ankles.

How many times had she dreamt of doing this? How many times had she been tempted to run into the waves and swim naked only to stop herself because she knew someone would somehow manage to get a picture of her?

But tonight she wasn't thinking about that.

Tonight, no one knew where she was and she was thinking of nothing but the moment as she plunged forward and felt the cool water close over her head. She came up gasping and laughing to find him standing there holding a damp mass of something unrecognisable in his hand. 'What's that?'

'Let's just say you're no longer a redhead.'

'Oh, no! The wig!' She made a grab for it but he threw it onto the beach and turned back to her.

'Now you're finally naked.'

And so was he. She gasped as he scooped her up and ploughed into the waves and tightened her arms around his neck.

'Drop me and you're dead, Tomas.' But she knew he wouldn't drop her and she buried her face in his neck and breathed. 'You smell good.'

'Comes from spending the day herding sheep.' But his voice was husky and, as he lowered her into the waves, his mouth found hers. They sank under the water, kissing, desperate for each other.

There was only the moonlight but it was enough for her to see powerful shoulders above the surface of the water. His hair was slick and wet, his eyes gleaming in a face that was so wickedly handsome just looking at him made her stomach flip.

'You're looking good, Tomas.'

'Taylor Carmichael skinny-dipping. Who would have thought it? Finally the woman in the maze that day has come out to play.'

Taylor Carmichael.

Her stomach gave a little lurch and just for a moment she heard her mother's voice telling her she shouldn't be doing this, that she should be thinking of her image, that she shouldn't be trusting a man, but the voice seemed further away than usual, barely a whisper, and when

Taylor listened again it was gone. Smiling, she pulled away from him and plunged back into the water.

She'd waited too long for this. Too long to deny herself this moment and as her arms cut through the cool water she realised she was smiling.

The moon sent arrows of light onto inky dark water and she knew from the soft splash next to her that Luca was adjusting his pace to stay level with her.

They swam until her limbs felt tired and her eyes stung from the salt water. Reluctantly she left the water, picked up her T-shirt and dried her face. Then she twisted her hair into a thick rope and squeezed out the water, conscious of him next to her. Conscious of every beat of her heart and the movement of her breath through her lungs.

She'd thought she was immune to this. She'd worked with hot men for her entire career and these days had no trouble resisting them. But this was different and she knew it wasn't his looks that drew her—it was his hunger for living. He ate it up, devoured everything life had to offer without regret or apology, and she admired that and wanted it for herself. She wanted to live like this every day.

Her heart gave a little leap although whether it was nerves or excitement, she didn't know.

All she knew was that she wanted him.

She pulled his head down to hers and his mouth closed over hers with no hesitation, hot and demanding.

He scooped her wet hair away from her face, his sinfully clever mouth fierce on hers, and she kissed him back with the same desperation, feeling something unravel inside her.

Instead of hearing her mother's voice she heard nothing but her own heartbeat, her own desires, and she wrapped her arms around his neck, her body aching for his, so aroused she couldn't think straight. She held nothing back, gave him all that she was as they kissed hungrily, bonded together by mutual desire and chemistry. She sensed that he was no more in control than she was and she heard him groan as she slid her hands down his body, savouring the feel of hard male muscle.

'You're killing me, Teresa.'

Laughing, breathless, she pushed him backwards and they tumbled together onto the soft pile of clothes they'd abandoned before their swim. 'I haven't even started. You're driving me crazy.' She licked at his chest, tasted the salt of seawater on her tongue and then moved lower until his breathing changed, until his hands tangled in her wet hair, until he took control and shifted her onto him.

She straddled him in the moonlight, her damp hair trailing over his chest, her eyes fixed on his as she took him deep, her lips parting as she felt the thick, hot pulse of his erection inside her. His hands gripped her hips and they moved together in a perfect rhythm as if this intimacy was something they'd shared forever.

'*Cristo*, Taylor,' he moaned her name. Her name. Taylor, not Teresa. The pretence had long gone as had the humour. His passion was every bit as dark as hers. They were both deadly serious, wrapped up in each other, oblivious to anything and everything but the moment as they rode the excitement until it exploded and took them over the edge and he caught her head in his hands and drew her mouth to his. And she discovered a kiss wasn't always about sensual manipulation. Sometimes it was a gift.

And as the madness faded she curled against him, her body dampened by sweat and sea as her heartbeat gradually slowed and steadied.

'I've wanted to do this for so long.'

There was a pause and then his hand lifted to her hair and stroked it away from her face. 'Swim naked?'

'No.' Her words were muffled against his chest. 'Be myself. Be invisible for a night. Be able to do what I want, with who I want, without thinking of the consequences. When I was a kid I just wanted to run off and assume another identity.'

'You didn't want to be an actress?'

'I loved the acting. I hated everything that went with it. And I hated that all I was to my mother was a meal ticket.'

'She was ambitious for you.'

'No, she was ambitious for herself. She was determined I'd live the life she'd wanted and hadn't had.

She didn't want me to make any of the mistakes she'd made. She controlled everything I ate, everything I did, everyone I saw. Even the big Hollywood studios were afraid of my mother. She mapped out a path for me. She decided which parts I'd take, who I could be photographed with. And she played the media.' Taylor rolled onto her back and stared up at the stars. 'She'd start rumours, anything to make sure my name and face were always in the press. I felt suffocated. Stifled. The only thing I never felt was loved.'

'I'm surprised you didn't rebel in a big way.'

'I did.' She'd unlocked the dark and it came swirling over her. Shocked by how sharp and raw it still was even after so many years she sat up sharply, trying to push it back. 'I fired my mother as my manager and everyone labelled me as difficult. I wasn't. I was just horribly lonely and disillusioned about everything. I wanted someone to love me for me, not for what being with me could give them, but when I told her I didn't want her involved in my work any more, she told me to move out. And she gave all these stories to the press about how I'd betrayed her.' The agony was as raw as ever. 'She was my mom, but she was only ever interested in what she could get from being with me. And I soon learned that was true of everyone around me. There was no one I could trust.' She didn't give him the detail. Didn't spell out the embarrassing number of times she'd trusted a person only to find intimate details in the press the next day.

'Where did you go?'

Taylor wrapped her arms around her knees. 'I moved in with Rafaele. He was directing my film and he saw me falling apart under the pressure. He offered me somewhere to go.'

'In other words he took advantage.'

'It didn't seem that way at the time but yes. I made a bad decision. I was seventeen and up until that point my mother had made virtually every decision for me.' She could see now that she'd allowed her vulnerability to colour her view of the people around her. 'I was so lonely. So desperate for someone who would love me for myself and not for what they'd gain from being with me. The breakup with my mother was all over the press. It was horrible. And that was when my father saw his opportunity to come back into my life and play the hero.'

'Perfect timing.'

'Yes. Except I was pretty messed up by then. I couldn't see why he would want me when he hadn't bothered being in my life for the first seventeen years and I told him that. So then he milked the press interest for everything it was worth and told more stories about me being a spoiled brat. I kept the media going single-handed. Every day there was another story about me. It was vile. The only person who seemed to care about me was Rafaele.'

Luca took her hand in the dark. 'Bastard.'

It was exactly the right response. She didn't think she could have handled sympathy, although the strength of his fingers on hers felt good.

'Yes. He wasn't a nice man.' This was when she should tell him. She should confess about the phone calls, the threats, the sick feeling she lived with every day, the stuff she was terrified of people discovering, but she'd kept her secret for too long to part with it now.

Trust, even this degree of trust, was so new to her it felt unfamiliar so she drew her hand away from his. 'Enough of that. Tonight is about having fun.'

And she realised with a lurch that every moment she'd spent with him had been fun. Even when they were fighting, he made her laugh. Unsettled by that realisation, she lightened her tone. 'Good job the board can't see you now lying naked on a public beach. I think you're newfound respectability just died a death, Corretti.'

'What the board doesn't see the board can't moan about. And it isn't a public beach.' He wrapped his arms around her and hauled her back to him, showing no urgency to get dressed, and she relaxed against him. Why not? It was perfect lying here with only the sounds of the sea for company.

'What do you mean? If it isn't public, what are we doing here?'

'It's my beach. Private. There's a path that leads up to the house from here.'

'Seriously?' She lifted her head and stared at him through the semi-darkness. 'We're that close? So we could leave the car and just walk?'

'If you want to. But it's not easy to follow in the dark and it's steep. Car would be faster.'

'Then let's take the car.' Suddenly she wanted to be home with him and she sprang to her feet and tugged her clothes out from under him. 'I have no idea what happened to the wig.'

'Doesn't matter. It served its purpose.' The serious nature of their conversation forgotten, he took her hand and they sprinted back to the car.

Taylor sat, covered in sand and happiness, wishing her life could always be like this.

'I enjoyed being Teresa. It was fun.' And she rarely did anything for fun. Fun wasn't part of her plan.

'Having fun suits you. You were built to have fun.' He shot out a hand to steady her as the car lurched up the road. 'Only next time let's have fun in the Ferrari. I don't mind buying you a wig but I draw the line at driving this car again.'

'Where is the Ferrari?'

'Hopefully back in the garage with no damage to the paintwork.'

'I'm covered in sand. What if Geovana sees us?'

'She'll thoroughly approve, but I'd rather avoid that conversation if possible.'

Like naughty children, they sneaked into the house, trailing sand on polished wood.

'We are going to be in trouble tomorrow.' She gasped as Luca nudged her into the shower, removed her clothes for the second time in one evening and turned on the jets.

'Then it's a good thing I've never been frightened of trouble.'

Taylor opened her mouth to ask what would happen when everyone found out their relationship was fake, but then closed it again.

Tonight, she didn't want to think that this was fake. And this part wasn't, was it? The engagement—sure, that was fake. But everything else?

No, not this part, with his hands in her hair and his mouth hot and demanding on hers. This was definitely real, and she closed her eyes and let the water wash over her. Felt his hands move lower, gasped at the skilled slide of his fingers over the most sensitive parts of her and after that she stopped thinking at all and just let herself feel.

They fell into a routine—work during the day and each other at night. Neither of them used the word *relationship*, nor any other word that might have implied their arrangement had in any way veered from the original plan.

Taylor found working with Ella, the new director, fulfilling and fun.

Of Rafaele she'd heard nothing and even her phone was silent.

She started to relax for the first time in years. It occurred to her that maybe Luca had frightened him off.

And although she and Luca kept up their public appearances, he was remarkably good at protecting her privacy and giving her space.

It was several weeks after Rafaele's departure when she woke one morning to find herself alone in the bed.

Luca was standing on the balcony of the bedroom wearing nothing but a pair of hastily pulled-on jeans, nursing a cup of strong coffee as he stared into the distance.

Taylor slid out of bed and walked over to him. 'You have the board meeting today. Is that why you're awake?'

'I'm enjoying a few moments of smug satisfaction that my interior make-over has had such an impact on profits. Profits of Corretti Home are up by thirty per cent and I have a team working on a strategy for Corretti Bambino. Would it make you laugh to discover I was studying population forecasts yesterday?'

She laughed and slid her arms round his waist, enjoying the peace and the privacy. 'Have you always lived in Sicily? Did you grow up in this house?'

'No.'

His lack of response frustrated her and she drew away slightly. 'You never tell me anything about yourself.'

'There's nothing to say.'

'Of course there isn't. You had no life before you met me.' She kept her voice cool and his hand shot out and he hauled her back so that she was eye to eye with him.

'Don't do that. Don't pretend you don't care and that I haven't just hurt your feelings.' His voice was rough and sexy, his jaw dark with stubble. 'Don't tuck the real you back inside the fake you. It's too much effort to dig her out again, but if I have to I will, because there's only one version of Taylor that interests me.'

'Fine! If you want honesty I'll give you honesty. Yes, it hurts my feelings when you strip me naked and have sex with me all night, every night, and then won't answer a single question about yourself.'

They were eye to eye, nose to nose, flat up against each other and she could feel the warmth of his chest against her skin.

And then he released her and raked his fingers through his hair. 'Get dressed.' His voice was unsteady and she felt a sudden lurch of horror.

Was this it?

Was this the end of their 'engagement'? Had he de-

cided that now his project was safely reaching a satis-
factory conclusion he no longer needed her?

'Why do you want me to get dressed?'

'I'm taking you to meet someone.'

Luca parked the car outside the house and questioned
the impulse that had driven him to bring a woman to a
place he'd never brought a woman to before.

As if realising something significant was happening, Taylor gave him a puzzled look. 'Where are we?'

'This is my grandmother's house.'

'You visit your grandmother?'

Luca strolled round the car and opened the door for
her. 'What's wrong with that?'

'Nothing but—' she bit her lip '—I'm just surprised,
that's all. You don't strike me as the sort of guy who vis-
its his grandmother. I thought your family wasn't close.'

'We're not. But my grandmother makes my life hell
if I don't drop in and see her once in a while. She's
heard news of our engagement. She wants to meet you.
I'd appreciate it if you'd play the role of loving fiancée. She doesn't need to know our relationship consists
of numerous fake performances and endless nights of
hot sex.'

Endless nights?

The realisation hit him in the gut and he frowned
slightly but Taylor didn't comment on that.

'You care about her.'

Luca shrugged. 'I don't want to upset her. She lost my grandfather a few months ago. I try and visit whenever I'm not travelling. She'll be on the terrace at this time, eating breakfast.'

With Taylor's hand locked in his, he strode round the house to the vine-covered terrace and found his grandmother sipping coffee.

Every time he came here, the memories came with him but he'd already stayed away too long and he greeted her in Italian and stooped to kiss her wrinkled cheek. 'I brought Taylor to meet you, Nonna.'

'And about time too. Come and sit down.' His grandmother spoke in accented English and gestured to the chair next to her. 'I want to see the woman who finally stole the heart of my favourite grandson.'

'We're all her favourite grandson.' Knowing how wary Taylor was with people she didn't know Luca wondered if the barriers would come up, but she sank into the chair and faced the old lady with a smile.

'My Italian is terrible. I apologise. And I know how to say that…' She faltered slightly. *'Mi dispiace.'*

'No doubt you and Luca are finding other ways to communicate.' The old lady's eyes gleamed and Taylor laughed.

'His English is fluent.'

'Yes. He always was the cleverest of my grandsons. He just hid it well. So his reputation with women doesn't seem to frighten you.'

'I have a reputation of my own.'

'So I understand. You're the girl who fired her own mother.' His grandmother peered at her and Luca cursed under his breath, knowing how fiercely Taylor guarded her privacy.

'Nonna—'

'Yes, I did.' Taylor's voice was steady. 'She used me as a way of making money. She didn't care about what I wanted or what I needed. She wasn't good for me.'

Braced to defend Taylor from a lecture on the importance of family, Luca watched in surprise as his grandmother took Taylor's hands in hers. 'Family should be about giving unselfish support and that is particularly true of the bond between a mother and child. I'm glad you had the strength to remove her from your life. You obviously showed remarkably good judgement for someone that young. So tell me what you love about my Luca.'

'Nonna—' Cursing under his breath, Luca tried to interrupt but Taylor answered without hesitation.

'Lots of things. I love his sense of humour, his strength and the fact that he's proud of who he is. I envy that. I…' She hesitated. 'I want to be more like that. I'm trying to be more like that. It isn't easy.'

'You're an actress. Fortunately my grandson is used to drama. He was raised on it.' His grandmother gave him a meaningful look and Luca switched to Italian.

'I don't want to talk about that.'

'I know. You never do.' Her voice soft, his grandmother reached out to him and he frowned as he stared
down at her wrinkled hands locked tightly around his.

'Nonna—'

'You'll be perfect together. I sense it.' She patted his
hands and then released them. 'And now you'll stay and
eat breakfast with me.'

They stayed for an hour, an hour during which Taylor
talked about growing up in America, about her mother's ambition and her father's reappearance once she'd
started earning big money.

'I want you to come and see me often.' The old lady
patted Taylor's hand. 'Luca calls me Nonna, but if you
prefer you can call me Teresa.'

'Teresa?' Startled, Taylor glanced up at him and Luca
gave a dismissive shrug.

'It's a good name.'

She didn't speak until they were safely inside the car.
'I thought Teresa was some random name you picked
and it turns out it's your grandmother's name and she's
this wonderful, amazing person.' The choke in her voice
surprised him. He was so used to her hiding her real
feelings that this new Taylor unsettled him.

'She liked you a lot.'

'She'll hate me when she finds out this is fake.'

'It's me she'll be angry with.'

'I wouldn't be so sure about that. She adores you. I

didn't even know you had a grandmother. What did she mean that you were raised on drama?'

'We're Sicilian. Drama is in the genes. Why be calm when you can explode?' But he could see his smooth response hadn't fooled her and the tension of the morning reappeared.

'You never talk about your childhood. You've never told me anything.'

'I've never been one to coo over old baby photographs.' Luca felt sweat prickle at the back of his neck and started the engine. 'Let's go.'

'What was your mother like?'

He kept his eyes on the road. 'She was very beautiful. Still is.'

'I wasn't asking you what she looks like—I know she's beautiful, I've seen pictures. I was asking what she was like as a mother.' There was a wistfulness to her voice. 'What is she like as a person?'

Desperately insecure, volatile, a danger to herself. 'Why do you want to know?'

'I'm just interested. I guess I'm wondering why you're so freaked out about relationships. Is she the reason?'

*He doesn't love me, Luca. What do I have to do to make him love me?*

The sweat turned to a chill. 'Does there have to be a reason? Maybe I was just born with good instincts for staying out of trouble.'

'You've spent your whole life in trouble.'

'I would argue I've spent my life having fun and pleasing myself.'

There was a tense silence and when she turned to him the warmth was gone from her eyes. 'You never let your guard down, do you? You insist that I don't hide anything from you but when it comes to your own secrets you're as impenetrable as Fort Knox. I thought what we had here was more than just superficial, but clearly that was my mistake.' Her voice was tart. 'No worries. Forget I ever asked. I'm not used to trusting people anyway so I have no idea why I'd start with someone like you.'

'Taylor—'

'No, really, you've made it clear you don't want to talk and that's fine with me.' It was obvious from her tone that it wasn't fine. She was all business. 'I gather Santo and Ella have agreed to let you use the set for the photo shoot this morning. I'm not a model but if you tell me what you want I'll do it.' No self-doubt. No insecurity. She didn't hunt for compliments or press him for reassurance that she'd be able to do the job.

It occurred to him that not once in all the time they'd spent together had she asked for reassurance about her appearance. In fact, she hadn't asked anything of him except to be her fake fiancé.

He tightened his grip on the steering wheel. 'I just want you to be yourself. Taylor Carmichael.'

'Which version?' She was back to being her usual guarded self and although he knew he should have been relieved, he missed the laughing version of the night before.

'The real version. You're edgy, modern, strong. Sure of who you are. It shows in the way you carry yourself, in the way you deal with people and in the way you face the world. You're a self-sufficient high-achiever who has learned to depend on no one but yourself because everyone you've ever met has used you so you're not going to let that happen again.' He kept his eyes on the road as he described how he saw her. 'You were let down by your mother, by your father and by a man you trusted and every secret you ever had was blown over the pages of newspapers. It's left you vulnerable, but it's also given you strength because there's no way you're ever going to let anything like that happen to you again. You're so afraid of being hurt again you shut the world out and hide behind the tough-girl act. That's what I want to see when you're wearing the clothes.'

She was staring at him, her face pale. 'I—I've told you so much. Too much.' Her voice was a whisper. 'Why did I do that?'

'I don't know.' He was asking himself a similar question. 'Because you trusted me.'

'I don't trust anyone.' Her lips were bloodless and it took no effort to read her mind.

'You're worried I'll sell your story to the media?'

He was surprised by how much that hurt. 'Come on, Taylor—'

'You've remembered every detail. Every single detail I've ever told you.'

'Because I'm a good listener.'

'Why? So that you don't forget the juicy parts?'

'You know me better than that.'

'I don't know you at all. You haven't let me know you.' She was stammering in her panic. 'I have no idea what you're capable of when you're upset or annoyed and I've trusted you with information I would never have given to anyone else.' She pressed shaking fingers to her face and breathed deeply while Luca swore under his breath and tried to grab hold of a situation that was fast spinning out of control.

But they'd arrived at the docklands and already the usual crowd of journalists pressed around the car.

Luca yanked on the handbrake. 'We need to talk.'

'I've talked.' There was no missing her emphasis on the word. 'The problem is you haven't and I'm not interested in a one-sided relationship.' Before he could respond Taylor was out of the car, tall, long-limbed and beautiful as she walked gracefully to where the modelling shoot was to take place.

He wanted to remind her their relationship was fake. That confidences had no part in what they were doing here. But the whole thing was a confused mess in his head and there was no opportunity to sort it out because the photo shoot was already under way.

And she was as professional during the shoot as she was with her acting. She listened to what was required and worked her heart out and by lunchtime Luca knew that what he had was perfect. Even the exacting, hypercritical Gianni was happy.

He had no idea how Taylor felt because the mask was back up and he knew it was his fault. Not only had he stripped away her protective shell and frightened her, he'd shut her down when she'd asked him a personal question.

*I don't know you at all. You haven't let me know you.*

Her words stayed with him as he walked into the boardroom an hour later. Prepared for something close to adulation from them for the way his ideas were already increasing occupancy and profits, Luca opened the door and was greeted by stony silence. A few of the older members of the board avoided looking at him.

Deciding that this was a day that definitely wasn't going his way, Luca strolled to the head of the table and braced himself for trouble. 'Well, this isn't quite the fun afternoon I was anticipating.' He kept his tone light but he was surveying the room, trying to identify the reason for the frosty atmosphere. 'Something wrong?'

There was an awkward silence.

The chairman cleared his throat. 'You don't know?'

'Know what?'

'About your fiancée.' The older man's mouth was set in a thin, disapproving line. 'It seems her past was even wilder than the rumours suggested. An Italian magazine claims to be in possession of certain naked photographs.'

Everything fell into place. He had no need to ask who had taken the photographs. Had no need to ask for any detail because he could guess at the detail all too easily.

Luca kept his face impassive. 'Photographs?'

'So you don't know.' The chairman exchanged a relieved glance with the rest of the board. 'Naturally this won't reflect well on you or the company. I expect you'll want to distance yourself from her actions and break off the engagement. It's damaging for the Corretti name and even more damaging for you personally.'

Closeted on the film set, it wasn't until Taylor finished filming for the day that she saw the usual crowd of journalists gathered at the barrier had swollen to ridiculous proportions.

Remembering the studio's insistence on publicity and determined not to give them any reason to complain about her, she forced herself to walk across to them. Her intention was to allow them a few shots that would hopefully satisfy them enough to make them leave her alone, but as she approached she sensed the buzz of excitement that comes with a major story.

'Taylor, do you have any comment on the photographs that are going to be published tomorrow?'

'Photographs?' But she knew what photographs and it was like stepping off a cliff.

The cameras were clicking away, microphones ready to record her response, and all she could do was stand there, staring at them in silence as the reality sank into her brain.

He'd done it.

Rafaele had finally done what he'd been threatening to do for years. He'd sold the photographs. Photographs he'd had taken when she'd still thought there were people in the world who could be trusted. Photographs she hadn't even known existed until she'd broken up with him.

She'd often wondered how this moment would feel if it ever came but it felt nothing like she'd imagined.

She felt numb. Disconnected. As if she were watching events from the outside.

She'd expected to feel betrayed but she realised now the betrayal had come years before. And it had formed her. Influenced every choice she'd made since then. Tainted every affair and ruined every friendship.

'Taylor? The photographs are going to be published in an Italian magazine tomorrow.'

So not even somewhere far away. On Luca's home ground where it would cause him maximum humiliation. Soil his perfect shiny moment when his achievements were being lauded by the board.

Everyone was talking and the noise in her head grew and grew until she wanted to cover her ears and scream.

'I don't have any comment to make but I'll be contacting my lawyers.' But it wasn't her lawyers who she was thinking of as she forged her way to the black chauffeur-driven car that was always at her disposal during filming. It was Luca.

Luca, who was going to walk into that boardroom thinking that for once he had the upper hand only to be knocked unconscious by the weight of the secrets tumbling out of his fiancée's closet.

She knew he wouldn't care about the photographs—when had he ever cared what people thought—but he at least deserved some warning so that he was prepared to handle it.

Grateful for the blacked-out windows that gave her privacy, she leaned forward and ordered the driver to take her to the Corretti building as fast as possible.

The place was already swarming with press but with the help of the security team employed by the studio, Taylor made her way through the glass doors unmolested.

Once inside, she took the elevator to the top floor and was about to ask where the board meeting was taking place when she saw Luca emerge from a room as if he were sleepwalking. His shirt was undone at the collar and he looked as if he'd been hit by a passing car. His handsome face was pale and his usually smooth hair tousled.

Eyes glassy, he knocked into a passing PA, sent a pile of papers flying and didn't even seem to notice. He didn't send her his trademark slanting smile, didn't use the opportunity to appraise her bare legs or make any comment at all.

It was clear that he was in shock and the fact that he was shocked shook her to the core.

Nothing shocked Luca.

Nothing.

Her insides lurched.

Slowly, he focused on her. His handsome face turned a shade paler and he didn't seem quite steady on his feet and for a moment he didn't speak. Just stared at her in disbelief as if he couldn't believe what he was seeing.

That shaken glance sent a tide of humiliation flowing over her and she realised just how much she'd been hoping he'd simply laugh at the whole thing. How much she'd been hoping they'd laugh together.

This was Luca Corretti. Bad boy personified. He was the one person she'd felt understood her. She'd wanted him to wink and say something in that careless voice of his—something like 'I hope they got your good side, *dolcezza*.'

Never, in all the time they'd been together, had she seen Luca Corretti at a loss for words. He always had a smart comeback for everything. He was never bothered by anyone's opinion.

But he was bothered now.

In fact, he looked as if he needed to lie down.

As if to confirm that, he turned to his PA. 'Get me a whisky.' His usual smooth, sexy voice was rough and shaky and when his stunned PA handed him a glass he drank it in one gulp, his hand trembling so badly he could barely hold the glass.

Then he looked at Taylor. 'I just found out— I had no idea— I learned something—' He was uncharacteristically inarticulate and Taylor suddenly found she had a lump lodged in her throat.

'I know you did.' She snapped the words, horrified to hear her own voice crack. 'I came to tell you myself. I'm sorry I was too late.'

'What did you come to tell me?' He looked distracted and she stared at him in exasperation.

'Well, obviously that— Oh, never mind—you already know. You found it out yourself.'

'Yes. Yes, I did and—*Cristo*, Taylor…'

The sight of him so shaken up unsettled her more than she wanted to admit. He'd seemed to understand her so well. Better than anyone ever had before. Why wasn't it obvious to him that Rafaele had taken advantage of her? He knew about her controlling mother and the way her father had used her. He knew she'd been vulnerable at the time. He knew all that and instead of defending her or even encouraging her to tell, he was shocked.

But of course he was.

Because he was thinking about himself, not her, the way people always did.

He'd agreed to the engagement as a means of gaining respectability and these revelations had just blown that out of the water. The board had probably just fired him, which would explain why he was reacting so strongly.

Taylor lifted her chin. 'I'm sorry you feel this way.'

'You are?' His voice was raw. 'You're sorry?'

'Of course! It wasn't what either of us wanted. It wasn't part of our arrangement.' *I wanted your support.* Suddenly she was desperate to leave before she made a fool of herself.

'It's over, Luca. Done. Finished. The terms of our agreement have changed so that's the end of it. There's nothing more to be said.' She walked towards the door and then, because she just couldn't help herself, she made the mistake of looking back. And wished she hadn't because Luca was staring blindly into the distance, looking like a man who had lost everything.

# CHAPTER NINE

TAYLOR LAY IN a sodden heap on her bed in her trailer where she'd spent the night, too drained to get up and face the press. She hadn't slept at all, just lain there, hoping desperately to hear from Luca. Hoping desperately that once he'd had time to think about it, he'd revert to his usual indifferent self and come and laugh with her.

But she heard nothing from him.

It seemed everyone in the world had called her except him. Everyone wanted her comment on the impending publication of the photographs, everyone wanted to know her side of the story and how she felt about the world seeing her naked. And she didn't even care. Each time her phone pinged with another message she grabbed it hopefully but it was never him. He didn't communicate. Not even a single text saying how sorry he was that she was in this mess.

She'd had no idea the pretence of respectability had mattered so much to him and the image of his shocked expression was jammed in her brain.

It wasn't just the thought of the whole world seeing her naked that upset her, it was the fact that Luca didn't care about how she felt. All he'd thought about was himself and how it was going to affect him. When she'd walked into his office yesterday she'd wanted him to defend her. Instead he'd looked shocked.

Luca Corretti, shocked.

He'd done shocking things in his life but clearly he was like so many men. He had double standards when it came to his own behaviour.

The weird thing was she didn't even care about the photographs any more. Even though it was what she'd dreaded for so long, she didn't care about the embarrassment and the humiliation. All she cared about was that her 'engagement' to Luca was over. No more dinners. No more skinny-dipping in the sea. No more Tomas and Teresa. No more…

Fat, scalding tears slid down her cheeks.

Reaching for another tissue, she blew her nose hard, acknowledging the truth with a sick lurch of her stomach.

She loved him.

Really loved him. All of him, from the fun outrageous side of him to the hurt, lonely boy who didn't trust anyone.

Somehow, somewhere, her feelings had shifted from fake to real whereas he—he didn't have any feelings at all.

There was a hammering on the door of her trailer but she covered her ears and screwed her eyes shut, ignoring it.

She'd faced the press alone so many times in her life, why did it feel harder this time?

But she knew the answer to that.

She'd allowed herself to trust Luca. For the first time since her teens, she'd lowered her guard. She'd believed he was a friend. But when trouble had landed he'd cut her loose and tried to distance himself.

She yanked another tissue out of the box. What had she expected? That he'd stand up and fight for her?

The hammering grew louder. It sounded as if they were actually going to kick the door down and anger flashed through her misery.

Why couldn't they leave her alone?

'Taylor! *Cristo*, open this door!' Luca's voice thundered through the door and Taylor jumped in shock.

'Go away! You are a hypocritical bastard and I never want to see you again.'

'Open the door or I'll break it down.'

'Fine! Whatever. If that's what you want.' Springing from the bed, she wrenched open the door and Luca immediately barged his way past her and slammed it shut, blocking out the cameras.

He swore in Italian. 'It's crazy out there.'

'Probably safer out there than in here.' Defensive anger bubbling up through the misery, Taylor folded her arms and tapped her foot on the floor but the words on her lips died as she took a proper look at him. 'You look awful. Isn't that the same suit you were wearing yesterday?'

'What? No. Yes.' He looked down at himself blankly and then back at her, tension in his features. 'I don't know. I do know there are things I need to say to you.'

'If "sorry for being a hypocrite" isn't on that list then you can save your breath and get out now.'

'Hypocrite?'

'Oh, come on, Luca—I saw your face yesterday. You were shocked.' The words choked her. 'How dare you be shocked? After everything you've done in your life.'

'But I've never done this.' His voice was hoarse. 'I just didn't think this would ever happen to me. I didn't want it to happen.'

'"This" being involved with someone like me? Well, I'm sorry to have disturbed your perfect life.' Tears of frustration and humiliation stung her eyes and she pointed to the door. 'Leave, before I sully your reputation even more. If you think you're such a saint, get out now. And it didn't happen to you, it happened to me. That's my naked butt up there on the Internet, not yours, so stop being so sanctimonious. You've done far worse, Luca Corretti. You are many things but I had no idea you were a hypocrite.'

He raked his hand over the back of his neck, his expression bemused. '*Cosa?* What are you talking about?'

'You! I just can't believe you're shocked to see naked photographs! You're the one who almost ripped my dress off at the wedding.' That revelation was met by tense silence.

'You think I'm shocked about the photographs?' Looking slightly dazed, he lowered his hand from the back of his neck. 'That's why you're calling me a hypocrite?'

'I saw you, Luca. Yesterday, when you stumbled out of the boardroom, you could barely speak you were so shocked.'

'Yes, but not about the photographs. I was shocked because—' he broke off and licked his lips '—because I...'

'Because what?'

He looked like a man who was about to step off a cliff. 'Because I'd just discovered I was in love with you. *Cristo*, that is the first time I've said it out loud and it sounds as weird as it feels.' He sank onto the edge of her bed and stared down at his hands. 'Look at me—I'm shaking.' He held out his hands as evidence but Taylor simply stared at him, stunned into silence by his raw confession.

Her mouth opened and shut but no sound came out and he looked at her helplessly.

'I've never been shocked by anything before but I was shocked by this. I still am. I'm a guy who has never fallen for a woman. I never intended to fall for a woman.' His voice was as shaky as his hands. 'When you started this engagement farce I thought I was going to hate every minute of it. Instead I loved every minute of it. I loved every minute of being with you. You're bright, sexy, funny, confident, sexy, strong, warm— did I say sexy?'

'Wait a minute.' It was Taylor's turn to shake. 'Are you really telling me you love me?'

'Yes and last night you said you were sorry I felt this way which, by the way, was not the most sympathetic comment I've ever heard.'

'Last night I thought you were shocked because there are going to be naked photographs of me everywhere. You're shocked because you love me?'

'Yes. And there won't be photographs. That's where I've been all night. With the Corretti family lawyers. We've stopped the photos being published.'

It was her turn to be shocked. 'How can you do that? The Italian press are notorious for not caring about rules and regulations.'

'There are some advantages to being a Corretti. We stopped it. That's all you need to know. No one gets to see my wife naked but me.'

'W-wife?'

'You have to marry me.' He was on his feet, his expression strained. 'Until I met you I'd never spent a whole night with a woman and now I can't stand being parted from you even for a moment. Even when I'm not with you I'm thinking about you all the time. I know you find it hard to trust people and I understand why, but I wanted to prove to you that you could trust me. I made sure those photographs won't be used.'

'But our engagement was fake. We did it because it gave us both respectability.'

He gave a humourless laugh. 'And how did that work for you, *dolcezza*? Because I hated every minute of being respectable. I don't care what anyone writes about you. I never have and never will.'

The fact he hadn't sold her out to the press meant almost as much as hearing him say he loved her. 'He told me I was beautiful. Rafaele...' The tears were falling again and she brushed them away with her palm. 'I was homeless and I had no one—my own mother had turned her back on me and my father had sold his story to the press, and he was there for me. Except that he wasn't. I trusted him—'

'Shh...' Luca wrapped her in his arms. 'He doesn't deserve a moment of your time and he certainly isn't worth your tears. Don't cry.'

'He's held it over me for so long. He didn't even tell me he had the photographs until after our relationship ended. He paid someone to take them from the garden of the house we were using in California. I had no idea. I thought it was just the two of us. I thought we were alone.' She pressed her face against his shirt and felt safe. 'And then I ended it and he told me what he had. How he'd use them. No matter where I went or what I did, he found me. And I always knew he was just waiting for the right time.' She swallowed, relieved to finally be able to tell someone. 'And the pressure got to me. Do you know how it feels to wake up every day wondering if this is the day the world is going to see you naked? It's just horrible. And finally—well, I had a sort of breakdown.'

'I know. I saw the pictures of you but no one knew what happened or where you went.'

'It wasn't drugs or drink. It was just the pressure. I wanted to get away. I flew out of LA and on the plane I met Zach.'

'Zach the friend?'

'That's all he ever was. He served in Iraq. We got talking and in the end I went back with him to DC and volunteered in a rehab unit. They didn't care who I was, they were just grateful for the help. I felt good about myself for the first time in my life. It was Zach who helped me separate the acting from all the mess that surrounds it.'

'I'm starting to almost like Zach.' Luca stroked her hair gently. 'So what made you come back to acting?'

'I read this script. And Zach helped me see that I love being an actress, I just hate being in the spotlight when I'm not on set. I hate that feeling that everyone is waiting to tear me down. And because of our engagement you'll be pulled down with me.' She felt sick when she thought of it. 'I dread to think what the board said to you.'

'They told me I had to distance myself from you and that's when I realised I didn't want to. I didn't want it to be fake. I want it to be real.'

'Are you sure?' Her smile was wobbly. 'The real me gets me in trouble every time.'

'Never with me. You're forgetting that I grew up with fake. I grew up watching my mother turn herself inside out in an attempt to please my father.'

Taylor touched his face. 'You've never talked about her.'

'She worked so hard to make him love her.' His raw confession startled her and she eased away so she could look at him.

'You don't have to tell me this.'

'I want to. I want you to understand. But I'm not good at this—I've never talked to anyone.'

'Why do you say she was fake?'

'He hurt her again and again and she just came back for more and tried to be who she thought he wanted her to be. He travelled a lot and I used to dread him coming home. She went from being a relatively stable normal parent to an insecure mess. She'd walk into my room at all hours, sometimes she'd even wake me up, and she'd always be dressed in something different, wanting to know how she looked. "You have your grandfather's sense of style, Luca, tell me if this works. Will he like me in this?"' His handsome face revealed the strain. 'For a while, when I was very young, I actually thought that to be loved you had to wear the right clothes. And every time my father rejected her she'd study his latest girlfriend and try and copy the look and she'd ask me again, "Is this better? Do you think he'll like this?" And when he didn't I always blamed myself. Maybe if I'd told her to wear pink instead of cream. Or wear her hair up instead of down. Maybe if I'd got it right, she wouldn't have spent the whole night crying.'

Appalled, Taylor slid her fingers into his.

He'd shouldered responsibility for his parents' marriage. He'd taken on his mother's pain.

'No wonder you didn't want commitment.'

'To me, commitment meant being responsible for someone's feelings. It meant tying yourself in knots to be what someone else wanted you to be. It was about losing your sense of self. I had to watch her suffer every single day of my life growing up.' His voice was raw. 'I saw that love was manipulative and painful. I decided early on I didn't want that.'

'No. I can see why you wouldn't.' Taylor hesitated

and then put her hand on his cheek. 'I'm no expert, but if love exists I don't think that was it.'

'I know it wasn't.' He leaned his forehead against hers and she gave an unsteady laugh.

'What a pair we are. We did this to give us both re-spectability. Thanks to me, your respectability has been blown apart. I don't think it quite worked out the way either of us planned.'

'I'm bored with being respectable. It makes me irri-table. I want to be who I really am and I want to be it with you.' Sliding his hand around her back, he pulled her hard against him. 'How do you feel about doing this for real?' He breathed the words against her lips. 'We can spend the rest of our lives being disreputable together. We can live wickedly ever after.'

It sounded so impossibly good that tears filled her eyes and she blinked them away. 'Is that really what you want?'

'Yes. I love you, Taylor Carmichael Corretti. I love you for better and for worse—preferably worse, by the way.' His eyes glittered into hers. 'I love a bad girl. Think about it—if I marry you we can spend the rest of our lives shocking people.'

She kissed him, half laughing, half crying and lov-ing him more than she'd thought it was possible to love a person. 'We'll be tomorrow's headlines.'

'You're with me now. You don't care if you're to-morrow's headlines. Come on, Teresa, let's go and break a few rules together, with or without clothes. Your choice.'

She was smiling but the feeling of warmth grew and spread through her veins. 'Do you mean it? What you just said?'

'About it being real? About wanting to marry you? Definitely.'

'No one has ever loved me before. No one. You're not just worried about losing the new face of Corretti?'

'This isn't just the face of Corretti—' he stroked her cheeks with his thumbs, his eyes warm as he looked at her '—it's the face I want to see every night when I go to sleep and the face I want to see every morning when I wake up.'

The lump grew in her throat. 'I never knew you were so poetic.'

'Neither did I. I'm shocking myself.' He grinned and kissed her on the mouth until she pulled away.

'I love you too, but I'm worried I'll destroy your reputation. What about the board—'

'The board can sort themselves out. I've proved I can do it. I've increased their profits. Besides, hotels are boring.' He stifled a yawn. 'It's time my brother Matteo came back and got on with the job he's paid to do. All this respectability is making me uncomfortable. The other day they used the word *sobriety* in the same breath as my name. Can you believe that?'

Taylor gave a choked laugh. 'But what will you do?

You're so brilliant and talented—will you focus on the fashion business?'

'I'll do what I do best which is living life to the full. Want to live it with me, *dolcezza*?'

She didn't need to think about it. Not even for a second. 'Yes,' she said simply, 'yes, I do.'

'*Bene*. In that case I take you, Taylor Carmichael, to have and to hold, to sin and misbehave with until too much hot sex doth leave us breathless and knackered. How does that sound to you?'

Laughing, unbelievably happy, she wrapped her arms round his neck. 'It sounds just perfect.'

\* \* \* \* \*

*Read on for an exclusive interview
with Sarah Morgan!*

## BEHIND THE SCENES
## OF SICILY'S CORRETTI DYNASTY:

### with Sarah Morgan

**It's such a huge world to create—an entire Sicilian dynasty. Did you discuss parts of it with the other writers?**

Whenever you take part in a series like this it's important to be consistent and link the books so, yes, there was discussion between the writers. We emailed back and forth discussing various aspects of the setting and characters and how we might bring it to life.

**How does being part of the continuity differ from when you are writing your own stories?**

When I write my own stories I create everything, including the setting, the characters, the backstory and the conflict. I don't have to think—or worry—about anyone else. In a continuity, the authors are given a large volume of background information to work with and that can be very challenging. Although there is some flexibility and freedom within the brief, I have to remember that any changes I make might impact on someone else's story. But I'm still writing a love story between two people and the focus is on their emotional journey so the basic process is the same.

**What was the biggest challenge? And what did you most enjoy about it?**

The biggest challenge is always being given an outline for two characters and the main plot points. Fortunately, I fell in love with these characters. From the moment I read the brief they came alive for me and I could "see" who they were and how their conflict would play out in the story.

**As you wrote your hero and heroine, was there anything about them that surprised you?**

I was surprised by just how bad Luca was. But I wasn't alone in that. Taylor was surprised, too. So we spent the book being surprised together!

**What was your favorite part of creating the world of Sicily's most famous dynasty?**

It was lovely to spend my day dreaming of Sicilian blue skies and the sparkling ocean, but the best part for me was writing the dialogue between the hero and heroine. I call this my "banter book." Taylor and Luca had so much fun together, even during the most emotionally charged intense moments of the story, and I had so much fun writing it.

**If you could have given your heroine one piece of advice before the opening pages of the book, what would it be?**

Beware of wickedly hot men bearing champagne.

**What was your hero's biggest secret?**

I never reveal a person's secrets! I can tell you that Luca is not a man who feels the need to hide who he is from anyone, but there are things he prefers not to talk about.

**What does your hero love most about the heroine?**

Apart from her legs? That she's every bit as bad as he is.

**What does your heroine love most about your hero?**

That he doesn't care what other people think of him.

**Which of the Correttis would you most like to meet and why?**

Luca! He's one of the most wickedly gorgeous heroes I've written and I love his sense of humor. I know a night with him would be something no woman would forget!

Please read on for a sneak peek at the next book in
**SICILY'S CORRETTI DYNASTY,**
*A Shadow of Guilt* by Abby Green, which features in
***The Correttis: Revenge***
available in June 2013.

# A SHADOW OF GUILT

**Abby Green**

Gio lifted his arms and brought his hands to Valentina's face, cupping her jaw, his thumbs wiping away the moisture from her cheeks. She knew she must look a sight, and Gio's shirt had to be sodden from her tears and runny nose. But she didn't care. A fierce burgeoning desire was rising within her, something which had been there before but had been put on ice for seven years.

For a long time it had been illicit and forbidden, *guilty*. But from the moment she'd seen him again it had flamed to life. Yet the contradiction had duelled within her: how could she hate him and want him at the same time? But now those questions faded in her head. *Hate* felt like a much more indefinable thing and the desire was there, stronger than hate, rushing through her blood and making her feel alive.

She lifted a hand and touched Gio's hard jaw. He clenched it against her hand. Desire thickened the air around them, unmistakable. As if questioning it, Gio looked down at her, a small frown between his eyes, 'Valentina?'

It was the same look he'd given her the other night when she'd exposed herself and she understood it now. He'd been asking the question then, unsure of what she'd been telling him with her body language. The knowledge was heady. He *wanted* her.

One of Valentina's fingers touched Gio's bottom lip, tracing its full, sensuous outline. Words were rising up within her, she couldn't keep them back. 'Gio…kiss me.' She'd wanted this, *ached* for this for so long.

It was only after an interminable moment of nothing happening that she looked up into Gio's eyes and saw something like torture in their dark green depths. He shook his head. 'This is not a good idea. You don't want this, not really.'

He wanted to kiss and plunder this woman before she changed her mind but he knew he couldn't. She hated him already, she would despise him forever for this.

Valentina's gaze narrowed on his. A light was dawning in her eyes. He braced himself for the moment when she would pull herself free and demand to know what the hell he was doing.

And then she said, 'Damn you, Gio Corretti, *kiss me.*'

© Harlequin Books S.A. 2013

Special thanks and acknowledgement are given to Abby Green for her contribution to the Sicily's Corretti Dynasty series

# The Correttis

**Introducing the Correttis, Sicily's most scandalous family!**

On sale 3rd May

On sale 7th June

On sale 5th July

On sale 2nd August

Mills & Boon® Modern™ invites you to step over the threshold and enter the Correttis' dark and dazzling world…

Find the collection at
**www.millsandboon.co.uk/specialreleases**

*Visit us Online*

0513/MB415

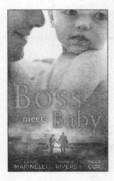

## The World of Mills & Boon®

There's a Mills & Boon® series that's perfect for you. We publish ten series and, with new titles every month, you never have to wait long for your favourite to come along.

---

### Blaze®
*Scorching hot, sexy reads*
4 new stories every month

### By Request
*Relive the romance with the best of the best*
9 new stories every month

### Cherish™
*Romance to melt the heart every time*
12 new stories every month

### Desire™
*Passionate and dramatic love stories*
8 new stories every month